THE SEDUCTION OF THE
CRIMSON ROSE

THE SEDUCTION OF THE
CRIMSON ROSE

Lauren Willig

DUTTON

DUTTON
Published by Penguin Group (USA) Inc.
375 Hudson Street, New York, New York 10014, U.S.A.
Penguin Group (Canada), 90 Eglinton Avenue East, Suite 700, Toronto, Ontario M4P 2Y3, Canada (a division of
Pearson Penguin Canada Inc.); Penguin Books Ltd, 80 Strand, London WC2R 0RL, England; Penguin Ireland, 25 St
Stephen's Green, Dublin 2, Ireland (a division of Penguin Books Ltd); Penguin Group (Australia), 250 Camberwell
Road, Camberwell, Victoria 3124, Australia (a division of Pearson Australia Group Pty Ltd); Penguin Books India
Pvt Ltd, 11 Community Centre, Panchsheel Park, New Delhi - 110 017, India; Penguin Group (NZ), 67 Apollo
Drive, Rosedale, North Shore 0632, New Zealand (a division of Pearson New Zealand Ltd); Penguin Books (South
Africa) (Pty) Ltd, 24 Sturdee Avenue, Rosebank, Johannesburg 2196, South Africa

Penguin Books Ltd, Registered Offices: 80 Strand, London WC2R 0RL, England

Published by Dutton, a member of Penguin Group (USA) Inc.

First printing, February 2008
1 3 5 7 9 10 8 6 4 2

 REGISTERED TRADEMARK—MARCA REGISTRADA

LIBRARY OF CONGRESS CATALOGING-IN-PUBLICATION DATA
Willig, Lauren.
    The seduction of the crimson rose / Lauren Willig.
        p.   cm.
    ISBN 978-0-525-95033-2 (hardcover)   1. England—Fiction.   I. Title.
    PS3623.I575S43   2008
    813'.6—dc22
                                                        2007043044

Printed in the United States of America
Set in Granjon with display set in ITC Novarese Book & Bernhard Tango
Designed by Leonard Telesca

PUBLISHER'S NOTE

To Nancy M. Flynn,
Setting the standard for best friends since 1982

Acknowledgments

I don't know what possessed me to believe that starting a new book and a new job at the same time would be a good idea. Demons, most likely. Many thanks go to my editor, Kara, and all the folks at Dutton who waited patiently for delayed installments of the manuscript; to my parents, who made sure I had groceries to eat and a table to rest them on and even volunteered to put on a blond wig and pretend to be me at work; to Brooke, who put up with more Mary and Vaughn than anyone not writing about them ought; to Nancy, Claudia, Abby, Liz, and Jenny, who talked me down off a variety of tree limbs; and to my friends and colleagues at Cravath, who kept their senses of humor—and by extension, mine—through cite checks, doc reviews, and assorted fire drills. Big hugs go to Emily, Alexi, Sarah, and the 12:30 lunch group. Thanks, guys. I don't know why you put up with me, but I'm glad you do.

THE SEDUCTION OF THE CRIMSON ROSE

Prologue

November, 2003
The Vaughn Collection, London

"Four pounds," demanded the fourteen-foot-high statue of Hercules.

For such a big man, Hercules had a surprisingly high-pitched voice. It took me a moment to realize that it wasn't actually a piece of classical statuary demanding the contents of my wallet, but a very human-size woman seated at a small desk at its base. When you're confronted by a twice-larger-than-life statue of Hercules, wielding a club and wearing little more than a strategically draped serpent, you tend not to notice much else.

To be fair, it wasn't all Hercules' fault. I had spent the morning in a state of utter uselessness, nearly gotten run over by a cab on my way to the archives, and given a pair of confused German tourists directions to Westminster Abbey when what they wanted was Kensington Palace.

The cause of all this chaos and confusion? I had a date. A real, live date with a real, live boy.

If this doesn't seem exactly stop-the-presses sort of stuff, then you've clearly never experienced the soul-sucking self-doubt that comes of a year without so much as an attempted grope. And the boy in question . . . Think a blond Hugh Grant without the sketchy past, or Errol Flynn without the tights. Unlike my other exes (and most Robin Hoods), he actually spoke with an English accent. Which made sense, because he was

English, born and bred on the scepter'd isle, as British as HP Sauce, crooked teeth, and the Queen Mum's hat collection. What single Anglophile of a certain age wouldn't be smitten?

In my own defense, I hadn't come to England looking for romance. As a fifth-year graduate student with an increasingly angsty dissertation advisor and a research grant that didn't quite pay my rent, I didn't have time for men—at least not live ones. Unfortunately, the dead ones could be just as frustrating as the live ones. After three months hunched over a desk in the British Library Manuscript Room, three months of endless train rides to obscure county records offices, three months of assuring my advisor that, yes, everything was going just brilliantly and of course I would have a chapter for him by January, by November I had still been no closer to my goal: the unmasking of the Pink Carnation, the flowery spy whose very existence gave Napoleon an intense allergic reaction.

The fact that a whole legion of intensely interested nineteenth-century French agents, as well as several successive generations of scholars, had also failed ought to have clued me in.

But when has that ever stopped anyone? It's like the search for the mines of Solomon or the Lost City of Gold; that no one else has found it before just adds to the challenge. I'm sure the men who perished in the jungles of Mexico didn't say, "Oooh, let's go die on a hopeless quest!" No, they dreamed of coming home draped in gold and covered with glory. My goal wasn't gold but footnotes, the coin of the scholarly realm. Otherwise the impetus was the same. The fact that many scholars smugly insisted that the Pink Carnation had never existed in the first place, that he was an imaginary folk hero invented to sell papers, or a sort of shadow puppet invented by the War Office in the hopes of scaring Napoleon, only spurred me on. I'd show them.

Or not. For a while, it was beginning to look like not.

But every now and again, once in a hundred years, despite all the nay-saying and the accumulated weight of scholarly truths, someone gets lucky. This time, it was me. I don't know what it was that made Mrs. Selwick-Alderly decide to allow me access to a cache of family papers never before open to the public. Perhaps I reminded her of a long-lost daughter. Or she might simply have taken pity on me for my pathetic and bedraggled air (I'm frequently bedraggled, and after three months of fruitless dissertation research, I was feeling pretty darn pathetic). Whatever the cause, in her cozy sitting room, I had found not only the secret identity of the Pink Carnation, but something more, something that came in a tall, blond, and, at that point in time, very irate package.

That's where Colin came in.

Ah, Colin. I was staring happily into space, contemplating the wonder that was Colin, when an annoying, squawking noise permeated my reverie.

"Four pounds," the receptionist repeated, clearly taking my blank stare for either a linguistic barrier or just chronic stupidity.

"Huh?" I said brilliantly, still mentally wandering hand in hand with Colin in a Technicolor wonderland complete with dancing munchkins. I was wearing a floaty frock that flitted daintily about my knees as Colin swung me in a happy circle beneath the cerulean sky. All that was missing was Dick Van Dyke, although, given the look in Colin's eye, Dick would have been decidedly superfluous.

Still tap-dancing through daydream, I favored the receptionist with a big, beaming smile.

"Oh, I'm not here for the museum," I said brightly, confirming her impression that a village somewhere back in the States was missing its idiot. "I'm here for the Vaughn Collection."

"This *is* the Vaughn Collection."

I knew I should have had that extra cup of coffee before leaving my flat. I thought of pretending that I didn't speak English, but it was a little too late for that.

"Sorry," I said, with that super-ingratiating smile that works on Americans but falls flat in the British Isles, "I didn't mean the art collection. I meant the documentary collection—the archives. I spoke to your archivist?"

I'm not sure why it came out as a question. After all, if I didn't know whether I'd spoken to the archivist, she surely wouldn't know, either. From the look on the receptionist's face, she seemed to share this opinion.

Trying a different tack, I said, more assertively, "I was told the archives were open between one and six on Saturdays."

Dismissing me as a bad job, the receptionist jerked her head to the right. "Straight through down the stairs at the back if you want to see the museum it'll be four pounds." The fact that she said this without pausing to draw breath rendered the performance even more impressive.

"I'll be sure to keep my eyes shut as I go."

This earned me another fishy stare. Deeming it wiser to quit while I was ahead, I hoisted my bag higher on my shoulder and headed in the direction the receptionist had indicated. The caryatids arrayed on either side of the door looked down on my brown wool pants and baggy green Barbour jacket with a decided sneer. I don't know what they were so supercilious about; their marble draperies were a good two thousand years out of fashion.

Dotted with little glass cases, the room beyond must have been a ballroom or something equally grand once upon a time, when Vaughn House was still inhabited by genuine Vaughns rather than the remnants of their art collection and a scraggle of hardcore art historians and scruffy tourists. You could have fit five of my flat into it and still had room for a good-size coffee shop.

With a fine disregard for atmosphere, the curators had plunked a series of glass and chrome display cases throughout the room, each containing a motley collection of personal effects of long-deceased Vaughns. In the largest case, in the very center of the room, the curators had displayed the pièce de résistance, an impressive collection of Edwardian underwear, from lace-edged drawers large enough to swathe the backside of a baby elephant to a pair of stays that looked like they might have been used to tow the *Queen Mary* back into port. Next to them, the curators had helpfully positioned a sepia photograph of a formidable dowager with a waist cinched into nothingness and a bosom that could smother a small city.

With four months of fish and chips weighing heavily on my midriff, I cast a speculative eye over the stays. Unfortunately, I didn't think they would fit under my going-out pants, which were designed for something a bit lighter in the way of undergarments. I wondered what the curators of museums would be displaying a hundred years hence. Would we have glass cases filled with fire-engine-red thongs and leopard-print bras, along with a carefully printed white card explaining their sociocultural significance?

The gentleman who occupied the better part of one wall seemed to share my qualms. His gaze was fixed upon the underwear display with a decidedly jaundiced air. He had been painted, according to the conceit of the time, in a classical wasteland, with a broken pillar wedged beneath one elbow and vague suggestions of a decaying Roman temple in the background. It was an evening scene, in which the rich black brocade of his coat would have blended with the deep indigo of the night sky if not for the silver threads that ran through the weave like condensed moonlight. The entire ensemble had a supernatural shimmer reminiscent of old-fashioned ghost stories featuring family phantoms.

Even with all the shimmer and silver, it wasn't the eerie glow of his attire that first caught my eye, but his face. I would be lying if I said it was a handsome face. The nose was too long—the better for looking down at you, I suppose—and the lips were too thin. There were interesting hollows beneath his sharp cheekbones and paunches beneath his eyes, not unlike those one sees in pictures of the Duke of Windsor, the last word in aristocratic dissipation. His thin lips were curved in a cynical half-smile, and the sideways slant of the eyes suggested that he had just noticed something that both appalled and amused him—or amused him because it appalled him. Either way, I wanted to be let in on the joke.

The artist had chosen to color his eyes nearly the same shade as the silver that ran through his coat. The effect was unusual and arresting. Those silver eyes glinted with a sardonic amusement that even two centuries of hanging on a wall couldn't dim. He looked as though he had seen it all before, including the undergarments. He probably had. Those slender hands, elegantly poised on the head of an ebony walking stick, seemed more than capable of unlacing a pair of stays in about three minutes flat.

I didn't need to read the swirly script on the brass plaque affixed to the frame to know who he was.

Sebastian, Lord Vaughn, eighth Earl Vaughn, Baron Vaughn of Vaughn-on-Tweed, and a host of lesser titles, all of which nicely filled up the space of half a page in *Debrett's Peerage* & *Baronetage*. A grand Whig aristocrat of the old school, member of organizations as diverse as the Royal Society and the Naughty Hellfire Club, intellectual and wastrel—and quite possibly a French spy.

I had come across Lord Vaughn in a number of highly suspicious circumstances. His name kept popping up in the annals of the Pink Carnation. Wherever he appeared, he brought with him death, destruction, and a devastating way with a quizzing glass.

The first time Vaughn's name had intruded upon my notes, it was in connection with the death of an operative of the War Office, who had been placed in Vaughn's household as a footman. No one ever really explained that one. The assumption was that the footman had been murdered by the Marquise de Montval, the deadly French operative who worked for the even deadlier Black Tulip (and by the time you've gotten to two levels of deadly, you're talking pretty deadly).

Did I mention that the Marquise had been Vaughn's mistress? The association might have been purely amorous—or it might not have been. It was Vaughn who had released the Marquise from the custody of the English War Office, and Vaughn in whose company she had traveled to Ireland to foment rebellion on behalf of France. In short, Vaughn was looking pretty darn suspect. Add to that a decidedly sinister manner of dress, an extended stay on the Continent, and rather flippant ideas about the value of King and country, and you had a likely candidate for Traitor of the Year.

I had been thrilled when I discovered that the choice art museum, the Vaughn Collection, had belonged to that Vaughn. I'd heard of the

Vaughn Collection—it had been prominently featured in my guide-book as a must-see for the serious student of art along with the Wallace Collection and the Sir John Soane's Museum—but it took a while for the connection to click. Vaughn, after all, was a fairly common name.

But while Vaughn was a fairly common name, there weren't all that many Vaughns with family mansions in snooty Belliston Square. In fact, there was only one. By a miracle, Vaughn House had remained in the family, escaping both the Blitz and bankruptcy, until the twelfth earl had left instructions in his will for its conversion into a public museum upon his death, apparently for the sole purpose of irritating his children. From what I was able to make out on the Web site, the bulk of the Vaughn Collection had been acquired by Sebastian, Lord Vaughn—my Vaughn—who seemed to have made his way across the Continent by buying up everything in his path.

A cover for other activities? Or merely the acquisitive instincts of a born connoisseur? I intended to find out. At least, I hoped to find out. Whether I would or not was another story entirely.

I hadn't been entirely honest with my new buddy, the receptionist. It hadn't been the archivist I had spoken with on the phone the day before, but a sort of assistant. He had sounded utterly baffled by my wanting to visit the collection. This did not inspire me with confidence.

The archives, he had informed me, around a yawn, were mostly documents establishing provenance of the artwork and all that sort of thing. There were, he allowed, some family papers still floating around. Yes, he thought there might be some from the late eighteenth, early nineteenth century. He supposed if I *really* wanted to come see them . . . The implication, of course, being that any sane person would rather spend a Saturday afternoon watching a cricket match, or watching paint dry, which amounts to much the same thing, as far as I've been able to tell. The whole conversation had been pretty much the professional equivalent of sticking your fingers in your ears and chanting, "Nobody's home!"

Between the receptionist and the guy I had spoken to on the phone, I got the impression that the Vaughn Collection wasn't awfully keen on visitors. Which is a little counterproductive when you're a museum. I was fervently hoping that the archivist's assistant's attitude (I dare you to say that three times fast) was born more of laziness than of the fact that there just plain wasn't anything there.

I did have at least one other option. The Vaughns hadn't donated their family papers to the British Library, or printed up one of those nineteenth-century compilations with all the good bits expurgated. They did still own a rather impressive family seat up in the wilds of Northumberland, currently operating as a leisure center for corporate trainings—the sort of retreats that involve dumping people in a lake and giving them points for how efficiently they get out of it again and other such acts of socially sanctioned torture. The family documents might still be housed up there, but even with the miracles of modern transportation, Northumberland was a ways away. Depending on how things went with Colin . . .

Ah, Colin.

Dodging through the obstacle course of glass display cases, I shook my head at my own foolishness. If I turned into a useless blob of goo every time I thought of him, how was I ever going to maintain a coherent conversation for the duration of dinner?

Every time I relaxed my concentration, there I was again, off in daydream land, in a glorious summer landscape with a man as perfect and plastic as a Ken doll. I knew I was being absurd. Outside, it was late November, bitter cold November, only three days after Thanksgiving. Yet, in my daydreams, we strolled hand in hand beneath a gentle June sun while the birds chirped away in the trees above. In real life, one of them would probably crap on his head. So much for romance.

Logically, I knew that the man was just as imaginary as the scene. The Colin I knew—or, rather, the Colin I had met, since I couldn't really presume to know him at all, despite a rather intense acquaintance to date—was far from perfect. In fact, he was mercurial to the point of being schizophrenic, warm and flirty one minute, cold and distant the next. When I'd first met him, he'd practically bitten my head off for having the nerve to accept his aunt's invitation to go through the family archives; the next thing I knew, he was refilling my champagne glass and looking at me in a way that made me go all wobbly (although four glasses of champagne will do that to a girl).

At least he'd had an excellent excuse for his most recent Jekyll and Hyde performance. What I'd thought was a case of Colin simply blowing me off because of, well, me, turned out to be a panicked rush to Italy, where his mother was unconscious in a hospital after a particularly nasty car accident. I hadn't even realized Colin had a mother.

Naturally, I knew he must have had one at some point (yes, we all took sixth-grade bio class), but in novels, heroes never seem to have parents, at least not living, breathing ones who get sick or have accidents. Occasionally they have parent issues, but the parents are always conveniently off somewhere to stage left, usually dead. Can you imagine Mr. Rochester trying to explain to his mother how he burned the house down? Or Mr. Darcy promising his mother he won't marry that hideous Bingley girl? I rest my case.

Even writing off Colin's last mood swing, I still hadn't found out just why he had reacted quite so violently to my excursions into his family's archives. Most of the hypotheses that occurred to me were far too ridiculous to countenance. Even if Colin's great-great-grandparents had founded a sort of spy school on the family estate, there was no way that the family could have remained continuously in the spying business since the Napoleonic Wars.

Could they? My notions of modern espionage had a lot to do with James Bond movies, complete with low-slung cars, talking watches, and women in bikinis with breasts like helium balloons. Colin drove a Range Rover and wore a Timex. As for the helium balloons, let's just say that if that's what Colin was looking for, he wouldn't be going out to dinner with me.

Occupied by these fruitful speculations, I managed to make my way through the series of linked rooms that led to the back of the house, which petered out into a narrow corridor: Someone had painted the walls a utilitarian white that somehow managed to look more depressing than an outright gray.

There was a door with a big sign on it that read PRIVATE in all capital letters in four languages (presumably, if you didn't speak English, German, French, or Japanese, this prohibition didn't apply to you), with a rope strung across the entrance for emphasis. I cleverly deduced that that was not the door I was looking for.

An anemic red arrow pointed visitors down a narrow flight of stairs with shiny reflective tape beginning to peel back from the treads. Clutching the warped handrail, I picked my way carefully down and came straight up against—the bathrooms. The little stick figures were unmistakable.

Next to them, however, a plain white door had been marked with the word REFERENCE. It was just the tiniest bit ajar, presumably for ventilation rather than hospitality. I pushed the door the rest of the way open and made my way in, the heels of my boots slapping hollowly across the linoleum floor.

In contrast to all the gilt and rosewood upstairs, the reference room wasn't a very impressive setup. The room was small and square, furnished with two rickety aluminum folding tables, each supplied with four equally rickety folding chairs with hard plastic seats. Padding might have encouraged people to linger. At the far end of the room, a small counter, not unlike those in drugstores, separated the reference room from the archives beyond. Through the gap I caught a tantalizing glimpse of utilitarian metal shelves piled with a variety of acid-free boxes and big black binders.

At the desk, a man in a hot pink T-shirt guarded the gap. I use the word "guarded" loosely. He was so deeply absorbed in whatever he was reading that I could have vaulted over the desk without his noticing me. The thought was tempting, but that kindergarten training dies hard. I didn't vault. Instead I coughed. When that didn't work, I coughed again. Loudly. I was afraid I was going to have to resort to more drastic measures—like sneezing—but the third cough finally broke through his literary absorption. As he hoisted himself up, I took a peek at his reading material. It was a copy of *Hello!* magazine, open to a fine showing of airbrushed celebrities.

Somehow, I didn't think this was the archivist. In fact, I had a pretty shrewd guess as to who he was.

"I believe we spoke on the phone," I said.

Clearly, he also remembered our conversation fondly. His face went from lascivious to hostile in the space of a second. "Oh. You."

So much for being a goodwill ambassador for America, or whatever else it is that the Fulbright people expect you to do. Fortunately, my grant was a Clive fellowship, not a Fulbright, so I was off the hook. As far as I could tell, Mr. Clive had harbored no pretensions about his grantees fostering international amity.

That being the case, I felt no guilt at all about saying crisply, "I'm here to see the papers of Sebastian, Lord Vaughn."

The boy gave me a look as though to say, "You would." Levering himself up with obvious effort, he trudged wearily off into the blazing desert sands, five hundred miles across rugged terrain, to the metal shelves right behind the desk. There, he made a great show of studying the labels on the binders.

"That's Vaughn, v-a-u-g-h-n," I said helpfully. "Sebastian, Lord Vaughn."

"Which one?" asked Pink Shirt dourly.

It had never occurred to me that there might be other Sebastian, Lord Vaughns floating around. "There's more than one?"

"1768 or 1903?"

It was a bit like ordering a hamburger. "1768."

After a moment, his head popped back around again. "Do you want the 1790 box, the 1800 box, or"—his head ducked back down for a moment—"the everything else box?"

Next, he was going to ask me if I wanted fries with that. I made my choice, and the 1800 box was duly shoved into my hands. The tape on one end bore a label that descriptively stated, "Seb'n, Ld. Vn., Misc. Docs. 1800–1810."

I began to wonder if the archivist actually existed, or if they just pretended they had one for the sake of show. Not only was that one of the less convincing classificatory systems I had ever encountered, there had been no effort made to put the contents of the box in any sort of order; small notebooks, loose papers, and packets of letters were all jumbled, one on top of the other. Given that Vaughn had lived well into the reign of Victoria, my hunch was that the everything else box wasn't so-called because there wasn't much there for the next forty years of his life, but simply because no one had gotten around to sorting through it yet.

Settling myself down at the more stable of the two tables, I reached for the first packet in the 1800 box, gingerly unwinding the string that bound the letters. There's nothing like peering into someone else's correspondence. You never know what you might find. Coded messages, plotting skullduggery, passionate letters from a foreign amour, invitations to a late assignation . . . These turned out to fit none of the categories above. They were all from Vaughn's mother.

What was this with everyone having a mother all of a sudden?

Shoving my hair back behind my ears, I skimmed through the letter on the top of the pile. After one letter, I decided I liked Vaughn's mother. By the end of three, I really liked Vaughn's mother, but reading about Vaughn's spinster cousin Portia who had run off with a footman ("She might at least have picked a handsome one," opined Lady Vaughn) wasn't getting me any nearer to ascertaining the identity of the Black Tulip, so I reluctantly put the pile aside for future perusal and dug back into the box.

I toyed with the notion of Lady Vaughn herself as the Black Tulip, spinning her webs from the safety of Northumberland as she sent out her minions to do her dirty work. Sadly, it didn't seem the least bit probable. From her letters, Lady Vaughn was far too busy bullying the vicar and terrifying her family to be bothered with international espionage. Another great opportunity wasted.

I flipped quickly through the usual detritus of a busy life. There were love letters (using that term broadly); invitations to routs and balls and Venetian breakfasts; an extensive correspondence with his bankers (which generally seemed to boil down to "send more money"), and, at the very bottom of the box, tucked away where one might never have noticed it, a nondescript black book.

It wasn't a little black book in the modern sense. There was no list of addresses, conveniently labeled, MEMBERS OF THE LEAGUE OF THE BLACK TULIP (LONDON BRANCH). But the reality was nearly as good. I had found Lord Vaughn's appointment book. All of Lord Vaughn's movements, recorded in his own hand. His writing was just like his appearance, elegant, but with a sharp edge to it. I paged rapidly through it until I hit 1803, watching the place-names change from the exotic (Messina, Palermo, Lisbon) to the familiar (Hatchards, Angelo's, Manton's). Vaughn, I noted, had had a particularly close and personal relationship with his tailor; he saw him nearly once a week.

I was ruffling lazily through, wondering idly if I could make something out of those tailor appointments (there had, after all, been a round of spies rousted out of a clothiers establishment the year before), when a familiar name struck my eye: Sibley Court.

Sibley Court . . . I knew I had encountered that name before. After a moment staring into space, it finally clicked. Sibley Court was the family seat of the Viscounts Pinchingdale.

I bolted upright in my uncomfortable chair. Viscount Pinchingdale, at least the Viscount Pinchingdale in possession of the title in 1803, had been second in command of the League of the Purple Gentian, from which he moved on to aiding in the endeavors of the Pink Carnation. He was no fan of Lord Vaughn.

What might the potential Black Tulip be doing at the family seat of a known agent of England?

Well, that was a silly question. Spying, one presumed.

I would never know one way or another unless I read on. The entry was terse, but it was enough for a start. Especially once I recognized the names involved, including that, prominently featured, of Miss Jane Wooliston, otherwise known (although not to many) as the Pink Carnation.

14 Oct., 1803. Sibley Ct., Gloucestershire. Immured in Elizabethan horror in G'shire. Forced to play hunt the slipper with Dorrington and wife. Selwick going on about days of glory in France. Interesting proposition made to me by Miss Wooliston. . . .

Chapter One

Sing in me, Muse, of that man of many turnings. . . .

—Homer, *The Odyssey*

October, 1803
Sibley Court, Gloucestershire

Sebastian, Lord Vaughn, stood beside a rusting suit of armor, a dusty glass of claret in hand, wondering for the tenth time what evil demon had possessed him to accept an invitation to the house party at Sibley Court. It had to be a demon; Vaughn held no truck with deities.

The house, which had been closed for well over a decade, was a masterpiece of Elizabethan handicraft—in other words, an offense to anyone with classical sensibilities. Vaughn regarded a series of carved panels with distaste. The repetition of Tudor roses had undoubtedly been intended as a heavy-handed compliment to the monarch. The tapestries were even worse than the paneling, lugubrious depictions of the darker moments of the Old Testament, enlivened only by a rather buxom Eve, who seemed to be juggling her apples rather than eating them.

Sibley Court had slumbered among its memories and dust motes since the death of the current Viscount Pinchingdale's father and had only just been hastily opened for the accommodation of the viscount and his new bride. Vaughn had no doubt that the new viscountess would soon have the ancient flagstones gleaming. She was the managing sort.

So far, she had already managed her guests through supper, a game of hunt the slipper, and an abortive attempt at blindman's buff that had come to an abrupt halt when the hoodsman, one Mr. Miles Dorrington, had blundered into a suit of armor under the delusion that it might be his wife, bringing the entire edifice crashing down and nearly decapitating the dowager Lady Pinchingdale in the process.

Undaunted by her brush with death, the dowager Lady Pinchingdale and her newest relation by marriage, Mrs. Alsworthy, appeared bent on engaging in Britain's Silliest Matron contest. So far, the dowager Lady Pinchingdale was ahead four swoons to three. The only one of the lot who seemed to have two brain cells to rub together was the long-suffering Mr. Alsworthy. He had proved his intelligence by promptly disappearing just after their arrival.

Between the dowager and his fellow guests, Vaughn was considering a spot of decapitation himself. Starting with his own head. It was beginning to ache damnably from the combination of inferior claret and worse conversation.

Nursery parties—for that was what the gathering at Sibley Court felt like—weren't usually in Vaughn's line. He ran with an older, faster set, men who knew the way of the world and women who knew the way of those men. They played deep, they spoke in triple entendres, and they left their bedroom doors open. In contrast, the crowd at Sibley Court was sickeningly unsophisticated. Part of that insipid breed spawned by the new century, Pinchingdale's set uttered words like "King" and "country," and had the poor taste to mean them. No one dueled anymore; they were all too busy gadding about France disguised as flowers. Or named after them, which was nearly as bad. Lord Richard Selwick, currently occupied in propping up the enormous Elizabethan mantelpiece, had only recently been unmasked as the notorious Purple Gentian, a flower as obscure as it was unpronounceable. The youth of England were fast running out of botanical monikers. What would they do next, venture into vegetables? No doubt he would soon be forced to listen to dazzling accounts of the adventures of the Orange Aubergine. It all showed a marked lack of good *ton*. Vaughn might be less than a decade older than his host, but among this company he felt as ancient as the tapestries lining the walls.

The blame for his presence fell squarely on the woman standing next to him, looking deceptively demure in a high-necked gown of pale blue muslin embroidered with small pink flowers about the neck and hem. With her smooth brown hair threaded with matching ribbons and her gloved hands folded neatly around a glass of ratafia, Miss Jane Wooliston looked more like a prosperous squire's daughter than that many-petaled flower of mystery, the Pink Carnation. It was her summons that had sent Vaughn jolting through the back roads of Gloucestershire clear off the edge of the earth to this godforsaken relic of Bonnie Olde Englande. And he wasn't even sharing her bed.

At the moment, Jane was occupied in examining a dark-haired girl who posed becomingly in front of the light of a twisted branch of candles. Like Jane, the girl was tall, tall enough to carry off the long-lined classical fashions swept across the Channel by the revolution, with the sort of finely boned features that showed to good effect in the uncertain light of the faltering candles. But there the resemblance ended. There was nothing the least bit demure about the girl across the room. The light struck blue glints in the smoothly arranged mass of her black hair and reduced the fine fabric of her muslin gown to little more than a wisp.

"She is lovely," remarked Jane, in a considering sort of tone.

Lovely wasn't precisely the word Vaughn would have chosen. It implied a sweetness that was utterly lacking in the self-possessed stance of the woman in white. Luscious didn't serve, either; it suggested Rubenesque curves and dimpled flesh, whereas the woman by the candles had the perfectly carved lines of a marble statue. Wanton? No. There was a discipline in both her straight-backed posture and the proud set of her head that gave the lie to the suggestive cling of her dress. Whatever her revealing gown might have been meant to convey, to the astute observer she was more Artemis than Aphrodite.

There was one word, however, that Vaughn had no difficulty at all applying: notorious.

Vaughn hadn't followed the Pinchingdale Peccadillo (as the scandal sheets had unimaginatively dubbed it), but it had been impossible to avoid learning the basic outline of the story. It had entirely eclipsed Percy Ponsonby's latest fall from a window as the gossip of choice as the Season lurched to a close. Attempting to elope with the famed beauty, Miss Mary Alsworthy, the besotted young Viscount Pinchingdale had somehow erred and managed to dash off with the wrong sister. Suffering from a foolish adherence to propriety, Pinchingdale had marched up to the altar with the compromised sister, one Laetitia, who was chiefly famed for boasting the largest collection of freckles this side of Edinburgh. It was the sort of absurd bedroom farce that couldn't fail to appeal to the jaded palettes of London's bored elite.

In the end, the hubbub had died down, as it always did. London's elite had trickled away to their country estates, to amuse themselves sneering at the local assemblies and irritating the wildlife (sometimes the two pursuits were nearly indistinguishable), while the new Viscount and Viscountess Pinchingdale wisely removed themselves for an extended wedding journey—or so the story went. The genuine version, to which Vaughn was reluctantly privy, was a good deal more complicated, involving spies, Irish rebels, and exploding masonry, from all of which the new viscount and viscountess had emerged more pleased with each other than otherwise. In fact, they had returned from Ireland rather sickeningly smitten with each other, Lord Pinchingdale's prior passion for the elder Miss Alsworthy conveniently forgotten.

Vaughn raised his quizzing glass and ran it along the elegant sweep of Miss Alsworthy's neck, cunningly accentuated by three long curls that fell from hair swept into a knot in the Grecian style. Standing in the light of a branch of candles, her sheer muslin gown left very little of the elegant lines beneath to the imagination.

A woman would have to be either a saint or a fool to harbor a rival beneath her own roof. Especially a rival who looked like that.

"If I were the current Viscountess Pinchingdale, I would not be overjoyed by Miss Alsworthy's presence."

"Letty's strength is as the strength of ten," replied Jane whimsically.

"Because her heart is pure? Never place your trust in aphorisms, Miss Wooliston. They are more for effect than substance."

The same, he reflected, could be said of the lovely Miss Mary Alsworthy. Some men had an eye for horses; Vaughn had one for women. No matter how fine a collection of points Mary Alsworthy might have, there was a glint to her eye that foretold an uncomfortable ride. It didn't take an expert to tell that she was highly strung and all too aware of her own good looks. That sort tended to be damnably expensive—not to mention possessed of an unfortunate tendency to buck the rider. He had encountered her kind before.

"Well?" inquired Jane. "What do think?"

"I think," he said deliberately, "that if you have dragged me out to this inhospitable corner of the earth on nothing more than a bout of romantic whimsy, I shall be entirely unamused."

"My dear lord Vaughn, I never matchmake." Jane smiled to herself as though at a private memory. "Well, very rarely."

Vaughn arranged his eyebrows in their most forbidding position, the one that had sent a generation of valets scurrying for cover. "Don't think to number me among your exceptions."

"I wouldn't dare."

From the woman who had invaded Bonaparte's bedchamber to leave him a posy of pink carnations, that pledge was singularly unconvincing. "I believe there are very few things you wouldn't dare."

Jane was too busy scrutinizing Miss Alsworthy to bother to reply. "Have you noticed anything particular about her?"

"Only," said Lord Vaughn dryly, "what any man would be expected to notice."

Jane tilted her head to one side. "She doesn't remind you of anyone? Her skin . . . her hair?"

He had been doing his best not to notice the resemblance, but it was impossible to ignore. That sweep of ebony hair, the willowy form, the graceful white dress were all too familiar. *She* had worn white, too. White, to draw attention to her long black hair, straight as silk and just as fine.

It had been more than a decade ago, in a room all lined with glass, from the long doors leading out to the garden to the tall mirrors of Venetian glass that had lined the walls, cold and bright. That was how he had first seen *her*, sparkling by the light of the candles, flirting, laughing, Galatea remade in ebony and ivory. Every man present had been panting to play Pygmalion. He had been no different. He had been young, bored, running rapidly out of dissipations with which to divert himself. And then she had turned to him, holding out one white hand in greeting—and challenge.

There had been a ruby, that first night, strung on black velvet so that it nestled tightly against the hollow of her throat. Sullen red welling against white, white skin . . .

Vaughn let his quizzing glass drop to his chest. "The resemblance is purely a superficial one. A matter of coloring, nothing more."

"That might be enough."

"No," said Vaughn flatly.

"If," said Jane, ignoring him as only Jane dared, "someone were to speak to her; if someone were to suggest . . ."

"Ah." Vaughn's lips compressed, as the whole fiasco suddenly fell into place. "That's what you want of me. To play Hermes for you."

"We can't all be Zeus," Jane said apologetically.

Prolonged exposure to Jane was enough to make anyone take to Bacchus. "I'm afraid I've left my winged shoes at home. Forgive me for suggesting the obvious, but why not approach the girl yourself? Why drag me into this fiasco?"

"Because," said Jane very simply, "I don't want her to know who I am."

Vaughn regarded her with reluctant appreciation. Lulled by the peaceful symmetry of her fine-boned face, it was easy to forget that that pink and white complexion masked a mind for strategy that put Bonaparte to shame. It seemed unlikely in the extreme that Miss Mary Alsworthy was a French agent. Her interests, thus far, had tended more to millinery than politics. But hats—and all those other furbelows that tricked out the willowy forms of society's beauties—were expensive.

The identity of the Pink Carnation was a commodity for which more than one person would be willing to pay dearly.

"A wise decision," Vaughn granted. "If you persist in going forward with the plan, I suggest you set one of your entourage to the task. Dorrington, for one, appears in need of occupation."

Jane gave a slight shake of her head. "Unlike Dorrington, you have something Miss Alsworthy wants."

Jane didn't need to specify. Her meaning was horrifyingly clear. Vaughn could feel the parson's noose dangling just shy of his neck.

"Which," replied Vaughn pointedly, just in case Jane had forgotten certain crucial facts, "she is not going to get."

"No," agreed Jane. "And yet . . ."

Vaughn polished the lens of his quizzing glass, squinted critically at it, and swiped at an invisible blemish. "Yet, my dear Miss Wooliston, is a treacherous jade. She'll lead you astray if you let her."

"Yet" kept men gambling when they ought to have thrown in their cards; it outfitted expeditions for cities of gold and fountains of youth; it dulled the critical faculties with false promises, as bright and baseless as the towered palaces of an opium dreamer's paradise. Yet led one into absurd situations such as this.

Jane wagged an admonishing finger. "You have a very low opinion of conjunctions."

"Of all kinds." His brief marriage had been enough to convince him of that.

"No one is suggesting you engage in a conjunction of a permanent sort," said Jane mildly. "I'm sure we could persuade Miss Alsworthy to lend us her talents with less drastic inducements. And she would be perfect for our purposes."

"You mean, for your purposes."

Knowing well the power of judicious silence, Jane chose not to answer. She simply continued to look at him, with an expression of calm conviction designed to persuade most men that they had always agreed with her in the first place and were simply being given time to voice it. Vaughn had to admire her cheek. It was one of the few reasons he tolerated her. Her complete lack of interest in his matrimonial value was another.

So he was to lure Miss Mary Alsworthy into Jane's schemes with his title as bait, was he? The idea was almost entirely without merit.

And yet . . .

Ah, there she was again, that treacherous jade, that will-o'-the-wisp, that yet. Vaughn pondered the monumental boredom of Gloucestershire and decided that will-o'-the-wisps were the lesser evil. One needed to do something to enliven the stifling ennui of the human existence. And one could only beguile so many empty hours by bedeviling one's valet or seducing the serving girls.

And then there were his own purposes. . . .

"How could I possibly deny any lady such a simple request?" With an unhurried gesture, Vaughn shook out the lace of his cuffs before adding, "Even a fool's errand is preferable to being forced into another round of hunt the slipper."

"But my dear Lord Vaughn"—Jane blinked innocently up at him— "isn't that exactly the game you have been playing?"

MARY DREW HER LIGHT GAUZE SHAWL more closely around her shoulders, which were beginning to show unbecoming signs of gooseflesh. The wrap, which had been perfectly adequate for London's overheated ballrooms, did very little to ward off the October chill that pervaded the Great Chamber of Sibley Court. Next to her, a twisted branch of candles did more to cast shadows than spread light. Any attempt at illumination disappeared into the depths of the dusky tapestry on the wall beside her, which appeared to depict one of the gorier episodes from the Bible. At least, Mary hoped it was biblical in origin. Otherwise, that girl really had no business holding aloft that man's severed head.

Mary might, she told herself, have endured the cold with equanimity. She might have smiled with tolerant condescension upon the antiquated furnishings and dour tapestries, graciously endured the drafty chambers, and equally accepted the lack of any local society—any local society worth knowing, that was—within twenty miles, were it not for one small problem.

Her problem sported dark blue superfine and wore his dark hair cropped close to his head. He was also walking right towards her, moving with a soft stride that seemed to swallow sound rather than create it, a shadowy presence in the dim room. He was Geoffrey, Lord Pinchingdale, Second Viscount Pinchingdale, Eighth Baron Snipe, owner of Sibley Court and all its lands and appurtenances.

Once upon a time, it had been simply Geoffrey.

Once upon a time, he hadn't been married to her sister.

Pausing in front of her, her new brother-in-law bowed briefly over her hand, their first private contact since the hot days of July, when they had met in the sunshine of Hyde Park while her maid kept lookout three trees away.

In the drizzling gloom of October, it felt a lifetime ago, like a summer flower found pressed between the pages of a book.

"Miss Alsworthy," Geoffrey said softly.

It did seem a tad formal after "beloved."

"Mary," she corrected demurely, retrieving her hand and smiling as prettily as any young girl at her first Assembly. "After all, you are my brother now."

He looked so relieved that Mary almost wished she had said something less conciliatory. She couldn't have, of course. It would have been bad *ton* to make a scene. Unlike her sister, she knew what was required of her. But it would have been nice to see even a touch of remorse—or, even better, of regret—rather than pure relief at being so easily released from his former bonds.

Slicing the wound wider, he said, "Letty and I were both so pleased that you were able to join us here."

What was it about married couples that always made them speak for the other person as well? Didn't he have any thoughts of his own anymore? Or was that not allowed? Letty always did have opinions enough for two.

"The pleasure is mine," Mary lied, making her eyes as limpid as nature would allow. "I have always been eager to see Sibley Court."

That struck home, at least. She could see guilt flicker across his face as the barb struck—or perhaps it was nothing more than the uneven flick of the candle flame, playing tricks with her eyes.

Well, he ought to feel guilty. He had been the one who had promised to bring her home to Sibley Court as its mistress. Over dozens of dances he had spun endless stories of the wonders of the family home: the ghost who stalked the battlements, the trees he had climbed, the scent of the ancient herb garden after a spring rain.

"Miss Alsworthy . . ." Mindless of the company around them, Lord Pinchingdale looked earnestly down at her, groping for words. "Mary . . ."

They had stood that way so often in the past, his dark head bent to hers, a private haven in the midst of a crowded room. Mary lowered her eyes against a sudden pang. Not of the heart, of course. A heart had no business engaging in practical transactions. Half the time, she reminded herself, she hadn't listened to a word he had said, mentally cataloguing the dances she had already promised and devising new ways to play off her admirers one against the other.

Call it memory, then, or nostalgia. He might have been dull, but he had still been hers. She had gotten into the habit of him.

"Mary . . ." His voice scraped along the back of his throat, as though he spoke only with difficulty. "I'm sorry."

Sorry, sorry, sorry. She was sick of sorry. Letty had been sorry, too. They were sorry, but she was alone. So much for sorry.

"Don't be. It all turned out for the best." If her smile was a little sour around the edges, Geoffrey didn't appear to notice. "Practically enough to make one believe in Fate." Or just very meddling relations.

"Not many would be so generous."

Any more generosity and she would choke on it. Lowering her lashes, Mary took refuge in modestly murmuring, "You are too good." That much, at least, was true. He and Letty deserved each other; they were both sickeningly virtuous. Their children would probably be born with halos already attached. "If you would excuse me? I promised Mama I would roust Papa out of the library before the supper tray is brought in."

As always, he believed every word. Geoffrey had always believed her, no matter what flummery she spouted. It had been one of his greatest assets as a suitor.

"Certainly. Do you know your way? Sibley Court can be a bit confusing on a first visit." There was no mistaking his pride in the drafty old pile.

"If I get lost," replied Mary lightly, "I'll simply call on one of the family ghosts to show me the way."

"Make sure you find your way back, or Letty will worry."

"Letty always worries."

"I know." Geoffrey smiled a private smile that made Mary feel as hollow as the elderly paneling that lined the walls. "She told me to make sure you get enough supper."

His eyes slid over her shoulder to where Letty was bustling from group to group, making sure everyone had a good time whether they wanted to or not. Letty might be a viscountess now, but she looked like a prosperous squire's wife, with her gingery hair frizzing out of its haphazard arrangement of curls and her fichu askew across her ample bosom. As she moved, the candlelight threw her shadow in grotesque parody against the wall, adding chins and lengthening her nose.

It didn't seem to matter to Geoffrey. His eyes followed his wife as she made her way across the room, his lips tilted up on one side in a smile so intimate that it hurt to observe it. There wasn't anything lustful about his gaze. Mary had seen enough lust in her time to become inured to its expression. It was something much more personal, that spoke of genuine fondness.

He had never looked at her like that.

"Must find Papa!" said Mary brightly, sweeping up her skirts in one hand. "Until supper, then."

For a man who had once haunted her steps and doted on her smiles, he barely seemed to realize she had gone.

Knowing the importance of a good exit, Mary kept her head high and her back straight as she moved deliberately towards the heavily carved door that led out to the gallery that overlooked the Great Hall. She let a slight smile tease the edges of her lips, the sort of smile that always made gentlemen wild to know what she was smiling about. It drove women equally wild for entirely different reasons.

Pausing in her leisurely progress, she stopped to examine a particularly busy portion of tapestry with every sign of antiquarian absorption. Two paces away, she couldn't remember a single thread of it. All she could see was Geoff's dark eyes drifting away over her shoulder towards her sister.

A woman scorned had a certain grandeur to it; a woman forgotten was merely pathetic.

Only when she had achieved the empty space beyond the door did she allow herself the luxury of defeat. Letting her seductive smile melt into blankness, Mary trailed one pale hand along the worn wood of the balustrade that ran along the upper gallery of the hall below. According to Geoffrey, a Pinchingdale bride had flung herself from that balcony rather than submit to a loveless marriage. More fool she, thought Mary. What was it about idiocy that attained veneration through sheer age? Mary had never understood why Juliet refused to marry Count Paris. He was a far better match than that silly young Romeo. And then to drink poison . . . well, there was just no accounting for some people. Mary would have taken Count Paris and his Veronese palazzo in a heartbeat.

The walls of the upper gallery had been paneled in dark wood, each square carved with a portrait head in profile. Wattle-necked women in stiff headdresses and long-nosed men glowered at Mary from their coffered prisons. The fabric of Sibley Court hadn't changed much since the Armada. It suited Letty brilliantly. She looked right against the finicky paneling and the musty old tapestries, right in a way that Mary never would have. If Mary had had her way, she would have torn the whole monstrosity down and started all over again in good clean marble.

Lucky for Sibley Court, then, that Geoffrey hadn't married her. Lucky for Geoffrey, lucky for Letty, lucky for everyone.

If she was being honest, lucky for herself as well. All through the era of his adoration, Pinchingdale had been a crashing bore.

Even a boring husband was better than being left on the shelf, forced to rely on the charity of her relations, pointed at and whispered about by giggling girls fresh in their first Season.

Reaching the end of the upper gallery, Mary slipped beneath an elaborately carved lintel, no proper destination in her head except away. She found herself in a seemingly endless corridor, where the plastered ceiling stabbed down in regular points like pawns suspended upside down. After a moment of disorientation, she realized where she was. Originally constructed during the reign of Henry, before being "improved" during the tenure of his daughter, the house had been built in the shape of an H, in a rather obvious compliment to the monarch. She was in the crossbar of the H, a long and narrow gallery that connected one wing of the house with the other.

On either side of her, narrow-faced Pinchingdales gazed superciliously down on her, their gilded frames spotted with age. There was at least half a mile between the two wings of the house, long enough to display three centuries' worth of relations and even one or two particularly prized pets. Mary wandered aimlessly among them, absently noting the dull sheen of painted jewels, repeated over and over. There was the large pearl that hung from the waist of an Elizabethan Pinchingdale; the three matched sapphires set into the collar of Spotte, *A Faithfull and Lovinge Companyon* (there was something decidedly smug about the set of Spotte's paws); the emeralds that adorned the neckline of a woman with tight curls and a simpering mouth, holding tight to the hand of a cavalier in a plumed hat (one assumed from her grip that he must be the donor of the emeralds);

and the famous diamond parure worn by Geoffrey's grandmother to the coronation of George II, impressive even rendered in oil and dim with dust.

Those diamonds made up for a great deal of boredom.

At the time, it seemed like a fair trade. She got the diamonds and Pinchingdale got her, an ornament for an ornament, each with its price. She knew her price and she set it high.

What else, after all, was there to do? She didn't have it in her to be a bluestocking and write dour tracts. She had no interest in educating other peoples' brats. The days when a woman could make a career as a royal mistress had long since passed. Mary had always thought she would make an excellent monarch—the skills required for international diplomacy were much the same as those that Mary used to keep the various members of her entourage in check—but no one had had the consideration to provide her with a kingdom. There was only one game to be played, so Mary played it and, she had always thought, played it well.

Obviously, she had been wrong. Because, in the end, she had lost the game.

She had also come to the end of the gallery. Ahead of her, an immense, mullioned window looked out onto blackness. In the daytime, it was no doubt a pleasant prospect, looking out over the vast sweep of gardens and park that stretched out from the back of the house. At night, the leaded panels glistened like a hundred obsidian eyes. On either side of the window, doorways led off to realms unknown, unlit by either candle or moonlight. A sweeping curtain of red velvet shielded each opening, dragged back on one side like a cavalier's cloak.

Mary lowered herself slowly onto the matching red velvet that cushioned the window seat. Ordinarily, she never sat at parties. It wrinkled one's dress. Tonight, she couldn't bring herself to care. It felt good to relax into the well-worn velvet of the ancient cushion, good to stare into nothingness and not have to smile and pretend that she didn't mind that her sister had married her best chance at matrimony. Her short, plump, practical, managing little sister. Who had nonetheless learned the secret to catching a man's heart and holding it. Mary had failed to master the holding bit.

With the moon obscured by clouds, the prospect in front of her loomed as blank as her future. It didn't matter that she had been voted Most Likely to Marry an Earl three years running in the betting books at White's. No earl had proposed. Not marriage, at any rate.

What was she to do with herself? For the first time in her life, Mary simply didn't know. Her beauty had always provided both means and goal, ever since her nurse had first leaned over her cradle and clucked, "Eh, she'll marry a prince, that one, see if she doesn't!" But she hadn't. She wasn't going to. The results of three Seasons didn't lie.

Mary rested her elbows on the stone of the windowsill, staring sightlessly through the phantom tracery of her own face. What did it matter if her elbows wrinkled? She had three sonnets to them already. Four would be superfluous.

Behind her, the worn boards of the gallery creaked. Not ghosts, as Geoffrey had promised all those months ago, but a human tread. Someone else had escaped to the quiet of the Long Gallery.

Mary would have preferred a ghost. A specter might be ignored, while a fellow guest would expect conversation, might even try to persuade her back into the discomfort of the Great Chamber. Hadn't she smiled enough for one evening?

Holding herself very still on her bench, Mary hoped her presence might go unnoticed in the uncertain light. Torches had been lit at intervals along the walls, set into iron brackets placed well away from the more important portraits and flammable items like velvet swags. Her window seat was safely in shadow, aside from the dim reflection of light on glass.

Oh, go away, Mary thought irritably. Was it too much to ask to be allowed to brood unmolested?

Apparently, it was. The measured tread continued inexorably onwards, one creak following another with the rhythmic beat of an executioner's drum. Whoever it was must have seen her. Her dress was too painfully pale to do anything but stand out against the grim crimson of the cushions. The footsteps stopped a scant distance behind her—and showed no sign of reversing themselves.

Mary could feel the prickle of scrutiny scuttle across the bare skin of her shoulder blades as she sat resolutely deaf and dumb, willing the intruder away.

"Admiring the view?" inquired a masculine voice.

Chapter Two

For thou thyself art thine own bait,
That fish that is not catch'd thereby,
Alas, is wiser far than I.

—John Donne, "The Bait"

Mary rose reluctantly from her cocoon among the cushions. She drew it out as long as she could, unfolding limb by limb, waiting until the very last moment to turn her head and face the intruder. The longer she avoided looking at him, the longer she had to compose her face along appropriate lines. She didn't want this man—this man in particular—to see her at a disadvantage.

She had known him from his voice, a slow drawl flavored with the arrogance of the last century. It was the sort of voice that had known duels and red-heeled shoes, that was as comfortable with a rapier as a powder box.

Behind him, the half-drawn velvet curtain looked as though it had been designed merely as backdrop for his presence. He stood with one foot set carelessly in front of the other, one hand resting lightly on the silver head of his cane. The cane had been cunningly fashioned in the shape of a serpent, the long silver tail writhing in spirals down the ebony shaft. At the top, the snake's mouth yawned open, bored after a long day of tempting souls away from paradise. The heavy-lidded eyes looked uncannily like those of its owner.

"Lord Vaughn." Through her prolonged ascension, he hadn't said anything at all. He just stood there watching her with detached interest, as though she were a new entr'acte at Drury Lane presented for his delectation. "I didn't hear your approach."

"Next time I shall contrive to tread more heavily." Instead of removing himself, he strolled towards her, glancing over her shoulder at the dark carapace of the window. The sleeve of his jacket skimmed again the unprotected skin above her glove. "You show a curious taste in landscapes."

"I call it A Study in Solitude." Mary leaned heavily on the last word.

Vaughn dismissed both the hint and the landscape with a wave of one ringed hand. "Better to label it Ennui."

Mary tilted her head, and found herself in far too intimate proximity with the clean line of his jaw. For a dark-haired man, he was ruthlessly well-shaven, without any of the distressing stubble one often found on other men. She hastily turned her attention back to the window.

"You don't find the party amusing, my lord?" she inquired of his reflection.

Vaughn's eyes glinted silver in the window. "I haven't—until now."

That was an invitation to a flirtation if Mary had ever heard one. What she couldn't understand was why.

Vaughn had never shown himself susceptible to her charms before, and it wasn't for want of trying. Vaughn certainly wasn't perfect— there were rumors that he had murdered his first wife—but ghosts were insubstantial things compared with three estates, one of the finest mansions in Mayfair, and the famous Vaughn rubies. He was wearing one now, buried deep in the snowy folds of his cravat, the one touch of color in his otherwise midnight-hued ensemble. Even the buckles of his shoes reflected the cold glint of diamonds, like flecks of distilled moonlight. The ruby smoldered against the white linen, pinned a hand's breadth away from the heart.

If Vaughn did have a heart, Mary hadn't been able to get anywhere near it.

Oh, she had laid her snares very delicately, very discreetly. It was simply a matter of conveniently dispatching her admirers on errands as

Lord Vaughn happened by; of finding herself in his vicinity just before the supper dance; of declaring, in her most carrying tones, that she simply must have some fresh air—and making sure the balcony door remained open. These methods had all worked for her in the past. Vaughn, fresh from years of dissipation on the Continent, undoubtedly in want of a wife to perpetuate his ancient (and wealthy) line, was sure to be easy prey. Older men were always flattered by the attention of a pretty young thing. Mary wasn't as young as some, but she was still younger than Vaughn. Bat your lashes a few times, ask breathless stories about the triumphs of their youth, and they were yours.

Vaughn ignored every single lure. He had continued walking as she sent her other suitors running off for lemonade and fans and he left her to cool her heels through the supper dance. Oh, he had gone out onto the balcony—but it had been the balcony on the other side of the ballroom. Alone.

If he had deliberately followed her out of the Great Chamber, his ennui must be quite overwhelming indeed. Well, he was just going to have to find other entertainment. She was not for hire. Not by him, at any rate.

"You might beguile the time with contemplation of art," she suggested primly. "There is a great deal in the gallery of interest to the educated eye."

"How very true." Vaughn's quizzing glass traveled the sweeping circumference of her neckline. "I consider myself something of a connoisseur."

Mary rather doubted they were discussing the same type of art. "My brother-in-law informs me there are several fine works by Mytens, as well as the Holbein portrait of the first Baron Pinchingdale."

Vaughn rolled the head of his cane idly between his fingers. "I was seeking something a bit more modern. Perhaps you might be able to assist me."

Mary seized the opportunity to drift away from the confines of the window embrasure. With Vaughn standing next to her, the arch felt uncomfortably close. She waved a graceful hand at the portrait of Spotte, liberally spotted with dust. "Sibley Court tends to the antique."

"You mean the antiquated." Vaughn strolled easily in her wake. Mary felt as though she were being stalked by a particularly graceful beast of prey. "I find that being surrounded by decay generally renders one all the more eager to gather one's rosebuds."

Mary paused in front of a painting of a sour-faced dowager holding a sullen pug. "You've come at an inauspicious time for rosebuds. I'm afraid in winter we must be satisfied with the memory of summer's bounty."

Vaughn moved to stand directly behind her, so close that she could feel the tickle of his cravat against her bare shoulder, the burr of his breath against the nape of her neck.

"But my dear Miss Alsworthy," Vaughn's cultured vowels teased the edge of her ear, "it is not winter yet."

Mary's skin prickled with a heat that had nothing to do with the few sullenly smoldering torches that lined the unheated gallery. His posture echoed hers so closely that all it would take would be the merest whisper of movement to bring them into embrace. If she tilted her head just the slightest fraction, if she permitted her taut shoulders to relax . . .

She would be the greatest fool in all the West Country.

"I assure you, my lord," Mary said frostily, staring straight ahead at the dowager's bad-tempered pug, "there is a definite chill."

And so there was. One minute he was looming behind her, the next he had casually strolled away, as though they had been discussing the weather! Which, in fact, they had been. Mary's lips quirked in sour amusement.

"I could offer to warm you," Vaughn said meditatively, as though it were a matter of intellectual speculation, "but that would be far too commonplace."

Mary's sapphire eyes narrowed as she faced him across the width of the gallery, where he leaned casually against the plinth of a marble bust. "Not to mention unwise."

Vaughn wagged his quizzing glass approvingly, a miracle of urbane detachment. "I couldn't agree more."

Where was the man who had been oozing illicit intentions a moment before? At the moment, his demeanor was positively avuncular. Mary's head was beginning to ache in a way that had nothing to do with the smoke from the torches.

"Good," she said shortly. "I'm glad we agree."

"How agreeable," drawled Vaughn.

Mary felt rather disagreeable. Disgruntled, even. Had he never intended to seduce her? It wasn't that she wanted him to seduce her—of course not!—but it was very off-putting to be defending one's honor one moment and spiraling through empty space the next. She certainly hadn't welcomed his interest. A flirtation with Lord Vaughn was the very last thing she needed.

Mary had the uncomfortable feeling that the entire interlude, from that very first honeyed compliment, had been an extended joke. On her.

Pasting on her very best social smile, Mary gathered her skirts and swept past the painted faces of a censorious crowd of Parliamentarian Pinchingdales. She hoped all of them were preparing a particularly thorny berth in hell for one Sebastian, Lord Vaughn. "If you would be so kind as to excuse me, my lord, I should be getting back. My sister does fret so."

Vaughn's soft voice interrupted her just short of Praise-God-For-Your-Salvation Pinchingdale (Proggy, to his friends), a grim fellow in black chiefly famed for having even more warts than his friend Cromwell. "Before you go . . ."

It was said very quietly, but it carried all the authority of a command. Mary found herself pausing, her skirt drawn back over one white satin slipper. The toe, she noticed, was beginning to show signs of wear, the fabric rubbing thin over the stiffened frame.

"Before you go," Vaughn repeated, in that same, well-modulated tone, "you should know that I was, in fact, sent to seek you tonight."

"To seek me?" Vaughn, being dispatched, must have decided to amuse himself with a little spot of dalliance along the way. It was all beginning to make a certain amount of sense. Mary allowed herself the luxury of a small eye roll. "I suppose my sister sent you. She seems to think I ought to be fed."

"Does she?" Vaughn's gaze moved lazily over Mary's form in a way that suggested he found nothing whatever the matter with her proportions. "No. Your sister had nothing to do with it."

Mary looked at him quizzically. Her mother? Mary couldn't see Vaughn voluntarily playing lackey for her mother; he would more likely just shrug and walk away. As for the rest of the party, most of them were better pleased by her absence than her presence. She was under no illusions as to that.

"I don't understand," she said.

"I rather wish I didn't," murmured Vaughn. Bracing his cane on the ground between his knees, he looked at Mary over the silver serpent's head. "What do you know of the current blight of flower-named spies?"

"As much as anyone here," Mary said shortly, and couldn't for the life of her understand why that seemed to amuse her companion so. "I do know how to read, my lord. Occasionally, I even employ that skill. Why do you ask?"

"I come here tonight as emissary."

"From a flower-named spy." Mary didn't bother to keep the skepticism out of her voice.

The only flowery spy at Sibley Court, as far as Mary knew, was Lord Richard Selwick, the spy formerly known as the Purple Gentian. The likelihood of his seeking her out for anything—other than a good gloat—was nonexistent. Lord Richard had all but ordered fireworks in celebration when he discovered that his best friend had escaped from her clutches (his words, not hers) and married her younger sister instead.

"What does our esteemed Purple Gentian want of me?" Mary asked.

"Oh, it's not the"—Vaughn coughed discreetly, as though the name came with difficulty to his tongue—"the Purple Gentian for whom I happen to be acting."

"Oh?" said Mary acidly. "Have we been honored with the presence of other flowers? A Roving Rosebud, perhaps?"

Vaughn spread his hands wide. "Ridiculous, isn't it? But the most ridiculous tales are often the truest."

"Unless one were to deliberately invent a ridiculous tale, trusting that others might follow that reasoning."

"Why would I go to the bother of such invention? Unless . . . oh no. Oh no, no, no." Vaughn chuckled, a rich full sound that resonated along the vaulted ceiling.

To her horror, Mary felt the color rise in her cheeks. With anger, she assured herself. She never blushed—and certainly not for the likes of Lord Vaughn.

The lines around Vaughn's eyes deepened with sardonic amusement. "You didn't truly believe . . . you and I? No, no, and no again."

"I find myself exceedingly relieved," Mary said stiffly, "to find that we are once again in agreement."

Vaughn wasn't the least bit fooled. He smiled lazily. "My dear, if I had wished to arrange an assignation, I would hardly have been so clumsy as to leave you in any doubt of my intentions. This matter is purely business."

"But whose business is it, then?" Mary challenged. "Why didn't they contact me directly?"

"My dear girl, if you were meant to know, why do you think our friend would have sent me?"

"I find it even less likely that you would agree to play errand boy, my lord."

Vaughn refused to be baited. He contemplated the serpentine head of his cane, twisting it so that the fangs glinted in the light. "I prefer go-between. So much less menial."

"Whatever you choose to call it, you still haven't explained why."

"Wouldn't you rather know *what*?" Vaughn inquired lightly. "I should think the substance of my communication ought to interest you more than my motivations, which are of no concern to anyone at all other than myself."

"Aren't they?" asked Mary, but left it at that. Vaughn's tone might have been casual, but there was a fine edge of steel beneath that forbade further inquiry. "All right, then. What does your Roving Rosebud want of me?"

Vaughn winced. "A better name, I should think. No, no, don't bother. It will do for present. My friend seeks your assistance in the removal of a particular thorn. A thorn called the Black Tulip."

Mary took great pleasure in saying, "You are mixing your horticultural metaphors, my lord. Am I meant to know who this unusually thorny Tulip is?"

"If any of us knew who it actually was, there would be no need to enlist you." Having scored his retaliatory point, Vaughn went on: "The Black Tulip is the nom de guerre of a spy in the employ of the French government. He started off, in the usual way of such creatures, by leaving arch notes in inconvenient places. Along the way, however, he developed an irritating habit of skewering English agents. The, ahem, Rosebud would like to see him removed."

"And you want me to bring you his head on a platter?" Mary made no effort to hide her derision.

"Metaphorically speaking. I gather that the platter is optional these days." Vaughn paused to admire the effect of his rings before adding, "You have, shall we say, certain attributes that would be most advantageous to the goal in question."

Men had admired Mary's attributes before. This was, however, one of the more ingenious stories she had been presented with.

"You must think I am very green," she said gently.

"Oh, not so very green." Lord Vaughn's eyes danced silver. "Just a trifle chartreuse around the edges."

"Inebriating?"

"Unschooled."

That would teach her to fish for compliments from Lord Vaughn. "Not so unschooled as to believe that any spy would seek me out to serve as his personal assassin."

"Ah, that explains it." Lord Vaughn's understanding smile was a miracle of polite derision. "Your role would be merely a—how shall I put this? A decorative one. You do have some experience in that field, I believe. Your services are required not as assassin, but as bait."

Well, that certainly put her in her place. Mary raised a brow. "Weren't there any other convenient worms to hand?"

"None so well suited as you." Oh, bother, she had walked right into that one. Before Mary could come up with a suitably cutting rejoinder about snakes and their habits, Vaughn went on: "The Black Tulip has a curious conceit. He makes it a point to employ women with your particular coloring. They are"—Vaughn paused for good effect before delivering the pièce de résistance—"the petals of the Tulip."

"How poetic. And how entirely absurd."

"My dear girl, the whole lot of them are absurd, from the Purple Wonder in the other room to every fop in London who pins a carnation to his hat and tells his friends he's turned hero. Nonetheless, they still manage to cause a good deal of bother."

Torchlight slashed in a jagged angle across Vaughn's face, slicing across his nose, leaving his eyes in shadow. In the orange light, the lines around his mouth seemed more deeply graven than usual.

"A very great deal of bother," he repeated.

Despite herself, Mary's attention was caught. The improbable tale of rosebuds and tulips might have been nothing more than a polished line of patter, designed to capitalize on the current craze for gentlemen spies. But a man didn't feign that sort of bitterness. Not a man like Vaughn, at any rate. To acknowledge pain was to acknowledge that one was capable of sustaining a wound—in short, that one was capable of deeper feeling. It wasn't in Vaughn's style. Or, for that matter, in hers.

"And so," said Mary, "you introduce the bait."

"The Tulip," explained Vaughn, "is currently running rather short of petals. Unless his habits have changed, the Black Tulip will be in want of fresh recruits. Women of your coloring are rare in this part of the world. Hence my errand tonight."

"I see." Mary took a small turn about the corridor. The train of her dress whispered along the floor behind her, dragging with it a decade's worth of dust, undoubtedly turning her hem as murky as her musings. "You do realize that this is all highly irregular."

"To say the least," Vaughn agreed calmly. "There's no need to rush to a decision. Take some time to think about my proposition. Mull it over in the deepest depths of your maidenly bosom. I would, however, advise against unburdening yourself to your friends."

Mary nearly smiled at that. Friends. Ha. Her "friends" had been the first to claw her reputation to shreds when word of Geoffrey's defection exploded through the *ton*. That was one lesson one learned quickly on the bloody battlefield of Almack's. Confidantes were a luxury a clever woman could ill afford. To confide in others was to invite betrayal.

Mary lifted her chin. "I keep my own counsel."

"A wise choice. Should you accept, your duties will be minimal. There is, of course, the appeal of *patria* to be considered," Vaughn added as an afterthought. "Rule Britannia and pass the mutton."

Vaughn had obviously never tasted mutton. If he had, he wouldn't joke about it. "How could one help but be swayed by such a rousing appeal?"

"Spoken like a true and loving daughter of our scepter'd isle."

"I can do no better than to model myself on you."

"Alas for England." There was something oddly engaging about the way his mouth twisted up at one corner in self-mockery. "Sharper than serpent's tooth . . . There is something else, however, that might quicken your filial piety."

"What could possibly move me more than mutton?"

Beneath their heavy lids, Vaughn's pale eyes glinted with pleasurable anticipation, like an experienced cardplayer about to lay down a winning hand. "Something we haven't yet discussed. The small matter of remuneration."

Mary schooled her face to stillness, but she wasn't quick enough. Whatever Vaughn was looking for, he found it. His tone was insufferably smug as he added, "You will be paid. Handsomely."

Crossing his arms, he leaned back against a bust of the sixth Baron Pinchingdale and waited for her assent, the silver threads on his cuffs winking insolently in the torchlight.

He looked so vilely sure of himself—so vilely sure of her! So he thought that was all is would take to get her to say yes, did he? All he needed to do was dangle a few pieces of gold in front of the venal little creature and watch her jump.

Well, she wasn't going to jump for him. Not for an unspecified sum, at any rate. He'd have to do rather better than that.

Striking her most stately attitude, Mary raked her sapphire gaze across Vaughn's face with royal scorn.

"An amusing proposition, my lord, but I'm afraid you will simply have to ask elsewhere." Without waiting for his reaction, she turned on one heel, using the sweep of her long skirt to good effect. "I cannot imagine any recompense you might offer that would be of any interest to me."

Basking in self-satisfaction, Mary swished regally down the long corridor, giving Vaughn an excellent view of her elegant back and graceful carriage. Ha! There really was nothing quite like a good exit.

Except, perhaps, for a good last word. Vaughn's amused voice snaked after her as she sailed imperiously down the gallery.

"Can't you? I can. . . ."

Chapter Three

Alack, when once our grace we have forgot,
Nothing goes right; we would and we would not.

—William Shakespeare, *Measure for Measure*, IV, iv

Mary stubbed her toe.

Fortunately, she managed to turn her stumble into a flounce, using the momentum to propel herself forwards, away from the mocking echo of Vaughn's voice. Even the architecture appeared to be in league with him. The words bounced off the arched vault of the ceiling, following Mary clear down the length of the corridor.

He would have to get the last word, wouldn't he?

Mary had to admit to a certain grudging admiration for his technique. It had been beautifully done. He had waited until she was just far enough away that she would have had to stop, turn, and screech like a fishwife if she wanted to get a last word in. And what could one possibly reply to "I can"? The only response that came readily to mind was, "Well, I can't." Sophisticated stuff, that.

Scowling, Mary swished beneath the heavily carved arch that marked the end of the gallery. She was sure Vaughn would have enjoyed nothing more than to see her embroiled in a lengthy round of "cannot . . . can, too," baiting her on in that languid drawl of his.

What exactly was "I can" supposed to mean?

It was one of those hideous phrases that said nothing but implied a good deal. That was the brilliance of it. It left all the insults to the imagination of the hearer, playing on the hidden insecurities the speaker could only guess at. She could only fume and wonder at what he might have meant—when, in fact, he probably meant nothing in particular at all.

On the other hand, she could certainly imagine recompense that would interest her. And she was sure he could as well. She wondered how much he had been about to offer her. "Handsomely" was such an indeterminate term.

Whatever the amount might have been, it was a moot point now. Mary's pace slowed as reason began to return. After her grand exit, she couldn't very well go back and negotiate. It was a pity she had reacted so hastily. At the time, however, it had seemed far more important to wipe that smug expression off his face than to consider the merits of his offer.

It wasn't like her to react so irrationally. So emotionally. Mary made a face at herself as she paused to lean against the balcony overhanging the Great Hall. During her three years in London she had managed to sail unsullied through barbs from her friends, indecent propositions from her admirers, and assorted irritants from her loving family. The trick, she had learned long ago, was simply not to react. Nothing blunted malice—or lust, or jealousy, or anything else—like impassivity. One simply stayed silent and waited for the speaker to start to stumble and stutter.

One didn't throw a temper tantrum and sweep out.

It had been a trying few days, Mary reminded herself, running one gloved finger through the furrow created by an ancient gash in the walnut balustrade. First there had been the long trip from London to Gloucestershire, perched on a lumpy pile of her father's books, half-smothered by her mother's shawls, while her mother went into squealing raptures over Letty's new situation and her father fired off sarcastic comments that went clear over her mother's head. Once the journey ended, there was the joy of seeing the happy couple together for the first time since the tangled events of July, Letty lording it over them as mistress of Sibley Court and Geoffrey beaming with affection— affection for Letty, not for her.

And then that strange interlude in the Long Gallery, with the smoke from the torches thick in the air and Lord Vaughn's breath warm against the back of her neck. For a moment . . . well, that didn't matter, did it? None of it had been real.

Mary lifted her hands to rub her aching temples. In retrospect, the conversation with Vaughn seemed even stranger than it had at the time. Flowers and spies and a flirtation that wasn't. Had that original seduction scene been a form of test, a way to try her wits and her resolve? Or merely an attempt to throw her off balance?

If it had been the latter, it had worked.

Mary peered sideways, towards the entry to the Long Gallery, but the corridor lay as quiet as the crypt. Vaughn wasn't going to ruin a perfectly good parting line by following her. And it was too late to go back.

There were half a dozen questions she ought to have asked, and would have asked if she had had her wits about her. She was almost entirely convinced that he had been telling the truth about his odd offer, but there was a great deal that still didn't make sense. How, for example, was this spy, this Black Tulip, to know that she was available for hire? Any spy who made a practice of propositioning any young lady who fit his aesthetic requirements would not remain in business for long.

Unless . . . could it be a double blind? The tale of the Roving Rosebud might have been nothing more than a front, not for seduction but for more treacherous purposes. Closing her eyes, Mary re-created the image of a black jacket, black pantaloons, black cane, all limned with silver. Vaughn's chosen emblem was a serpent rather than a flower, but a man would have to be an idiot to proclaim his purpose on his sleeve, like that silly boy who had dubbed himself the Purple Pansy and gone off to France with his signature flower splashed right across his waistcoat. The French had jeered over that one for weeks.

Mary didn't know terribly much about Vaughn, but she did know that he had spent the past decade on the Continent, reputedly doing all the dreadful and dissipated things one did on the Continent. No one was ever entirely clear about just what those dreadful and dissipated pursuits were, but they appeared to involve large quantities of pasta and loose women. After being whispered from ballroom to ballroom, the stories had gotten rather garbled in translation.

Dissipation would make an excellent cover for treasonous activities. And she had certainly not displayed an excess of patriotic fervor.

Pushing away from the balcony, Mary straightened her shawl around her shoulders and permitted herself a resigned sigh. There was nothing for it but to rejoin the others, an activity she looked upon with about as much pleasure as entertaining a personal firing squad. Tentatively, she touched a hand to her hair, checking for flyaway strands. After her meeting with Vaughn, she felt frazzled, disarrayed. But a cursory inspection confirmed that all her ribbons were neatly tied and the three long curls that had taken her maid an hour to arrange still fell gracefully over one shoulder. All frayed edges were entirely internal.

Reassured that her armor was still sound, Mary walked resolutely to the carved double doors that fronted the Great Chamber, wishing she didn't feel quite so much like Marie Antoinette ascending the steps to the guillotine. Like so much else, the immense double doors were a sham. Within the massive, carved carapace was one normal-sized door, set into the larger edifice. Easing it open, Mary could hear the cacophony of chatter that marked a successful party, the shrill tones of the dowagers in their corner underpinned by the bass rumble of male conversation.

The clink of silver against china accented the clatter of voices. In her absence, the supper tray had been brought in. An array of delicacies had been set on a long trestle table at the far end of the room, blackened with age and supported by a series of curiously contorted Titans. One of them was most definitely sticking out its tongue. The scent of richly spiced game warred with the perfumes of the women above a musty undertone of damp tapestry and warped wood. Keeping country hours, they had had their dinner at six, eating in state at the battered old table in the Great Hall below, with Letty at one end and Geoffrey at the other. At least the appearance of the supper tray meant that the hideous evening was almost over.

Until they were forced to repeat the whole process tomorrow.

Mary paused to consider her options. The thought of more food rather turned her stomach, but at least a plate gave her an excuse for avoiding conversation. Directly in front of her, Lady Henrietta Dorrington and Lord Richard Selwick's wife—what was her name again?—were deep in animated chatter. Mary rather doubted they would welcome her company.

"I never thought it was a wise idea," declared Lord Richard's wife, jabbing her fork into a piece of cold game pie. "But you know Jane—"

"—and her choice in bonnets!" finished Henrietta Dorrington brightly, driving an elbow into her companion's ribs. "I never understood why she insisted on buying the yellow, when yellow is the one color that doesn't flatter her complexion. Hello, Miss Alsworthy. Have you had anything to eat yet?"

Mary had had quite enough humble pie for one day. She had never liked Lady Henrietta, and Lady Henrietta had never liked her.

"As much as anyone can be expected to stomach," she said with a smile just as bright as Henrietta's. "My sister sets an excellent table."

Lady Henrietta gave Mary a slightly wary look. "Well, you should really try the braised duck. It's excellent." Turning to Amy Selwick, she asked, "Will you and Richard go to Scotland for the shooting?"

Lord Richard's wife shook her head, setting her short dark curls bouncing. "No, we're straight back to Sussex. We plan—" Glancing at Mary, she abruptly broke off. "Um, that is, we have obligations that keep us close to home."

Increasing, thought Mary. How dull.

"You and Miles will come visit, won't you?" Amy said eagerly, confirming Mary's diagnosis. "Before Christmas? It would be such a help to us. Jane will be visiting, too."

"You know we would like to," said Lady Henrietta, with a pointed glance over her shoulder, to where their respective husbands propped up opposite ends of the mantelpiece, conspicuously ignoring each other. At least, Lord Richard was conspicuously ignoring Mr. Dorrington. Mr. Dorrington looked a bit like a dog hoping to wiggle his way back after having been booted off the hearth rug. Mary did vaguely recall hearing something about a falling out between the two men, something to do with Lady Henrietta's marriage, but with Geoffrey's defection following only a day behind, the domestic dramas of the Selwick clan had been the least of her concerns.

Amy made a face. "Don't worry. Richard is coming round. Slowly, but . . ." She shrugged in a way that proclaimed her French ancestry.

"But aren't they always," Henrietta finished for her, with a grin. It was clearly an old and well-established conversation. Whatever the rift between their menfolk, Lord Richard's wife and younger sister were clearly on excellent terms. "Slow, that is. At least they are speaking now, even if it is mostly in grunts."

"Someone ought to prepare a dictionary," chimed in Letty, settling herself on the settee next to Lady Henrietta. Mary had known they were friends—the less popular girls did tend to band together—but she had never realized they were quite that cozy with one another. "It would vastly improve communications between the sexes."

"Your disadvantage was in never having older brothers," said Lady Henrietta smugly. "It does wonders for one's fluency."

"I do have one," protested Amy. "What about Edouard?"

"But he's French," countered Henrietta, who had met him. "They can't be trusted to make the right sorts of inarticulate noises."

"The French are scarcely articulate at the best of times," put in Mary, just to have something to say.

Instead of tittering the way they were supposed to, the other three women just looked at her, as though they had forgotten she was there and were less than pleased to have been reminded.

"I believe I'll have some more of that duck," said Henrietta, rising with more energy than grace from her perch on the settee. "Letty?"

"I shouldn't." Mary's sister glanced ruefully down at her waist.

"But you will," concluded Lady Henrietta cheerfully, threading her arm through Letty's.

"You," protested Letty laughingly, "are an evil influence."

"I know," said Lady Henrietta complacently. "It's one of my more loveable attributes. Oh, look, there's Penelope with Miss Gwen! I wonder what mischief she's been getting into now?"

"Penelope or Miss Gwen?" demanded Amy, a dimple showing in one cheek.

"Either," replied Lady Henrietta with relish.

Laughing, the group swept on ahead, leaving Mary standing like so much detritus in its wake.

Only Letty hung back. She tilted her head up at Mary with what Mary privately thought of as her country housewife expression, a militant gleam that presaged someone being washed, fed, or otherwise ordered about. "You are going to come eat, aren't you? You didn't have a thing at dinner."

"I ate a whole jugged hare." Perhaps it hadn't been an entire jugged hare, but it had certainly been the better part of one. Including an ear Mary was quite sure wasn't supposed to have been there.

Mary could tell Letty didn't believe her. "Would you like some tea? Or coffee? Perhaps a lemonade? We still have some lemons left in the orangery—"

"No. Thank you." Mary cut her off before that hideous *we* could grow and spawn, birthing a litter of *ours*. "I believe I can contrive to carry on without a beverage."

Letty refused to be balked. "Are you comfortable? Are you quite sure you have everything you need?"

Except a husband, preferably titled. Mary managed a brittle smile. "Really, Letty, you needn't fuss. I'm quite as comfortable as I can be."

The words "under the circumstances" didn't need to be voiced. They seeped out like smoke, poisoning the air and scorching a deep furrow between Letty's brows. Guilt charred across every inch of her guileless face. Even her freckles looked guilty.

Mary bit back a wordless noise of annoyance. Why did Letty always have to be so earnest about everything? She was welcome to her dreary viscount, if only she would stop looking at her with that hangdog expression, the one that positively panted for expiation. What did Letty expect her to say? *No, darling, I don't mind in the least that you've quite ruined my prospects. I always wanted to be made a laughingstock in front of the* ton. It only made it worse that Letty hadn't done any of it on purpose. Outright malice would have been easier to bear than blundering virtue.

"What about a biscuit? We have some lovely gingery ones. . . ."

Mary just looked at her.

Letty sighed. "Perhaps, later, we might speak privately?"

Mary's expression didn't change. "Perhaps."

"I have some good news for you."

"I shall look forward to it."

There was nothing Letty could say to that, so she simply furrowed her brow at Mary one last time—her concerned expression, as opposed to her feeding or washing expression—and went off after her friends in pursuit of refreshments. From the supper table, Mary heard the flurry of chatter abruptly peak in volume as Letty rejoined her friends. Like a flock of geese squawking, she thought unpleasantly.

Vaughn still hadn't returned.

He couldn't still be in the gallery, could he? Mary's eyes narrowed as she glanced at the narrow sliver of floor revealed by the half-open door. She couldn't blame him for wanting to avoid the rest of the house party—but where was he? Without his saturnine presence, the gathering felt oddly flat.

"Darling!"

The same could not be said for the maternal bosom, which was currently swollen with unabashed glee and an entire carafe of ratafia. Mary fought her way free of her mother's embrace.

"Isn't this above all things splendid?" gushed Mrs. Alsworthy. "Oh, your darling, darling sister."

So, noted Mary dispassionately, Letty had risen to two darlings.

Bring out the Pinchingdale diamonds and she might attain the giddy heights of three endearments at a time. In the space of one wedding ceremony, Letty had gone from disappointment to favorite daughter. As for Mary, she had been demoted down into the depths of parental purgatory. Not hell, since she still had a chance to redeem herself by an advantageous match, but she had quite definitely been booted out of paradise pending further developments.

"Such a house!" Mrs. Alsworthy exclaimed, her cheeks pink with pride and wine. "Have you ever seen anything like it?"

"It is certainly something out of the ordinary." Unless, of course, one happened to live between the covers of a novel by Monk Lewis or Mrs. Radcliffe.

"And the park! I've never seen anything so grand. Why, I'm sure you could fit half of London into it!" Mrs. Alsworthy beamed gleefully about her. "Your sister has done very well for herself, very well, indeed."

"Hasn't she," murmured Mary.

"I do wish we could have found as comfortable a settlement for you," fretted Mrs. Alsworthy, conveniently forgetting that Lord Pinchingdale had originally been intended for her older daughter. "I don't understand it. Three Seasons! One would have thought you would have caught someone by now." Mrs. Alsworthy preened, one ringed hand rising to pat her green silk turban. "I secured your father without even *one* Season."

"At the Littleton Assemblies," Mary supplied, having heard the story more times than the Prince of Wales had consumed hot dinners. "I know."

"I was wearing my blue brocade, with my hair all piled on top of my head—that was the fashion then, you know, and very becoming it was to me, too—and the sweetest little stomacher all embroidered with purple pansies, and your father was smitten, smitten on the spot."

People who waxed rapturous about love matches clearly had never been privy to the aftermath of one. Her parents' great love had lasted all of a year; the marriage itself had been limping along for three decades.

"Of course," Mrs. Alsworthy was still rattling on, "I was never so tall as you, and we all know that men don't like tall girls. It makes them feel small. You really must get in the trick of looking up at them, like so."

Mrs. Alsworthy hunched her shoulders, stuck out her neck, and attempted to look dewy-eyed.

Mary wasn't quite sure how impersonating a myopic turtle was supposed to help her secure a husband, but it was easier not to argue. "Yes, Mama."

Mrs. Alsworthy squinted thoughtfully at her. "And perhaps a bit more trim on the bodice . . . Gentlemen do so appreciate a nicely trimmed décolletage."

"I don't think it's the trim, Mama," said Mary.

As she had known she would, her mother ignored her and carried on with her own train of thought as the ribbons on her own exuberantly trimmed bodice trembled in sympathy. "So fortunate that Letty has offered to fund another Season for you—but this will have to be the last, you know. To have five Seasons looks like desperation."

"*Letty* is paying for my next Season?"

"Why, yes. Isn't it lovely of her to take such notice of her sisters now that she is a viscountess? A viscountess!"

"Just lovely," repeated Mary flatly. It was one thing to make the same tired rounds a fourth time, batting her eyelashes at the same rapidly diminishing crop of men, but it was quite another matter to do so on the sufferance of a younger sister. To know that every shawl, every dress, even the food on the table had been magnanimously donated by Letty for the worthy cause of helping her older sister to a husband.

On those terms, she would rather remain a spinster.

Only she wouldn't. Either way, she would be choking on her sister's charity. She could accept Letty's munificence now—and meekly submit herself to being organized as Letty saw fit—in the interest of one last, desperate bid for the comparative independence of the married state. Or she could remain unwed and be a perpetual dependent upon her parents. Which, in the end, meant being Letty's dependent, since her father's income was scarcely enough to keep him in new books and her mother in turbans. Between the two of them, they neatly dissipated the revenue from her father's small estate before one could say beeswax.

It was rather galling to face a future as a petitioner in the house where she had thought to be mistress.

"And Lord Pinchingdale will be paying Nicholas's fees at Harrow! Harrow! Can you imagine! We could never have done so much."

"Nicholas must be overjoyed," said Mary.

Nicholas would be miserable. Her little brother was the despair of the local vicar, who had been enlisted to teach him the classics. Fortunately for Nicholas, the vicar was as nearsighted as he was hard of hearing, as well as being prone to drifting off at odd moments, a habit Nicholas had done his best to encourage. Mary would be very surprised if Nicholas knew how to read, much less in Latin. Being sent to Harrow would do wonders for him—if they didn't expel him first. It was undoubtedly the right thing to do. Letty always knew the right thing to do. But it set Mary's teeth on edge.

She was the eldest. She was the one who was supposed to be magnanimously funding her brother's education and using her social consequence to bring out her younger sisters. Not the other way around.

It wasn't *right*.

"Have you tried the duck?" Mary cut in, just to put a stop to the catalogue of all the benefits Letty planned to confer on her family now that she was a viscountess—a viscountess! Her mother enjoyed the title so much that the word had acquired an inevitable echo every time she uttered it.

"Duck?"

Mary took her mother by the arm and steered her towards the refreshment table. "Yes, duck. I hear it's very good. There's also game pie."

Unfortunately, she didn't think food would do much to fill the hollow feeling that seemed to have settled into the pit of her stomach. It was the same feeling she had had in the gallery before Vaughn appeared, only ten times worse. In the space of three months, she had become superfluous. The grand match she had intended to make had been made by Letty; the benefits she had intended to graciously bestow upon her family were already being bestowed—by Letty. What was there left for her? Nothing but to sit and wait and be an object of charity, fed on Letty's leavings.

As if she had read her mind, Letty spotted Mary and their mother and began to bear down on them. In her hands, she held a plate piled high with food, and her face bore its most determined housewife expression. Someone was going to be fed, and they were going to be fed now.

It wasn't going to be Mary. Without a qualm, Mary tossed her mother to the wolves. "Look!" she called out cheerfully, giving her mother a little shove in the direction of her sister. "Isn't Letty lovely? She's prepared a plate for you."

"Darling!" Mrs. Alsworthy exclaimed, and made for Letty with both arms outstretched, although whether to embrace her or to snatch up the plate was largely unclear.

Mary didn't wait to find out.

Leaving her relations to it, Mary hastily made her exit stage left, back into the relative quiet of the upper gallery. It should take Letty some time to extricate herself from the maternal embrace. Well, it was only fair, Mary decided. If Letty wanted to be a two-darling daughter, there was a price to be paid.

Mary had her mind set on a very different sort of price. Lifting her skirts clear of the dusty floor, she made straight across the upper hall into the Long Gallery. The painted Pinchingdales held no fascination for her this time. She strode rapidly past them, seeking the living rather than the dead. There was no one standing between the torches, no one sitting on the window seat. The gallery was empty, deserted.

Mary reached the window and turned, thwarted. Where was he? She would have seen him had he returned to the Great Chamber. There had been no sign of movement downstairs in the hall. Of course, he might have retired to his room or gone out to the gardens or climbed up to the battlements to howl at the moon. He could be anywhere in the vast old pile. He might even have left—really, truly left.

That was too dreadful a prospect to be thought of. She had to find him. Because anything, anything at all was better than spending the winter hearing her mother sing an endless chorus of the wonders of her sister, while she herself faded into something not quite alive. She would see just what sort of price Lord Vaughn's theoretical flowery friend was willing to pay. And if Vaughn himself was the Black Tulip . . . well, then, surely the government must provide rewards for that sort of discovery.

But where had he got to? She couldn't very well seek him out in his bedchamber. That would spell ruin, and Vaughn, Mary could tell, was not the marrying kind.

Not like Geoffrey.

Of course, even being truly ruined would be more interesting than another evening of game pie.

Hands on her hips, Mary stalked over to the red velvet curtain by which Vaughn had posed when he first appeared earlier that evening— and stopped, her eye caught by a glimmer of light where there had been none before. The archway half-concealed by the curtain led off into the western half of the wing that fronted the garden, the bottom half of the second long stroke of the H. Earlier that evening, both corridors leading off the gallery had been dark and still. Now, lamplight seeped across the floor, coming from a partially open door just a little way down the corridor.

A superstitious shiver snaked down Mary's spine. Framed in red velvet, the deserted hallway might have been a stage set for *Don Giovanni*, black as a scoundrel's heart except for the reddish tint of hellfire to come. She could, of course, go back to the safety of the Great Chamber.

She could fix her mother's plate and listen to her tales of success at the Littleton Assemblies.

Brimstone, it was.

Squaring her shoulders, Mary set off to strike her bargain with the Devil.

Chapter Four

Better to reign in hell, than serve in heav'n.

—John Milton, *Paradise Lost*, The First Book

A skull made a very restful companion.

Stretching one leg out in front of him, Vaughn settled more comfortably into the squashy interior of a squat wooden chair. In front of him, paired peasants shouldered the burden of the hooded mantel, grinning at an unpleasant rural secret. The little room must once have served an undistinguished purpose, antechamber to a grander room or perhaps even a privy, but at some point in the last century the room had been converted into a private den, lined with books and tricked out with the latest in the Gothic style. A blackened walnut table had been fitted out with an illuminated medieval manuscript, placed next to a decanter and goblets hammered out of semi-precious metal and set about with misshapen chunks of colored glass meant to look like a prosperous chieftain's hoard. The skull, grinning winningly from one corner of the table, completed the scene. A tentative tap of the fingernail confirmed that it was not, in fact, a plaster facsimile.

No detail had been neglected. Gargoyles stuck out their tongues from the joins in the vaulted ceiling, and a mirror had been cunningly angled above the fire to mirror and magnify the stained-glass window hung above the door. The distorted reflection transformed the tiny chamber into a towering cathedral, licked at the edges by the orange flames of the hearth. A cunning illusion, reflected Vaughn, as long as one didn't look away from the mirror.

But then, that was the way of illusions, wasn't it? All charlatans, whether the stage magician or the amorous rake, relied upon man's yearning to be deceived, to gaze in the mirror of his own desirings and be gulled by the image therein. It was a tempting prospect, to look and believe, like Faust panting after Helen's shadow. In the end, however, the mirror always cracked, revealing the images for the shams they were. Loyalty, love, the joys of home and hearth—no more substantial than an opium dream and just as debilitating while they lasted.

Of course, none of the earnest young people cavorting in their innocent frolics in the Great Chamber would admit a word of it. They all believed in fates worse than death, True Love in capital letters, and the innate goodness of man. Even Jane, for all her perspicacity, suffered from an unaccountable attachment to abstract notions of honor. Except, perhaps, for Miss Alsworthy.

Now there was something out of the ordinary.

Hooking an arm over the side of the chair, Vaughn gazed reflectively into the mirror. He was, he realized with some surprise, suffering from an entirely unaccountable sense of disappointment. But, then, the whole evening had been entirely unaccountable. Enjoyable, even. Her opening jab about solitude had been nicely done, very nicely done indeed, although she had lost ground later on by letting herself be rattled by his abrupt switch away from seduction. Conversation, when conducted properly, wasn't unlike a good fencing match, a constant attempt to sniff out one's opponent's weak spots and throw him off guard. Under that carefully cultivated mask of vapidity, Miss Alsworthy harbored a natural knack for the sport. In want of training, certainly, but with an acid tongue that boded well for future bouts.

The last thing he needed just now was yet another black-haired beauty getting in the way of his plans. And yet, the complications might have been adjusted to his advantage. He might have sworn off raven-haired agents, but surely one more, employed in just the right way . . . What were vows for, but to be broken? No one knew that better than he.

Ah, well. After the way their little interview had ended, the point was decidedly moot.

Drumming his fingers against the blackened wood, Vaughn addressed his new friend, Yorick Redux. "Another lost opportunity, my dear chap. I would imagine you know something about those."

"My lord?"

It wasn't Yorick. Not unless Yorick had suddenly become a good deal more talkative and female. The voice was a woman's voice, low and imperious. A voice recently heard and even more recently remembered. A shadow swayed over the table, falling across Yorick's bald pate and the barbaric splendor of silver and gems.

Vaughn stilled, his hands closing over the arms of the chair. Beneath his languid demeanor, anticipation thrilled through him, sharp as a foeman's steel. It was merely an antidote to the grinding ennui of the past week, the anticipation of a verbal duel with an unexpectedly adept opponent, nothing more.

"Miss Alsworthy," he murmured, rising smoothly from his chair.

Lapped in shadow, her graceful figure looked insubstantial and oddly fragile. The hearth light picked out the hollows beneath her collarbones and the shadows under her eyes, whittling away the armor of the flesh to the brittle bone beneath.

He had, reflected Vaughn wryly, been spending altogether too much time in the company of corpses if he could look at a beautiful woman and think only of the grave.

He moved swiftly to shut the door behind her.

"What a pleasant . . . surprise."

Miss Alsworthy's shoulders stiffened as though the door had thudded into her back rather than its frame. She hid it well, though, taking the moment to stroll forwards, one pale hand trailing lightly along the edge of the table. Only her shoulder blades betrayed her, brittle as glass above the scalloped back of her dress.

"A friend of yours?" She nodded to the skull with commendable sangfroid.

Vaughn closed the short distance between door and table. Resting a caressing hand on Yorick's bald pate, he traced the brow with a deliberation that would have brought a blush to a more susceptible maiden's cheek. "I've only just made his acquaintance. A decent enough sort, although his conversational style appears to be somewhat lacking."

"I thought all men desired such a complaisant companion." Mary's deep blue eyes glinted up at Vaughn from beneath lowered lids. "Someone to offer unconditional agreement."

" 'The grave's a fine and private place, but none I think do there embrace,' " Vaughn recited meditatively, lingering on the last word. "Rather a high price to pay for unwinking devotion, don't you think?"

"One pays a price for everything."

"And what, Miss Alsworthy, is your price?"

He had expected her to answer with coy digressions, but she surprised him. "A dowry," she said abruptly, the train of her skirt whispering against the table leg. "The cost of a Season."

"Is that all?"

"All?" Mary glanced back at him, bitter humor lengthening the corners of her lips. It was, he thought, more becoming to her than the mask of placid sweetness she donned in front of society. "You might ask the same of the young man who begs the cost of a commission, or a sea captain in want of a ship. Trifles to you, but ruin to those who lack them."

"Surely, you have a sister."

"And now a brother, too," Mary said grimly. "Would you take charity on such terms?"

Having spent the better part of a month in Dublin in enforced proximity with Miss Alsworthy's estimable relations, Vaughn would sooner bunk with Methodist missionaries. But he certainly wasn't going to afford her the gratification of saying so.

Vaughn stretched lazily, setting the silver strands in his lace sparkling. "I can only be grateful such a situation has never arisen."

"Not all of us have that luxury."

"This sudden interest in my company . . ." Vaughn propped a shoulder against the wall, affecting an expression of well-bred surprise. "Are you trying to tell me that you have reconsidered the merits of my little offer?"

"Yes," said Mary shortly, her head bent low over the illuminated manuscript on the table.

"Despite your, er, earlier objections? I wouldn't want to force you to anything you find unworthy of your energies."

"It is I," murmured Mary, "who am unworthy of such solicitude from so great a personage as yourself."

"Brava," said Vaughn gravely. "There are few who condescend so well to condescension."

Without looking up, Mary flicked over page of the manuscript. Sturdy peasants cavorted in a pastoral fantasy on the red, blue, and gold page. "It is not, however, a marketable skill."

"Not on the marriage market, at any event," agreed Vaughn. "Philistines, the lot of them."

Mary lifted her chin, her gaze like a gauntlet. "Are you offering to remedy their lack of discernment?"

With the words quivering in the air between them, Vaughn caught her gaze and held it. He met her stare for stare, challenge for challenge, before saying, slowly and very deliberately, "No."

Mary smiled without humor. "I didn't think so."

Well done! applauded Vaughn. He found himself seized with a most unusual desire to render genuine praise. Since praise might be taken for approbation and approbation for encouragement, he quashed the impulse and turned instead to the assortment of barbaric drinking vessels. Raising the decanter, he poised it above a misshapen silver goblet.

"May I offer you a glass of brandy—in the spirit of our future partnership? Our future *business* partnership, that is."

Mary closed the Book of Hours with a decided snap. "Hadn't we better come to an agreement before we celebrate it?"

Vaughn lifted his glass in a toast. "A lady as shrewd as she is beautiful." It wasn't intended as a compliment, and she was astute enough to know it. "To business, then. I assume you have no objections if I prefer not to commit the terms to paper?"

"As long as I can trust you to abide by them." Her tone suggested that she couldn't.

It was lovely to see cynicism in one so young. It positively restored his faith in human nature. Vaughn placed his hand over his heart. "You may trust to my honor, dear lady, as you would to your own."

She rose beautifully to the insult, like a trout to the hook. "Do you ever come to the point, my lord?"

"Not when I can avoid it." Vaughn toyed with the stem of his glass, sending the amber liquid swirling within the bowl. The metal, while picturesque, lent the brew a tinny flavor. "I prefer the circuitous route. The scenery is more entertaining."

"Linger too long," Mary said, angling her head pointedly towards the door, "and the scenery may change."

"The gods would weep," replied Vaughn politely.

A branch cracked in the hearth, sending reddish sparks flaring up-wards. Mary's eyes strayed from the hearth towards the skull. "I doubt God has anything to do with this."

"You don't believe in divine providence, Miss Alsworthy?"

"Only when He is on the side of the strongest battalion."

A glimmer of Vaughn's pale eyes acknowledged the quotation and the point. "The clash of arms is merely a diversion. The real battles occur in little rooms such as these. That," he added smoothly, "will be your task."

"What sort of little room did you have in mind?" Mary asked warily.

"Not a bedchamber, if that was worrying at your conscience."

Vaughn had to give her credit; she didn't flush or affect maidenly flutters. Having determined to do business, Miss Alsworthy was noth-ing if not direct. "My conscience," she said levelly, "isn't the problem. My reputation is."

"Not virtue, but the appearance of it," Vaughn agreed with all seri-ousness, saving the sting for last. He smiled pleasantly as he added, "One wouldn't want to risk being compromised . . . again."

Mary's fingers clenched almost imperceptibly within the folds of her skirts, but there was no sign of it in the perfectly sculpted lines of her face. "I don't believe you would enjoy the outcome any more than I would."

"Touché," Vaughn acknowledged the point with a fragment of a nod. "Your solution?"

Mary addressed herself to the fire rather than him, her expression remote. "It would be the last word in foolishness to obtain the means to get a husband only to render myself unmarriageable. In order to prevent that occurrence, I must insist on the presence of a chaperone at all times."

"As you are chaperoned now," murmured Vaughn. "Our presence in this room is in itself highly suspect. Alone. A closed door. Tsk, tsk, Miss Alsworthy."

"In my sister's house." Mary shrugged. "None of her guests would dare make a fuss. Letty wouldn't allow it."

"And you?" Vaughn braced both hands against the table, closing the distance between them. "You don't feel the least bit uncomfortable?"

"In a business discussion?" Mary cast back at him.

"Business, my dear Miss Alsworthy, is a very broad term. And this"—Vaughn's voice dropped to a slumberous murmur—"is not a very broad place."

Mary stood straight and still, a perfect marble figurine. He might have believed her entirely unaffected, except for the telltale flutter of the pulse at her throat.

"Are you quite finished, my lord?" she asked coolly.

It took more strength than he would have liked to pull casually away, to shake out his cuffs with every appearance of unconcern. "For the moment. I have no objection to the notion of a chaperone in principle—as you say, it could be deuced inconvenient to us both otherwise—but you may find yourself in some odd situations."

"All the more reason for a chaperone," countered Mary.

"Have you one who is blind, deaf, and dumb?" asked Vaughn sarcastically. "Such a one would be perfect for our purposes."

Mary's eyes lit like stained glass. "I believe I might," she murmured, her mouth quirking with private amusement.

Vaughn knocked back the remains of his brandy with uncharacteristic haste. Tense and guarded, she was magnificent. Alight with mischief, she was . . .

A tool to be used for a limited set of circumstances, he reminded himself, gulping down the astringent brew. And those circumstances did not include his bed, his settee, his carriage, or any other horizontal surface his undisciplined mind might devise.

Vaughn set his glass down on its tray, locking his hands behind his back as he paced rapidly away from the table. "I leave the procurement of a chaperone to you. At the end of the house party, you will return to London with Lord and Lady Pinchingdale."

"I hadn't heard that they were planning to return to London."

"Hadn't you?" Vaughn shot over his shoulder. A few words from Jane would rapidly put the Pinchingdales' plans to rights. There were benefits to being associated with the Pink Carnation. "I imagine the new viscountess will wish to avail herself of the shops. If you are lucky, you might even share in the largesse."

All animation fled Mary's face, faster than a ship before a gale. Regarding him with a hauteur that Vaughn found immensely reassuring, she demanded, "Once I return to London, what then?"

Once in London . . . Vaughn banished thoughts of beds, lounges, and settees. He tapped a finger lightly against Yorick's bald skull. "Once in London, we bait our trap."

"With me."

Vaughn smiled at her in a way that would have sent any sensible bait scurrying for cover. "Precisely."

"And if your fish doesn't bite?"

"Don't worry. You will still be paid."

This time, Mary didn't flinch. "In full."

"As agreed. You have my hand on it. Or shall we, as our feudal ancestors would, seal it with a kiss?"

Mary had no doubt that Vaughn would delight in exercising his droit du seigneur. "Your hand will do."

The crispness of her tone brought a smile to his narrow lips. Lifting her proffered hand, Vaughn held it suspended for a moment, cool and pale in his own, before very deliberately turning it over and brushing a kiss against the tender skin of her palm.

What use was fire, after all, if not to be played with?

With the skill of long practice, Vaughn folded her nerveless fingers around the palm, pressing her hand in his own before releasing her. "There. A doubly sealed bargain."

Snatching back her hand, Mary said briskly, "I need no further assurances." Her skirts whispered secrets against the Turkey carpet as she swept grandly towards the door. "Good night, my lord."

It would have been a magnificent exit but for the intransigence of the doorknob. Turning the moment to good account, she glanced regally back over her shoulder as her fingers grappled with the knob. "I look forward to a profitable partnership for us both."

Lord Vaughn's lips spread over his teeth in a decidedly wolfish smile.

"As do I, my dear. As do I."

Chapter Five

Someone tapped me on the shoulder, sending my pencil skidding clear across the page. Fortunately, it was my notebook page rather than Lord Vaughn's appointment book. I glanced up irritably, one arm still shielding the page I'd been working on, like a fifth grader in a French exam.

The man in front of me embodied the essence of officialdom. Despite the fact that it was a Saturday, he wore a sport coat that was just a matching pair of pants short of being a suit. His dark hair was going gray at the temples in a way that might have come out of a packet labeled FOR THAT DISTINGUISHED LOOK. Even his tie fit the image, a conventional deep blue scattered with dozens of tiny shields that undoubtedly ought to have signified the identity of an august institution if I only were properly up on the iconography of the English educational system.

"I'm sorry to have startled you," he began. That struck me as a remarkably silly comment, considering that the whole point of tapping someone is to startle them. "I'm Nigel. Nigel Dempster."

Ah, the missing archivist. So much for my stern librarian with the pince-nez on her bony bosom.

"I'm Eloise. Eloise Kelly." He did seem to be standing there for a reason, so I began haphazardly piling up my papers. "I'm sorry if I've overstayed. I wasn't sure what the hours would be on a Saturday. . . ."

"No, no, nothing like that." Dempster held out a soothing hand, which went admirably with the strips of gray in his hair. I relapsed back into my metal chair as he cast an unfavorable look at the now-empty desk at the back of the room. "I only regret that I wasn't here when you arrived." His nose twitched like a cat's whiskers. "I really must apologize for Rob. He is still in the process of being trained."

Next, he was going to say that it was so hard to find good help nowadays.

He didn't. But I could tell he was thinking it.

Instead, he tilted his head towards the jumbled mass of documents in the box in front of me. "Rob mentioned to me that you had asked for Sebastian, Lord Vaughn."

"Was I not supposed to?" I cast an anguished glance in the direction of the ecru box. The papers hadn't looked particularly frail, but every institution had its own peculiar rules. It's all part of the fun of historical research. At the Bodleian, before even letting me near a manuscript, they had made me recite a little pledge that sounded remarkably like the Pledge of Allegiance, only involving not ripping, scarring, immolating, or otherwise violating the documents for which they stood, so help me God. It would be too cruel to have known those papers existed and then have to give them back—or wait endless months for the proper forms and permissions to be processed. I wanted them, and I wanted them now.

"No, no," he said, and I began breathing again. "We do have some earlier papers that are in a much worse state. Those we loan out only in microfiche."

I nodded knowingly, trying to repress the impulse to grab the box and bolt. "But these are perfectly capable of being handled, right?"

Instead of answering my question, he surveyed his fiefdom with all the pride of a Norman knight with his very first keep. "This is a new project, you know. The Vaughn Collection's primary mission has always been the care and preservation of the objets d'art accumulated by the Vaughn family." He conscientiously rolled the *r* in art.

"It is a pretty amazing collection up there," I said, surreptitiously scooting my notebook closer to me, like a stallion at the starting gate. Ready, set . . . only the blasted man didn't go.

Instead, he shook his distinguished head with a practiced look of professional resignation. "The written records, except when needed for matters of provenance, were sadly neglected. When I started here last year, the records room was a shambles."

"You've done an incredible job," I lied. Always be polite to archivists. It was one of the first principles my advisor had pounded into me in my first-year research seminar. A little flattery never hurts, either. "The catalogue at the BL isn't half this accurate."

"It isn't, is it?" If he had been a woman, he would have patted his hair. Being a man, he just preened a bit, touching a hand to his already perfectly straight tie. "We do have a much smaller source base," he said modestly, showing no inclination to move. "Although several of the Vaughns did keep up a very broad correspondence."

"I'm sure they did," I said glumly. Occasionally, flattery backfired. I braced myself for a lengthy disquisition on the Hon. Miss Arabella Vaughn (1868–1918) and her raptures over the loveliness of the seaside. [N.B. There is no Arabella Vaughn, honorable or otherwise. I just made her up for illustrative purposes. Historians aren't really supposed to do that, but we always do, anyway.]

"Sebastian was one of the most prolific," he added, with a nod towards my work.

Thank goodness it wasn't Arabella. "I hadn't realized you were on first-name terms. I got the impression that Lord Vaughn wasn't on first-name terms with anyone at all, including himself."

That went right over his head. He gave me a hearty smile that stopped just short of being a pat on the head. "One gets a very strong sense of his personality after working with his papers."

"That one does," I agreed, just as heartily. "He's quite the character."

"What brings you to our Sebastian?"

"I'm doing research for my doctoral dissertation," I parroted, for what felt like the thousandth time since I had arrived in England. I could do it in my sleep by now. "On espionage during the Napoleonic Wars."

"Ah," said Dempster, smiling at me in an intimate way that made me wonder if my sweater had come unbuttoned. "So you're also looking for the Pink Carnation."

The room was so quiet, you could have heard a jaw drop. Mine, for starters.

Also? What in the hell did he mean by *also*?

The Pink Carnation was mine. All mine. There was no also.

I began to wonder if one could publish before one had anything written. I certainly wasn't going to allow this, this *archivist* to pip me to the post. My Pink Carnation. Mine, mine, mine.

"Of course," I jabbered, doing everything but hug my notebook to my chest, as if the identity of the Pink Carnation might somehow have leaked across the page, "my dissertation is on espionage more broadly. I'm looking at the means and manner of all sorts of different organizations over that twenty-three-year period between 1792 and 1815.... You said *also?*"

Dempster shrugged, in a nonchalant gesture worthy of Vaughn himself. "My own background is in history of art, but the Pink Carnation has become something of a hobby for me. Working among these papers"—he gestured broadly back towards the muniments room— "it's very hard not to take an interest. One of history's great mysteries here, at my disposal."

"Of course," I said, relief oozing out of every pore of my body. It was a pity he hadn't taken up the Princes in the Tower instead, but as long as his interest was genuinely that of a bored amateur, it was all fine.

"We might," he suggested delicately, "even be of use to each other. I might be able to direct you to areas of the Vaughn Collection of interest to you."

"Mmm," I said noncommittally. Considering I already knew who the Pink Carnation was, I would be of far more use to him than he to me. As for keeping it secret, my own skills at subterfuge were what one might tactfully call less than well developed. My sister, Jillian, would say it went with the red hair. Did I mention that Jillian is brunette?

On the other hand, if this Nigel Dempster really did know his way around the Vaughn papers as well as he claimed . . . well, it couldn't hurt to pick his brain just a bit, could it?

I firmly shut out the echo of Jillian's mocking laughter. Little sisters have no respect these days.

Dempster waved a hand at the box in front of me. "If you're looking for spies, I'm afraid you'll find Sebastian a bit of a disappointment."

"Really?"

Dempster perched familiarly on the edge of the table. I could see a bit of striped sock poking out beneath his trouser leg, patterned with discrete red blobs. "For a man who wrote so fluently on politics and art, Sebastian is remarkably chary with the details of his personal life. He remains, even within his own collection, a bit of a shadowy personage."

Were we talking about the same Sebastian? Lord Vaughn? It was the Vaughn collection, after all. I didn't think Lord Vaughn would have tolerated the infiltration of extraneous Sebastians.

Dempster gazed pensively off into space, a pose I recognized from far too many BBC documentaries: historian waxes informative about lack of information. At length. It's amazing how much screen time historians can eke out of the absence of evidence.

"Sebastian's diaries place him in France at suspect times, but never say why. He attends meetings of underground societies, but leaves unspoken to what end. Do you know"—he leaned confidingly forward—"I quite suspect Sebastian himself of being the elusive Pink Carnation." His plummy voice lent "elusive" all the pomp and circumstance of Alistair Cooke introducing *Masterpiece Theatre*. "But I have no confirmation, no—as it were—proof."

And then it hit me. He didn't know who Jane was. And if he didn't know who Jane was, then none of the rest of it made the least bit of sense. That list of names at the house party that had sent a hundred bells ringing for me wouldn't mean anything at all to someone who hadn't known about the circumstances of Lord Richard's marriage, Lady Henrietta's involvement in the search for the Black Tulip, and the peculiar circumstances of Lord and Lady Pinchingdale's so-called honeymoon. Based on what was available in the public record, all an outsider would know was that Lord Richard, guest at the same house party, had at one point been the Purple Gentian. That was all. And while that might tend to suggest that there might be something more going on than hunt the slipper, it wasn't enough to implicate Jane or inform one of much of anything at all.

Almost all my revelations—the missing bits that enabled me to decode Vaughn's terse notations of his activities—had come as a result of a particular set of privately owned papers. The Selwick papers, to be precise.

Oh dear. Selwick. Colin. Me. Him. Dinner.

All systems accelerated to red alert. Oh God, what time was it? I had been in the basement for what felt like years, but it couldn't have been more than a few hours, could it? There were no windows down there, just those plain whitewashed walls. For all I knew, it could have been anytime between noon and midnight.

"I've often thought," mused Dempster, in uncanny echo, "that the answer must lie in the Selwick papers."

Oh, damn, damn, damn. I needed to take a shower, and pick an outfit, and shave every part of my body that could possibly be shaved, whether he was going to see it or not. In short, all the requisite predate preparations that men never notice, anyway, but without which we can't make it out of the door of the apartment.

"Do you know what time it is?" I asked abruptly.

Dempster was taken aback, but the influence of the old school tie prevailed. "Six o'clock."

I had been there for five hours? Thank goodness he had interrupted me, or I might have turned into an archival Rip Van Winkle. I could picture Colin standing there . . . slowly turning old and gray . . . while I moldered away forgotten in the basement of the Vaughn Collection, just transcribing one last document. Of course, he wouldn't be standing there all that while. Some other lucky woman would undoubtedly snatch him up in the meantime. Intelligent Englishmen with decent dental work don't come along every day.

"Will you excuse me?" I blurted out. "I really have to run. I have a dinner engagement—lost track of time—really don't want to be late."

"And it's a Saturday night," Dempster finished for me, looking less stiff than I had seen him. He really wasn't a bad-looking man once he dropped the posing. If you liked that sort of type. "Don't worry. I'll put these away for you."

"Are you sure?" I began shoving my personal effects pell-mell into my bag before he could change his mind. "That would be beyond kind of you. Thank you."

"I'm assuming you'll be back?"

"Absolutely! First thing on Monday." I grinned at him. "And I promise not to make you clean up my mess next time."

Sweeping my bag onto my shoulder, I wriggled out of my chair, all but overturning it in my haste.

Dempster edged gingerly off the table so as to cause the minimum creasage in his Savile Row slacks. "There is a fee."

"A fee?" Swiveling back around, I tripped over the pointed toe of my own boot. Had I missed the small print somewhere?

"Coffee," Dempster elaborated, looking far too pleased with himself. I suppose it wasn't every day that he got to send a girl staggering.

"Uh, sure. Coffee." He'd made me lose precious minutes for that? "That would be great. I'll look forward to it." I paused in the doorway just long enough for a haphazard wave. "Bye!"

The faint echo of "next week" followed me up the white-walled stairs. Fortunately, I knew the type. It wasn't my personal attributes that spurred him on, it was the prospect of an informed audience as he trotted out all his pet theories about the Pink Carnation. There would be no need to invoke the specter of an invisible boyfriend to ward him off.

Unless, by that point, it wasn't an invisible boyfriend anymore, but a real one. One with toffee blond hair and square, capable hands . . .

The jolt of my bag bumping against my hip brought me abruptly back to my senses. No point in getting ahead of myself when we hadn't even had our first date yet. Although I could imagine just how comfortable it would be to curl up together on the couch on a Sunday morning, matching coffee mugs perched on the coffee table, a half-eaten bagel sitting askew on a copy of the *Sunday Times*.

Hitching up the strap of my bag before it could bump me again, I got myself firmly in hand. I didn't even have a coffee table. And I wasn't sure if they sold bagels in London. In fact, I was pretty sure that the whole idyllic image came straight out of a *New York Times* commercial. Reality wasn't like that. Reality was spilled coffee and newsprint on one's fingers—and being too comfortably snuggled up against a warm shoulder to care. I didn't need the bagel or the coffee table. I didn't need the paper. All I wanted was the man.

And if I kept this up, I was going to work myself up into a proper state of first-date nerves, the type where you can barely muster a hello, much less impress the other party with your wit, charm, and long-term entertainment potential. It would be lovely if one could just circumvent the whole process and skip straight to coupledom. No excessive grooming, no wardrobe panics, no blurting out idiotic things and praying the other person will be too busy agonizing over blurts of their own to notice. Of course, then, as my friend Alex (short for Alexa) is fond of pointing out, you miss half the fun of it.

Easy for Alex to say. She's been with the same guy since freshman year of college. It only seems fun if you don't have to do it.

Hurrying away from Belliston Square in what I hoped was the right direction, I found myself smack in front of an array of footware. Like a homing pigeon with expensive tastes, I had gone in precisely the wrong direction, landing myself on New Bond Street, directly in front of Jimmy Choo. Oh well, it wasn't a disaster. At least, it wouldn't be as long as I didn't go in and buy anything. One shoe there could wipe out my stipend for the entire month. A pair would be completely out of the question.

Fortunately, I had made my way to Bond Street before. All I needed to do was follow New Bond Street all the way up past the glossy shop fronts until I hit the grotty hubbub of Oxford Street, and from there it was a straight twenty-minute walk back to Leinster Street and my basement flat. I wasn't taken any chances on the tube. If it knew I had a date, it would be sure to break down.

I was just scurrying off in that direction, when two men stepped out into the street right in front of me. They were coming out of Russell & Bromley, that most veddy British of men's shoe stores, and my first thought was, Ha! So men do go shopping together in pairs, too.

My second was much less coherent and involved ducking around or under or behind things, if only there had been anything to duck around or under or behind. Somehow, I had the feeling that crashing through the plate-glass window of Jimmy Choo would be far more conspicuous than staying put. The fight-or-flight instinct had taken hold, and flight was well on its way towards winning.

Because those weren't just any two men.

The one carrying a shoe box, who looked as if someone had just shot his pet dog, I vaguely recognized from the night of my disastrous blind date with the man of Grandma's choosing. But I wasn't concerned with him. It was Colin who worried me; Colin, who was strolling blithely along beside him, right in my direction. My unshowered, ungroomed, decidedly unkempt, anything but seductive direction.

In the glow of light from the shop windows, cutting against the November dusk, Colin's hair shone like tawny gold of an old coin, back before they started diluting the currency with lesser alloys. Next to his stockier, darker friend, he looked like a Plantagenet monarch with Thomas à Becket in tow, ready to conquer France at a single blow and sweep single heiresses off their feet. I, on the other hand, looked like a mugwump.

Since it was too late to duck or flee, there was nothing to do but brazen it out. "Hey, there!" I called out, waving my arms like a one-woman semaphore competition. "Yoo-hoo! Colin!"

I'm not sure if it was the yoo-hooing or the waving that did it, but his tawny head turned in my direction and his face broke into a great big smile. It looked rather nice that way. He didn't seem to notice that my hair was greasy or that my Barbour jacket was two sizes too big, or that I was wearing pants that had probably been designed for a circus clown. He just seemed genuinely glad to see me.

How very bizarre.

"What are you doing here?" he asked, with real interest.

"I've been archiving in the area," I explained airily. "I was just on my way off home."

"Archiving?"

"I archive, you archive, he/she archives. . . ."

"Naturally," Colin said with a grin. "I ought to have known." Belatedly remembering his friend, he turned and gestured in his direction. "Eloise, have you met Martin yet?"

"No, I haven't," I said pleasantly, rather liking that "yet" and the sense of inevitability that came with it, as though it was a matter of course that I would be introduced to his friends. On the other hand, I was also friends—or friendish—with his sister, so the odds were that I would meet them socially sooner or later, even if not through him.

As you can tell, I analyze way too much, especially when there's nothing there to analyze.

I held out a hand to Martin. "Pleased to meet you."

Martin held out a hand back. It was a nice enough hand, but his clasp lacked conviction. He looked, quite frankly, as though he were somewhere far, far away. Wherever that place was, it wasn't a pleasant one.

"So, I see you've been shopping?"

Martin nodded.

"Shoes," said Colin informatively.

"Useful things, shoes," I commented.

Martin nodded again. His conversational repertoire appeared to be limited.

"Well, if you two are still in the middle of shopping, I wouldn't want to keep you," I said, beginning to edge away. I pointed a finger at Colin. "I'll see you at eight?"

"There's no need for that," said Colin.

I frowned. Did this mean he had noticed the lack of shampoo and rather inadequate application of deodorant?

"We're just finished," Colin clarified. "So if you're hungry now . . . ?"

I could hear my friend Pammy's voice in my head, whispering,

"Hungry for what?" I made it stop. Dinner early was an awful idea. I still needed to shower and change and shave—not necessarily in that order.

"I was just off home, anyway," Martin put in, proving he could manage not only words but whole phrases.

I looked at him worriedly. If he were my friend, there'd be some serious "Is everything okay?" going on. But men don't operate that way—at least not in the presence of members of the opposite sex.

"Are you sure?" I asked, looking from him to Colin, which was the closest I could get to an "Is he going to be okay?" without actually saying it.

Martin answered by raising the hand not holding the shoe box. "Cheers."

"Cheers," Colin responded.

Neither of them sounded particularly cheery.

"Is he going to be all right?" I murmured. "He looks like his dog just died."

Colin glanced down at me in complete comprehension. "Not his dog, his girlfriend. She gave him the shaft last week."

"Oh!" I said, as memory hit. "Martin. The one who just had the bad breakup."

Colin nodded. "He's not exactly at his most sociable right now. They were together for four years."

"Ouch." I craned my head back over my shoulder, much the way one might rubberneck at roadkill, but Martin had already been obliterated by the shifting patterns of the crowd. "Poor guy."

Colin looked grim. "She rang him while we were in the store."

Since another ouch would be redundant, I said, "Does she want him back?"

"No. She wants to be friends."

"Poor Martin," I said softly. There's nothing worse than being strung on by an ex. Not that I would know. When I dumped Grant, I had done it cleanly—if it can be called cleanly to fling a ring in someone's face and hang up on all his subsequent calls. But at least I left him in no doubts as to my sentiments. Once you've called someone lying, cheating scum who belongs under the nearest rock, and called him that loudly and in public, there's just no going back.

"So," said Colin, looking down at me in a way that banished both Martin and the memory of evil exes from the horizon. "Shall we?"

Absurd as it sounds, we'd been so companionably chatting about his friend's angst that I'd nearly forgotten we were supposed to be on a first date. And that I was unshowered, untweaked, and otherwise unkempt.

I looked down at the silly pants, at my computer bag bumping against my hip, and thought of a hundred reasons to say no. I could tell him I wanted to drop my things off at my flat. Even half an hour would buy me enough time to hastily shower, put on a sweater without dyed-in deodorant stains under the arms, and give myself an extra inch with a pair of super-tottery going-out heels. I could make the usual big, predate fuss.

Or I could just go along with Colin.

"Sure," I said, smiling up at him through the tousled strands of my greasy hair. "Let's."

Chapter Six

Nine coaches waiting—hurry, hurry, hurry.
Ay, to the devil.

        —Cyril Tourneur, *The Revenger's Tragedy*

It had been very clever of Lord Vaughn to wait until she was already ensconced in his carriage before he announced the location of their first foray. Since the alternative was leaping out into traffic, Mary chose to disbelieve him instead. The very idea of her, going to a . . . well, it was palpably absurd.

"All right," she said tolerantly, since nothing needled more than amused forbearance, "you've had your joke. Now where are we really going? Or would you prefer to tell me another tall tale?"

Whatever his valet had used to polish his boots, it had created a mirrorlike sheen that reflected Vaughn's smug expression with unnerving accuracy. "My dear lady, would I jest?"

Mary didn't even need to stop and think about it. "At my expense? Certainly."

Mary was surprised the English government hadn't leased Vaughn out as a secret weapon of torture. They could make a fortune in fees. He needled; he baited; he drawled. His eyebrow rose more regularly than Pauline Bonaparte's hemline, and he never spoke directly when a means of confusion was to be had. If Vaughn swore the sky was blue, it probably meant it had turned green when no one was looking.

It made for a refreshing change. After a week of living with Letty and Geoff, Mary welcomed the distraction provided by Lord Vaughn's mercurial shifts. Having her sister and brother-in-law tiptoe around her made Mary feel as though she were suffering a slow death by cotton wool, smothered in good intentions. They were painfully solicitous of her feelings, with the sort of solicitude that did far more for the giver than the recipient. It wouldn't sting nearly as much watching them hold hands beneath the breakfast table as it did when they instantly sprang apart as soon as she entered the room, exchanging a look more intimate than any handclasp, a look, that in the private matrimonial lexicon, roughly translated to, "Mustn't upset Mary." That upset Mary. It was pure wormwood and gall to be treated as an emotional invalid needing cosseting and special care. For the first time, Mary understood what drove animals to bite the hand that fed them—sheer irritation at being patronized. It made her want to growl and snap.

With Lord Vaughn, she could growl and snap as much as she liked. He might mock—in fact, he invariably did mock—but he never said, "Oh, Mary," or suggested that a nice cup of hot milk would make her feel just the thing. She could be just as beastly as she liked in the comfort that he would be beastly right back.

Across from her, Lord Vaughn spread out his hands, palms up. "Today, I am all honesty."

Mary waded comfortably into the fray. "And I am all amazement. I doubt there is such a place as this Common Sense Society."

"Until recently, there wasn't. It was called the Paine Society until some perspicacious soul pointed out that the original title came too close to the actuality. Paine's writings are bad enough. His disciples elevate dullness to a new order."

"If such an organization exists, why subject us to it?" If Vaughn was telling the truth, she was to be making her intellectual debut at the heart of London's most rabid disciples of political philosophy, mingling with rough, desperate men who read John Locke for fun and wallowed hedonistically in the illicit pleasures of Rousseau and Thomas Paine. It sounded about as exciting as eggs on toast.

"Because, dull though most of these philosophers may be, there are always some few bold enough to translate idea into action. In the nineties—before your time, my dear—there were quite a few such groups, all scrabbling away for *liberté, egalité,* and *fraternité.* Corresponding Societies, they called themselves."

"I've heard of the Corresponding Societies," Mary interjected. Before her time, indeed! The nineties hadn't been all that very long ago, and she was rather older than the usual run of debutante, although that latter was something she generally deemed it wiser not to bring to the attention of men searching for a nubile young wife. "My father belonged to one."

"Radical tendencies in the family, Miss Alsworthy? Tsk, tsk." On Vaughn's tongue, the syllable became a caress. A caress with a sting in its tail. "I had no idea I was clasping a revolutionary to my bosom."

"I thought we agreed that there would be no clasping of any kind," Mary countered crisply, earning a light chuckle.

"Fair enough." Across from her, Vaughn raised a sardonic eyebrow. It was always the same sardonic eyebrow. Given its repeated use over their short acquaintance, she was surprised he hadn't suffered a strain.

It would have been flattering if he could have contrived to look just a little disappointed. But he didn't. He never did. One moment, his heavy lidded eyes would burn with seductive promise and the next they would be as amused and detached as any bored young buck in his box at the theatre. It was both infuriating and intriguing.

Carrying calmly on with their previous topic as though clasping and bosoms had never entered into it, Vaughn said, "The Common Sense Society is the last gasp of the old Revolution and Constitution Societies. They're a fairly bloodless lot, but rumor has it that they still retain some ties with the agents of the French Republic. And if they do . . ." Vaughn cast her a glance pregnant with meaning.

"You do realize," said Mary darkly, "that this will be nearly as bad for my reputation as being compromised. No man wants to marry a bluestocking."

"Cheer up. Perhaps you'll meet a gentleman of a reforming nature. Idealists generally make easy prey."

"I take it you know this from personal experience?"

Vaughn leaned back lazily against the black velvet squabs. No dull beige for Lord Vaughn in his custom coach; the appointments were all that money and imagination could devise, complete with silver tassels dangling from the hangings at the windows and a trompe l'oeil painting of a stormy sky decorating the ceiling. The painter had arranged it so that a bolt of lightning angled straight at Lord Vaughn's irreverent head. Another case, thought Mary, of art imitating life. If anyone deserved to be skewered by a bolt from above, it was undoubtedly her companion, who was doing his best to live up to his rakish reputation as he drawled, "I never waste my time on the easily won. The sooner had, the sooner bored."

Mary toyed with a tassel, twining the silver thread around the finger of her glove. "How do you know you will be bored?"

"Anything one can acquire is seldom worth having. Wine. Horses. Women."

The ranking was so deliberately intended to outrage that Mary couldn't do anything but chuckle at it. "I suppose I ought to be grateful that our association is purely of a business nature. Lest it otherwise go flat."

"Yes." Vaughn's pale eyes settled on her face, his expression unreadable. "Quite."

Breaking eye contact first, Mary glanced out the window, asking casually, "Whom should I expect to see at this afternoon's gathering?"

Odd how not looking could increase one's other senses, the rasp of fabric, the masculine scents of starch, cognac, and cologne. In comparison, the vista of identical white houses, gray from coal smoke, seemed distant and insubstantial. She could hear the rub of wool against velvet as Vaughn shrugged. "The usual mix of bored dilettantes and wild-eyed reformers."

"Including your Tulip?" Mary asked delicately. Vaughn had only told her where they were going; he hadn't bothered to specify why.

"Good God, no. No sensible spy would waste his time with this lot. They're a bunch of prosy bores and half-mad fanatics. It's only the latter who make the former bearable."

"Into which category do you fall?"

"I? I am but a humble spectator of the human comedy."

Mary refrained from making the obvious comment about his humility or lack thereof. "You seem remarkably well-informed for a mere bystander."

Vaughn's lips curved in the bland smile that Mary had already learned meant he had no intention of answering her question. His countenance was as polished and unyielding as a well-cut piece of marble. "My dear girl, at my age there's very little with which I'm not familiar. Regrettably."

"Your age?" Mary mimicked. For all his world-weary airs, Lord Vaughn was no more than thirty-five. So said *Debrett's Peerage,* and Debrett's never lied. One could set one's clock by it—if it had anything to do with clocks. "Prior to the flood, I'm sure. I can just picture you frolicking about in your antediluvian idyll."

Vaughn looked down the length of his slightly crooked nose. "I assure you, the ark was highly overrated. Full of livestock and not a decent claret to be had." He looked just a little too pleased with himself as he added, "Not unlike Almack's."

"It isn't any more pleasant for the cattle," retorted Mary acidly. It was one thing to talk about the marriage market, quite another to be taken for a cow.

"I would have thought that your devoted swains would have contrived to keep you better entertained." It was quite obvious that Lord Vaughn was not referring to poetry readings.

Mary's lips twisted cynically. "They tried."

Lord Vaughn's voice unfurled smoothly as black velvet. "Clearly not hard enough."

Mary caught the edge of the seat as the carriage jolted to a stop. "If you meant to offer to remedy the defect, it's too late," she said, somewhat more tartly than she had intended. "We appear to have arrived."

"Pity," yawned Vaughn, as if the prospect couldn't have interested him less. Which it probably couldn't, Mary reminded herself. Vaughn flirted as naturally as he breathed; the mistake would be to take any of it seriously.

"Quite." Mary pointedly diverted her attention to the seat next to her and her remarkably silent chaperone. "Aunt Imogen? Aunt Imogen!"

Aunt Imogen might not be quite deaf, dumb, and blind, but with her broad-brimmed hat dipping low over her eyes and her utter refusal to employ an ear trumpet, she was as close as could be found. The expression on Vaughn's face when Mary had propelled Aunt Imogen into the entryway that afternoon had made up for a week's worth of sarcastic remarks. For one glorious moment, the great Lord Vaughn had been rendered genuinely speechless. Mary considered Aunt Imogen one of her better inspirations.

The famous profile that had once entranced Gainsborough was all but hidden beneath a picture hat that had been all the crack when Mary was a toddler, and the broad-skirted dresses that had once emphasized her stately figure hung loosely from her reduced frame, the formerly rich brocades beginning to fray and fade. Despite the passage of time, Aunt Imogen clung to the fashions of her heyday, either from nostalgia or because she couldn't afford to replace them. Aunt Imogen, Mary had been told, had been one of the great beauties of her day, an intimate of the Duchesses of Gordon and Devonshire, painted by Gainsborough, and ogled by the aging George II. It was a chilling thought.

It was partly penury and partly stubbornness that had reduced Aunt Imogen to her current state. Properly Lady Cranbourne, Aunt Imogen had been an old man's fancy, second wife to an elderly earl with a large fortune, grown children, and a taste for pretty young things. When Lord Cranbourne cocked up his toes, Aunt Imogen had been left a jointure that made the earl's children gnash their teeth and mutter darkly about undue influence. They had booted her out of the family mansion forthwith. Returning to London, Aunt Imogen had merrily dissipated her jointure on two decades of lavish entertainments, younger men, and amateur theatricals. Penniless and passé, she had finally been forced to batten on the generosity of friends, making the rounds of a shrinking circle of acquaintances as eccentric as herself.

Aunt Imogen made her home with Lady Euphemia McPhee, a distant connection of the royal family via one of Charles II's many illegitimate children and quite as mad as Aunt Imogen. Mary had only secured her great-aunt's services as chaperone by promising to take part in Lady Euphemia's latest production, *A Rhyming Historie of Britain*, although she hadn't thought it necessary to confide that little detail to Vaughn.

"Aunt Imogen!" Mary repeated. Decades of sitting too near the orchestra at the opera had wreaked havoc on Aunt Imogen's hearing, and the angle of her hat rendered lip-reading an impossibility.

Vaughn regarded the tilted hat without favor. "Are you quite sure she's still sentient?"

"Only just barely—but isn't that the point?"

"A hit. A palpable hit." Vaughn sighed. "Bring out your aunt. The proprieties, after all, must be maintained."

Grasping what she assumed to be the general vicinity of Aunt Imogen's shoulder, Mary essayed a gentle shake. Happily dreaming of handsome footmen, Aunt Imogen snored on. Abandoning gentle, Mary shook her again. Aunt Imogen might look fragile, but she had the constitution of a carthorse and was harder to wake than the seven sleepers. Aunt Imogen's crumpled lids crackled open over bloodshot eyes. From her open mouth came a noise that sounded like, "Wuzzat?"

A pronounced Whig drawl, the chosen dialect of the previous century's upper classes, made her all but impossible to understand. When in her heyday Robert Burns had written her an ode, the critics had promptly hailed it as "the unpronounceable in praise of the incomprehensible."

"The political meeting, Auntie," Mary shouted. "Lord Vaughn has escorted us to a meeting of the Common Sense Society. Shall we go in?"

"Arrr-bar," pronounced Aunt Imogen imperiously.

Mary chose to interpret that as, "Do let's." It might even have been so. Aunt Imogen, if rumor was to be believed, had harbored quite a weakness for radical politicians in her day, canoodling with the elder Mr. Fox and flirting with the masses at the hustings. She and the late

Duchess of Devonshire had scandalized society by trading kisses for votes during the general election of 1784. At least, Aunt Imogen claimed she had been trading kisses for votes; malicious gossip maintained that she hadn't insisted very hard on securing the latter before bestowing the former.

Lord Vaughn climbed out first, holding out his arms to Aunt Imogen, who revived sufficiently to bat her eyelashes coquettishly in his general direction. An earl was an earl, after all.

"My lady," murmured Vaughn, ushering her forwards.

Aunt Imogen gurgled appreciatively, although whether in response to Lord Vaughn or at the footman holding the door, whose finely turned calves she was unabashedly ogling, remained unclear.

Shaking her head, Mary helped herself out of the carriage. If she was to be a bluestocking for the afternoon, in the model of that dreary Wollstonecraft woman, she might as well start acting the part. It wasn't their message Mary objected to; it was that they dressed so shabbily as they delivered it.

Pausing on the second step, Mary stared in dismay at the scene before her. She wasn't quite sure where she had expected a philosophical society to meet, but her imagination had conjured a great white-walled room, ringed with pillars and decorated with the marble busts of great men. Instead of a temple to learning, the building before them was built of brick in the lower story, surmounted by crossed timbers set in plaster above. A sign creaked above the door, displaying a frog with a five-pointed crown on his head, crouching within a ring of feathers.

In short, it was a tavern.

"Welcome," said Vaughn, "to the Frog and Feathers."

Mary tugged her bonnet down forward over her face, wishing she had worn a cloak and hood instead of a fashionable spencer. The short jacket might display her figure to admiration, but it provided very little extra material for the purpose of hiding her face.

"A tavern?" she demanded.

"What did you expect? The Royal Academy?"

Since that was sufficiently close to the truth, Mary chose not to answer. Putting her nose in the air, she swept grandly down the final steps.

Vaughn wasn't fooled for a moment. Holding out his arm directly so that she had no choice but to take it, he said in an undertone, "Such meetings are illegal twice over. Our friends would be fools to hold them in a more noticeable venue. Besides," he added mockingly, "they have precedent behind them. The tavern has always been the preferred meeting place for illicit activities. Cavaliers, Jacobites, revolutionaries . . . all of history's schemers find their way sooner or later to the alehouse."

Despite the inclusion of Cavaliers with their dashing taste in haberdashery, Mary wasn't sure that was a list she wanted to join. "I do hope you know what you're doing."

"Only on alternate Tuesdays." Wrapping her arm through his, Vaughn guided her through the main room as Aunt Imogen swept unsteadily along in front of them, her trailing skirts picking up dust, crumbs, and a rancid sausage roll. "Ask me again next week."

Mary caught a brief glimpse of trestle tables set around a low-ceilinged room before Vaughn turned her sharply to the right. "If I'm still speaking to you next week," Mary cautioned.

"Oh, you will be," said Vaughn confidently, using the head of his cane to push open another door. Ushering her through ahead of him, he added, "If you want to be paid."

Mary would dearly have loved to have decimated him with a cutting comment, but it was too late. She was already inside. Revenge would have to come later.

Preceding her escort into the private parlor, Mary automatically adjusted her posture as several pairs of male eyes swiveled in her direction. She might have saved herself the trouble. The gentlemen milling about the room didn't seem the sort to be swayed by feminine pulchritude, unless she came bearing a tricolor in one hand and a bloody axe in the other, preferably with one foot planted on a pile of dead aristos. They were just as Vaughn had described, the sort of social detritus one would expect to adhere to an outlandish cause, paunchy, myopic, and with the habitual hunch of men who spent more time in the study than in the saddle. They wore ink-stained waistcoats and carelessly tied cravats. Many still sported the longer hair of the previous decade, scraped back with bits of string or, for the more soigné, black velvet ribbon. No wonder they belonged to a revolutionary society intent on the overthrow of the current regime; most of them would be laughed out of any ballroom in London.

There was, however, one man who didn't fit the general mold. It wasn't that he was taller than the rest, for the room boasted its share of scarecrows. He was only slightly above medium height, perhaps an inch taller than Mary's escort, but there was something that made him stand out from his fellows. It was, Mary realized, that he looked healthy. His golden brown hair had the sheen of health rather than grease, and his skin had the warm brown tint that marked an outdoorsman rather than the unwholesome white of his fellow disciples. He might be just above medium height, but he held himself well, without the scholarly stoop that hunched the others, and his red-figured waistcoat stretched across a quite respectable expanse of chest. There was something open and friendly about his face, with its straight nose, wide mouth, and broad cheekbones. Compared with the saturnine visage of her escort, it was an endearingly boyish countenance.

He was also, Mary noted, already taken. As she watched, he bent solicitously over a woman in a dark bonnet who sat in a chair at the far corner of the room. From the distance, it was impossible to make out anything of her features, but given the man's attentive stance, there had to be something worth seeing to under the voluminous crape that veiled her bonnet. Remembering Vaughn's comment about reforming gentlemen being easy prey, Mary made a wry face. Someone else had obviously beaten her to it.

Abandoning the couple in the corner, Mary scanned the rest of the scene. Someone had gone to some effort to decorate the room for the occasion. Colorful—and most likely treasonous—bunting in red, white, and blue draped the edges of a table, on which rested the Society's seal, a battered gavel, and a signed engraving that could only be of

Thomas Paine himself. He wore a suitably grave expression and toted a pamphlet on which the words "Common Sense" could be seen emblazoned in flowing script. In one corner of the engraving, the enterprising artist had added several illustrative emblems, including a pair of stays. Mary could only assume the corset was meant to convey an abstruse allegorical meaning.

Nudging Vaughn's arm, Mary nodded at the engraving and murmured, "The underpinnings of state?"

Vaughn's lips quirked. "Or simply underpinnings. Before he started peddling revolutionary ideals, Mr. Paine's trade was corsets. To wit, the construction thereof."

From what Mary could make out of the stays, either the engraver had never seen a woman's undergarments or Paine had made a very poor job of his original profession. "I hope he is more adept with his pen than his needle."

Vaughn answered with a droll expression that made Mary smother an inappropriate chuckle. "Why do you think women's fashion in France changed so dramatically after Paine descended upon them?" He shook his head in mock regret. "A whole revolution just to do away with a set of stays."

"I don't think that's *common sense*," protested Mary, casting a watchful eye around them.

"Certainly not," rejoined Vaughn, with a private smile. "I could think of far simpler ways to remove stays."

"I'm sure you could," said Mary repressively. "But now is not the time."

Vaughn raised an eyebrow. "Is that an invitation?"

"Don't," Mary whispered. Two men had abandoned the cluster in front of the engraving and were heading their way. They did not look hospitable. One was tall and gaunt, his nose curved in an arrogant arc like the beak of a bird of prey. With his spare frame and too-bright eyes, he reminded Mary of an El Greco painting of a saint on the verge of martyrdom, half-mad and more than a little smug. Next to him, his friend faded into insignificance, a blur of round cheeks and thinning hair. Mary rapidly arranged her face into a dewy-eyed simper. "You'll have us booted out before we've begun."

"I'll take that as a no." Without missing a beat, Vaughn extended a graceful hand to the two gentlemen approaching. "Gentlemen! How delightful."

"May we help you?" asked the taller man forbiddingly. With that nose, Mary reflected, he couldn't help but look forbidding, no matter how benign his intentions might be. Up close, he looked even more like a saint returned from forty days in the wilderness. Rather than the closely tailored coats in fashion, he wore a long frock coat in a rusty black that bore an uncanny resemblance to a cassock. Hollows beneath his cheekbones gouged triangular gashes in his long face.

"We do find ourselves among the distinguished members of the Common Sense Society, do we not?" Vaughn drawled, deploying his quizzing glass in a way that suggested he hoped the answer would be not.

The thin man regarded him warily. "You do. And since you appear to have the advantage of us . . ."

Vaughn made an elegant leg, lace fluttering and jewels glinting. He was as out of place in the rough-hewn room as a tiger in Hyde Park.

"I am Vaughn," he announced, with the unconscious arrogance of three hundred years of being able to introduce oneself by one name alone. "I had the pleasure of meeting your estimable Mr. Paine many years ago through the good auspices of my cousin, Lord Edward Fitzgerald. It was . . . an unforgettable experience."

The hawk-nosed man inclined his head, his dark eyes never leaving Vaughn. "I am Mr. Rathbone. This"—he indicated the shorter man—"is Mr. Farnham, who acts as chairman for our Society."

The round-faced man bobbed and mumbled his pleasure at the introduction. It seemed, thought Mary, a rather curious disposition of roles. Mr. Rathbone, with his automatic habit of command, appeared unlikely to take second chair to anyone, much less so insignificant a figure as the pink-cheeked Mr. Farnham, who was beaming welcome and goodwill through his chipped teeth. Either there was some title higher than chairman in their little Society, or Mr. Farnham possessed unexpected talents beneath his humdrum façade.

Vaughn must have entertained similar questions, because he trained his quizzing glass lazily on the taller man, in a way that made the hollows beneath Rathbone's cheekbones go even hollower. "And you, Mr. Rathbone? What role do you play?"

"I have the honor to serve as vice-chairman," said Rathbone shortly.

"Vice . . . chairman," mused Lord Vaughn, separating the one word into two. "What a very pleasant position that must be. Such . . . scope."

"Are you, too, a reformer, Lord Vaughn?" inquired Rathbone. He seemed to have difficulty wrapping his tongue around the title. Ah, one of those, thought Mary. The problem with revolutions was that they scraped up all sorts of ideologues with ridiculous ideas about doing away with hereditary honors and giving land in common to the masses and all that sort of rubbish.

Polishing a corner of his quizzing glass, Vaughn neatly avoided the question. "I do what little I can. I have," he added modestly, "been fortunate enough to be admitted into the august company of the Societé des Droits des Hommes."

Mary had never heard of it, but it worked an immediate magic upon the shorter man, who in his excitement rose to the balls of his feet and flapped his hands like a chicken.

"The SDH! Our sister Society in Paris," he explained to Mary, for want of anyone else to explain to. His voice emerged in a nasal squeak, too high-pitched for his amply padded frame. "Our model, our guide . . . I'd always hoped to visit the SDH someday," he finished wistfully.

Rathbone was less impressed. "Then you know Monsieur Delaroche, of course."

"Of course," Vaughn assured him blandly. "Excellent fellow. A bit quick with the guillotine finger, but always good for a spot of revolutionary rhetoric. His extemporaneous harangues were quite the rage when I was last in Paris."

Rathbone looked at Vaughn sharply, but Farnham cut in, bobbing in front of the other man. "How lucky you were to be in Paris during such stirring times! How did it feel," he demanded eagerly, "to breathe the clean, pure air of liberty?"

"Rather fetid, actually. The French, you know," Vaughn replied, touching his handkerchief delicately to his nose.

Farnham's face fell, but after a moment's deep reflection, he nodded in understanding. "Of course," he said. "We are so frightfully cut off here. Did the resolution pass?"

"Which one? Sausages for all, or death to the aristos?"

Farnham frowned uneasily, as though not quite sure whether Vaughn were bamming him. "The latter, of course."

"Oh, indubitably. Four frogs to one. We adjourned just before midnight, and had a bang-up sausage fest at Mme. Lefarge's pie shop."

Farnham looked wistful. Unmoved by culinary considerations, Rathbone's eyes narrowed. "You seem to treat our goals with a certain levity, Lord Vaughn."

"Far be it from me to impart undue humor to so serious a cause. I am simply giddy with the delight of being here among you tonight. Do tell me, Mr. Farnham, have you read Mr. Paine's latest pamphlet?"

"You mean . . ." Farnham's head sunk until it seemed to have nearly disappeared into his cravat, leaving nothing but a pair of eyes peering out.

"Precisely," said Lord Vaughn.

"I'm afraid I don't understand," interjected Mary.

"His new pamphlet," whispered Farnham, his piggy eyes swiveling madly from side to side. "It is about . . . It suggests . . ."

"Invasion," declared Lord Vaughn.

Chapter Seven

—William Shakespeare, *Richard III*, II, iv

The word shivered in the air among them.

Lord Vaughn hefted his cane as though testing its weight. "Invasion," he repeated, rolling the word on his tongue as Mr. Farnham wrung his hands and Rathbone's eyes continued to narrow until they were all but swallowed up. "A French invasion to bring about the glorious benefits of the revolution to those of us here at home. Mr. Paine has generously offered himself and his expertise to Bonaparte as guide in helping us create a new form of representative government in our degenerate state. A bold prospect for a new age."

"Indeed," squeaked Mr. Farnham, clasping his hands together and peering over his shoulder. "But to speak of it . . . easy enough for Mr. Paine to write from the safety of America, but to talk of such a thing, here . . ."

"Come, man," said Vaughn jovially, his diamonds winking incongruously as he dealt the other man a hearty clap on the back. "We are all friends here, are we not, Rathbone?"

"So we have been given to believe," replied Rathbone tightly. "And you, Miss . . ."

"Alsworthy," supplied Mary, with a modest droop of her bonneted head.

"And you, Miss Alsworthy? What do you think of our prospects for a French style of government?"

"I think," said Mary demurely, "that if it comes with a French form of fashion, I shall like it very well indeed."

Lord Vaughn took refuge behind his handkerchief.

"The dust, you understand," he explained innocently, flapping the lace-edged linen in illustration. "Damnable to the delicate nose."

Mr. Rathbone was unconcerned by the state of Vaughn's sinuses. "A very light response, Miss Alsworthy, to such weighty events. Am I to understand that you view the fate of nations as nothing more than a diversion? A parlor game, perhaps?"

"It was certainly not my intention to give you that impression," hedged Mary, even if it did fall close to the truth. Did this scarecrow of a man truly believe he could command the destiny of empires? It would have been laughable if he hadn't been quite so serious about it. He would, reflected Mary, have made a brilliant Grand Inquisitor, if only he had had a Spanish accent and a small goatee.

Even without those props, he managed to radiate disapproval, all of it in Mary's direction. "We prefer our members to demonstrate a certain seriousness of purpose."

Mary struck her Joan of Arc pose, one hand clasped to the bosom and the head tilted slightly back towards the heavens. Or where the heavens ought to be if there weren't a ceiling in the way.

"I pray you, sir, do not judge me by my mere façade. Beneath these meaningless rags beats a heart that burns with the injustices perpetrated by an unequal society"—it was, in fact, entirely unfair that some girls should get husbands while other, prettier girls did not—"and I have pledged myself in whatever humble way I may to doing my own small part to remedy those iniquitous inequities."

Mary was quite proud of the alliteration at the end. All those tedious years of playing poetic muse did have their benefits. She could also do an excellent epic simile if the occasion called for it, but she thought that might be a bit much, even for a revolutionary society.

Rathbone shifted so that they stood a little apart from the others. "Perhaps your part, Miss Alsworthy, may be larger than you think."

"I would be honored to think that might be the case," replied Mary carefully, trying not to notice the way his dark frame walled her away from the rest of the room. The expanse of black broadcloth barring her path emitted an unpleasant smell, musty wool with an acrid overtone of wood ash, like a damp fire. Mary darted a glance past him at Lord Vaughn, but Vaughn was arm in arm with Farnham, bending over the man with exaggerated solicitude. She hadn't really expected him to ride to the rescue, had she? That hadn't been in their arrangement— and saving embattled maidens wasn't much in Vaughn's line.

She was, after all, here for a specific purpose: to roust out French spies. It wasn't as though Vaughn were squiring her about for the pleasure of her company. She would do well to remember that.

With that in mind, she asked, "What do you think, Mr. Rathbone, of this talk of invasion?"

"I?" There was something cruel about the curve of Rathbone's lips, a secret knowledge that made Mary, for the first time, wonder at the wisdom of toying with world affairs. But it was too late now. She was committed. And she was damned if she would cry coward before Lord Vaughn. "I think that more subtle methods might be employed to achieve the same ends."

"I, too, am a great believer in subtlety, Mr. Rathbone." Steeling herself to rest a hand lightly on his arm, she added pensively, "It has long been a sorrow to me that the disposition of society prevents my playing a larger role in events of so much moment to us all."

"If the spirit is willing, the opportunity will present itself."

"I do so hope so." Mary looked up at him through her lashes. "But how will one know opportunity when it comes to call?"

His too-bright eyes raked her face, probing at the levels of pretense. Mary returned his scrutiny without faltering. Some people thought they could read another's thoughts from their eyes. Mary knew that to be sheer bunk. She could lie with her eyes just as effectively as her lips.

Whatever Rathbone saw, it seemed to satisfy him. Enough so that his thin lips relaxed, opening to say . . .

"Hallo!"

Mary started as a cheerful voice shattered the silence, interrupting whatever it was that Mr. Rathbone had been about to confide. The breath Mary hadn't realized she was holding went out in a rush, leaving her vaguely light-headed as her gloved hand dropped from Rathbone's arm.

Straightening, Rathbone nodded coldly to the newcomer. It wasn't Lord Vaughn, come to intervene, but the gentleman she had noticed from across the room, the one in the red patterned waistcoat with the exuberant golden brown hair. Up close, he was older than he had appeared, with white lines scarring the tanned skin around his eyes. Unlike Lord Vaughn, this man's wrinkles were the sort that came of squinting at the sun, rather than too many late nights in too many ladies' bedchambers.

Strolling up beside Rathbone, he clapped the other man on the back, beaming genially from Rathbone to Mary and back again. "Rathbone, won't you do me the great honor of an introduction?"

"Miss Alsworthy, Mr. St. George." The vice-chairman looked more than ever like a Grand Inquisitor as he looked down his nose at St. George. "I would remind you both that the meeting will be called to order in precisely two minutes."

"No need for reminders, Rathbone, old chap. We shall attend faithfully, I promise you."

For a moment, the vice-chairman looked as though he might like to object, but the other man's smiling regard was too much for him. With a stiff "See that you do," he stalked off in the direction of Paine's painting, collaring Farnham as he went. Mary watched him go, not sure whether to be relieved or annoyed by the interruption.

Either way, there was nothing to be done now but accept the setback gracefully.

"How do you do," said Mary, putting out a hand.

"Incredibly relieved," said Mr. St. George, bowing over it with evident relish. "I don't know if I could bear another evening with only the faithful for company. You're not, are you? If so, I'm most terribly sorry—for multiple reasons."

"Not so bad as that, at any rate," said Mary laughingly, nodding towards Mr. Rathbone's stiff back. "This is only my first meeting."

"I've been to at least twenty," confessed Mr. St. George glumly. "It's m'sister. Never been quite the same since her husband stuck his spoon in the wall. She's taken to *causes*."

So that explained the woman in the black bonnet. Tilting her head in sympathetic understanding, Mary's tone warmed considerably. "And you are forced to escort her?"

St. George squared his shoulders. "Someone has to."

They both jumped as the gavel resounded against the wooden table, calling the meeting to order.

"Gentlemen!" called Farnham breathlessly from his perch next to the framed engraving of Paine. "Ladies! I hereby call this meeting of the Common Sense Society to order. If the secretary would rise and read the minutes from last week's meeting?"

A shabbily dressed man shuffled to his feet next to the table, pieces of paper drifting to the floor as he rose. "Th-thank you, Mr. Chairman . . . ," he began.

St. George lowered his voice to a whisper as he and Mary, in silent accord, melted back towards the far wall, as far away from the gavel as they could get. "At least this lot is better than my sister's last go. All August it was homes for aged governesses."

Mary cast a doubtful glance at the stuttering secretary, who was being harangued by hecklers who disagreed with his rendition of their speeches from the previous week. "Somewhat more decorous than this lot, surely?"

Propping a shoulder against the wall, Sr. George said darkly, "You don't know what true horror is until an aging harridan tells you you're not to have any sticky toffee pudding until you recite all your multiplication tables. Brought me out in hives. I couldn't remember a thing after the sevens. And before that it was the Society for the Protection of Turtles."

"Turtles?"

"Saving them being put into soup, that sort of thing." Mr. St. George looked like a man who knew all too much about that sort of thing for his own liking. "I'll tell you one thing I've learned: French chefs have a deuced annoying habit of carrying very large knives. It's not sporting."

"I'm sure you've earned your place in heaven—with the path all paved with turtle shells."

"It's felt more like that other location, especially when one chap dumped boiling broth on me. I tell you, in that moment, I felt myself in genuine sympathy with the turtle."

"Enough to give up turtle soup?" inquired Mary archly.

"There's no need to be extreme," St. George hastily assured her. "I just close my eyes and think of the governesses."

"Have you any notion what your sister will choose next?"

"She seems to be pretty well stuck into this at the moment. Can't move half a foot without tripping over a pile of prosy treatises."

"Don't you mean informative pamphlets?"

St. George grinned at her. "Just so."

Behind them, the gavel clattered down. "*If* those in the back would care to pay attention . . . ," squawked Mr. Farnham. Mary and St. George exchanged guilty smirks, united in delinquency.

Even as she smiled, Mary was figuring sums of her own. His clothes weren't at the height of fashion, but they were of good fabric and decently made. The cameo stickpin in his cravat was Italian, unless she missed her guess, and worth a pretty penny. That sort of complexion generally betokened time spent outdoors, and time spent outdoors generally happened on an estate. From the outward indicia, she would reckon his income at about five thousand pounds a year, perhaps slightly more. A widowed sister might be a liability, but not if, as it seemed, she had her own income. He was not unattractive, appeared good-natured, and was most definitely flirting. Given her current lack of prospects, she could do much worse.

A life spent watching Letty and Geoffrey holding hands beneath the breakfast table, for example.

After all, Lord Vaughn had advised her to set her cap at a gentleman of a reforming nature. From far away she could hear Vaughn's voice echoing in mocking memory. *You and I? No, no, and no again.*

He needn't have bothered with three nos. One would have been enough to get the point across.

In that case, he could have no objections to her cultivating the interest of Mr. St. George. As long as it didn't interfere with their *business* arrangement.

Mary's lips curved in the beatific smile that made her admirers weak at the knees and her family distinctly nervous.

"... a special treat," Farnham was saying in his high-pitched voice. "A letter all the way from Pennsylvania from our revered brother in exile, Dr. Priestley." The announcement was greeted with applause from some and loud hisses from others.

"Who?" whispered Mary to St. George.

"One of the founders of the old Constitution Society," St. George whispered back. His breath smelled of cloves, like a country kitchen at Christmastime. Pleasant enough, if one liked that sort of thing. Which, Mary assured herself, she most definitely could. It was simply a matter of acquiring a taste. Like brandy or olives. "That was before my time. At least, before my sister's time, which amounts to the same thing."

As Mary watched, Mr. Rathbone stalked up to the podium, a rolled piece of paper tucked beneath one arm.

St. George groaned. "That's torn it. If Rathbone's going to read one of old Gunpowder Priestley's letters, we could be here till next week."

"Gunpowder?" Mary asked, diverted. "I assume his parents didn't christen him that."

"No. It's something dull and biblical. Joseph or Joshua ... The gunpowder bit was entirely his own doing, from what I understand. You know about the Gunpowder Plot, don't you? Guy Fawkes crouching under the House of Lords and all that?"

Tilting her head, Mary quoted the old nursery rhyme, "'Remember remember the fifth of November; Gunpowder, treason and plot ... '"

Adding his voice to hers, St. George finished with relish, "'I see no reason why gunpowder, treason should ever be forgot'! Brilliant rhyme, that. Sticks in one's head, you know."

Mary wasn't particularly interested in treason two centuries old. That had been a different world, a world of religious wars and dynastic squabbles. It was hard to believe that only half a century before, men had fought and died to try to restore a Stuart king to the throne in place of a Hanoverian one. Compared with the tumult of revolution across the Channel, the quibbles over which royal brow should bear the Crown seemed rather quaint and entirely irrelevant.

Tilting her head up at St. George, she firmly steered the conversation back to the present. "But the Gunpowder Plot was two hundred years ago. Surely, your Dr. Priestley can't be quite that old."

"Well," continued St. George, visibly expanding under her attention, "in one of his political rants, old Priestley started thundering on about blowing up 'the old building of error and superstition.' Some chaps got the notion that Priestley was referring to a literal building. Like the Gunpowder Plot, do you see? The poor old duffer had no idea—he was just speaking metaphorically—but it got about, and the man was pretty much run out of the country. Before he could light the match, as it were."

"Metaphorically or literally?"

"I doubt the rioters stopped to inquire. It didn't help that he dabbled in natural philosophy. It was something to do with air and fire—the sorts of things that go bang in the laboratory. So he might have been coming up with infernal machines, for all his neighbors knew." St. George waggled his eyebrows. "It was a combustible combination."

Mary cast him a chiding glance. "That was too bad of you, Mr. St. George."

"You can't fault a chap for trying."

"It's the results I object to," replied Mary, with an arch glance that took the sting out of the words. Before they could wander further off the topic, she donned her best expression of melting confusion, the one designed to make men feel big and strong and completely miss the fact that they were being led about by the nose. "But what of Mr. Rathbone?

What does he have to do with this gunpowder fellow? I fear I've lost the thread of the story."

Lord Vaughn would undeniably have said something cutting, but St. George hastened to explain, "Rathbone was one of Gunpowder Priestley's disciples back in the old days. Assisted in his laboratory, sharpened his quills, beat off the maddened hordes, that sort of thing. The old boy was quite cheesed off when Priestley had to scurry off to Pennsylvania just ahead of the authorities. It was quite some time ago, too," St. George added reflectively. "You'd think Rathbone would be over it by now."

"How long ago was it?" asked Mary.

"Thirty years, give or take." St. George laughed at Mary's horrified expression. "I know! The man is in want of a wife. Only not," he added hastily, "my sister, please God."

"I couldn't imagine having to face that across the breakfast table every morning," commented Mary, salting away the information about Rathbone for future consideration. Philosophical convictions and chemical knowledge could, in her companion's flippant phrase, make for a combustible combination. Vaughn had mentioned something earlier in the week, about the Black Tulip's use of explosive materials in a recent rebellion in Ireland. . . . "I believe your sister ought to be safe."

"I'm afraid old Agatha isn't as discriminating as you. You should have seen the first husband."

"Not exactly the beau ideal?" she asked, although her focus was elsewhere. Where *was* Vaughn? Mary spotted Aunt Imogen holding forth to an entirely unappreciative audience about her latest theatrical production, but there was no sign of her escort.

St. George leaned forward confidingly. "He looked just like a turtle!"

"At least that explains the soup," teased Mary mechanically. Had Vaughn just gone off and left her in a room of fanatics with incendiary tendencies?

Turning slightly to scan the room for her erstwhile escort, the strap of her reticule caught on something that abruptly gave. Mary caught the gleam of gold as it tumbled to the ground with a small, reproachful ping, spinning several times before toppling over onto one side.

"Oh dear!" Mary hastily stooped to retrieve it, nearly bumping heads with Mr. St. George, who had dived forward at the same time. Straightening, Mary held out the golden disc in one palm.

"I'm afraid I've broken off your watch fob," she said remorsefully. "I'm sorry."

St. George waved away her apologies. "Don't even think of it. The chain wanted repairing."

It wasn't a coin, but a medal, engraved on both sides, the glitter of the gold dulled with time and frequent handling. The surface of the disc was so worn that Mary could barely make out the picture that had been incised on the front. Beneath a film of grime, she could just distinguish the form of a man—at least, she thought it was a man, since it appeared to be wearing armor. A spear held jauntily in one hand jutted diagonally across the coin. One foot was slightly elevated, poised atop an oblong lump that might have been any number of things. Around the sides, capital letters spelled out an unfamiliar Latin phrase.

"*Spes tamen est una?*" Mary relinquished the medal into St. George's outstretched palm. "I'm afraid I have no Latin." Her father's scholarly inclinations hadn't extended to engaging a proper governess for his daughters.

"'There is still one hope,'" translated St. George. He traced the letters that ran around the circumference of the disc. "A father's admonition to his son. He gave me the medal on my tenth birthday. The figure in the middle is a play on our name. St. George, you know," he explained unnecessarily.

That explained the lump, at least: a recently slain dragon acting as footstool. Mary watched as St. George tucked the medal into his waistcoat pocket. "What does your father think of your sister's causes?"

She knew the answer almost as soon as she had spoken, for a shadow darkened his face.

"Oh," said Mary. "I'm so sorry. I didn't mean—"

"No, no." Unconsciously, St. George's hand closed over the small lump in his waistcoat pocket. "Quite all right. It was some time ago."

"You must have been very fond of him."

"He was a king among men," St. George said simply.

In the face of such uncompromising devotion, Mary's wiles and platitudes failed her. She quite simply did not know what to say.

Nobility just didn't come into her own family. Her father needled her mother; her mother scolded her sister; her sister badgered her brother; and so on, all around the twisted circle of familial relations. She wondered what it must be like to feel that sort of uncomplicated affection, without stings and barbs and hidden meanings to complicate matters.

Uncomfortable in the face of emotion, Mary retreated to commonplaces, "Do tell me about the rest of your family. Do you have only the one sister?"

She had asked such questions a dozen times before, delicately probing into a gentleman's means and circumstances. With very little effort, she rapidly ascertained that Mr. St. George had a respectable estate in Wiltshire, an aging mother in Bath, and only the one sister.

"For which I thank God on my knees fasting," he finished, with a feeling glance at the black-bonneted figure in conversation with Mr. Rathbone.

For lack of a fan, Mary fluttered her lashes coyly instead. "Surely sisters can't be all that bad."

"It wouldn't be if any of them were anything like you," averred Mr. St. George engagingly.

"My little brother wouldn't agree with you."

"How old is he?"

It took Mary some time to remember. "Eight."

"Too young to know a good thing when he sees it."

"Or just old enough to be wise," drawled a new voice, just behind Mary's ear.

Chapter Eight

Exit, pursued by a bear.

—William Shakespeare, *The Winter's Tale*, III, iii

The hairs on Mary's neck prickled as she recognized the speaker, and the mingled rush of irritation and anticipation that inevitably attended his appearance.

Turning, Mary dipped into an exaggerated curtsy. "My lord Vaughn," she intoned. "Might I have the great honor of presenting to you Mr. St. George?"

Vaughn inspected and dismissed Mr. St. George with two quick sweeps of the quizzing glass before bending his glass on Mary. "I trust you are enjoying yourself," he said, in a voice like cut glass.

Clearly, the only acceptable answer was an emphatic negative.

Mary put her chin up. "Yes. Quite."

"How very pleasant for you," clipped Vaughn. "Alas, I find myself in the unfortunate position of having to break up this happy colloquy. Your aunt wishes to depart."

Across the room, Aunt Imogen had wrested the podium from Rathbone and was giving a spirited, if incomprehensible, rendition of the Prologue from *A Rhyming Historie of Britain.*

"Does she?" asked Mary caustically.

"She was quite emphatic about it," Vaughn drawled. "Insistent, even."

"It runs in the family," returned Mary, a dangerous glint in her deep blue eyes. "Insistence, that is."

"And here I thought you referred to her dramatic tendencies." Flipping open the lid of his snuffbox with a practiced gesture, Vaughn scattered a few grains on the side of his wrist. "A fascinating thing, heredity."

Mary's eyes narrowed as Vaughn raised his wrist gracefully to his nose and essayed a delicate sniff. "Particularly inbreeding," she retorted.

Before Lord Vaughn could reply, St. George intervened. Possessing himself of Mary's gloved hand, he said winningly, "I'm sure it wouldn't do to keep your aunt waiting. I have a few of those myself," he added with a smile, "and I know they mustn't be kept from their naps."

"You're very good," said Mary warmly.

"Positively saintlike," murmured Lord Vaughn, snapping shut the lid of his snuffbox. "Pity there aren't any dragons in the vicinity."

Mary silenced him with an elbow to the ribs. "Are you in London long, Mr. St. George?"

"I have business concerns that will keep me in town at least till the opening of Parliament. And then, of course, there is my sister."

"And her turtles," twinkled Mary, favoring him with a private smile designed to irritate Lord Vaughn. Its effect on Lord Vaughn was unclear, but it caused St. George to blink rapidly and forget whatever it was he had been about to say.

"And you, Miss Alsworthy?" stammered St. George, recollecting himself with visible effort. "Will you be staying in town?"

Mary kept her head tilted away from Lord Vaughn, an angle that gave him an excellent view of her profile. "Yes, at least for the present. With so few people in town this time of year, I'm sure our paths must cross again."

St. George swallowed hard and squared his shoulders. "I shall make sure of it, Miss Alsworthy, and that you may be sure of."

"Surely?" echoed Vaughn in saccharine falsetto.

St. George flushed, a deep mauve creeping up beneath the browned skin of his cheeks. "I meant . . . that is to say . . ."

He was saved from disgrace by Aunt Imogen, who swept grandly into their midst, her entrance only slightly marred by her hat flopping forwards. Pushing it back with one crooked hand, she smiled coquettishly up at St. George as Mary performed the necessary introductions.

Aunt Imogen clutched at St. George's arm, uttering a series of sounds that resolved themselves into, "What did you say your name was, young man?"

"St. George?" said St. George diffidently.

"Yes!" cried Aunt Imogen, her hat tipping drunkenly. "You shall be my Saint George!"

"That is my name," said Mr. St. George hesitantly, not wanting to give any offense.

"What Aunt Imogen means," said Mary hastily, well aware of Vaughn's sardonic gaze, "is that she wants you to take part in Lady Euphemia McPhee's latest play. It is a history of Britain." Avoiding Vaughn's eye, she got out the worst of it. "In rhyme."

Vaughn's lips quivered at the corners. "A rhyming history of Britain, in fact?"

Mary couldn't quite control an answering smile. "Some have called it that."

"Will you be taking part?" asked St. George earnestly.

"I play a princess of ancient Britain," said Mary, smiling at him.

"Preferably painted blue," drawled Lord Vaughn. "As princesses of ancient Britain were wont to do."

"In that case," said St. George, oblivious to mockery or rhyme, "I shall most decidedly accept."

"Lovely, lovely." Vaughn cut off further declarations by the simple expedient of shooing Aunt Imogen along in front of him. "I'm sure you'll rhyme brilliantly, St. George. Say your good-byes, Miss Alsworthy. There's a good girl."

Acceding to the inevitable, St. George bowed over her hand. "Good day, Miss Alsworthy."

"The company made it so." Mary lifted one hand in a little wave as Lord Vaughn propelled her towards the door. In an undertone intended for Vaughn's ears alone, she added, "Some company much more than others."

"I shan't demand to know which is which." Vaughn ushered her after Aunt Imogen. "I doubt my *amour propre* could survive the experience."

"I wouldn't be so sure of that," murmured Mary, waiting just that crucial moment before adding, "I would have thought your self-regard was too firmly rooted to be struck down by such an insignificant creature as myself."

In a tone drier than kindling, Vaughn said, "You appear to have made an impression, even if not the one intended."

Mary slid her arm out from Vaughn's grasp. "I was seen. Wasn't that the point?"

"It would have been better had you been seen to take an interest—in something other than St. George and his dancing turtles."

Mary glanced up at Vaughn from under her lashes. "Jealous?"

Vaughn stifled a yawn with one jeweled hand. He made no move to reclaim her hand—in any sense of the word. "My dear, I've never had any aspirations to sainthood. Or hard-shelled amphibians."

Mary matched his tone of brittle boredom. "I hear they make excellent soup."

Holding the door open, Vaughn ushered her through into the main room of the tavern with an elaborate sweep of the arm. It was still early enough in the day that only one ale-sodden sot sprawled across the hard wooden benches. "I'm sure I can find hot water enough for you, if you so desire."

Mary cast a glance back over her shoulder at the gaunt figure still orating in the next room. "Haven't you already?"

"Ah, yes. I noticed your little tête-à-tête with Mr. Rathbone."

Mary lowered her voice. "Apparently, he has some background with incendiary devices, as well as radical politics."

"Did he have anything interesting to impart?" Beneath the well-tailored elegance of his clothes, Vaughn's lean frame was taut, alert, like a swordsman poised for an attack.

"He might have done. We were interrupted."

Vaughn's lip curled. "For which you can thank your estimable St. George. The man appears congenitally incapable of ignoring a maiden in distress."

"Aren't the dragon jokes a bit too easy?" scoffed Mary, but her heart wasn't in it. She frowned down at the worn planking. "If we hadn't been interrupted, I might have learned whether he was our quarry."

"St. George?" Lord Vaughn raised a sardonic brow.

Vaughn knew very well what she meant. "Rathbone," replied Mary, with a quelling glance.

"No." Vaughn dismissed the vice-chairman of the Common Sense Society with a brisk flick of his fingers. "He's all bluster. Not the sort to manage a delicate operation and keep it secret for a decade."

Unlike someone else she knew. Mary favored Vaughn with a brief, sideways glance. "You seem remarkably sure of his character for such a short acquaintance."

Vaughn placed a hand on her back to boost her into the carriage, his touch warm through layers of linen and twill. "One should never speak unless one intends to do so with conviction."

"Even when there is nothing on which to base that conviction?"

"The one has nothing to do with the other."

Mary moved aside to make room for Aunt Imogen. Twitching out the folds of her skirt, she said irritably, "And what you say seldom has anything to do with what you mean."

Lord Vaughn paused in the act of climbing into the carriage. With one hand on either side of the door frame, he stood silent for a long moment, his eyes fixed thoughtfully on Mary's face. "On the contrary, sometimes I say exactly what I mean."

Despite her better judgment, Mary couldn't help but be drawn in. "Such as?"

"Tomorrow. Five o'clock. We ride in the park." Vaughn swung himself into his seat, resting his cane between his knees. "Is that direct enough for you, Miss Alsworthy?"

"Eminently." Mary squirmed to the side as Aunt Imogen's brim scraped across her cheek. "Do you intend to tell me what we mean to do in the park, or must we play twenty questions for that, too?"

"What does one always do in the park?"

Mary had conducted a series of clandestine meetings, in the interest of arranging an elopement, but she decided not to bring that up. Lord Vaughn had already made quite clear his feelings on the subject of matrimony.

"Whatever my esteemed employer wishes me to do—or isn't that the correct answer?"

"A bit testy this afternoon, aren't we? Fear not, my dear, I'm sure your hero will sally forth eventually to rescue you from the big, bad dragon."

"The park?" Mary asked pointedly.

"We go to see and be seen. Just as everyone else does."

By whom they went to be seen was another matter entirely. Mary had some notions of her own on that score. It was not beyond the realm of possibility that a sporting gentleman, missing his usual country pursuits, might take to the paths of the park on a sunny autumn afternoon for a brisk canter.

Mary resolved to tell the maid to set out her most becoming habit. After all, as Mr. Rathbone had said, if the spirit was willing, the opportunity would present itself.

Across the carriage, Vaughn was gazing idly out the window, hands resting loosely on the head of his cane. In profile, he resembled nothing so much as a portrait medallion of one of the Roman emperors, austere and slightly alien, accustomed to pomp and no stranger to intrigue. Plots and counterplots, alliances and betrayals had all left their mark on his form. They were written on the thin, flexible line of his lips, designed to laugh or sneer as the occasion required; the hooded lids that shielded his eyes from scrutiny more effectively than any number of hats; the lean swordsman's body disguised beneath an incongruous armor of lace and jewels. Vaughn, Mary thought, would have made an excellent Caesar, raw power clothed in deadly pomp.

Mary leaned forward, swaying with the motion of the carriage. "Why did we leave so early?"

Vaughn waved a lazy hand. "*Pas devant*, my dear."

"*Pas devant* whom? Aunt Imogen? She can hardly hear a word. And she wouldn't care if she did." Mary leaned towards Vaughn. "Had we stayed longer, I might have prized more particulars out of Rathbone."

Vaughn's posture was just as lazy, but there was something watchful in his silver eyes as he countered, "Come, come, Miss Alsworthy. You can't expect me to believe that Mr. Rathbone was the primary attraction."

In any other man, Mary would have suspected jealousy. But in Vaughn, nothing he said was ever as it sounded. If he pretended jealousy, it was clearly for some ulterior motive. Why bring her there and dangle her in front of Rathbone only to pull her away again? Unless, of course, Vaughn was playing a game of his own, quite different from the one he had represented to her.

"I was merely following your advice," returned Mary primly. "Finding myself a reforming gentleman, as you suggested. Can you think of any reason why I should do otherwise?"

"If you cannot think of it on your own," said Vaughn very softly, "there's very little point in my telling you."

Mary could think of several reasons, but she wasn't at all sure they were the ones Vaughn meant. She was about to say as much, when an imperious voice rang out like an impromptu cannonade, bringing the carriage to a jarring halt that made Vaughn's hat tip forwards over his face and Mary's elbow bang against the wall hard enough to bring tears to her eyes. As Mary rubbed her aching elbow and righted Aunt Imogen, a gargoyle galloped up to the window.

It took Mary only a moment to determine that the object floating in the window frame was not a gargoyle but merely a singularly ugly woman, her craggy face contorted into an expression of extreme distaste. Reining her horse alongside them with the ease of a practiced horsewoman, she stuck her head imperiously through the window frame. She looked like one of the gnomes Mary's childhood nursemaid had warned her about, the ones who snatched up naughty children and bore them away deep beneath the earth.

"So it *is* you," she rasped, in a voice as low as Mr. Farnham's had been squeaky. "I thought I recognized your carriage, but I had hoped to be mistaken."

Vaughn bowed as elegantly as any man could from a semireclining position. "It is an ill wind, my dear Lady Hester. I hear it blows nobody good."

"One of these days," replied Lady Hester icily, "it will blow you straight to perdition."

"Before that happy day occurs, may I introduce my companions to you? Lady Cranbourne and her niece, Miss Alsworthy."

"Alsworthy?" Lady Hester nearly cracked her head on the window embrasure. "But I thought—" Her eyes narrowed, and she pulled back slightly, her broad shoulders rasping against the window frame. "No. No. I see that it is not. How very curious."

"Miss Alsworthy," broke in Lord Vaughn, seeming to apply undue emphasis to the repetition of her name, "you have the honor to be addressed by none other than Lady Hester Standish."

"*The* Lady Hester Standish?" inquired Mary breathlessly, since such a reaction seemed to be called for.

This time, it was Vaughn's turn to look a warning. "Yes," he said pointedly. "*The* Lady Hester. Meddler, schemer, occasional republican— except, of course, when it gets in the way of the proper order of precedence. One would not, after all, wish to make do with a lesser seat at dinner. Have I left anything out, dear lady?"

"Pots and kettles," returned Lady Hester disdainfully, before turning her icy gaze back to Mary. She looked her up and down with the sort of piercing assessment that made Mary wonder if she had remembered to don clean linen. "So you're Imogen's niece, are you? Paugh."

Mary had never actually heard anyone say "paugh" before. It grated off Lady Hester's tongue like sandpaper on granite.

"Lady Cranbourne is my great-aunt, yes," Mary said carefully. "I hadn't realized you were acquainted."

Lady Hester's nostrils flared, highlighting her resemblance to her horse. She had very large, square teeth. "She nearly caught my brother," she rasped, speaking of Aunt Imogen as though she wasn't within two feet of her. "Might have got him, too, but she never could stay the course. Always was a flibbertigibbet, was Imogen. Kisses for votes, dashing about with Scottish poets—deuced rackety sort of gel."

"And a pretty one, I hear," put in Mary helpfully, and watched the gargoyle features harden to granite. "One of the great beauties of her day."

"Only men put store in beauty," retorted Lady Hester, her masculine voice even harsher than usual. "Weak vessels, the lot of them. Always ready to be led astray by the next pretty face."

"Wouldn't know about that, would you, Hester?" cackled Lady Imogen from under the depths of her hat, causing Lady Hester to crack her head rather satisfyingly on the top of the window frame. "Frumpy as ever!"

Lady Hester's rough features turned a very unbecoming red, although that might have been due largely to the blow to her head. "Some of us put store in greater things."

"Hopeless spinster," murmured Aunt Imogen to herself, although, with the uncertain volume of the mostly deaf, her murmur could be heard halfway to Hyde Park.

"My brother had a lucky escape. And *you*." Lady Hester turned on Vaughn with an expression that wouldn't have looked amiss on Medusa during one of her crankier days. "What would Teresa say to your strutting about with this chit?"

Vaughn's face didn't change, but Mary could see his fingers tighten on the handle of his cane. "It is very difficult," he said mildly, "to strut while sitting. And," he added, "equally difficult to ride with one's head stuck in a window."

"Don't think you've seen the last of me, Vaughn."

"I know," yawned Vaughn. "You'll be back."

Lady Hester didn't deign to answer. Wheeling about, she cantered off in the direction of Hyde Park, her horse's hooves striking an angry tattoo against the paving stones.

"Never liked her brother, anyway. Dull old stick," contributed Aunt Imogen in a deafening aside. Poking her great-niece in the arm with a bony finger, she added, "If Hester gives you trouble, come to me. I'll soon set her right. Heh."

And she subsided once more beneath her hat, a smug smile visible just beneath the brim. It boded ill for Lady Hester.

Rapping to the coachman to drive on, Vaughn returned to his perusal of the passing scenery as though he were accustomed to a daily diet of threat and invective. Given his winning manners, the prospect wasn't all that unlikely. Mary was sure there were many people who would be delighted to see Vaughn tumble off a cliff . . . or down a flight of stairs . . . or out a window.

"And what did you do to alienate Lady Hester Standish?" inquired Mary lightly. "Not the same as Aunt Imogen, I trust."

"No," replied Vaughn at long last. "Don't be fooled by that display. Lady Hester was—and remains—a very clever woman. A clever woman, and a determined one."

Mary had her doubts about the former part of that description. Between her face and voice, Lady Hester's gender was entirely unclear. Her habit, cut to accommodate her wide shoulders and angular frame, accentuated the impression. But for the fact that she was riding sidesaddle, Mary could have easily taken her for a man.

"Clever?" she prompted.

"Do they discuss nothing more exigent than the properties of lemonade at these soirées you attend? Lady Hester was, at one time, one of our foremost philosophers. She schooled Wollstonecraft in the rights of women, flirted with physiocracy, corresponded with Jean-Jacques Rousseau and Mme. de Stael—you do know who Mme. de Stael is, don't you?"

Mary thought Mme. de Stael might have something to do with poetry . . . or was it painting? Nor could she have said with any confidence just what physiocracy entailed, other than a vague notion that it was something to do with political economy. But she wasn't going to let Vaughn know that.

"Of course," she said, putting her nose up in the air. "Doesn't everyone?"

"My apologies," said Vaughn ironically, in a way that made it quite clear he had seen through her bluff. "Perhaps later we might discuss some of her works. At your convenience, naturally."

Mary made a mental note to raid her brother-in-law's library for anything by a Mme. de Staël. "I shall look forward to that," she said coolly. "I gather your friendship with Lady Hester was an intellectual one?"

"It certainly wasn't amorous. Before the war, Lady Hester hosted one of the most celebrated salons in London. As her views became more radical, her guests trailed off to more peaceable pleasures."

"Like you?"

The only answer she received was an infuriating little shrug, which might have meant anything from assent to an unidentified itch.

With the carriage pulling up before the portico of Pinchingdale House, Mary abandoned the subtle approach. "Why does she hate you so? Not simply for abandoning her salon, surely?"

Lord Vaughn swung his long legs onto the folding steps as a footman rushed to open the door. "Do you doubt the power of politics?"

"To produce that sort of venom?" She accepted Lord Vaughn's hand as he reached up to help her descend. "Yes."

There was no sound as he handed her to the ground except for the swish of her hem against the bottom step. His reserve was so marked, his withdrawal so complete, that Mary thought he meant to abandon the topic entirely, as he had so many others.

She was framing a suitably light and flippant farewell when Vaughn said with studied blandness, his arm stiff beneath the light touch of her fingers, "Lady Hester's brother was the Earl of Petworth."

"I see," murmured Mary.

And she did. Even before Vaughn added, with chilling finality, "Lady Hester is the aunt of my wife."

Or, more accurately, *was* the aunt of his wife. Even now, over a decade later, dowagers still whispered over the mysterious death of Lord Vaughn's wife. No wonder Lady Hester resented her presence in the carriage with Vaughn. Another woman, taking her niece's place . . . or, as Lady Hester had so vividly put it, strutting about in her niece's place.

Only one thing niggled at her. In preparation for her debut, Mary had pored over *Debrett's*, memorizing the lines of all the great houses, their spouses, their offspring. She could see the page as though it were in front of her, the paper creased from wear, the print small, the ink smudged, but still readable for all that. A list of all Vaughn's titles and honors—followed by the name of his wife. Lady Anne Standish, daughter of the Earl of Petworth.

Lady Hester had mentioned a woman's name. But it hadn't been Anne.

Behind them, one of Lord Pinchingdale's footmen helped Aunt Imogen from the carriage. Mary looked quizzically at Vaughn. "I had thought," she said slowly, "that your wife was named Anne."

Lord Vaughn's eyes followed Aunt Imogen as she ascended the short flight of steps into the house. No hint of emotion illuminated his features. His countenance was as still and cold as a plaster saint's.

"She was."

Chapter Nine

I know you what you are;
And, like a sister, am most loath to call
Your faults as they are named.

—William Shakespeare, *King Lear*, I, i

Who, then, was Teresa?

Mary slowly followed Aunt Imogen into the foyer of her brother-in-law's London mansion. All around her, white marble nymphs sneered down at her from their niches, arrogant in their chilly perfection. One held an urn as though ready to dump water over the head of anyone so unwary as to walk directly past. No hint of color enlivened the entry hall, not so much as a black tile on the floor. The octagonal room had been executed all in icy white, like a Roman temple—or a tomb for the living.

Mary's boots echoed sharply on the white marble floor, in counterpoise to her thoughts. She could picture Vaughn, his hand clenched on the head of his cane in the sort of reaction she herself had failed to elicit. What had this Teresa been to him? Or, rather, Mary corrected herself, what was she to him. There was nothing to indicate that a use of the past tense would be more appropriate to the occasion.

Was this Teresa Vaughn's mistress? Mary hadn't heard any rumors linking Vaughn to a particular member of the demimonde, but that would explain Lady Hester's use of a first name alone, without title or honorific. It was a form that might indicate either familiarity or contempt.

A devoted aunt might be deemed to have reason for reviling her niece's husband for his extramarital antics.

But Vaughn's wife had been dead. For ten years. Most men didn't remain constant in wedlock, much less after it. The only reason Mary's father hadn't strayed was that he was more interested in his books than in women. And an income of three hundred pounds a year didn't leave much room for supporting a mistress.

Mary became aware of a certain bobbing and fluttering on the corner of her vision. A maid, in a neat gray dress and white cap was trotting along beside her, jogging anxiously up and down in an unsuccessful bid for her attention.

"Yes?" Mary asked sharply.

The maid melted into relief. "It's her ladyship. Her ladyship said as to tell her—"

"Yes, yes." Mary cut her off with a wave of one hand, and the maid subsided into alarmed silence. Mary had a feeling she knew all too well what it was her ladyship wanted. She seized on the most expedient means of delaying the inevitable. "I'd like a bath brought up to my room."

Chewing on a hangnail, the maid hovered indecisively, torn between following her original orders and the unmistakable tone of command. Mary's back stiffened. Someday, she was going to have her own household, where her servants obeyed her orders. The operative word being hers. Hers, hers, hers. Not her parents'. Not her sister's.

"Sometime today," added Mary, with a pleasant smile ringed with steel. Vaughn's conversational habits appeared to be catching.

They were also effective. With one last anxious glance over her shoulder, the maid went. A moment's observation confirmed that she was, in fact, heading for the nether regions where servants and hot water were to be had and not to her mistress's chamber to tattle. That should earn her at least fifteen minutes before Letty came banging on her door.

Tugging in turn at each finger of her glove, Mary proceeded pensively up the broad marble stairs. Even without the added incentive of delaying her sister, a bath wasn't a bad notion. She could still feel the grime of the tavern like a film on her skin, laced with the nauseous scent of stale beer and day-old sausage rolls.

She wondered, idly, if Lord Vaughn was doing the same. She couldn't imagine he liked the stench of sausage any better than she did. Lord Vaughn with his impeccable lace and linens. And yet . . . Mary closed the door of her temporary bedroom behind her, tossing her gloves onto the bed. And yet, Vaughn had seemed awfully at ease with the group of radicals in the tavern. For a man who had been on the Continent for the last decade, he had been surprisingly familiar with their proceedings.

Yanking free the ribbons of her bonnet, she sent the straw and silk confection skimming after the gloves onto the white eyelet bedspread that Letty had chosen for her. Embroidered with a twining frieze of white flowers and vines about the edges, the coverlet was all that was pristine and virginal, a perfect haven for an innocent young girl's maidenly dreams. Mary hated it. It jeered at her of her failure, frozen at twenty-five in an inappropriate and attenuated girlhood.

She took pleasure in tossing her spencer onto the coverlet, the braided twill creating a wide blue blot on the pristine white. It was a petty sort of revenge, but it was better than nothing.

There were times her palms ached to close around a china ornament and fling it against the wall just as hard as she could, for the satisfaction of hearing it smash into a thousand tiny pieces. She would take the Dresden shepherdess on the mantel, blond and smug, and she would hurl it at the pink-patterned paper on the walls, that hideous pink paper covered with rosebuds that would never bloom, frozen in artificial sterility from here to eternity. And she would exult as the porcelain shattered, as the pattern cracked, as a million little pieces sifted sparkling to the muffling calm of the carpet.

There were times when just the thought of crashing china was all that kept her from running screaming down the hallways of Pinchingdale House. The idea of making a scene, causing a fuss, cracking all the codes that had held her all these years, watching her sister's and brother-in-law's faces as they came running in . . .

Followed by the inevitable clucking. The sideways glances, the concerned conferences, the smothering solicitude.

The Dresden shepherdess was safe on her perch.

At least now she had her little agreement with Vaughn to distract her. Whatever else Vaughn's faults might be, he worked excellently well as a diversion. As long as she took care to remember that a diversion was all he was. As Beatrice had said of the Prince in *Much Ado About Nothing*, he was too costly for daily use.

Mary reached back to untie the ribbon that held a sapphire cross in place against her neck. The sapphires were glass, of course, like all of her jewelry. An impressive gleam on the outside; worthless within.

As Mary let the black velvet slide into a small heap on her bedside table, a knock sounded tentatively against the door.

Servants never knocked, even such ill-trained ones as her sister employed.

Mary stiffened, fighting a craven desire to slip out through the dressing room and keep going.

"Mary?" her sister's voice called. It couldn't be anyone but her sister. No one else in the household called her by her first name. Even her brother-in-law had retreated into a respectful Miss Alsworthy, as though by that belated formality he could eradicate their embarrassing past.

Mary retreated hastily to her dressing table, sliding onto the low bench with its embroidered cover. Pitching her voice low, she called out, "Not now, Letty. I'm bathing."

The door cracked open, and a gingery head of hair poked through. It was followed by Letty, insufferably tidy in a green wool dress that brought out all of her freckles. "No, you're not," she said. "The water hasn't been heated yet."

The maid had gone straight to Letty, then. Ah, well. It was her own fault for being so careless as to neglect to follow up her request with a sixpence. A little bribery always worked wonders.

Without turning from the dressing table, Mary began taking the pins from her hair, letting the long, dark mass unroll down her back, section by section. "But I will be."

Letty rolled her eyes in the mirror. "Don't worry. I'll leave when the water arrives. I just wanted to talk to you about—"

"Lord Vaughn," Mary finished for her. Lifting her brush, she held it suspended, waiting. Her eyes fixed on her sister's in the mirror. Letty's eyes, usually as easy to read as a child's primer and just as wholesome, shifted uneasily away.

Letty shrugged uncomfortably. "Well, yes. It's just that . . ."

"You don't like him," said Mary flatly.

Letty flung up her hands. "I am capable of finishing my own sentences, you know."

Mary didn't bother to respond. She simply set the bristles of the brush against her hair, drawing it deliberately through the shining length. One stroke . . . another . . .

In the mirror, Letty made a face of annoyance. "It's very hard to carry on a conversation by oneself," she said.

Mary waited, drawing the brush downwards in long, languid strokes, the only sound in the room the swish of the bristles against her hair. If Letty was set on lecturing, lecture she would, whether she received any encouragement or not.

Letty shook her head at her in the mirror. "Oh, Mary . . ."

There it was again. That "Mary." That long-suffering, long-drawn-out rendition of her name that made her nails sharpen into claws. When had that begun? Five years ago? Six? Before that, Letty had been such a complaisant child, so easy to entertain with a bit of ribbon or an old doll, beaming all over her freckled face at the chance to play dress-up in her sister's clothes and have her hair dressed like a big girl's.

That had been a very long time ago.

Letty drew herself up to her full height, just a shade over five feet, her bosom puffing out like a pigeon's. "I need to talk to you about Vaughn."

"Do you?" Mary's voice dripped acid.

Letty frowned at Mary in the mirror. "He's . . . not trustworthy."

"Is that all?" Mary laughed derisively. "I've known that for ages. It's hardly news."

Letty plunked both her hands on her hips. "Mary, you must see—"

Dropping the brush, Mary swung around on the bench. "I don't see that I *must* see anything. Must I?"

Letty shook her head. "I didn't mean it like that. It's just . . ."

"What? That you're older and wiser?"

Letty had the grace to flush, but she soldiered stubbornly on. "When I was in Ireland," she blurted out, "Vaughn was there, too."

"A hanging offense, to be sure," Mary drawled, in her very best imitation of Vaughn.

The furrows in Letty's brow dug a little deeper, but she didn't allow herself to be deterred. "There was a woman . . ."

"With Vaughn, I imagine there would be," replied Mary thoughtfully, abandoning the drawl. "He's that sort of a man."

"You almost sound as though you admire him for it."

"I do," said Mary coolly, and was surprised to realize she meant it. He was a man who knew what he wanted and took it. She had had enough of poets and moralists, the sort who sighed and yearned and never had the backbone to act. It had taken months to coax, wheedle, and maneuver Geoffrey into taking the final steps towards elopement, and even then he had done so with a heavy conscience and an inauspicious eye. A conscience, Mary decided, was a damnably unattractive trait in a man.

Letty was determined to make her see sense. "Vaughn won't . . . that is, he isn't . . ."

Mary's lips twisted into a crooked smile. "The marrying kind? He's never made any misrepresentations on that score."

"You don't want to be compromised. Or worse." Letty bit down on the last two words, her teeth digging into her lower lip as though she feared she had already said too much.

Mary's eyes narrowed. "Why not? It works remarkably well for some."

Letty backed up a step, stumbling over the hem of her own skirt. "That's not fair," she protested.

"But true," countered Mary pleasantly. Flexing her hand, Mary languidly examined the perfect curve of her fingernails. "After all, *you* were compromised. And everything you do is always right. Ergo . . ."

Letty shoved her hair haphazardly behind her ears. "It wasn't like that. You know I never meant any of this to happen. Mary . . ."

Watching Letty's lips move, her hands twisted in the folds of her skirt, Mary felt a surge of impatient pity for her little sister. If only Letty wasn't so damnably earnest. She could have her Geoffrey and good riddance to him. Just so long as she stopped talking about it.

"This woman Vaughn was with," Mary interrupted abruptly. "Was her name Teresa?"

"What?" Caught midsentence, Letty blinked several times at the abrupt change of subject.

"Her name," Mary repeated, as though to a very slow child. "What was it?"

"I don't remember her Christian name," Letty said distractedly. "I'm not sure I even heard it. I knew her only as the Marquise de Montval. That is, I knew *of* her. I didn't actually know her. Not as such."

"French?" Mary tucked that bit of information away for future use. The name meant nothing to her, but it might be of use in conversation with Vaughn.

"No, English. At least, she *was* English." Letty raked her hair back from her face with both hands. "But that's not the point. The thing I wanted to tell you—that is, the Marquise de Montval—she—"

"So she married a Frenchman, then." Teresa wasn't exactly the most common name for an Englishwoman. It certainly wasn't as popular as Charlotte or Caroline or even Mary, but it wasn't unknown. They could be one and the same.

"Ye-es, but—" Letty stumbled to a halt, scuffing one sensible shoe against the pastel flowers of the Axminster carpet.

Mary raised a quizzical eyebrow. "Surely a married woman shouldn't be so miss-ish? I assure you, I shan't swoon at the mention of a mistress. I have heard of such things, you know, despite my spinster state. Are you trying to tell me that she and Vaughn were lovers?"

Letty's honest face was a study in consternation. "I wish that were all, really, I do. But the Marquise—"

Letty broke off as a scuffling noise at the door attracted her attention. Looking almost relieved, she called, "Yes?"

Around the corner of the door appeared an undersized figure in a neat gray dress and a white cap, the same maid Mary had neglected to bribe. She was holding out a heavy sheet of cream-colored paper, the fine stationery an incongruous contrast against her work-reddened hand. On the reverse of the paper, Mary's name had been scrawled in a bold, black hand. There was no direction, no frank, just *Miss Mary Alsworthy* in thick black ink. The bottom of the *y* snaked back under the whole like a sea serpent twining around a hapless ship.

"This just came for you, miss," the maid murmured, lowering her eyes under Mary's unblinking stare. "Under the door, like."

Mary and Letty both moved forwards at the same time. There were some advantages to having longer legs. Mary crossed the room and plucked the letter out of the maid's hands before Letty could get to it.

"I believe this is meant to be mine," she said, looking pointedly at her sister's outstretched hand.

The pads of her fingers tingled with anticipation against the textured surface of the paper. Through the thick stationery, it was impossible to see what was written within. The hand was an unfamiliar one.

To the maid, Mary added, "You may go."

She would have liked to have said the same to her sister, but she doubted it would have any effect. The maid looked to Letty for confirmation. Letty motioned for the maid to stay.

"Under the door?" Letty asked, wrinkling her nose. "What do you mean, Agnes?"

As Letty quizzed the maid, Mary smuggled her prize to the far side of the room, standing beneath the shelter of the curved fall of the drapes as she cracked the black wax that sealed the paper shut. There had been a signet of some sort pressed to the wax, but the die had slipped as it was applied, smudging the imprint and rendering it unrecognizable. She could make out a snippet of a curve at the bottom. It might have been anything from the bottom of St. George's shield to one of the serpents of which Vaughn was so fond. Or the ornamental sweep at the bottom of a large *R*, for Rathbone. Did revolutionaries patronize such expensive stationers?

Knowing that her time was limited, Mary hastily cracked the seal, impatiently brushing aside the broken bits of dried wax that scattered across her skirt. The missive was only one page, seeming thicker only due to the quality of the paper. And that one page contained only three words, scrawled dead across the center of the page, between the two lines made by the folds.

Vauxhall. Tomorrow. Midnight.

And that was all. There was no salutation, no signature, no explanation, only that abrupt summons—for summons it must be. But from whom? And why? She doubted St. George would be capable of couching a simple request in anything less than a paragraph. Rathbone, perhaps. But Vauxhall, pleasure palace of the idle rich, hunting ground for the amorous, all flimsy fantasy and decaying decadence hardly seemed to be Rathbone's métier.

Vaughn, on the other hand . . . Oh, yes, Vaughn was a creature of Vauxhall if ever there was one. And the peremptory nature of the summons smacked of his oratorical style. Vaughn lifted a finger and the rest of the world obeyed. Or so he liked to think. It was all of a piece with the way he had invited her to the park the following afternoon. Anticipation tingled through her like heady wine thinking of Vauxhall, with its dark walks and even shadier inhabitants, dusted over with fireworks that dazzled rather than illuminated.

Mary snuck a sideways glance towards her sister, still deep in conversation with the maid, who was spinning a complicated tale of underfootmen and misplaced correspondence. Letty would be sure to disapprove.

Letty would not have to be told.

She might even, Mary thought, her head spinning with possibilities, be able to do away with the indifferent chaperonage of Aunt Imogen. At Vauxhall, hooded, masked, who was there to recognize her and go tattling back to society? She could be free for a few precious hours.

But why hadn't Vaughn mentioned anything a mere hour ago, when he had all but ordered her to the park with him? And why fail to sign the note? He might be arrogant enough—no, Mary corrected herself, he *was* arrogant enough—to assume that he would need no introduction, but she would have expected at least a V, sprawled at the bottom of the page in seigneurial splendor.

Pursing her lips, Mary squinted down at the letter, drawing out the three folds to their full extent. The paper crumpled beneath her fingers as she saw it, there, on the lowest right-hand corner of the paper. At first viewing she had taken it for nothing more than a blot, a careless drop of ink spattered by an impatient pen.

But it wasn't.

On the lower right side of the page, where a signature ought to have been, someone had sketched a small black flower.

Chapter Ten

... But that was in another country,
And besides, the wench is dead.

—Christopher Marlowe, *The Jew of Malta*, IV, i

In Belliston Square, Lord Vaughn had received a letter of his own. Vaughn could see why his fastidious butler had pointedly buried it at the very bottom of the pile, beneath an invitation to the Naughty Hellfire Club's annual Fall Frolic (breeches optional) and a circular advertising a two-for-one sale at Mme. Pimpin's House of Pleasure (bed one wench, get the next one free). The paper was the cheapest sort of foolscap, stained with trails of ink and the oily imprint of grubby fingers, presumably those of the bearer, since the letter itself bore no frank. It must have been delivered by hand, and a decidedly dirty hand, at that. Beneath the streaks of grime, the enclosing sheet was puckered and snagged where the writer's impatient quill had jabbed through in her haste. The writer had driven the nib clean through the base of the V like a swordsman running his opponent straight through the heart.

Not that the heart was an organ with much bearing on the affair. Not for a very long time, at any rate.

Vaughn didn't need to crack open the wax to know the identity of the writer. There was no seal imprinting the wax, no telltale scent wafting from the folds (other than a slight tang of mud, courtesy of the bearer), no distinguishing curlicues twining from the base of the letters, but even blotted and smeared, he knew that handwriting. There had been a time—a time he preferred to ignore—when he knew it as well as his own.

With the finicky care of a cat, Vaughn lifted the letter by one corner. It was all of one sheet, folded over, sealed, and addressed on the blank side, curiously insubstantial for something that pressed against him like the weights used to crush accused traitors, stone by painful stone, gasping for air from their constricted lungs until their organs crumpled one by one beneath the pressure.

The seal crumbled off with the flick of a finger, red wax flaking onto the table like drops of wine. Slowly, deliberately, Vaughn spread open the page.

"Sebastian—" it began.

A name no one addressed him by anymore. His acquaintances, his enemies, even his own mother called him Vaughn, in proper deference to his rank. The boy Sebastian had been outrun years ago, abandoned somewhere in Paris.

If the use of his name were an attempt to soften him with reminders of past intimacy, it was in singularly poor taste, given the terms on which they had parted. Vaughn's eyes flicked past the salutation, to the letter itself. The ink she had used was as cheap as the paper. Diluted with water, it turned the words into a gray wash on the page. Even so, one phrase burned from the blur.

Did you really believe I was dead?

Vaughn pressed his eyes closed, but it didn't help. He could still see the words blazoned against the backs of his lids.

Grimacing, Vaughn looked down his nose at the letter. She needn't sound quite so snippy about it. It had, after all, been an impression she had gone to a great deal of trouble to secure.

Believe it? Yes. No. Perhaps.

Letting the paper drift to the table, Vaughn rubbed two fingers against his temples. Belief had had nothing to do with it. At the time, it had been far easier to take the situation as it appeared, without wasting time on trivialities like confirmation, accepting it because he wanted it to be so. A quest after proof bore far too great a chance of kicking up inconvenient truths, like slut's wool under the rug.

He hadn't reckoned with resurrections. When someone went to that much bother to appear dead, they generally stayed dead. At least, so one would hope.

Believed? Perhaps not. Hoped? Oh God, yes. He hadn't realized just how much, until now, with the disappointment of it wrenching at his gut, filling his mouth with ashes and his breast with bile. Since returning to England, he had found himself contemplating the very banalities he had long since abandoned: a wife, a nursery, speeches in the Lords and a well-worn chair at Brook's. What a grand irony it would be, after all his years of wanderings, to settle down like Odysseus at his own hearth with a faithful Penelope on his knee. And yet, there it was, beckoning, taunting him with the possibility that the past might be rolled up and bundled back into Pandora's box; that he could, after all this time, start again and redeem the years he had lost.

He ought to have known better.

Exposure, the letter threatened. A full accounting, unless he acceded to her as-yet-unspecified demands. Never mind that by exposing him, she would expose herself as well. She had less to lose. He didn't doubt for a moment that she meant what she threatened. She was, and always had been, entirely ruthless when it came to achieving what she desired; ungracious in victory, vengeful when thwarted, like the goddesses of classical drama, who thought nothing of destroying an empire for an imagined slight.

Rising, Vaughn stalked to the window. Outside, the autumn twilight had deepened to full dark, smudged with coal smoke. All around Belliston Square, lamps were being lit, curtains drawn, fires built against the October chill. Narrow chimney pots sent out their dense smoke to coat the arrogant stone of the great houses and film white woodwork with gray.

Vaughn breathed deep of the tainted air, savoring the scratch of smoke against his nostrils, scraping the back of his throat. It was, he supposed, as close as one could get to brimstone without actually being in hell.

Reaching for a decanter, Vaughn poured himself a splash of smuggled French brandy, contemplated his glass, and splashed in some more.

"Where I fly is hell, myself am hell," he murmured, and raised the glass in sardonic salute to his own reflection in the window, a shadow figure who nodded and drank in concert, watching him with wary eyes. The shadow image was filmed by the soot that streaked the window. Every day, the servants wiped it away, and every day the stain returned.

He had been a fool, at this late date, to think he could settle to domesticity, warm his toes by the fire and cultivate his garden in gouty old age. Like Milton's Satan, he carried the seeds of his own destruction with him wherever he went.

Taking up the letter, Vaughn held the corner with the signature to the candle flame. The flimsy paper caught instantly, the paper blackening and curling, obliterating the name he had hoped never to see again. As the paper twisted and charred, one word stood out against the shrinking background. *Dead.*

Did you really believe I was dead?

Wincing, Vaughn dropped the burning letter onto the silver tray, where it smoldered like one of the salamanders of medieval alchemy, a twisted, blackened thing with glowing red embers for eyes, until those, too, winked out into a pile of ash.

He poured more brandy to stop the pain in his head, marveling at the diabolical impishness of the workings of providence. Tossing it back, he poured another, settling himself down in a wide-armed chair, balancing his glass on one arm as he contemplated the bloody fiendishness of fate.

Closing his eyes, Vaughn let his head drop against the back of the chair. Against the backs of his lids, he could see the firelight striking blue lights in Mary Alsworthy's hair as she stood in that tiny Gothic chamber in Sibley Court, coolly bargaining over terms. It reminded him of another fall of blue-black hair, spread against the arm of a settee. . . . Without opening his eyes, Vaughn applied the brandy to his lips and found the liquid chased the vision away. Instead, like a necromancer's potion, it supplied him with another image of Mary Alsworthy, canoodling in a corner of the room with that bloody St. George, fluttering her lashes for all she was worth, and doing it bloody well. What a courtesan she would have made, what an actress. What a countess.

Mary Alsworthy, Vaughn reminded himself, reaching for the decanter without bothering to open his eyes, was not auditioning for a role as his countess, or even his mistress. She was there for a task, a task that might be more easily accomplished if he let her get on with it, rather than rushing forwards like an overprotective duenna the minute danger threatened.

Danger, indeed! The Common Sense Society was a toothless lot, so harmless that even the government hadn't bothered to swoop down and close them down. A bunch of idle dreamers, ink-stained scribblers, each more ineffectual than the last, led by poor, mad Rathbone who spent most of his time solitary in a laboratory, endlessly tinkering with the elements. The point of their presence at the society had been merely to establish Mary's radical bona fides, to have her seen in the company of known supporters of the revolution, in the hopes that word would spread to the right quarters. They ought to have stayed longer, made the rounds of the room, established Mary firmly as part of the group. Instead . . .

Vaughn set the decanter back down with an abruptness that made the stopper rattle against the lip. He had no excuse for his actions, nothing except a fleeting, unreasoning impulse to which he had even more unreasonably given way. Balancing his brandy balloon on his chest, Vaughn contemplated his own folly. Standing there, in the corner of the low-beamed room, with her dress a long streak of white against the smoke-stained walls, Mary had looked uncannily like Teresa. It was more than coloring, more than clothing. She had that same trick of angling her head, that same proud tilt of the chin. She had looked so slight next to St. George, so vulnerable, with nothing but a thin layer of linen between her skin and an assassin's stiletto. With a clarity that had made his skin prickle with cold in the overheated room, Vaughn had seen Teresa as he had last viewed her, superimposed over Mary, the red lips slack, the pale skin gone gray, eyes filmed and staring. Only this time, it wasn't Teresa, but Mary Alsworthy.

Foolishness, of course. He wouldn't allow it to happen again. He had hired her to do a job, and there was no sense letting mawkish qualms get in the way. It was a contract, a transaction, a business arrangement.

And if he kept reminding himself of that, he might actually believe it.

It was no wonder he was damned, when he willfully repeated the same pattern over and over again, like a little illustration of the fall of man. Not just a fool, but three times a fool. First Anne, then Teresa, and now Mary Alsworthy. All apples from the same tree. Beautiful, yes; clever, yes; selfish and scheming—ah, there were the qualities that drew him, time after time. And why not? Like called to like.

"'Haste still pays haste, and leisure answers leisure,'" Vaughn recited, enjoying the roll of the words on his tongue. There was nothing like a bit of the Bard to add depth and grandeur to one's petty peccadilloes. "'Like doth quit like, and Measure still for Measure.'"

"Very true, my lord," a bland voice commented.

Vaughn spilled brandy on his shirtfront. He opened one eye, regarded two of his butler, decided it wasn't worth it, and closed it again.

"What the devil do you want, Derby?" he inquired, letting his head fall back against the chair.

"No devil, sir, but certainly a maid."

It had clearly been a mistake giving his butler the run of his library. It was one thing to utter ambiguous bits of Shakespeare oneself, it was quite another thing to be bedeviled by inapposite paraphrases from one's butler.

"In plain English, Derby," ground out Vaughn, wondering at the bizarre properties of brandy, which, rather than shrinking his headache, had simply bloated his head, thus spreading the pain across a larger area.

"You have a visitor, my lord," intoned Derby, in the sonorous tones for which Vaughn had hired him.

"At this hour?"

"A *woman*, my lord," intoned Derby, placing the full weight of his disapproval on the second word.

Did you really believe I was dead?

It was an odd hour to call. Unless, of course, one were a ghost.

"She didn't waste any time, did she?" muttered Vaughn.

"My lord?"

Dragging a deep breath into his lungs, Vaughn ignored his butler and contemplated his options. An oubliette would solve his problem nicely, but town houses seldom came equipped with such amenities. He would have to go and hear her terms, there was no avoiding it. But there was no reason to make it easy for her. A bit of intimidation would do wonders for their negotiations. Nothing too overt, nothing too heavy-handed . . . just a taste of what it meant to cross swords with a master.

When the solution arrived, it was so obvious that he wondered he hadn't thought of it straightaway. Levering himself up on both elbows, Vaughn's lips curled back in a singularly unpleasant smile.

The great diamond on his finger sparkled like frost as Vaughn gave his butler his orders.

"Take our unwanted guest to the Chinese chamber."

ALONE IN THE GREAT CENTER HALL of Vaughn House, Mary tapped a booted foot against the marble floor.

The sound echoed back to her in a series of phantom taps, mocking her impatience and only making the great room feel even emptier. The imperious personage who had opened the door to her had departed a good ten minutes ago, essaying only a chilly, "If you would be so good as to wait here," before disappearing into the uncharted depths of Vaughn House, leaving Mary without chair or refreshment.

Mary made a face at the coffered archway through which the butler had departed. He might at least have shown her to a parlor. Surely, that wouldn't have been too much of a strain upon his dignity. The entrance hall was pointedly bereft of seating.

Drawing her cloak closer, Mary warily examined her surroundings. She had visited Vaughn House before, for the great masquerade ball Vaughn had hosted to celebrate his return from the remoter bits of the Continent. It had been July then, and the hall had thronged with parti-colored Pierrots, plumed cavaliers, and gold-breasted Roman generals, the room so crowded that the great green columns that paced at intervals along the walls had scarcely been visible for the press of bodies and the intricate scagliola work that decorated the floor had been entirely blotted out beneath the stampede of slippered feet. The warmth of the July night, the heavy perfumes worn by the guests, and the steam of incipient intrigue had all met and mingled to create a heavy musk that draped across the crowd like the smoke from the hundreds of candles that glittered in their silver-gilt sconces.

Vaughn House, alone, on an October night, was a different prospect entirely.

Empty, the room was much larger than she remembered. Only one branch of candles had been lit, held by one of the two great ebony blackamoors that guarded the entrance to the central rotunda, where a great curved stair stretched towards the upper stories, like a snake stretching itself. The meager light cast strange shadows off statuary and gilt-topped columns, turning the marble inlay of the floor into a sinister pattern of shifting shapes.

It was cold, too, colder than she had realized on the brief walk over, a cold that emanated from the floors and walls and chilled all the way down to the bone. Inside, somewhere in the inner reaches of the house, there must be warmth and light; Mary couldn't imagine Vaughn depriving himself of any of the creature comforts. But the entry had been designed to chill, to intimidate, to overawe.

It was working.

Crossing her arms tightly across her chest beneath the cover of her cloak, Mary lifted her chin, affecting a hauteur she was far from feeling. Above, the gilded figures who perched on the tops of the columns seemed to be leering down at her.

This had not, Mary admitted to herself, been one of her better ideas.

Why hadn't she just sent a note? That would have been the prudent course to take, and just as effective. The Black Tulip's proposed assignation wasn't until the following night; there would have been plenty of time for Lord Vaughn to receive her note and reply. There had been no reason to come herself, none at all—other than the hectoring tone of her little sister's voice as she warned her away from Lord Vaughn. Mary's brows drew together in annoyance at the recollection. What did she know of it, anyway? Just because she had a husband—Mary's lips pressed together in a tight, hard line, stopping up that line of thought before it could go any further.

It had seemed, at the time, like a very good idea to thwart her sister and steal away the short distance to Lord Vaughn's. The expedition had been laughably easy to organize. All it took was snapping that she had the headache. No, she didn't want her maid; no, she didn't want a soothing posset; all she wanted was to be left alone. Was that *too* much to ask? Letty had retreated with a reluctant backwards glance, her anxious, earnest face peering around the edge of the door one last time before the panel had finally clicked shut. After that, it had been the work of a moment to draw all the drapes, pile up cushions beneath the bedclothes, and slip out down the back stairs. Letty might knock, she might lurk anxiously in the hallway, she might even peek around the corner of the door, but she wouldn't enter without invitation.

It was exhilarating to whisk down the back stairs and know that there was not a person in the world who knew where she was, to be entirely, gloriously free—if only for five minutes. Vaughn's residence had been a world away from last season's lodgings on the borders of Bloomsbury, but it was a mere stone's throw from her brother-in-law's house in Grosvenor Square. At long last, she was of Mayfair. And at the end of the journey, there would be Vaughn.

It had never occurred to her that he might not be home. Or, that being home, he might not want to see her.

She wasn't quite sure what she had expected, but it had something to do with being shown into a warm room, with a fire in the hearth and Vaughn lounging arrogantly in a chair. When she entered, he would draw deliberately to his feet and drawl out a remark that might sound like an insult, but contain within it a hidden kernel of welcome, equal to equal. And she would insult him back, in perfect harmony and understanding, no fussing, no false politeness.

None of which could happen if he weren't there.

Mary twisted her head and contemplated the great front door. Perhaps tonight hadn't been the best time to call. All it would take would be a quick twist of the knob and a good, strong shove with one shoulder. If the butler hadn't seen her face . . .

"Madam?" It was too late. The erstwhile butler had reappeared.

Mary gave him her haughtiest glance, trying very hard to look as though she hadn't been caught contemplating a precipitate flight back out into the night.

The butler was not impressed.

"If you would be so good as to follow me?" he intoned, in the sort of voice that would have filled Drury Lane Theatre twice over.

Mary gathered her cloak about her with as much dignity as she could muster and followed. They proceeded through a stately procession of reception rooms, each more ornate than the last. The butler's single candle struck gold glints off the ornately curled frames of innumerable pictures, hung one above the other in a dazzling display of connoisseurship and raw wealth. Overhead, the passing light revealed glimpses of azure sky. Pink-skinned goddesses, bearded patriarchs, and dimpled nymphs yawned down upon Mary and her guide as they passed below, disturbing their slumber.

Even the very shadows seemed shinier than the ordinary run of shadow, richer and sleeker. That might merely have been the effect produced by the smooth sheen of Venetian mirrors and silk-hung walls, Gobelin tapestries and floors polished to so slick a sheen that the light wriggled in the amber surface like fish swimming just below the surface of a river. Mary's boots seemed even older and shabbier against the glowing patina of the parquet floor, and her woolen cloak rasped dully against Savonnerie carpets that must have cost more than all the contents of her childhood home put together.

At the end of the last room, the butler opened a door in the paneling that Mary hadn't seen before, cleverly cut to blend into the rest of the wall. Beyond lay a short stretch of hallway that seemed dark and dull in comparison to the richness of gilded woodwork and painted ceilings in the chambers through which they had passed. There were no windows on either side, merely a series of matched sconces set at intervals down the wall, paired serpents whose open mouths each held the base of a candle, while their tails twined together in a love knot below.

At the far end, Mary could make out the shadowy shape of a stairway. Not the grand stair that curved around an immense statue of Hercules in the central rotunda, but a plain, workmanlike stair, narrow and steep, leading up to the upper stories.

Mary covertly eyed the staircase, wondering just what Vaughn intended. Upper stories tended to contain more private sorts of room. Like bedchambers.

Instead of the staircase, however, the butler turned the knob of a door in the center of the wall, so insignificant that Mary hadn't noticed it. With an inclination of his head, the butler gestured her into the room.

Mary swept regally past him, so intent on her grand entrance that it took her a moment to realize that it was being wasted on empty walls.

Mary came to an abrupt halt, the sole of her boot squeaking against the polished floor. She scarcely noted the click of the door as it closed behind her. There was no Vaughn. The room was empty.

Revolving in a slow circle, Mary took in her surroundings. There was certainly no place for Vaughn to hide. The room was scarcely larger than her dressing room at her brother-in-law's house, the walls paneled in a polished rosewood inlaid with precious porcelain plaques painted with scenes of life in the Orient. There were eight panels in all, angling inward to form an octagon. The parquet of the floor echoed the shape of the walls, sloping inward in an ever-narrowing pattern that drew the eye towards the center of the room, where a fancifully carved table held a silver salver.

Everything in the room was rich and strange, from the unexpected shelves that held vases made of jade so fine that Mary could see the light reflecting through it, to the Oriental dragons who stood in pairs beside the crimson-cushioned benches that sat at the base of seven of the eight walls. The eighth wall was occupied by a mantel of rare red marble, in which a fire had been laid but not lit. Even without the fire, the room didn't feel cold. Candles had been lit in gold filigree holders at even intervals all along the eight walls, and their light reflected warmly off the rich rosewood and the pale parquet floor, striking off the hidden gold threads in the shot-silk crimson cushions and turning the lolling tongues of the brass lions red-gold.

Standing in the center, beside the carved teak table, Mary felt as though she had been placed in a velvet-lined jewel box. There were no windows, no door, nothing but rosewood and porcelain, filigree and marble. Even the ceiling had been plastered and painted in imitation of the roof of a pagoda, tricking the eye with the illusion of successive layers of intricate architectural detail rising ever upwards.

Tipping her head back, Mary squinted at the ceiling, knowing that it had to be flat no matter how her eyes insisted otherwise.

The only warning she had was a light click, and then the door burst open, followed by a velvety voice drawling, in tones of barely veiled menace, "How very kind of you to call. It saves me all sorts of trouble."

Mary dropped her head so quickly she nearly wrenched something in her neck. It was so like Vaughn, to catch her at a disadvantage, gawking at the ceiling like some poor provincial who had never seen trompe l'oeil before.

Drawing herself up, she slowly turned to face him with all the outraged dignity of Elizabeth I confronting a disorderly courtier. She was doing quite well at the regal outrage until Vaughn came into view. The stinging rejoinder Mary had prepared fell unuttered from her slack lips.

Vaughn lounged in an expansive pose, the billowing white folds of his shirtsleeves filling the doorway. Without waistcoat or cravat, the ties of his shirt undone, Lord Vaughn looked more like the caricaturist's ideal of a dissolute poet than a belted earl. His shirt hung open at his neck, revealing the strong lines of his throat and a surprisingly impressive display of musculature, the smoothly honed physique of a swordsman rather than a pugilist. The shirt had been loosely tucked into his pantaloons, but seemed to have come free in the back, the shirttails hanging over the tight kerseymere of his breeches. The large diamond still winked on his finger, its richness only serving to underline his shocking dishabille.

Mary found herself incapable of doing anything but stare. It was impossible to envision Lord Vaughn without his armor of brocade and lace, but there he was, in little more than his linen, the lithe grace of his form admirably displayed by the sheer folds of fine fabric. It was . . . Mary blinked rapidly. It was unmistakably Lord Vaughn, but a Lord Vaughn such as she would never have imagined. And yet, it was undeniably he. Who else could be so arrogant even in dishabille?

In the meantime, Vaughn seemed to be having equal difficulties comprehending her presence. At the sight of her face, he rocked back on his heels, taking an inadvertent step back and catching at the door frame for balance in a movement that made his sleeves flatten against the corded muscles of his arm.

Regaining his usual self-possession, he propped himself against the door frame, folding his arms across his chest.

"Well, well," said Vaughn mockingly. "What have we here?"

Chapter Eleven

What hath night to do with sleep?
Night hath better sweets to prove. . . .

—John Milton, *Comus*

"I believe the usual greeting is good evening," returned Mary, as Vaughn wavered in the doorway.

"My most abject apologies," drawled Vaughn, sauntering into the room and kicking the panel shut behind him. "I had expected someone else."

Mary stood primly beside the marble mantel, her hands clasped at her waist. "I'm sorry to disappoint you."

Vaughn's eyes conducted a leisurely inspection of Mary's person, from the scuffed toes of last season's kid half-boots straight up to the folds of the hood draped around her face.

He lifted one eyebrow in a lazy tribute. "Did I say I was disappointed? On the contrary. I am merely rendered dumb by the unexpected apparition of such loveliness in my humble bachelor abode."

Easing back her hood, Mary wrinkled her nose at the inlaid porcelain plaques, straight from the Orient, the gilded dragons, the precious rosewood carelessly used to line the walls. "You have a curious notion of humility, my lord."

"And what of bachelordom?" Vaughn propped himself against one of the priceless porcelain plaques as carelessly as if it were common plaster. "Now, there's a curious thing, bachelordom."

He was properly a widower, not a bachelor. Not that it made any difference. Either way, he could marry if he chose. He simply chose not to.

Mary permitted herself a sour smile. "I wouldn't know. My only experience is of spinsterhood."

"You sell yourself short, my dear." With no regard for the antiquity
of the materials behind him, Vaughn pushed away from the wall.

The movement overset his balance, and he stumbled a bit, putting
out a hand against the wall to catch himself. Mary revised her earlier
opinion of his dishabille. Not mere insolence, then, but—could the un-
flappable Lord Vaughn possibly be in his cups?

It was a practically unimaginable notion, but there was no denying
the uncharacteristic flush lighting his cheekbones and his slight un-
steadiness, almost but not entirely masked by the studied deliberation
of his movements. But even that deliberation was just the tiniest bit
miscalculated, like a drawing with the proportions off by the fraction
of a hair. And what she had assumed was a shadow, in fact, upon closer
viewing, looked suspiciously like spilled wine, a dark blot against
Vaughn's otherwise immaculate linen, in the general region of his
heart.

The white linen of his sleeve billowed dramatically about his arm as
he gestured grandly at Mary. "What mere mortal could aspire to such
loveliness?"

"Anyone with ten thousand pounds a year," said Mary caustically.

Vaughn clucked disapprovingly. "Can the world buy such a jewel?"

"And a case to put it into." Mary matched his quote and topped it.
Every now and again, Shakespeare actually said something sensible;
Mary had always taken that particular line as her personal motto. "No
one has offered me a suitable case yet. My lord, I did come here for a
reason."

"To see me," Vaughn provided, with a winning smile.

"To convey some intelligence to you," Mary corrected, with a frown.
Inebriated men needed to be dealt with firmly, since they had a way of
wandering from the point.

Of course, Vaughn had a way of diverting the conversation even sober. And for a man in his cups—if he was, indeed, in his cups—he sounded surprisingly lucid. Ever since that first stumble, his posture would have been the envy of any dancing master, and all his sibilants were exactly where they should be.

"Wounded!" cried Vaughn. "Struck to the heart! Did you think I had not intelligence enough already?"

"I think, my lord, that you could fright an academician out of his wits," began Mary carefully. "But—"

"Child's play," Vaughn interjected. "Academicians are a witless lot to begin with. I require more of a challenge. What of you?" he asked silkily. "Could I deprive you of your wits?"

"I wouldn't be of much use to you in that event, would I?"

"I wouldn't be so sure of that," murmured Vaughn, with a decidedly improper glint in his eye.

Mary could all but hear Letty's *I told you so* echoing in her ears. What was it Letty had called him? A reprobate? A rake? Whichever it was, he was doing his best to live up to the appellation.

She had enough of her wits left about her to nip that right in the bud. Straightening her spine, Mary cast him her best dowager-in-training expression, the one designed to cow dogs, servants, and small boys.

"I must beg your pardon for calling at such an unorthodox hour. I would not have done so had the circumstances not been exigent."

"Exigent." Vaughn rolled the word on his tongue as he strolled towards her. "The imagination quivers with anticipation. Have you left the hounds in hot pursuit? Shall I find a pack of creditors panting at my door? A love-maddened marquess anxious to sweep you away to his mountaintop lair? Or, perhaps," he added delicately, raising one brow, "a jealous wife, baying for your blood?"

Mary knew exactly which wife he meant.

"Neither," she snapped, biting off the word on her tongue. "Merely an overworked French spy, seeking an assignation with a likely operative."

The statement had an effect, even if not necessarily the desired one. Vaughn went still, his expression remote.

"Ah," said Vaughn.

"I had expected some response other than 'ah,' my lord," Mary pointed out with heavy sarcasm.

Instead of replying, Vaughn twisted a piece of filigree, revealing a cunningly constructed cabinet hidden behind the porcelain plaque. The opening of the cabinet had been cut in the shape of the plaque, the filigree edging hiding any break in the wall. Within sat a crystal decanter with a delicately rounded base and two matching glasses.

The number of glasses made a certain amount of sense. More than two people and the room would start to feel crowded. All the same, Mary couldn't help but wonder just whom Vaughn had entertained in the Chinese chamber before—and whom he had been intending to entertain tonight. Her eyes strayed to the little red cushioned benches that lined the walls. They were too narrow to support two comfortably, too shallow for dalliance of a more relaxed nature. Private the room might be, the furniture was inappropriately constructed for impropriety.

Looking up, Mary encountered Vaughn's amused gray eyes, watching her as though he knew exactly what she had been thinking.

Holding up the decanter, Vaughn enquired, "Claret?"

It was amazing the innuendo the man managed to pack into an entirely innocent word.

Lifting her chin, Mary gave a sniff worthy of a spinster chaperone. "I don't indulge."

Vaughn paused with the stopper poised above the decanter, one eyebrow raised. "No?" he said softly, and Mary had the uneasy feeling that they were talking about more than wine.

"No," she said shortly. "If we might return to business . . ."

"Business is it? How extremely . . . lowering. And just what sort of business would you care to transact?"

"Exactly the sort you engaged me to pursue. Or, rather, the individual you engaged me to pursue. The Black Tulip."

"And if I told you my interests had changed? That my circumstances had altered?"

Mary frowned at him. "We have a bargain, my lord."

"Bargains change. People change."

"How poetic." Mary's voice was so acid it nearly burned a hole in the exquisite marquetry of the table.

Setting down the decanter with a decided thump, Vaughn's face spread in a grin of genuine appreciation. "Well said, Miss Alsworthy. And as we all know, the truest poetry is the most feigning. *As You Like It*," he added, for Mary's edification.

"I don't like it," Mary said repressively.

Glass in one hand, Vaughn gestured expansively. "Don't all young ladies love poetry?"

"Not this one."

Vaughn's voice dropped intimately. "Generations of cavaliers have spun pretty lies for pretty faces—and what face prettier than yours? Would you prefer an epic, with ships dashed across a foreign shore in your honor? A ballad, perhaps. 'Come live with me and be my love / And we will all the pleasures prove . . .' "

Mary cut through Vaughn's recitation before he could enumerate them. "The Black Tulip has suggested a meeting place."

Vaughn bowed to the inevitable. "Very well," he sighed, motioning with his glass. "Since you seem determined to do so, tell me about your spy."

"*Your* spy has summoned me for an audience tomorrow night at Vauxhall Gardens."

"Vauxhall," mused Vaughn, as the reflected points of light in his claret sparkled like candles of a drowned city. "An interesting choice."

"An obvious one," Mary countered. "With masks and dark walk-ways."

"I am familiar with the gardens," replied Vaughn, his lips curving reminiscently. "More so than you, I imagine."

Judging from the glint in Vaughn's eye, he had made good use of the darker corners. "Far be it from me to challenge your great experience, my lord. My own little knowledge of the world certainly can't compare."

Vaughn's face darkened. He abruptly put down his glass. "Don't even wish it. You are better served without my experience. It would put lines on your pretty face. Here." He ran a deliberate finger down her cheek, his every move a challenge. "And here. It would be a shame to mar a thing of such beauty." His hand moved to cup her chin, angling her face with the dispassionate expertise of a collector examining a miniature. "Such exquisite beauty."

Mary steeled herself not to react, even as his touch tingled against her cheek.

"I know," she said coolly. "Others have told me so before."

Their eyes locked and held in an unspoken battle of wills, each daring the other to give way. With a rough laugh, Vaughn broke first, releasing his grip on her chin, staggering slightly as he did so.

Sweeping up his glass, Vaughn saluted her. "To women who know their own worth."

With one fluid motion, he knocked back the contents.

"Enough to know when to leave." Mary dragged the corners of her cloak around her and turned to look for the mechanism that operated the hidden door.

It couldn't be that complicated; architects seldom had much imagination when it came to concealing such things. It was the fourth panel from the fireplace; Mary had marked that much when Vaughn entered.

She poked cautiously at a particularly protuberant curlicue.

"Don't." Vaughn spoke softly, and yet his voice seemed to carry to fill the whole room, like mist at twilight. "Don't go."

Mary's fingers stilled on the filigree border, the finely chased gold biting into the pads of her fingers. "Why should I stay?"

Mary heard the chink of crystal against wood as he set down his glass on the teak table. His soft-soled slippers made hardly any noise on the polished floor.

Staring at a Chinese village, a long-poled house poised beside a hypothetical river, Mary was reminded inescapably of the Long Gallery at Sibley Court, that very first night of their association. He had come up behind her just so then, standing so close that his shirtfront brushed her back, so close she could feel the warmth of his skin, so close that his breath stirred her hair. They had so stood so then, and he had stepped away, another calculated move in a game played more for intellect than passion. It had been a feint, a ruse.

But this time, Vaughn didn't step away. He smelled of soap and sandalwood and spilled spirits.

He bent his head, and whispered in her ear, "Because I want you to."

Mary made a Herculean effort not to squirm.

"It isn't good for you to always get what you want," she said primly.

"Perhaps not," Vaughn agreed solemnly, his breath ruffling the hair at the nape of her neck. His hands cupped her shoulders, warm even through the wool of her cloak. They moved downwards, exploring the shape of her upper arms through the fabric. There was something mesmerizing about the movement, the power of human touch. "But so very, very pleasant."

Swallowing hard, Mary twisted in his grasp, turning to face him, the porcelain plaque hard and cold against her back. "Lord Vaughn—"

"Sebastian," he corrected.

There was something in his face as he said it, something raw and vulnerable, that robbed the words from Mary's tongue.

She bit down on her lower lip in confusion, not knowing what to say. It was one thing to spar with Lord Vaughn, sleek and polished, but this Sebastian, with his hair tousled and his shirt open at the throat, was another matter entirely, and infinitely more unsettling.

Taking advantage of her bewilderment, Vaughn ran an exploratory finger along the curve of her cheek, like a master sculptor marveling at his creation. Even his very breath seemed to intoxicate, rich with the smell of heady foreign wine. Mary seized on the scent with the last vestiges of common sense.

"You're foxed," she protested.

"Intoxicated," Vaughn corrected, using his fingers to trace the arch of her brows. His lips formed the words very deliberately. Mary couldn't take her eyes off the sight of them. "Drunk on the sight of you."

Mary tilted her chin, looking him straight in the eye. Her show of bravado might have been more effective if her heart wasn't pounding quite so hard, all but drowning out the sound of her own voice. "Eyes don't inebriate."

"Yours do. Stronger than port wine, sweeter than champagne, more biting than brandy. One gaze and a man is left staggering, sotted."

"I think you confuse me with the claret, my lord," she managed.

"Who needs claret?" His hand infiltrated the carefully arranged locks of her hair, twining through the long strands with a fine disregard for her hairdresser's art.

"You did, an hour ago."

Vaughn's thumbs smoothed over her eyelids, coaxing them closed. " 'Drink to me only with thine eyes,' " he murmured, his voice pitched deep and fathomless as midnight, " 'and I will pledge with mine.' "

One finger brushed across the sensitive skin of her lower lip in a pledge of things to come. They both knew how the verse ended, but Mary found herself waiting breathlessly for the final line, like the final words of an incantation.

Vaughn's voice dropped to something scarcely above a whisper, his breath soft against her lips.

" 'Or leave a kiss but in the cup, and I'll not ask for wine.' "

She could taste the claret he had drunk, headier from his lips than from the glass. He gave her a sporting chance to pull away, his lips a mere whisper on hers, his hands braced on the wall behind her. She could so easily have leaned away, have broken the fragile contact, as good sense and all her upbringing commanded. There was no profit in his kisses, no prospect of matrimony to follow.

That, at least, was what she should have been thinking. Instead, she found herself leaning forwards, sharing the draft he was offering. She could feel the warmth of his skin through the fine linen of his shirt as her hands moved up his arms to his shoulders, the muscles tensing beneath her touch, moving to hold her closer. His skin was warm, so warm, warding off the chill of the cold porcelain behind her back, the echoing gilded rooms, the night outside. His hands slid beneath her cloak, molding themselves to her waist, drawing her nearer, warming wherever they touched. Perhaps it was the wine, tingling on her tongue, inebriating by extension. Or perhaps it was just Vaughn—Sebastian— cradling her as though she were more precious than the porcelain on the walls, his lips exploring hers with the skill of a decade of assorted debaucheries.

At the nape of his neck, his hair feathered against the back of her hands, surprisingly soft, just as the skin beneath his collar was warm and supple, a world away from the starched shirts and stiff coats with which the Lord Vaughn she knew always barricaded himself. Mary let her hands slide further beneath his collar, feeling the muscles of his back undulate beneath her touch. Her fingers roamed over his shoulder blades, like an explorer traversing a mountain range in a strange, new land, and she could hear a roaring in her ears like the fall of a distant waterfall.

Until the hands holding her abruptly pulled away, and she opened her eyes to see Vaughn, her hair tousled and his eyes the color of an old silver coin.

Blinking a few times, Mary touched her fingers to her lips. She had been kissed before, more times than she cared to admit to. In her first Season, fresh from the country, she had allowed liberties in the hopes it might bring someone up to scratch—and, if she were honest, because she had been curious. It hadn't always been unpleasant. There were men who knew what they were doing, who didn't grab, who didn't slobber, who didn't try to colonize her vocal cords with their tongues. But it had never, ever so absorbed her attention or scattered her senses.

Despite her four Seasons, Mary suddenly felt as callow as any girl on her first balcony, all her worldliness in tatters around her.

Perhaps it was the claret.

"My lord—" she began, before realizing that she no idea where the sentence was supposed to end. "Sebastian . . ."

The name felt awkward on her tongue, despite the license he had given her to use it.

Vaughn's arm stiffened beneath her hand. Stepping back with un-flattering promptness, he stared at her as though seeing her for the first time, his gaze raking her face as though he were seeing straight through the skin.

Pressing his eyes tightly shut, he took a deep breath. "Mary—" he began, and then stopped, scraping a hand through his hair in an entirely uncharacteristic gesture of confusion.

"Yes?" said Mary, trying to keep her voice neutral and failing utterly.

Vaughn's lips twisted. "I can't say I never intended it, because I did. When I saw you standing there, I thought . . ."

Mary waited for him to finish the thought, but Vaughn turned abruptly away. "The time has come to restore you to the bosom of your family. I'll have Derby ready my sedan chair to take you home. You shouldn't be abroad at this time of night."

Bending, he yanked violently on the tongue of one the gilded dogs. The tongue rolled forwards. Somewhere in the depths of the door, a catch clicked and the panel sprung smoothly open.

"What of Vauxhall?" Mary asked.

Vaughn paused with one hand on the panel. "Vauxhall," he repeated, as though it were an unfamiliar term.

"The reason for my visit," Mary reminded him lightly.

Vaughn's brows drew together. "Of course. I knew that."

He looked rather adorable when he was befuddled, Mary thought giddily, although whether he was befuddled with claret or the kiss was unclear. She preferred to credit the latter.

Drawing himself up with exaggerated dignity, Vaughn addressed the air somewhere beyond her left shoulder. "There are arrangements to be made for our trip to Vauxhall. I'll see to them. It is," he added, with a crooked smile, "the least I can do."

"Until tomorrow, then?" Mary asked archly.

"Yes," Vaughn said, and there was nothing to be read in the silvered mirrors of his eyes. "Until then."

Chapter Twelve

"So...," Colin said.

"So," I agreed, nodding heartily.

Now that I had him, two hours before schedule, I had no idea what to do with him. Here we were, out in the middle of Mayfair, me in my sloppy archive clothes, Colin as dishy as ever, and all I could do was bob my head like one of those Chinese dolls.

Needless to say, I had had it all planned out. There was a charming little Greek restaurant next to my flat—well, Cypriot, but close enough—with coarse red tablecloths, heavenly food, and a rough but surprisingly potent Greek wine. Between the impact of the wine, the conveniently dim lighting, and the exotic strains of Greek music playing softly in the background, it was the perfect place for a first date, the sort of place where they would let you sit for hours, intruding only to refill your wine glass and bring you yet another plate of olives.

I had pointedly ignored my friend Pammy's advice to spend the week practicing seductively extracting pits from olives. I didn't see anything the least bit seductive about an olive pit. That was, Pammy informed me, precisely my problem. On the other hand, trying to ditch the olive pit could provide an icebreaker if conversation ever got slow.

But my little Greek restaurant—and my sleek, black going-out pants, my deodorant, and my hair dryer—were all back in Bayswater. We were in Mayfair. It was what one might call a slight logistical problem.

"So," I repeated, since it seemed to be the word of choice. "What shall we do?"

"Eat?" Colin suggested, with a little lift of the eyebrow that made the grainy November dusk as bright as any Technicolor fantasy land. It was, I realized, going to be okay. In fact, it was all more than okay.

"Squirrel stew?" I suggested, pointing to one who was regarding us curiously from his perch on a metal railing.

"I'm sure we can do better than that."

And it was as easily done as that. In one moment, his hand was at my elbow, as if it had always belonged there. Either he was, as my friend Pammy would say, a first-class smooth arse, or he liked me. Like really *liked* liked me. That's also Pammy, only circa sixth grade.

"True," I agreed giddily, leaning happily into the hand on my elbow and feeling the brush of his Barbour jacket against mine. Perhaps our Barbour jackets could give birth to a litter of lovely little Wellies. "There must be a pigeon or two somewhere. We could have pigeon pie."

"You have to be fast," cautioned Colin. Away from Bond Street, in the gloom of a residential street, I couldn't quite make out his face, but I knew the glint was there. "They're speedy little buggers."

"Dangerous, too. There was one time—my little sister had just left to go to school. Next thing we know, poof! She comes back in, absolutely covered—" I broke off with something that was half-hiccup, half-snort, trying to choke down the silly giggles.

I couldn't believe I was launching the Date to End All Dates with a disquisition on pigeon poo. I'd never read *The Rules*, but I was sure there had to be something in there about saving scatological humor for the third date. After all, he'll never respect you if you give it to him on the first date. And there was no reason Colin needed to know about Jillian's close, personal acquaintance with the Metro New York pigeon population.

"Um, how's your sister doing?" I gabbled quickly, in an awkward attempt at a save.

"Pigeon-free, last I heard," Colin said dryly.

I did what any sensible, adult person would do. I slapped him on the arm. Then I giggled. "You *know* that's not what I meant."

I'm sure I was batting my eyelashes, too, but fortunately it was too dark for him to see. In the space of five minutes, I had regressed straight to middle school. It could have been worse. I could have been wearing leg warmers and a My Little Pony sweatshirt.

"You've seen her more recently than I have," Colin pointed out.

"By about two hours," I protested. Pammy had invited us all to an expat Thanksgiving dinner at her mother's posh town house in The Boltons, a quiet crescent in South Kensington. Needless to say, there wasn't anything the least bit expat about either Colin or his sister, but Pammy knew Serena from the all-girls school where they'd both gone to high school together, or whatever they call high school on this side of the Atlantic.

As for Colin . . . well, let's just say that Pammy had gotten fed up with my attempts to organize my love life for myself, and had decided to barge in, more like a charging herd of water buffalo than a fairy godmother. Bless the girl. All I could say was that it had worked. After all, I was here, wasn't I? More importantly, Colin was here.

"—the rest of the dinner?" he was saying.

"Oh, it was the usual thing," I said blithely. "We all ate until we felt ill, and then we had dessert."

Next to me, Colin chuckled, and I felt the boost of it go straight to my head, like a shot of Red Bull on an empty stomach. I was clever, I was charming, I was Super-Date!

Thus emboldened, I informed him, "It's not a proper Thanksgiving dinner unless you have to roll yourself groaning out the door at the end of the evening, swearing that you'll never eat again."

"I'm so sorry I missed it," he said blandly.

Making a face up at him, I made a big show of trying to recall what happened next. "Aside from the indigestion, you missed out on a great bit of social satire. All the financial people stared fishily at the fashion people and the fashion people made fun of the financial people."

"Which camp did you join?"

"Neither. Serena and I slunk off into the parlor and drank all the rest of the gin. We had a *lovely* chat."

Suddenly, the hand at my elbow had gone as limp as last week's lettuce. Trepidation came off him in waves. "Did you?"

"Oh yes," I said. "Serena told me all sorts of interesting things."

She hadn't, actually. Mostly, we'd talked about her job at a gallery, and then Pammy had barged in, and it had been all about Pammy's latest boy, who had gone off to Hong Kong and didn't seem likely to return. What with all that, there hadn't been much time for pumping Serena about Colin's childhood peccadilloes. But I was enjoying making Colin squirm.

In the shadows, I could see Colin mentally cycling through his catalogue of potential disasters. I was just grateful my own sister was safely on the other side of the Atlantic.

"Weren't we going to get dinner?" Colin asked hastily.

I made a mental note to myself to pump Serena for information in the not-so-distant future. Even better, I could have Pammy do it for me. With Pammy at hand, there's no need for thumbscrews. She could wring information from a turnip.

Taking pity on him, I indicated the quiet street around us with a sweeping gesture. "We seem to be in a restaurant-free zone. There's not even a Pizza Express in sight!"

"Impossible," returned Colin. "They're everywhere. I even have one under my pillow."

I wondered whether the pillow he was referring to was a Sussex pillow or a London pillow. The only times I'd seen him in London, he'd been staying with his great-aunt in Onslow Square, which would seem to imply that he didn't have a London flat of his own. There was the huge old family pile out in Sussex, a lovely Georgian mansion with a late Victorian library that I coveted with every last breath in my body, but it was hard to imagine someone our age actually living full time out in the country, all alone, in a house meant for a large family and hot-and-cold running servants.

"Are you staying with your aunt while you're here?"

"I usually do when I'm in town," he said, which didn't answer anything at all. I wanted to know what he did in town, where he lived when he wasn't in town, and what his views were on long distance relationships. Did London to Sussex count as long distance?

"Do you live at Selwick Hall full time?" I realized how silly it sounded the minute the words were out of my mouth. "Sorry. It's just that you don't usually see people without a family living out in a big house in the country. I mean, at least not in New York. Is London different?"

Damn. Open mouth, insert whole leg. Now I'd made it sound like he was some weird sort of family-less freak.

Fortunately, he took it in the spirit in which it was intended. "I used to live in London," he said easily. "Up until two years ago. I had a flat in Crouch End."

"I haven't been there," I said, just to say something.

"You aren't missing much. It's very modern, very trendy." He shrugged, in cynical commentary on life's little vagaries. "It seemed the thing to do at twenty-two."

"And then?" I asked.

"When my father died—" was it just me, or did his lips seem to pause over the words? "When my father died, someone had to look after the old place."

I touched a hand lightly to his forearm. "I'm so sorry."

"Don't be," he said lightly. He didn't make any effort to pretend that he didn't know what I was talking about. "It was a long time ago."

Two years ago. Not that long, in the grander scheme of things. I wondered if that had to do with why he was so inexplicably single— and why his sister was so painfully thin. Had there been a woman in the picture two years ago, back when he had the flat at Crouch End?

I couldn't even begin to imagine what sort of impact the death of a parent might have. Mine were both alive and well, back in New York, to be argued with over the phone, commiserated over with my little sister, and called whenever I needed reassurance, money, or both. I made a mental note to call them when I got home. Not because I needed money or reassurance. Just because.

"What did you do in the city before you moved?"

"I was in the City."

Hmm. I thought we'd already established that I knew he was in the city. "But what did you do there?"

"I worked in the City," Colin repeated. Then, as I stared blankly at him, his eyes crinkled at the corners in comprehension. "Not the city, as in London," he clarified. "I meant *the* City. The financial district. Like your Wall Street."

Who was it who said that Americans and Brits are divided by a common language? Well, whoever it was, they got it spot on.

"Oh," I said, feeling like an idiot. "Right. I knew that."

And I did—at least, I'd seen the term before, in books and magazines. The papers were always going on about scandals in the City. It's just that it's very hard to realize the difference when you don't have that convenient capital letter to clue you in.

"I never realized just how American I was till I got to England," I confessed. "So you did financial stuff?"

"Stuff was my specialty," teased Colin.

"Come on. That's not fair. How much do you ever really know about what other peoples' jobs are?" Warming to my theme, I waved my free hand in the air for emphasis. "I mean, my best friend's a lawyer, but I have no idea what she actually does, other than that she's always stuck in the office late, and her desk looks like it was eaten by a giant paper monster."

Colin looked bemusedly down at me. "A paper monster?"

"You know, big piles of paper." I sketched them out with one hand, like a mime with a nontraditional box.

"You have a very vivid way of putting things."

"Thank you. I think."

My compliment fishing went unrewarded. Instead of assuring me that I was the most amusing raconteuse he'd ever met, Colin said, "I know what you do."

I shook my hair back and said, just as archly. "Not all of it."

"Your secret life of crime?" speculated Colin. "Or are you undercover for the CIA?"

Considering that it's what I'd been wondering about him, it made me go redder than I'd otherwise have gone. I did notice that he had very cleverly routed the conversation away from his putative job in the City, and whatever it was he had done since. I'd have to get back to that once we'd had something to drink.

"Double-O Eloise? I don't think so. I'm just a humble Ph.D. student, trying to cobble together a dissertation before my committee kicks me out."

"Do you enjoy it?" he asked. He sounded like he meant it, like he really wanted to know.

"Sometimes more than others," I admitted.

We had been meandering quite slowly, along a quiet residential street lined with identical white-fronted town houses. Now, Colin slowed entirely to a stop, turning so that he was facing me.

He smiled right down at me in a way that made my graduate career seem like a purely academic topic. "And right now?"

"Right now I'm enjoying myself quite a lot," I murmured.

Anything louder than a murmur might have broken the fragile shell that surrounded us, that edged out the houses and the parked cars and the bustle of Bond Street just a few blocks away. We stood alone in the glow of a streetlamp, in a moment as round and perfect as the interior of a snow globe. It seemed perfectly natural when Colin reached out a hand to brush a strand of hair away from my eyes and tuck it behind my ear, and even more natural for his hand to linger against my cheek after the hair was safely tucked.

"Weren't we going to get dinner?" I asked breathlessly, shoving my hands into my pockets just to make sure I didn't do something stupid like fling them around his neck. "I mean, if you're hungry, that is."

"I'm always hungry," said Colin cheerfully, taking the change of subject in stride. "What do you fancy?"

Him, but that was beside the point. "There's a little Greek place near my flat if you don't mind a bit of a walk."

I wondered if he'd notice that crucial detail, "near my flat." Not that I was necessarily planning anything, but . . . just in case.

"Lead the way," he said.

"I would," I hedged. "Only I'm not quite sure where we are."

Colin gave me one of those "you've got to be kidding" looks. "We're three blocks from Bond Street."

"Which way is Bond Street?"

Colin pointed.

"I have no sense of direction," I confessed. "If it were up to me, we'd probably wind up in Edinburgh by accident."

"That's a long walk," said Colin, completely deadpan, except for the flicker of a dimple in one cheek that gave him away.

"Trust me, I've done worse. Actually, I got lost *in* Edinburgh once. It's a good thing it's not a large city."

"Where were you trying to go?"

"I meant to go to Holyrood House, but somehow I wound up by Arthur's Seat."

"You didn't climb Arthur's Seat, did you?" Colin was watching with amused fascination.

"Noooo. Not then, anyway. That was another night." I wafted that aside. "On the plus side, I find all sorts of interesting things that way. I stumbled on the Tollgate Museum when I was looking for the National Library."

"Aren't those in opposite directions?"

"It depends on where you're coming from," I lied cheerfully. In fact, they had been in opposite directions from the dorm where I'd been staying in Edinburgh. I'd just gotten entirely turned around and gone the wrong way. But, as I'd said, the Tollgate Museum had been more than worth it.

"Right." Colin settled back in the classic pose of the lecturer, weight evenly balanced on both feet, hands up and slightly parted. "This"—he pointed to the right—"is the way to Bond Street. If we walked that way"—he pointed straight up—"we would land on Oxford Street."

I rather liked the sound of that we.

"And there," he finished up, pointing left, "is Belliston Square. Grosvenor Square is just one over from that. If we keep going this way, we'll be at Hyde Park."

He'd lost me well before Hyde Park, partly because I was too busy admiring the strong shape of his hands as he gesticulated. They were awfully nice hands, broad without being beefy, permanently tanned from a lifetime spent in outdoor pursuits. I'd bet he was a brilliant skier. I already knew he was a rider; I'd seen a picture of him with a horse on his great-aunt's mantelpiece, looking sunburned, wind-blown, and utterly at ease. It was all my knight-in-shining-armor fantasies rolled into one very human package, minus the armor.

In order to hide the fact that I'd been so busy drooling over him that I'd paid no attention at all to what he'd been saying, I seized on the bit I did know.

"Belliston Square!" I exclaimed, with far more enthusiasm than the location warranted. "I was just there today. For the Vaughn Collection," I explained, pointing it out as we strolled into the square. "Have you been there?"

"Not for years," Colin admitted. "I seem to recall being dragged there by my mother as a small child, but I haven't been since. Serena tried to get me to go last year, but—" His lips closed very tightly over whatever it is he had been about to say.

"But what?" I asked, genuinely curious. Museums seldom elicit such violent reactions, unless they're the sort of museums that have installations of crosses suspended upside down in jars of urine, or photos of men in unnatural poses, which the Vaughn Collection decidedly was not. Gainsborough tended not to go in for that sort of thing.

Colin shook his head dismissively. "There was a chap—" he began, but before he could get any further into it, his attention was distracted by a man popping up out of the service entrance of the Vaughn Collection, practically under our noses.

The man was coming up the stairs of the sunken entrance known in the nineteenth century as "the area," the short flight of stairs that led down to the kitchen, scullery, and servants' hall. Or, in these days, the bathrooms, the reference room, and assorted offices and storage areas. He was a tall man, with an umbrella clamped beneath one arm and a briefcase in his hand, looking more like a City stockbroker than an employee of an art museum.

His eyes went instantly to where I stood with Colin, the streetlamp lighting my hair like a flaming brand. It's hard to inconspicuous when you're one of the few true redheads in a city of blondes and brunettes.

"Eloise!" Dempster exclaimed expansively. Umbrella sticking out from under his arm like a duck's tail, he advanced on me with his free hand outstretched in greeting. "Is there any way I can be assistance? Did you leave something—"

And then he saw who was standing beside me.

Colin hadn't said a word. He had just grown stiffer and stiffer until it was a bit like standing next to a barbershop Indian, a wooden cutout of a man painted to imitate life. His eyes were fixed on Nigel Dempster with a hostility that could only come from actual acquaintance.

The light from the streetlamp glinted wetly off Dempster's parted lips as he bared a full set of teeth in a broad smile.

"Not only Eloise—but Colin Selwick! What a perfectly lovely surprise. . . ."

Chapter Thirteen

The barge she sat in, like a burnisht throne,
Burnt on the water: the poop was beaten gold;
Purple the sails, and so perfumed that
The winds were love-sick with them; the oars were silver,
Which to the tune of flutes kept stroke, and made
The water which they beat to follow faster,
As amorous of their strokes. For her own person,
It beggar'd all description. . . .

—William Shakespeare, *Antony and Cleopatra*, II, ii

Mary lounged like Cleopatra in the back of Lord Vaughn's private barge. Reflected light from the lanterns hung on either side of the canopy unfurled across the dark waters of the Thames like silk ribbons as the prow pulled through the water, propelled by the efforts of half a dozen liveried oarsmen.

In front of her, Letty perched uncomfortably on the edge of her own seat, looking as out of place in her warm red cloak as a plump red hen at a court fete. She and Geoffrey had come along as chaperones, having firmly refused to countenance the notion of Vauxhall without their own protective presence. Aunt Imogen, Letty had declared, would just not do. Mary had accepted their escort with a good grace that caused her sister and brother-in-law to exchange a surprised glance.

Vaughn had added two others to the party, a widow and her daughter, both attired in shocking shades of purple that warred with the smooth black and silver of the barge. Between Miss Fustian's exuberant lace flounces and the large, ruffled parasol that Mrs. Fustian inexplicably insisted on carrying, the small cabin felt inordinately crowded.

The party was crammed beneath the tilt, or canopy, a half-cabin that the whimsy of Vaughn's craftsmen had shaped in the form of a small Greek temple, with a triangular pediment and two long Corinthian columns fronting either side, their complex pattern of icanthus leaves chased with beaten silver. Above Mary's head, the underside of the canopy had been painted in faithful reproduction of the night sky, the constellations reproduced in such painstaking detail that one could scarcely tell what was roof and what open sky, nature and artifice blended in brilliant illusion until the reproduction seemed the reality and the reality mere shadow. Rather, thought Mary, like Vaughn himself.

Along the open sides of the tilt waved long banners of rich black silk, embroidered in silver with Vaughn's own devise, a serpent contorted in an impossible spiral as it chased its own tail. Below it, on a curling sigil, rang out Vaughn's chosen motto: *Sic Semper Serpentibus*.

It wasn't, Mary knew, the family crest of the Vaughns. That, immortalized in print in *Debrett's Peerage* and in stone along the frontage of Vaughn House, consisted of a modified version of the lion of Scotland (a nice nod to their origins, another of the hangers-on who had followed James I from Scotland to England and been granted an earldom for their pains), demurely licking its paw among a field of gold balls, that the unkind claimed were meant to represent the coins that had come their way through the royal monopolies granted by the intemperate monarch. James I had always had a taste for handsome young men, and by all accounts, the first Lord Vaughn had been possessed of a particularly well-turned calf. The Vaughn motto was something equally mundane, the usual rot about perseverance and plenty, glorified by translation into Latin.

The silver serpent was Lord Vaughn's own private device, echoed in the livery of the oarsmen and rearing figure of a reptile at the prow, every scale outlined with painstaking artistry.

Vaughn had sensibly elected not to cram in with the others beneath the tilt. Standing just beyond the canopy, one jeweled hand resting against a Corinthian column, Vaughn looked every inch the Elizabethan grandee, lord of all he surveyed. While the fashion for swords had ended well over a decade ago, Lord Vaughn still carried himself as though he felt the weight of a hilt on his hip. He stood with a swordsman's stance, balanced and alert beneath his carefully cultivated air of languor.

Mary wondered what he had been like a decade ago, before his precipitate departure for the continent. A hot-headed young blood, eager to press his luck on the gaming table and the dueling field? A lace-frilled dandy with diamond buckles on his high-heeled shoes, all die-away sighs and languid airs?

It was impossible to imagine him as either, as anything other than what he was now, unchangingly, agelessly . . . Vaughn. A creature of contrasts. Lightless black and flashing silver, heavy lids and alert eyes, seeming indifference and . . . Vaughn's eyes caught Mary's above the purple feathers of Mrs. Fustian's headdress and something leapt between them that was anything but indifference.

Mary reclined against the rich velvet cushions like a satisfied cat. It didn't matter that he hadn't come to sit beside her, or that he had chosen to stand at the far end of the ship. It didn't matter that he had scarcely said more than good evening to her since she had climbed aboard. Vaughn, as well as she, knew how to bide his time.

With smooth skill, the oarsmen drew the barge up beside the Vauxhall Stairs. With murmured thanks, Mary took the hand Geoffrey offered her to lift her up from her seat, but her eyes were on Vaughn, as he helped his guests out of the boat. Now, surely, he would say something, give her some sign. Take her arm, walk with her along Vauxhall's shaded paths, as lovers had done for decades before them . . .

Pleasantly aware of her own fashionable white muslin, she watched as Vaughn's amused gaze skated over Miss Fustian's yellow bows and purple net. "My commendations to your dressmaker, Miss Fustian. I have never seen anything quite so . . . original."

Mary watched the silly chit simper in response, too dull to realize she had been insulted.

At last it was her turn to exit the boat, and she held out a gloved hand to Vaughn with her daintiest air, knowing that her shapely ankle in its fine silk stocking showed to good effect as she lifted her skirts a modest inch to effect her descent. As he handed her down, she glanced sideways up at him, the same sideways glance that had half the young bucks of the ton panting to get her out onto the balcony. It was a glance she reserved for very special occasions—or very titled men.

Lord Vaughn never noticed. His attention was unaccountably elsewhere. Not on her ankle—that, Mary could have understood; indeed, encouraged—but on the back of Mrs. Fustian's feathered head. Two fine lines showed between his brows, like the goal posts in a game of Pall Mall.

"You have a lovely barge, my lord," Mary murmured in her huskiest voice, arching one slippered foot to hunt for the ground with exaggerated care.

Vaughn's eyes flicked ever so briefly sideways as he handed her over the last step. "Your approbation is, as always, the light of my existence."

Mary hit dry land with a thud that reverberated from the bottom of her thin slippers right up through her legs.

When she turned her head back to Vaughn, to make some retort, something to make his eyes glisten silver with sardonic amusement, she found only the black wool of his back as he reached back to hand down her sister, exchanging snide comments with Pinchingdale about not caring to perform the same office for him.

He couldn't very well have simply walked away and left the last of his guests to fend for themselves, Mary reasoned with herself. It would have been bad form. Mary tried very hard to ignore the sharp little voice in her head that persisted in opining that Vaughn wasn't the sort to let himself be deterred from his desires by social niceties. The logical conclusion to that line of thought—that Vaughn didn't desire her, in any way at all—didn't bear consideration. There was last night.

Pasting a bright social smile on her face, Mary walked up to join the little group that clustered at the entrance to the gardens, as though that had been exactly what she had intended all along. After all, if he wanted her company, Lord Vaughn knew where she was.

Apparently, two could play at that game. At least, Mary hoped Lord Vaughn was playing. Having safely seen all his guests off the barge, Vaughn strode to the front of the group, offering his arm to the purple-bedecked Miss Fustian. With their number complete, the small party meandered down the lantern-decked alley that led from the water entrance into the slightly tarnished wonderland of the gardens. Walking behind Mrs. Fustian, who showed a very unmaternal lack of concern about her daughter's tête-a-tête with Lord Vaughn, Mary bided her time.

"I don't like this," Mary heard her sister whisper behind her in an aside meant for her husband.

Since there was a good foot between Letty's mouth and Pinchingdale's ear, the communication wasn't nearly as discreet as her sister had intended.

"You mean you don't like Vaughn," interjected Mary over her shoulder, and had the satisfaction of seeing her little sister flush.

"That's Lord Vaughn, to you, missy," snapped Mrs. Fustian, jabbing the point of her parasol into the gravel for emphasis. The steel of her voice warred with her floating layers of feathers and bows, like a dragon decked out in a lacy peignoir. "Of course, they don't like him! Liking is for ninnyhammers. Real men elicit rancor." Pausing for a moment of deep consideration, she added, "Loathing, even. But never liking."

"Hatred, perhaps?" suggested Mary's brother-in-law, hiding his amused smile behind a tone of excessive gravity.

Mrs. Fustian was not impressed. "Certainly not. Any common laborer can hate. True connoisseurs prefer more subtle shades of aversion."

Common was certainly a word no one would ever think of applying to Lord Vaughn. Tonight, in particular, he was uncommonly elusive, as glinting and inaccessible as the subtle silver threads that ran beneath the dark weave of his coat. He had taken the unaccountable step of devoting himself to the entertainment of the younger Fustian, heading up the party with her gangly form mincing along beside him.

Clinging to Lord Vaughn's arm, Miss Fustian stared goggle-eyed at him through her spectacles, looking as though she had never seen an earl before. Dressed like that, perhaps she hadn't, Mary thought crossly.

"If not hatred," put in her brother-in-law as the path broadened so that they could walk all abreast, "what of love?"

Out of the corner of her eye, Mary saw her sister and brother-in-law exchange a sickeningly speaking glance.

"Hmph," was Mrs. Fustian's eloquent opinion on that subject. For the first time that evening, Mary found herself in perfect agreement with her. "Good enough for shepherdesses, but not at all the thing for civilized folks. Love is a severely destabilizing emotion. Look at Paris," she finished, as though that said it all.

"The city, or the Greek?" inquired Letty in a tone of suppressed laughter, her arm twined possessively through her husband's.

"Either!" declared Mrs. Fustian.

"The late Mr. Fustian, then . . . ?" broached Geoff delicately.

"Fustian by name, fustian by nature," provided Lord Vaughn, pausing by the famous statue of Handel in the southern piazza with a simpering Miss Fustian on his arm as the little group collected around him. "Isn't that so, my dear?"

"Oh yes, my lord!" stammered Miss Fustian, overcome with the honor of his regard. "Very much so! Dear, dear Papa! How I do miss him." Miss Fustian took refuge behind a purple linen handkerchief.

"And a fine bit of fustian he was," concurred Lord Vaughn reminiscently.

Mary's brother-in-law made a noise dangerously close to a snort, earning him a quick squeeze on the arm from his wife.

With the uncomfortable sense that she had somehow been left out of a private joke, Mary looked quizzically at Vaughn. "You were acquainted with Mr. Fustian, then, my lord?"

Vaughn smiled blandly around the circle of lamp-lit faces. "As well as anyone here. Mr. Fustian was kind enough to accompany me on many of my wanderings."

Well, that explained it, then, thought Mary with some relief. Mr. Fustian must have been a tutor or a companion of sorts who had followed Vaughn around the Continent in his youth. That explained the undeniably underbred tone of the Fustian females. Naturally, Vaughn would think fondly of such a man and be kind to his widow and unfashionable daughter for the sake of his memory.

"I always found him," continued Vaughn meditatively, as the little group clustered in the lee of the brightly painted supper boxes, "an uncommonly resourceful fellow."

"Really?" Mary's brother-in-law raised an eyebrow at Lord Vaughn. "I would have said that he lacked depth."

Shaking off the importunate Miss Fustian, Vaughn matched Mary's former suitor eyebrow for eyebrow. "My dear Pinchingdale, at least he was constant in his inconstancy. Fustian never pretended to substance."

This time there was no mistaking the hard edge to her brother-in-law's tone. "You mean he never took the trouble to be honest."

Lord Vaughn's quizzing glass flashed mockingly. "My, my, how quick we are to condemn others. Imprudent honesty can do more harm than honest roguery. Wouldn't you agree, Pinchingdale?"

"Good intentions—" began Letty hotly, bristling to her husband's defense.

"Pave the road to hell," finished Vaughn smoothly. Extending an arm to Mary, he said, as though none of the previous conversation had occurred, "Shall we venture along the promenades, Miss Alsworthy? It would be sinful to allow such an uncommon fine night to go to waste."

"More sinful not to," cackled Mrs. Fustian, earning a scowl from Mary's brother-in-law.

Propelled by a look from Letty, Geoff took a step closer to Mary, an honor guard of one. "You needn't put yourself out, Vaughn. I would be more than delighted to accompany my sister."

The emphasis on the last word was wasted on no one in the ill-matched party, least of all Vaughn.

With a sardonic smile playing about his lips, Vaughn's eyes skated from Geoff to Letty and back to Mary.

"Such a charming family grouping," he murmured, and might have said more, had his attention not been caught by something just beyond Mary's left shoulder. Beneath Mary's fingers, his arm went stiff. Surprise and alarm chased across his normally polished countenance.

Following his gaze, Mary saw nothing to excite that sort of reaction. There was no one there but a couple in conversation. The man wore a full costume, in the fashion of the Venetians, an all-enveloping black cloak and pointed bird's beak of a mask. The woman was more conventionally garbed, a black mask tied across her eyes obscuring her features, blond curls peeking out from under a black hood.

As the pair walked slowly past, Mary could make out the interior of the supper box behind them, tenanted by a familiar set of gargoyle features, bracketed by a thicket of coarse gray hair, randomly studded with ruby-tipped combs that managed to look more like weapons than ornament. It was the woman who had accosted them in the coach the day before. And she was staring straight at Mary, with an expression of unmistakable venom on her face.

Mary was tempted to wave gaily back, but any such impulses were stilled by the abrupt interpolation of another person in their midst.

"Pinchingdale? Pinchingdale, old chap!" exclaimed Turnip Fitzhugh, slapping his old school chum on the back so hard that Geoffrey staggered.

Turnip's mother had optimistically christened him Reginald, but there was nothing the least bit regal about him. No one was quite sure how he had acquired his distinctive nickname, but even his friends had to admit that it was an accurate reflection of his mental powers. He was, everyone agreed, quite definitely a Turnip.

He also, thought Mary irritably, had the world's most inconvenient timing. By the time his uncoordinated form had surged past, Lady Hester's box was empty. Mary glanced uncertainly up at Lord Vaughn, but his face bore an abstracted expression that blunted all hope of private communication.

"Pinchingdale, old bean! Is that really you?" demanded Turnip.

"The last time I checked," replied Geoff pleasantly.

"I can vouch for that," agreed Letty, bumping her head affectionately against his arm. "He's definitely Pinchingdale."

Unconvinced, Turnip peered uncertainly at his old school chum. "I say, Pinchingdale, aren't you off rusticating?"

"If he were," pointed out Mrs. Fustian acidly, "would he be here?"

A furrow formed across Turnip's broad forehead as he pondered that problem. He opened his mouth, thought about it, and then closed it again.

Being of a generous disposition, Geoffrey put him out of his misery by explaining, "We were. We came back."

"Ah," Turnip's brow cleared as he mulled that over to his satisfaction. "Devilish dangerous place, the country. Don't like to stay out there long m'self. Cows, you know," he explained to Letty.

"Cows?" demanded Mrs. Fustian, taking a grip on her parasol that would have cast terror into the heart of a more perceptive man.

Caught up in unpleasant recollections of his own, Turnip shook his head, looking as grim as a man in a carnation pink waistcoat could contrive to look. "Deuced tetchy beasts, cows. Who knew?"

"Trust me," intervened Geoff, before the gleam in Mrs. Fustian's beady eyes could translate into words. "You don't want to know."

"Speak for yourself, Pinchingdale," sniffed Mrs. Fustian. "Unlike some, *I* have an inquiring mind."

"And I suppose inquiring minds want to know," concluded Geoff in tones of deep resignation. "Don't say I didn't warn you."

Turnip wagged his head earnestly up and down. "Everyone ought to be warned about cows."

It was only a matter of time before they descended to sheep. Mary edged carefully away from the group around Turnip. One could generally count on Turnip to natter on about nothing for an extended period of time, and while he did, she could slip away from the watchful eye of her sister and brother-in-law. Midnight, the Black Tulip had said, and it had to be nearly that now.

Poised to slip her arm through Vaughn's and stroll off together along the dark paths—with the Black Tulip as their object, of course—Mary found herself reaching for an arm that wasn't there.

Vaughn had disappeared.

Chapter Fourteen

O *where else*
Shall I inform my unacquainted feet
In the blind mazes of this tangled wood?
... O thievish Night,
Why shouldst thou, but for some felonious end,
In thy dark lantern thus close up the stars. ..."

—John Milton, *Comus*

Who dares not stir by day must walk by night.

—William Shakespeare, *King John*, I, i

Mary stared uncomprehendingly at the spot where Vaughn had been standing. He couldn't just go off and leave her. Except that he had. Vaughn was quite thoroughly and completely gone, leaving her with the task of keeping the assignation with the Black Tulip. Mary bit down hard on her lower lip, trying to tell herself that it didn't matter, just as if she hadn't spent the whole day anticipating the moment when she took to the shadowy paths with Vaughn, arm in arm, alone in a place legendary for illicit assignations.

Well, she was alone, all right. Alone with a task to accomplish.

Mary put her mask more firmly to her face and set about her own disappearance, determined to be well out of the way before her sister realized she was gone and, as she inevitably would, came after her, husband (and probably Turnip) in tow. Burrowing into the midst of a motley party, country cousins come to town judging by the antiquated cut of their clothes and the women's cries of pleasure at the brightly lit oil lanterns, the music floating from the Rotunda, and the cunning follies that lined the paths, Mary listed all the perfectly logical reasons why Vaughn might have disappeared. It had probably been silly of her to assume that he would accompany her in the first place, a notion born more out of daydream than logic. The spy might not show himself with Vaughn present—especially if the spy was Vaughn.

Mary lingered on that last prospect. If the Black Tulip were, in fact, Vaughn, then he would be waiting for her somewhere in the dark walks. That would explain Vaughn's distraction, his sudden disappearance while her attention was elsewhere. It was harder to explain why Vaughn would engage in that sort of subterfuge. But then, Vaughn seldom needed a reason for subterfuge. It came to him as naturally as breathing. Perhaps he wanted to test her loyalty, to see how far she could be trusted. Perhaps he simply enjoyed the drama of it, the masked meeting in a dark grove under an assumed identity. Stranger plots had been laid, by minds less convoluted than Vaughn's. He was a man who never took a straight route when a circular one was to be had. Look at his chosen emblem, the snake's tail twisted and twined in a mastery of controlled misdirection.

If Vaughn weren't the Black Tulip . . . Mary suppressed a shiver that had little to do with the bite of the October breeze that sent the dead leaves eddying along the edges of the walk. Not that there was any real danger, she told herself hastily. She was going to parlay, nothing more. She was only of use to the Black Tulip alive—and if the Black Tulip hadn't wanted anything to do with her, he need not have summoned her. Even so, there was something reassuring about the notion of Vaughn hiding himself in the crowds, following along behind her to her rendezvous with the French spy.

Mary shifted to the side, trying to keep in the shadow of the great sycamore trees that lined the sides of the Grand Walk. The Grand

Walk was far too bright for her taste, hung with the hundreds of oil lamps that had made Vauxhall such a wonder to those of her grand-parents' generation. With the colder weather drawing in, the crowds, even on this most popular of Vauxhall's walkways, were sparse. Those who had ventured out preferred to cluster in the relative warmth of the Rotunda. Another week, and Vauxhall would be deserted entirely, closed for the winter.

The golden statue of Aurora, one of the wonders of the gardens, glinted at the far end of the three-hundred-yard stretch. The light from the oil lamps reflected off the gold, turning the cul-de-sac nearly bright as day. That wouldn't do at all.

Mary abandoned the well-lit Grand Walk, heading towards the Rural Downs, where an overgrown lead statue of Milton stared forever blind across the sycamores that lined the sides of the walk. If the Black Tulip were, indeed, Lord Vaughn, Mary doubted he would be able to resist the symbolism of Milton's statue. The memory of Vaughn's voice, quoting *Paradise Lost*, sent a reminiscent tingle down her spine, and made her set off towards her assignation with a much lighter foot. If it were Vaughn, waiting for her among the trees . . .

Mary blundered through a stand of elms, towards a track still beaten enough to be a path but rustic enough to merit the name "rural," but there was no statue of Milton at the end of it to reward her labors, only a grotto whose dilapidated air appeared to be due more to neglect than de-sign. Through the screen of trees, the Grand Walk seemed very far away, the occasional burst of laughter or snippet of conversation the disjointed outbursts of Shakespeare's sprites. The gravel was harsh beneath the thin soles of her slippers, the ground uneven here, where nature had begun to rebel against art, hard clumps of weeds poking through the path.

If not the Rural Downs, perhaps this was the Druid's Walk? Mary began to wish she had taken the precaution of studying a plan of the gardens before they had left. In theory, in the close confines of Vaughn's luxurious Chinese chamber, losing herself among the paths at Vauxhall and waiting for the Black Tulip to come and find her had seemed quite simple. Lost on a rutted track amid a tangle of under-brush, Mary could think of several other words, also beginning with *s*. Silly was the mildest of them.

It was so dark, that she could scarcely see to avoid the outcroppings of ill-clipped shrubbery. There were lanterns here, too, but some enter-prising soul had smashed the glass bowls, leaving this part of the gar-dens in almost Stygian darkness. Ahead of her, a ghostly dome loomed among the trees, a folly meant to resemble a deserted pleasure palace. It was open on all sides, nothing more than a rounded roof supported by pillars, with a hard marble bench set in the middle, but Mary headed towards it gratefully. Among other things, a stubborn bit of gravel had worked its way into her left shoe.

Disposing herself on the bench, she eased the offending slipper off her foot, relieving her feelings by slapping it against the bench some-what more vigorously than the occasion required. It was ruined al-ready. The decaying leaves on the path had left dark smears on the white satin and either twigs or gravel had raised snags and rents in the delicate fabric. She would, she thought wryly, giving it a final whack, just have to add the cost to Lord Vaughn's account. If she ever found her way back to the Grove. At this point, regaining civilization seemed like a far more pressing problem than the whereabouts of the putative Black Tulip.

When the voice spoke behind her, she was caught like Cinderella, a shoe poised in one hand.

"So you came," the voice rasped behind her.

Mary instinctively started to rise, coming to an abrupt halt as her stockinged foot hit stone. She hastily dropped the hand holding the slipper, putting it behind her back in a motion as instinctive as it was counterproductive, considering that her visitor was standing be-hind her.

Flushing, Mary would have turned, but a heavy hand on her shoul-der forestalled her, forcing her back down onto the bench, the marble still warm from her body.

"No, no. Do stay where you are. I believe we shall both be more . . . comfortable that way."

The person behind her had spoken in French, perfectly accented despite the husky rasp that disguised what might have otherwise been a light tenor or even a deep alto voice. Mary's French was grammatical enough—most of the time—but her accent tended more to Hertford-shire than Paris.

"Wouldn't you like to sit?" she asked in English, hastily fitting her shoe back on her foot. Offered, as they were, to a ruthless spy in the middle of a dark wood, the words felt ridiculously mundane.

The Black Tulip must have felt the same way, because she could hear the current of amusement in his voice as he murmured, "I think not."

The pressure on her shoulder shifted but didn't subside as the Black Tulip settled himself more comfortably behind her, just out of her range of vision. It was infuriating to sense him behind her, to feel the warmth of a human body, to know he was there, but to have no image to put to it. Kneeling behind her, he robbed her of even an impression of height, and the hands heavy on her shoulders prevented any hope of surprising him with a quick turn.

So far, she thought grimly, she wasn't making a very good showing. With one movement, the Black Tulip had blinded and immobilized her. Of course, she reminded herself, he had been at this a great deal longer than she had. She wouldn't fall for the same trick again.

Staring straight ahead, Mary waited in tense expectation for the Black Tulip's next move.

"So," said the Black Tulip at long last, "you wish to be of service to the cause."

There was no need to explain what that cause might be.

"Oh yes!" said Mary innocently. "Did Mr. Rathbone tell you? I so hoped he would."

The fingers on her shoulders tightened, clamped down like a vise on wood, grinding straight to the bone. "Let us not play games, mademoiselle."

"Games?" She would have bruises to show for this, Mary thought vaguely, resisting the urge to squirm under the bruising grip. There would be no off-the-shoulder gowns for at least a week.

"Why do you wish to join our great enterprise?"

Mary did not need the pressure of his fingers to tell her that she needed to make her response convincing. On the other hand, if he weren't the Black Tulip at all, if he were a counterspy or a government agent, she risked more than a handful of bruises. The penalties for traitors had a medieval vigor about them.

Mary chose her words cautiously. "I have no love for the current regime."

"That does not mean you have any great love for us."

Mary pressed both her eyes shut. "Revenge is often a stronger motive than love, Monsieur."

"True." The grip on her shoulders loosened. "True. On whom do you wish to exact revenge, my little Fury?"

"That whole self-satisfied bouquet of flower spies." Mary's voice was as hard and cold as Lady Macbeth's decreeing Duncan's downfall. "They all laughed when Pinchingdale jilted me. Selwick, Dorrington, the lot of them. I'll see that they don't laugh again."

"The Pink Carnation, too?"

Mary shrugged, her shoulders rippling beneath his hands. "I don't know who he is, but they're all related somehow. That's why I've come to you. I want to tear them out, root and branch."

"And what of Lord Vaughn?"

The Black Tulip leaned so near that Mary could feel the brush of his breath across her cheek, fanning the fine strands of her hair. She could smell the rich leather of the glove that lay so heavily on her shoulder. A faint tang of cologne clung to his person, rich and familiar. She could even make out, ever so faintly, the impression of a ring pressing against her shoulder through the fine leather of the glove.

"What of him?" Mary questioned, wondering if the shank of the ring might, in fact, lead to a large diamond on an elegant-fingered hand, the same she had felt around her own less than half an hour before.

Half an hour was more than enough time to draw on a pair of gloves and a mask and follow her as she blundered about the unfamiliar walks.

"Does he . . . share your aspirations?" His breath teased her ear.

The hairs on the back of her neck prickled in the waiting silence. Holding herself very still, feeling as though her spine were made of glass, Mary replied carefully, "Lord Vaughn keeps his own counsel. He allows no one close to him."

The Black Tulip's gloved hand traced a path from her shoulder to her neck. For a moment, Mary relaxed into the brush of warm leather against her skin, the movement caressing, even tender. But he didn't stop there. His hand was moving up, firmer now, pressing against her throat, tilting back her chin, with an insistent pressure that was no less relentless for its measured progress.

Mary stiffened, but it was too late; with two fingers against her jaw, the Black Tulip tipped her head inexorably backwards, setting off the clean line of her throat and the perfection of her profile like a horse trader putting a beast through its paces. He tilted her chin until she thought her neck couldn't possibly bend any farther, and still the relentless pressure continued, pressing back, back, like a medieval inquisitor winding a rack until muscles and joints all split and cracked.

"Not even," the Black Tulip murmured, "a woman of such beauty as yourself?"

Mary's neck ached at the unnatural angle, and her throat felt tight. She was scared, more scared than she had ever been. With one careless movement, he could snap her neck back like a broken spring—and she sensed that he would do it, too, with no more regret than a small boy's tearing the wings off a fly.

It was only through a sheer act of will that she managed to keep her voice cool and level. "You flatter me, Monsieur."

With a deep chuckle, the Black Tulip released his bruising grip, letting her head sag forward.

"Do you know," he said musingly, as Mary sucked air into her tortured lungs, "you just might do. But that name," he added, "will not. Your predecessor called me by another name. She called me *mon seigneur*."

His voice divided the word into two, not the title of a lord of the church, but the old appellation for a sovereign or a liege lord.

"*Mon seigneur*," Mary repeated softly, wondering why it felt like the opening formalities to a pact with the devil. There was something about the archaic ring of it that awakened superstitions she had never known she had.

"It sounds well on your lips." Gloved fingers fleetingly brushed her lower lip.

Mary steeled herself not to clamp her lips shut. It was maddening being forced to sit still, maddening not being able to see his face, maddening knowing only a pair of hands and a warm, taunting presence in the dark.

Mad. The word clicked into place with uncomfortable clarity. Whoever he was, there could be no doubt that the person behind her was more than a little bit mad. The slide of his fingers across her face seemed to leave a trail of ooze in their wake, something unnatural and unhealthy.

The hand moved to her cheek, tilted her face first to one side, then the other. "I only knew one other who was your equal. But she proved false. Will you?"

"How can one possibly answer that?" retorted Mary, shaken into honesty. "If I make protestations of fidelity, you have no reason to believe me. I wouldn't."

"Well said, *ma belle*."

She didn't want to be his beauty. His careless words—was anything the Black Tulip said careless?—about her predecessor danced back before her. He might have only meant her prior counterpart, but Mary knew better. Whoever her predecessor had been, the Black Tulip meant the word literally. Deceased. Dead.

Like Bluebeard's wives, the Black Tulip's beauties had an uneasy time of it.

How had Bluebeard's last wife escaped? Mary rooted about in her memory of half-remembered nursery tales. It was something to do with a tower. *Sister Anne, Sister Anne . . .* That was it. Her loyal sister had stood watch in the tower, waiting for their brothers to come charging to the rescue. The beleaguered wife had called out to her sister, again and again, until her rescuers reached the castle, just in the nick of time.

Given that Mary had deliberately evaded her sister, she didn't think that was going to help her much. There was nothing for it but to try her luck with Bluebeard.

"Does that mean—you will accept me?" She didn't have to feign the slight tremor in her voice.

He enjoyed her fear, she could tell. Resting both hands again on her shoulders, his voice was rich with satisfaction as he mulled aloud, "I believe a trial is in order. A test of your loyalty."

"What would you have me do?" No matter how she bent her eyes, she couldn't see more than the very tips of his fingers, the black of his gloves blending with the black of her cloak.

The Black Tulip thought for a long moment, his palms pressing against Mary's shoulders. Mary sat very still, scarcely breathing beneath his weight. A trial—or a sacrifice? She had, after all, spoken of wanting revenge. What better way of testing her loyalty, that putting her to a test of her word.

Mary's fingernails bit into her palms.

"How may I serve, *mon seigneur?*" she asked softly, sounding as docile as she knew how.

The Black Tulip's fingers tapped thoughtfully against her shoulders. "The King proposes to review volunteers in Hyde Park the week after next—the twenty-sixth of October."

"Meet me in Hyde Park on the day for further instructions. You may," he added as an afterthought, "bring an escort. In fact, you should. The crowd will be rough."

"How will I know you?" Mary asked. "Won't you at least give some identifying characteristic, some sign?"

The Black Tulip laughed low in his throat, ruffling the back of Mary's hair. "Oh, don't worry. I'll make myself known."

The last thing Mary heard, before the world went black, was the Black Tulip's voice, in a whisper as lingering as a kiss.

"You won't be able to mistake me."

Chapter Fifteen

I pray you, do not fall in love with me,
For I am falser than vows made in wine.

—William Shakespeare, *As You Like It*, III, v

Whoever the Black Tulip was, he wasn't Vaughn.

It took Mary some time to extract herself from the black cloth the Tulip had taken the precaution of tossing over her head. It was a simple trick, but an effective one. In her panic at her sudden blindness, she had flailed out, expecting worse to come. Nothing did. Instead of a rope around her arms or a knife against her throat, Mary found herself striking at empty air.

By the time she plucked the piece of cloth from her eyes, the Black Tulip was long gone. As a means of frustrating pursuit, it was crude but effective.

She would be prepared for that trick next time, too.

Mary dropped the piece of black cloth beside the bench with unconcealed distaste, scrubbing her palms against her skirt. Straightening slowly, Mary drew her cloak more tightly about her, wishing she could climb into a tub of boiling water and scrub. Her throat stung where the Black Tulip had favored her with his iron caress, and she could still feel the imprint of his hands upon her shoulders.

With her companion gone, the little summerhouse felt echoingly empty, like a stage after the actors had gone. The pillars holding up the roof shone ghostly white against the night sky and the marble bench glowed palely against the leaf-littered surface of the floor. There was no indication that anyone else had ever been there—nothing except for the discarded pile of black cloth, bunched like a noxious toad beside the bench, and a slight disruption in the debris behind the bench, where the Black Tulip must have knelt. He had left behind no footprint or conveniently dropped handkerchief. No telltale buckle or jewel winked at Mary from among the dirt and cracked twigs.

Using the roof of the Orchestra as her guide, Mary tramped single-mindedly through the closely planted shrubbery, heading in the direction of the Grove. She craved bright lights and loud voices, shrill laughter and strong perfume. She wanted people around her, and lights so bright they hurt her eyes. But most of all, she wanted Vaughn. He would smile that twisted smile of his, and the Black Tulip would be reduced to his proper place, a man among men and no less foolish than any of them. There was something so comfortable about the fellowship of Vaughn's cynicism, which relegated everyone else to their places in the vast human comedy while she and Vaughn sat enthroned as audience, above the madding throng. She wanted the warmth of his hand on her arm; the reassurance of his lean swordsman's body by her side.

She very much wanted that barrier, or any barrier, between her and the Black Tulip. There was simply something . . . wrong about him. It wasn't the casual violence of his hands on her shoulders and throat that chilled her. She had known vicious men before, the sort of men who tried to lure one out onto a balcony and were inclined to get rough when repulsed. An animal, lashing out as an animal did, she could shrug aside. But the Black Tulip's concentrated control, the methodical nature of his actions . . . those made her glance back over her shoulder as she forged through the underbrush, wondering just what she had gotten herself into.

Breaking through a gap in the hedges, Mary found herself just where she had meant to be, on the edge of the Grove, with music drifting from the Orchestra and the smell of ham and spiced punch from the supper boxes. The narrow path spat her out near the Pillared Salon, almost exactly opposite the place where she had entered the Grand Walk what felt like a very long time ago.

Near the Orchestra, which stood in the center of the Grove, Mary could make out the broad form of Turnip Fitzhugh, bold in carnation pink, nodding his head appreciatively in time to a spirited rendition of "When Sappho Tuned the Lyre," but of Lord Vaughn and his silver cane there was no sign. Unless . . . Mary's eyes narrowed as she caught a flash of familiar silver just beside the entrance to the Pillared Salon. He and his companion stood in the shadow of the building, apart from the groups of people milling about the orchestra and supper boxes. Whatever it was they were discussing, it must have been absorbing; Vaughn's head was bent intently towards his companion. It wasn't Mrs. Fustian— those purple plumes would have been unmistakable—and the woman was too short to be the gangly Miss Fustian. Vaughn was no more than medium height but the blond head of the woman next to him barely reached the bottom of his chin.

"Miss Alsworthy!" Mary recoiled as a hand lightly descended on her shoulder.

But this hand bore a white glove, not a black, and the arm it was attached to quickly retreated at Mary's alarmed reaction.

"I do beg your pardon," said Mr. St. George, biting his lip in contrition. "I didn't mean to startle you."

"Mr. St. George!" said Mary brightly, doing her best to get her breathing back under control. "I hadn't realized you were at Vauxhall this evening."

St. George shrugged his shoulders self-deprecatingly. "I've been told it's one of the sights one simply must see before leaving London. So here I am."

"Leaving?" echoed Mary, her eye on the blonde beside Vaughn. "I do hope that doesn't mean that you will be leaving us."

"I am glad to hear you say that," said St. George earnestly. "But I do have responsibilities in Warwickshire that will demand my presence presently. I mean, presently demand my presence. Presently."

"Hmmm," said Mary, thinking absently that what he lacked was presence of mind. Who was that woman next to Vaughn? It was hard to make out anything of her features, due to the mask that covered her face from her eyebrows to the bridge of her nose, but even a hooded black cloak couldn't disguise a figure as prettily curved as that of the pink-cheeked shepherdess in the large Hayman painting behind her. "Will you pardon me? I must ask Lord Vaughn if he has seen my sister."

"We have that in common, then," said St. George pleasantly, strolling along with her towards the Pillared Salon. "I seem to have misplaced mine as well. Oh yes," he added, in response to the question Mary might have asked had she been paying him any attention at all. "She came with that Rathbone fellow."

Belatedly recalling her duty, Mary made a noncommittal noise in reply.

"The very thing." St. George grinned wryly down at her, taking inattention for distaste. "I feel much the same way. I would be delighted if she would only return to the governesses. The turtles, even," he added with a gusty sigh.

For once, even amphibians had ceased to be diverting. As Mary watched, the woman pressed something into Vaughn's palm. It disappeared just as quickly into Vaughn's waistcoat pocket, so quickly that Mary had only a glimpse of something pale against the figured fabric of Vaughn's waistcoat before it was gone.

Vaughn looked blandly up as Mary and her companion approached, as though it were nothing out of the ordinary to be receiving notes from masked women.

Perhaps for Vaughn, it wasn't.

Mary's lips pressed together in a tight line. As for the woman . . . Mary glanced sharply to the side, but the woman was gone, as rapidly and quietly as the note into Vaughn's pocket.

If that didn't signify skullduggery, Mary didn't know what did. She narrowed her eyes at Vaughn in implicit question, but if Vaughn noticed, he chose not to comment.

Instead, he raised his cane in languid greeting. "Ah, St. George, Miss Alsworthy. Have you had a pleasant coze?"

Mary fancied she could see the outline of the note, pressing against the closely cut fabric of his jacket.

With none of her usual finesse, she broke in, "My lord, I believe I had the pleasure of meeting a friend of yours this evening. After I was so unfortunately and accidentally separated from my sister."

"Indeed?" Vaughn raised a casual eyebrow. "My sympathies, then. Friends are a tedious lot. Enemies, on the other hand——"

Shrugging, Vaughn abandoned the topic as though bored with it. Reaching into his pocket he extracted, not the treacherous little piece of paper, but a silver snuffbox, as intricately pierced and chased as a medieval saint's reliquary.

"And I suppose you are an expert on the topic," said Mary crossly, as Vaughn wordlessly offered the box to a bemused St. George. Next to Vaughn, St. George seemed as tame and domestic as a plate of blancmange.

Snapping shut the lid of his snuffbox, Vaughn clicked his tongue in exaggerated deprecation. "Far be it from a dilettante such as my humble self to claim virtuosity in anything. I am but an eager amateur and unworthy of any such accolades." As his eyes met Mary's, his voice unaccountably dropped, took on a different cast. "Entirely unworthy."

Looking in polite incomprehension from one to the other, St. George shook his tawny head as though to clear it. "Would you be so kind as to excuse me? I really ought to see if I can find my sister. . . ."

His honest blue eyes lingered just a moment too long on Mary, as though waiting for her to forestall him.

"Happy hunting, my dear St. George," drawled Lord Vaughn, shattering the moment.

St. George forbore to respond in kind. With a polite nod to Vaughn and a warmer salutation to Mary, he set out in search of his lost sister and her latest pet turtle. But he could not quite resist casting a look back over his shoulder at Mary.

Seeing it, Mary smiled and waggled her fingers at him.

St. George continued on his quest with a spring in his step that hadn't been there before.

Lord Vaughn's dry voice broke into their byplay. "Don't worry. I won't keep you from your saintly suitor long."

Mary, who had been worrying about nothing of the kind, felt the color rise to her cheeks—with irritation, she assured herself. "You might have been more subtle with him," she said, hating the carping note she heard in her own voice.

"Subtlety is wasted on such as he," Vaughn said dismissively. Mary wished she could have detected jealousy in his voice, but it wasn't there. There was nothing but a faint tang of impatience, with St. George—or with her? Vaughn's eyes scanned the crowd beyond her shoulder.

Searching for the blond woman?

"I met your quarry," Mary said, her tone harsher than she had intended.

Vaughn's eyes dropped back to her, as though almost surprised to find her still there. Resting both hands on the head of his cane, he said mildly, for him, "So I surmised."

Was there nothing that would light a spark of interest in those pale gray eyes? She remembered the way they had flashed silver last night, in the cloistered confines of the Chinese chamber, where the whole room had closed about them until it had shrunk to the space of her arms around his shoulders, his lips on hers.

But that had been a different night, a different place. A different man. Her shoulders still ached from the Black Tulip's bruising grip. Mary's brows drew together dangerously as she regarded her supposed coconspirator, urbane and unruffled in his black brocade coat and immaculately tied cravat.

Where was he while she was being molested by dangerous French spies? It was one thing to stay out of sight, so as not to alarm their quarry, but he might at least have lurked in the bushes. But, no. Lord Vaughn couldn't be bothered. He was too busy engaging in tête-à-têtes with short blondes.

Mary folded her arms across her chest and favored Lord Vaughn with a look that would have felled a lesser man. "He wants to meet again," she said abruptly.

Vaughn lifted one brow. "You?"

Mary's temper frayed dangerously. "No, the Queen of Sheba. Do you think that could be arranged?"

Reluctantly, Vaughn's lips split into a lazy grin, his teeth white against his shadowed face. "A few draperies, a little blackamoor to carry your train, and we'll have Solomon himself swooning at your feet."

She didn't want Solomon and she certainly didn't want the Black Tulip. At the moment, she wasn't even entirely sure she wanted Vaughn, unless it was to strangle him.

Before she could pursue that happy line of thought, Vaughn spoke again, his voice brisk and business-like. "When?"

"The King has announced his plans to review recruits in Hyde Park on the twenty-sixth of this month. The—your friend has requested that I meet him there to receive further instructions." Mary couldn't quite suppress a slight shudder of distaste.

"The twenty-sixth . . ." Vaughn paused a moment for mental calculation, one hand on the head of his cane, head tilted in the classic pose of cogitation. "He gives us the better part of a fortnight."

"Us?" Mary arched an inquiring eyebrow, deciding to forgo strangulation for the present. She rather liked the sound of the word "us." It had a pleasant ring to it, almost as pleasant as "Lord and Lady Vaughn."

Tapping the end of his walking stick against the gravel, Vaughn turned abruptly to examine one of the large paintings by Francis Hayman that decorated the open portico of the Pavilion. Frozen in paint, falsely accused Hero swooned in the arms of her cousin Beatrice in a convincing counterfeit of death.

Vaughn's eyes dwelled on Hero's lifeless features as he spoke in a voice as flat as the paint. "I will, of course, escort you. It was, after all, part of our agreement."

Mary didn't like the sound of that nearly as much.

On an impulse, she scooped a glass of wine off the tray of a passing waiter. The liquid gleamed garnet red in the light of the lanterns, like the wine in Vaughn's glass in the Chinese chamber last night as he offered it to her. She had declined then. Now—Mary lifted the glass in a silent toast, an invitation.

She didn't need to explain what it meant; he knew, as he always seemed to know.

Vaughn propped himself against his cane, the picture of languid unconcern, but his pales eyes glittered like the diamond on his finger as they narrowed on hers.

"I thought you didn't indulge."

"Perhaps I've changed my mind," Mary said recklessly, tilting the glass to her lips without breaking their gaze. Using her tongue, she flicked a stray drop of wine from her lower lip. "It is a woman's prerogative, is it not?"

Taking care not to brush her fingers, Vaughn reached out and abstracted the glass neatly from her lifted hand.

"Some prerogatives, Miss Alsworthy, are best not employed."

"Why not?" Mary demanded, wishing she could stamp her foot as she had when she was a child and thwarted in some small desire. But one didn't stamp one's foot in front of a peer of the realm, however much one wanted to.

"Because"—Vaughn's lips twisted into a crooked smile—"they have grown out of date."

Placing the glass firmly back down upon the tray, he looked inscrutably down at her, in a way that made Mary wonder if she had a smudge on her cheek or had suddenly grown a third eye in the center of her forehead. "If you ask him, I'm sure Mr. St. George will fetch you a lemonade."

Over Vaughn's shoulder, Mary could see her sister bustle across the Grove, dragging her tall husband by the hand, anxiously scanning the crowd. Spotting Mary with Vaughn, Letty raised her hand in greeting, her pace quickening.

Mary made an impatient gesture. "What if I don't want lemonade?" she protested, her blue eyes urgent on his. "Lemonade is so . . . insipid."

"Perhaps." Vaughn's bland countenance was a study in indifference. "But it is far better for your constitution. Enjoy your lemonade, Miss Alsworthy."

With a curt nod to her relations, Lord Vaughn strode off into the glittering crowd and was gone, leaving Mary with nothing but bruised shoulders and the sour taste of lemons.

Chapter Sixteen

"**D**empster."

If the archivist was pleased to see us, the same definitely couldn't be said of Colin. Dropping his hand from my elbow, he shoved both hands in his pockets, his attention entirely fixed on Dempster. He looked like a gunslinger about to face off at the OK Corral.

Dempster's eyes went from me to Colin in open speculation. His lips curved at the corners in a way reminiscent of Siamese cats and other creatures generally associated with snatching canaries from cages.

"You never told me you knew the Selwicks, Eloise," he said, in a way that made it sound like we were old and intimate acquaintances, as opposed to our five-minute chat that day.

The implication was so entirely at odds with the reality, that I was rendered momentarily speechless. I looked at him sharply, but before I had time to phrase a reasonably coherent comment, Colin had jumped in.

"Small world, isn't it?" said Colin in a voice with an undertone that made the hairs on the back of my neck bristle. "Especially where certain people are concerned."

My head swiveled back around to Colin. I was beginning to feel like the monkey in monkey-in-the-middle—a very confused monkey. I wished someone would explain to me what was going on, instead of just glowering at each other through me. To be fair, Dempster wasn't glowering. His expression could be more aptly described as a gloat. And for Colin to have glowered, he might have had to use his facial muscles, which were frozen in an expression of such complete impassivity that I feared it would take a hammer and chisel to crack it.

"You two know each other?" I said belatedly and entirely inadequately.

Neither bothered to reply. I didn't blame them. It had been a completely inane question. If they didn't know each other, they were certainly putting on a pretty good pretense of it.

"Well, I certainly wouldn't want to keep you," Dempster said smoothly. "I look forward to our coffee, Eloise."

I wished he would stop saying my name. Every time he did, Colin moved just a little farther away. My elbow felt very cold without his hand there.

"Thanks." I smiled tightly. "See you then."

With his umbrella sticking out under his arm like the Kaiser's sword, Dempster trip-trapped smartly across the square. Even his back looked smug.

"What was that all about?" I demanded.

Instead of answering, Colin jammed his hands in his pockets and looked straight ahead. "Where is that Greek restaurant of yours?"

We were definitely back into Mr. Hyde mode.

"Leinster Street. In Bayswater."

"Right. Shall we?"

He didn't wait for a response. I trotted along after, wondering what the hell was going on, but Colin's pace didn't leave much breath for interrogation. It had to have something to do with the Pink Carnation papers, but I couldn't imagine what Dempster might have done to elicit that sort of hostility. Admittedly, Colin had reacted with an entirely unwarranted vitriol when I'd sent in my humble request to be allowed to view the family papers. And that was before he'd even met me in person. His reaction when he met me in person, on his aunt's drawing room floor with the papers scattered around me like a child surrounded by the crumbs of purloined cookies, had been even more extreme. That was just plain not normal. In fact, we were entering the realm of creepy. I don't care how proud you are of your family heritage; it doesn't justify treating perfectly innocent historians like psycho serial killers just because they want to have a peep at your papers.

I was getting pretty damn fed up with this whole Jekyll and Hyde routine. By the time we'd made it to Leinster Street, I was windburned, breathless, and thoroughly out of patience with Colin, his mood swings, and his little dog, too. Sailing past him as he held out open the door for me, I held up two fingers to the maitre d' and squirmed into the banquette he indicated, letting my bag slip from my shoulder and fall to the floor with a defiant thump.

"A carafe of your house red, please?" I asked, before the maitre d' could escape. Just because I was pissed with Colin was no need to be rude to the staff. Just because some people couldn't control their tempers didn't mean I couldn't. Just because . . .

I realized a waiter was standing over me, waiting for me to take the offered menu. Belatedly, I took it from him, glad for the dim lighting that hid my flush, part irritation and part windburn.

Taking the chair across from me, which looked ridiculously little and spindly with him looming over it, Colin sat himself gingerly down. Whether that was because he feared the staying power of the chair or because he had picked up on the ominous tilt of my menu was unclear. I suspected the former.

I had meant to continue in cold silence, blasting him with the frost of my displeasure, but irritation and curiosity got the better of me. Abandoning any attempt to read the menu, I tossed it aside and leaned forwards with both elbows on the table.

"What was all that with you and Nigel Dempster out there?"

Instead of answering the question, Colin planted both *his* elbows on the table. "How long have you known Dempster?"

"Since about six o'clock this evening," I answered automatically, and then kicked myself for it. What was I doing answering his questions? I had asked first. Just because his elbows were bigger than mine didn't give him any right to bag first answer.

"Really," said Colin, managing to inject a world of mistrust into that one simple word.

"Give or take half an hour," I added. "I wouldn't want to be anything less than perfectly accurate. How long have *you* known Dempster?"

"Awhile."

That was certainly informative. He was just lucky I had left my thumbscrews in my other bag.

"Right," I said. "Okay. I don't know what's going on between you and Dempster, but if you want to be mad at him, be mad at him. Don't get all pissy with me."

It wasn't the most elegantly phrased argument I've ever made, but it got the point across. Colin removed his elbows from the table and looked at me curiously. "You really don't know?"

"I don't even know enough to know what I'm not supposed to know," I said irritably. "I met Dempster for all of five minutes this afternoon while I was doing research at the Vaughn Collection. He's the archivist there, you know."

"I knew that," mumbled Colin.

"So if you'd like to sit here and fume about Dempster or whatever else it is that's eating at you," I said, warming to my theme, "feel free to go right ahead. I'll just head off home and spend the evening watching the snooker championships."

"It's not snooker season, actually," offered Colin, in a conciliatory way.

"Fine. Darts, then."

"Envisioning them thrown at my head?" he asked ruefully.

Despite myself, I smiled back. "We were getting there."

We both leaned back as the waiter appeared and placed the carafe of wine in the center of the table between us, expertly flipping glasses right way up. He took our order, too, but don't ask me what I ordered, or how I ordered. When he had sidled away again, we both leaned forward, as at an unspoken cue.

After a long moment, Colin said, "Would an apology do, or does it have to be the darts?"

I melted in an instant. But I wasn't going to let him off the hook quite that easily. "I'll accept an apology if it comes with an explanation."

Colin rubbed his neck with his hand, regarding me like a hopeful puppy dog. "Are you sure you wouldn't prefer just to fling something at me and get it over with?"

I leaned back against the cushioned back of the banquette, folded my arms across my chest, and waited.

"Dempster?" I prompted.

Colin considered for a moment, contemplated the olive plate, considered some more, and came out with, "We don't get on."

"That much I figured out on my own."

Colin shifted restlessly in his seat. "It's a long story."

I patted the side of the glass carafe. "We have a large carafe of wine."

Colin let himself relax into a rueful grin. "I really am sorry. I didn't mean to drag you into it."

"Since I've already been dragged," I suggested, grasping the carafe with two hands and tipping it forwards over his glass, "it would be nice to know what's going on."

"Thanks." Colin took the glass I held out to him. He raised it an ironic salute. "Cheers."

"So?" I urged. "Story?"

After a moment's consideration, Colin gave me the short version. "Dempster dated my sister."

That was not quite what I had been expecting.

But it did certainly make a lot more sense. For a man to leap to the defense of his archive was just kind of odd; for him to leap to the defense of a sister was really rather sweet. Especially when that sister had just gone through a particularly nasty, self-esteem-destroying . . .

From the dark reaches of memory, in a completely different part of my brain, a snatch of gossip came floating up to the fore.

"He's that one!" I yelped.

Colin gave me a look.

I shrugged. "Pammy told me."

"Pammy talks a lot."

"She means well. She just wanted to make sure I didn't say something that might upset Serena. Wait—let's not stray from the point. Dempster is Serena's evil ex?"

I was still grappling with this key concept. It wasn't totally inconceivable. He was a reasonably good-looking man, if one went for the tall, dark type, and the little bit of gray at his temples only gave him a distinguished look, reminiscent of up-and-coming politicians and the better-looking sort of college professor. I put Dempster's age at late thirties, early forties, but that wasn't too ridiculous a leap for a girl in her mid-twenties, especially one looking for a replacement father figure. Grant, of unlamented memory, had been thirty to my twenty-two when we started dating. He liked them young, young and adoring. Hence my eventual replacement. But that's another story. Grant had no business butting in on my date.

Colin was watching me over the small bulb of the candle, the uncertain light playing off the planes of his face, making his eyes seem even more shadowed and wary than they were. "How much did Pammy tell you?"

"Only that Serena had just gone through a particularly nasty breakup." I think Pammy's phrasing had been more along the lines of "royally dumped," but that wasn't something that needed to be repeated to Serena's brother. I can be tactful. When I remember to be.

"Right," said Colin. "Serena's always been a little bit . . ."

"Vulnerable?" I suggested.

"Quiet. Shy. Defenseless. Our family—" Colin broke off with a brisk shake of his head. "That's too much to go into. At any rate, Serena wasn't in a good way. She met Dempster at an arts course. Something to do with authentication. Ironic, really."

"I gather Dempster turned out to be in-authentic?"

"At the time, Dempster seemed like a good thing. Steady, devoted, solicitous."

"What happened?" I had an uncomfortable feeling I knew where this was going. Especially when I remembered the Dempster's plummy voice rolling over the words, *I think the answer lies in the Selwick collection. . . .* The memory gave me chills, and not of a good variety.

Watching me, Colin nodded once, as though something had already been asked and answered. "You can guess, can't you?"

I met his gaze straight on. "He was after her for the papers, wasn't he?"

"Got it in one." Colin poked at a small green olive with his fork as though the olive had personally offended him. "He was very clever about it, too. For the first few months it was all art and music and mutual acquaintances. He didn't mention the Pink Carnation at all, except offhandedly, as part of a paper he was writing on iconic representations of great English heroes, or something of that ilk."

"Hmm," I said. That sounded awfully like a line in my dissertation prospectus. That did not please me. "And then?"

"He asked Serena to 'help' with his research by looking for old family papers. She gave him one or two things—not much, but enough to whet his appetite."

That I could definitely understand. Just a glimpse of the yellowing papers in Colin's aunt's flat had been enough to set me drooling, provided the drool didn't damage the papers, of course. To know that the papers were there, just out of his reach, must have been maddening to Dempster, like a brioche dangled in front of a man who had skipped breakfast. Not that I sympathized with Dempster's methods, mind you. But I could understand the impulse.

I wondered what I would have done if Colin's aunt hadn't miraculously offered me carte blanche among her papers.

It wasn't at all comparable, I assured myself. I wanted Colin entirely for his extremely attractive self, not for his access to archives. Even though that had been a very intriguing pile of papers I had left unexplored up at Selwick Hall. . . .

Perhaps Dempster had been initially attracted to Serena in the beginning, too, before archival fever took hold.

"And then what?" I asked, preferring not to follow that line of thought to its conclusion. It was different. It just was.

With the air of a man getting through a necessary but unpleasant task, Colin said briefly, "Dempster applied to Aunt Arabella for permission to see the rest. She refused."

"She didn't refuse me," I said smugly.

Colin raised both eyebrows at me. "Aunt Arabella has excellent taste." As I preened, he added, "Most of the time."

I made a face at him.

"If you're not going to compliment me, you might as well go on with the story," I said resignedly. "I imagine Dempster didn't take the refusal well?"

"To put it mildly. He became more and more insistent. He even asked her if she couldn't just remove a few documents, and return them before Aunt Arabella noticed."

I made appropriate noises indicating extreme horror and shock. The waiter hastened anxiously our way, but having ascertained that the choking sounds weren't caused by an olive lodged in someone's larynx, he obligingly sidled away again.

"Naturally, Serena refused," announced Colin, sounding rather proud of his little sister.

"Naturally!" I echoed.

"When Serena refused, Dempster became abusive."

"Physically?" I asked.

Colin made a wry face. "He didn't need to be. Working on her mind was easy enough. She was ugly, she was dull, she was fat, no one would ever date her if she didn't have him—it was all an attempt to terrify her into doing what he wanted."

"But it stuck," I said softly.

"It stuck," Colin agreed. "It was nothing she didn't already think of herself."

"But she's . . ." I brought my hands together in gesture indicative of extreme skinniness. "Tiny. Teeny-tiny. Super skinny. And she's absolutely charming," I added, as an afterthought.

"Try telling her that," said Colin grimly.

"I will," I said, resolving to shower Serena with compliments the very next time the occasion arose. It wouldn't be that hard. She really was that charming, in that shy, slightly retiring way that tends to get plowed under when stronger personalities are present (i.e., just about everyone else).

"So that's why," I said. "That's why you reacted so badly when you saw me at your aunt's that first time."

"That was part of it," Colin agreed. "I wasn't feeling too kindly towards academics at the time."

"And now?"

Colin leaned back in his chair, looking at me from under half-lowered lids. "Let's just say I'm willing to admit there might be exceptions."

"How very generous of you," I drawled.

Colin's eyes glinted in the candlelight. "I try to be fair."

The sparks were coming along so nicely that I almost hated to spoil it by bringing it back to Dempster. "So when Dempster greeted me by name tonight, you must have assumed . . ."

"That you two were in cahoots," Colin finished.

"Wow." I shook my head to clear it. "That would be quite a plot. Dempster, having failed with your sister, goes and dredges up a female to try her wiles on the male half of the family. Since we all know men are notoriously susceptible to that sort of thing."

Colin's eyes crinkled in a way that suggested the joke was on him. "We are here, after all," he said, indicating the half-empty restaurant, with its dim lighting and cozy little tables.

"Right," I said sarcastically, trying to cover the little thrill that went through me at the implication that he might be susceptible to my wiles. "Me as Mata Hari."

For some reason, Colin didn't seem to find this idea nearly as absurd as I did. "Why not?" he asked.

"Did you really think I was interested in you only for your papers?" I demanded incredulously.

It wasn't until Colin raised one eyebrow, looking as smug as Lord Vaughn at his very smuggest, that I realized just what I had let slip.

I cast about for a last-ditch way to talk myself out of it.

"Um, what I meant was . . . would you like an olive?"

I thrust the little olive plate at him.

Colin took the plate and set it down, possessing himself of my hand instead of an olive. "It's nice to know that it's not just my papers you're interested in."

"Well, yes," I said, as red as the tablecloth. I dropped my eyes in front of his amused gaze. "I'm glad we've got that cleared up."

"Eloise?"

"Yes?"

"You're all red."

"That happens when I drink," I said hastily. "It's the Irish flush. We call it the Curse of the Kellys. Happens to all of us."

"Does it?"

"No," I admitted. "I just made it up to have something to say. Don't ask. I'll just go and get my foot out of my throat now, shall I?"

"Don't let that stop you. I think you're doing quite well," said Colin, not bothering to hide his grin.

"Do you know," I said inconsequentially, "that Pammy wanted me to spend the week practicing seductively spitting out olive pits?"

Colin looked deeply interested. "Is there a seductive way of spitting out olive pits?"

"That's exactly what I said! Pammy said I was hopeless," I added.

"Pammy doesn't know what she's talking about."

We broke off, grinning foolishly at each other, as the waiter arrived with the food that I couldn't remember ordering. It seemed almost a shame to clutter the space on the table between us with the half-dozen little plates that seemed to go with our starters, baby eggplant stuffed and stewed, gooey concoctions of rice and raisins wrapped in grape leaves, something pureed that looked like baby food for grown-ups, with bits of flat, heavenly smelling bread stuck artistically round it for dipping. With all the fuss and clatter, Colin discreetly released my hand, and we settled back demurely on our own sides of the table as the feast was arrayed before us, as if we hadn't just been holding hands like Lady and the Tramp with a strand of spaghetti between them.

Not being of a romantic disposition, the waiter professionally doled out plates and departed, leaving us again to our own devices, without so much as a serenade.

It's very hard to remain sentimental in the face of hot food. Giving in to the inevitable, I took a large spoon and began ladling pureed eggplant onto my plate.

"Why did Dempster want so badly to see the papers?" I asked, handing the spoon over, handle first, to Colin.

Accepting the proffered spoon, Colin raised his eyebrows at me over the eggplant. "Why did you?"

"That's different," I protested, poking a triangle of bread emphatically into the pureed eggplant. "I have a dissertation to write. What does he need it for?"

"Can't you think of more compelling reasons than a dissertation?"

I considered. "At the moment? No."

Colin leaned back in his chair, somehow managing to fill all available space. "Not even money?"

Chapter Seventeen

Sigh no more, ladies, sigh no more,
Men were deceivers ever. . . .
—William Shakespeare, *Much Ado About Nothing*, II, iii

It was nearly a week before Mary saw Lord Vaughn again, but that didn't matter. As Mrs. Fustian had so helpfully pointed out, hating was common, but had Mary been willing to take the time to do so, she might have been disposed to despise, loathe, and revile Lord Vaughn, all of which fell well within the permissible parameters of Mrs. Fustian's lexicon.

But she didn't. Because he wasn't worth the bother.

It wasn't as though she spent her spare hours reclining on her virginal bed, dreaming impossible dreams of what have been. Instead, she had spent them draped in white cheesecloth, reciting impossible rhymes, in Lady Euphemia McPhee's private theatre in Richmond. The theatricals had provided a welcome distraction, even if the sight of St. George's spear made her think longingly of running certain people through.

Unfortunately, Lady Euphemia wasn't the only one with a taste for the stage. On a miserable, rainy Tuesday, Mary found herself slogging reluctantly up the steps of the Uppington town residence, prepared to endure that ritualized horror commonly known as a musical entertainment.

Mary's slippers squelched against the black-and-white marble tiles of the entrance hall. She had landed with both feet squarely in a puddle when her brother-in-law handed her out of the carriage. She couldn't even blame him for neglect. There had been no patch of ground that hadn't contained a puddle. The Uppingtons' footmen were having a busy time of it, scuttling about after the guests with cloths to sop up the rainwater that created gleaming slicks on the shining marble floor. One unfortunate young lady had already gone into a skid that landed her flat on an unmentionable part of her anatomy.

A perfect day for a musicale.

They were among the earliest arrivals. Although Lady Uppington had engaged a celebrated soprano for the entertainment, her daughter, Lady Henrietta, was to sing first. Loyal friend that she was, Letty had refused to risk missing so much as one syllable of her friend's song.

Mary trailed along behind her sister and brother-in-law into the music room, where Lady Uppington was bustling about, overseeing the disposal of a regiment of gilt-backed chairs, designed to cause anyone over five feet tall severe cramps in various parts of their anatomy. The prime seats, the ones towards the back that allowed for easy escape, had already been taken, one by the Dowager Duchess of Dovedale's revolting pug dog, who yipped at the newcomers as though daring them to try to move him.

Mary generally gave the Dowager Duchess of Dovedale a wide berth. The antipathy had been mutual ever since Mary's first Season when the Dowager Duchess had trained on Mary her infamous lorgnette and pronounced, "I dislike showy looks!"

Mary, younger then, and bolder, had curtsied, replying with deceptive sweetness, "Isn't that better, ma'am, than having no looks to show?"

The reference to the Dowager Duchess's granddaughter, Lady Charlotte, sweet-faced but insipid, had been too obvious to ignore. Mary and the dowager had existed in a state of mutually acknowledged enmity ever since.

If she had it to do over, Mary admitted to herself, she might be more circumspect. The dowager was a rude old bag, but she carried a great deal of weight in the segments of society that mattered to Mary. Mary had always wondered how many of the admirers who had never come up to scratch could be laid at the dowager's door. All the Dowager Duchess had to do was whisper a few words in the right ears. A discreet hint that the chit wouldn't be received—at least not in the houses that counted, of which the dowager's was still one—and the word had gone out, from anxious mother to henpecked son. There had been at least three men her first Season who might have done, older sons from solid families with enough town polish to make the thought of matrimony more pleasant than otherwise. And all three had unaccountably moved, within the space of a month, from pursuit to apologetic retreat.

Mary defiantly took a chair in the same row as the dowager. Other guests had begun to filter in, pouncing on the seats along the sides. Mary caught herself looking for a silver-headed cane among the throng of dampened shoulders and rain-spotted frocks and made herself stop. It was unlikely that Vaughn would stoop to so insipid an entertainment as a musicale, even with the city still half-empty.

Miles Dorrington tottered into the room, wearing a beatific smile and bearing a large, padded chair, which he sat down with a satisfied thump just at the end of the front row.

"Helping yourself again, I see," commented Lord Richard.

The simple words produced a palpable tension among the family circle. Lady Henrietta dropped her roll of sheet music and Lord Richard's wife produced an indiscreet but heartfelt, "Oh dear."

Dorrington looked his former friend steadily in the eye, hurt and resignation written all over his straightforward face. Lord Richard's own gaze faltered beneath his steady regard. He looked, thought Mary, almost abashed.

"I don't think Hen would appreciate the comparison," Dorrington said quietly.

"She doesn't," chimed in Henrietta, taking her husband's arm. She jabbed an index finger into her brother's side. "You, sit. And you—" Henrietta turned to her husband, who beamed at her expectantly. "You sit, too."

Miles stopped beaming.

"And if you can't speak nicely to one another, don't speak at all. That means you," she added to her brother, just in case he might be under any misapprehension.

"Bossy as ever," complained Miles good-naturedly, but he sat.

"Completely power mad," agreed Lord Richard, sitting, too.

"Do you think that means they're speaking again?" demanded Amy of her sister-in-law, in a hearty whisper that carried clear across the room.

Henrietta rolled her eyes. "At least they've moved past words of one syllable. Whatever it is, it's an improvement."

"Power mad and indiscreet," amended Lord Richard from the front row, never lifting his eyes from the polished sheen of his Hessians.

"Agreed," grunted Miles, displaying an equal fascination with his own toes.

The two men exchanged masculine nods of commiseration before quickly returning to their contemplation of their boots.

Lady Uppington regarded her offspring with an expression of maternal satisfaction. It wasn't a look Mary could ever recall seeing on her own mother's face. Mrs. Alsworthy reserved her looks of satisfaction for the milliner and the mantua-maker.

"I do wish you would consider staying," Lady Uppington said to Henrietta. "Not long," she added, in the tone of someone taking up an old argument, "but just until you've refurbished Loring House. It would be such a blessing to have all of my children under the same roof again."

"What about Charles?" Lady Henrietta pointed out, referring to her oldest brother. As heir to the marquisate, he would have been a brilliant catch, but he had already been married by the time Mary made her debut, to the unobjectionable and uninteresting daughter of a minor baron.

Lady Uppington went a guilty pink about the ears.

Henrietta seized her advantage. "Ha! You always forget about Charles."

"Nonsense," Lady Uppington declared loftily. "Charles has children of his own now. He gets his own roof."

"Hmph!" snapped the Dowager Duchess of Dovedale from the back of the room. "Roofs are wasted on the young! Leave the lot of them out in the elements. Toughen them up, I say. Most of this lot wouldn't last the week."

The dowager jabbed her cane illustratively at the pastel-clad debutantes and dandies filtering into the room. Following the line of her thrust—it was either that, or be poked in the eye by her cane—Mary saw a diamond-buckled shoe cross the threshold, a glittering counterpoint to the muddy Hessian boots of the other gentlemen. The matching shoe followed, stepping across the parquet floor with a regal precision that practically demanded a fanfare. With one hand resting casually on the silver head of his cane, Lord Vaughn paused, surveying the crowd with the bored air of a visiting emperor.

Mary's chest tightened in a way that had nothing to do with the dowager's cane "accidentally" scraping her ribs. Who would have thought that Vaughn would so lower himself as to attend a musicale? Among the chattering debutantes and tousle-headed Corinthians, his aquiline profile looked as remote and as dangerous as the portrait of a Renaissance prince.

"*Caro!*" Mme. Fiorila greeted Vaughn with a cry of unfeigned pleasure, and Mary felt the little quiver of anticipation that had flared up in her chest blacken and crumble.

Without missing a step or sparing a single glance for Mary, Vaughn moved smoothly to the front of the room, taking the singer by both hands and bussing her smoothly on first one cheek then the other, in the decadent European fashion. In the candlelight, the opera singer's hair glowed pure red-gold, like the molten metal in a Byzantine emperor's mint. She laughed, and murmured something in a throaty voice that was lost to Mary's ears, something intimate enough to make Vaughn raise an eyebrow in amused reply, so at ease with this woman—this *opera singer*—that he didn't even need to bother with words.

Caro, was it? Just how caro was he to her? Not that it mattered.

Vaughn could prance through the beds of the entire Italian opera corps for all Mary cared. It was simply gauche to display such familiarity in public. One would have thought that a belted earl would have known better.

But not Vaughn. Oh no. He did as he pleased and damn the consequences, whether it was making a public spectacle of himself with a common opera singer or kissing—

"Miss Mary?"

Mary gave a decidedly undignified start at the sound of her name. A large male form cast a shadow over the program in her lap.

"Forgive me," said Mr. St. George, taking her alarmed look for one of indignation. "Miss Alsworthy, I should have said. It's simply that the other suits you so well. You look like a Madonna with your hair pulled smooth like that." His hands sketched the air in a gesture of masculine hopelessness at the intricacies of feminine coiffeurs.

"I thought Madonnas were usually blond," replied Mary, her eyes stealing to the front of the room. Mme. Fiorila wasn't really a blonde; her hair was closer to red, more Mary Magdalene than the Virgin.

"Not always," commented St. George mildly. "In Italy and Spain, one often sees the Blessed Mother portrayed with coloring more like yours. There is a picture by Velázquez in particular that puts me in mind of you. You have some of that same heavenly serenity."

"You flatter me, Mr. St. George," she murmured, donning serenity like a cloak. Beneath it, she felt about as serene as Beelzebub after a hard day in hell, and just as likely to start spitting bits of brimstone.

"Might I avail myself of the seat beside you? If my services might be of any use, I would be delighted to translate the Italian in the program for you."

Mary gestured graciously to the seat beside her. "That would be very kind of you. Our entertainer is Italian, is she not? I wonder why she styles herself *madame* rather than *signora*."

St. George shrugged good-naturedly, intent on the task of folding his long limbs into the tiny chair. "I'm afraid I don't pay terribly much attention to the opera, or opera singers."

Mary favored him with a smile of such warmth that the bemused gentleman nearly missed the chair. "That, Mr. St. George, cannot but show excellent judgment on your part." At the front of the room, Vaughn pressed a parting kiss to the back of Mme. Fiorila's hand. It wasn't a brief brush of the air, such as courtesy might demand, but a genuine press of lips against skin. "One wouldn't want to get mixed up with such people," Mary added waspishly.

As Lady Henrietta nodded to the accompanist, Lord Vaughn moved discreetly away, propping one shoulder against a painted panel depicting a young shepherd serenading his lass on a rather improbable lute. The opera singer didn't follow him; like the professional she was, she stood beside the spinet, waiting her turn to sing. But Vaughn had a clear view of her face from where he stood. As Mary watched, Lord Vaughn lifted his brows and the singer's cheeks creased with answering amusement.

Mary looked hastily down at her program, dry eyed and aching. Lady Henrietta's practiced trills felt like a barrage of artillery against her ears, all pounding home the same, unwanted message. Nothing Vaughn did was by accident, everything was deliberate, calculated. The way Vaughn snubbed her at Vauxhall—that hadn't been an accident or a mistake. There was no other explanation. He simply wasn't interested. He was grinding home to her, in the best means available to him, that she was nothing to him other than a business associate. Not even an associate, an employee.

"Do interpret for me, Mr. St. George," Mary purred, angling her shoulder closer to his. "What was that lovely phrase Lady Henrietta just sang?"

St. George tilted his head for a moment, listening. " 'Beat me, beat me, dear Masetto,' " he translated.

From the side of the room, Vaughn cast them an oblique, sideways glance.

"Indeed." Mary's lips curved upwards in an intimate smile. "Do tell me more, Mr. St. George."

" 'Meekly like a lamb will I stand . . .' "

"How charming."

Vaughn had left his position on the wall and was moving casually down the ranks of chairs, towards the back of the room.

St. George was still whispering in her ear, but Mary didn't hear a word of it. From the corner of her eye, she followed Vaughn's progress as he approached their seats, at the very end of the very last row of the room. And passed them by, so closely that the tails of his coat brushed the side of her chair. He didn't look down; he didn't look back. He simply left.

Mary's nails bit into the leather of her gloves. What further proof did she need? Vaughn was nothing to her, she reminded herself. Nothing.

Straightening her spine, she smiled upon her companion.

"How very faithfully you translate, Mr. St. George. Do go on."

THE APPLAUSE FOLLOWING LADY HENRIETTA's final note drowned out the light tap of the door shutting behind him. Alone in the entryway, once again pristine and puddleless, Vaughn turned unerringly along one of the two corridors that branched out off the entrance hall on either side of the great marble sweep of stairs. His instructions had been explicit.

Lady Uppington's musicale, third door on the left.

Aurelia was singing now; he could hear the familiar magic of her voice weaving its way through the cracks of the door as he prowled down the left-hand corridor, counting doors. It had been a relief to see her there, holding out both hands to him at the front of the room. Her company was always a source of solace. They had been lovers once, so long ago that he could not with any accuracy have named the year. Their liaison had ended by mutual consent, ripening instead into a friendship that was at once more satisfying and more lasting.

Aurelia's presence had never been more welcome than today, with Mary Alsworthy enthroned in the last row, sowing distraction and disorder like a siren of Greek myth. Five days of avoidance had done nothing to dim her fatal effect; they had merely been a panacea. It had taken all the force of five days of resolution, all the steadying influence of Aurelia's presence, to keep him from tossing that sickening St. George from his seat and claiming the place for himself.

The third door on the left was, in fact, the last door on the left. Vaughn helped himself to a candle from the sconce on the wall before turning the brass handle, a precaution that proved to be justified. The room in front of him was as dark as a dungeon. Rain streaked blackly down the windows lining two sides of the room, turning the surfaces slick and dark as polished ebony. The light of his candle reflected wetly off the dark surfaces, sending distorted images of the room wobbling in their depths.

Closing the door carefully behind him, Vaughn touched his candle to one of the mirror-backed sconces that flanked the door, and watched as a warm light flickered tentatively across the expanse of a pale yellow and blue rug. He didn't need the east-facing windows to tell him that this must be the morning room. The walls and furniture had been upholstered in a cheerful pale yellow stripe that seemed determined to hold the light and help it along.

Even in the uneven light, it was clear that he was the first one there. The furniture was all of the spindly and delicate variety, too dainty to conceal even the most delicate human form. The long cream and gold sofa was untenanted, and there was no room between the ormolu legs of the escritoire to hide so much as a cat.

On the mantel was arrayed a fine collection of Oriental porcelain, glazed cobalt blue and fitted, undoubtedly in France, with gilded trimmings. Hands clasped casually behind his back, Vaughn strolled towards the collection of vases, keeping a wary eye on the mirror above the mantel. It was clearly French in origin, unremarkable enough with its shell-shaped curves, but it served its purpose. It reflected the door behind him as the white panel slowly eased open and a slender figure slid through the resulting gap.

The angle of the glass blurred her features and elongated the pale column of her gown. Her dress was blue, a gray-toned blue that blended with the shadows, like a shade fleeing Hades. Like him, she had come prepared. The candle in her hand turned the fashionable frizz around her face into a distorted halo.

She lowered her light, placing it on a marble-topped Louis XV table, and the nimbus receded, bringing her face properly into focus.

It was a face he had known well, once. Even masked, at Vauxhall, he had known her. He could have traced from memory the familiar features, the short upper lip and small, straight nose. But she had changed. It wasn't only the polished surface of the mirror that lent a hard gloss to the once girlish features. The long curls that had framed and softened her face were gone, replaced by a fashionably short crop, held back by a bandeau to reveal a pair of dangling sapphire earrings that even by the uncertain light of the two candles were clearly paste, and a cheap version, at that, as flat and hard as the eyes that followed his in the mirror.

Vaughn could feel her eyes on his back, a palpable pressure against the layers of wool and linen.

"So you did come," she said, with no little satisfaction. She had always had the voice of a courtesan, low and throaty, with just a hint of a pout. The years had brought the pout into prominence.

Turning slowly to face her, Vaughn sketched an elaborate court bow, one leg cocked and one arm gracefully extended.

"As you can see," he drawled.

"I had thought you might not." Her words were meant to be coy, but her hands gave her away, locked tightly at her waist. She glanced quickly over her shoulder at the closed door to the hall.

"How could I resist such a summons? Beauty may be ignored, but threats tend to garner results," he added dryly.

Glancing in the mirror, she made a quick adjustment to one of the little curls on her forehead. "I wouldn't have resorted to them if I had thought there was any other way of getting your attention."

"Then how do you explain the visits I had from your charming Italian friend this spring?"

Taken off guard, she wasn't quick enough to pretend ignorance. "What did you do with Marco?"

Vaughn idly inspected the facets of his great diamond ring. "Was that his name? I must confess, we were never on those sorts of terms. One seldom is with one's blackmailer."

"You didn't—dispose of him?" she asked breathlessly.

"Let your fears be set at rest. The creature for whom you are so concerned—although one can hardly see why—is currently cooling his heels in the West Indies."

"Really, Sebastian! How could you?"

"More to the point, how could you? Then again," Vaughn added meaningfully, "you always did have appalling taste in men."

The woman in front of him stiffened, her teeth digging into her lower lip.

"How can I argue?" she retorted. Shaking back her blond curls, she looked provocatively up at him from under her lashes. "After all, I married you."

Chapter Eighteen

Claudio: *I am your husband, if you like of me.*
Hero: *And when I lived, I was your other wife:*

[unmasking]

And when you loved, you were my other husband.
—William Shakespeare, *Much Ado About Nothing*, V, iv

It wasn't every day that one had the opportunity of sparring with a ghost.

Crossing his arms across his chest, Vaughn smiled lazily at his dead wife. "Ah, the tender joy of the matrimonial bond. What do you want, Anne?"

She tilted her head at him in that practiced way she had had, eyes growing wide and misty in incipient supplication.

After all these years, it came back to him with a thud of recognition, collapsing the decade in between to the space of days. He knew that expression. Next would come an innocent flutter of the lashes, followed by a charmingly perturbed expression, as though she were searching for the right words. And, finally, the long, drawn-out, wheedling rendition of his name. *Sebastian* . . .

Vaughn's voice sharpened, cutting her off before she could get past the first flutter. "How much?"

Anne blinked up at him disingenuously. "It's not money I want, Sebastian," she said, dewy-eyed as a bride "I want to come back."

"Back," Vaughn echoed delicately.

"I want to come home," she repeated artlessly, resting a confiding hand on his sleeve. Against the dark wool, the small white fingers looked like claws, the bright rings like bits of a jackdaw's hoard. "I'm sick of abroad. All those foreigners with their smelly food. And their breath! If I never see another garlic clove again it will be too soon."

She tried to smile up at him, but the bright curve of her lips warred with the watchful tension of her eyes. Beneath the attempt at levity, her expression was as brittle as an eggshell, fine cracks showing in the lines around the corners of her mouth and eyes.

Dropping her eyes to his sleeve, she went on in a voice so low as to be almost inaudible, "I'm sick of it all. It was amusing in the beginning, but now . . . I've seen what happens to . . . to women when their looks begin to go."

"So have I," said Vaughn tonelessly. "There is one slight problem with your solution. You're dead, you know. You managed all that yourself, as you might remember."

Anne chewed thoughtfully on her lower lip, a habitual gesture that Vaughn had found seductive a long, long time ago.

"Well, we didn't want you following us," she said, as if it were only logical.

"Don't worry. I built you a lovely monument in the classical style. Persephone pulled down to Hades, I believe, was the theme. It seemed appropriate. In more ways than I knew, apparently."

Anne shrugged aside classical allusions. "Oh, monuments! It's all very well to talk about monuments, but one can't eat marble. Where am I to live, how am I to go on?"

"Who will keep you in jewels?" echoed Vaughn, sotto voce.

Instead of getting angry, she took a deliberate step towards him, tilting her head up in an intimate smile. "You haven't changed a bit, have you, Sebastian?"

Her voice was soft, nostalgic, deliberately drawing him back to shared memories, a shared past. He could see their once-upon-a-times reflected in the slick surface of her china blue eyes, like a rococo painter's fantasy of man and maid.

Everything had been pastel in those halcyon days: the soft shades of her clothes, sashed at the waist and topped with the filmy fichus demanded by sentimental fashion; the long, ash-blond curls tumbling clear to the great bow at the back of her dress; the muted straw of the great, sweeping hats that crowned her curls, shading her expression and masking her eyes. There had been boat rides, with servants to do the rowing; rural picnics, properly supplied with linen and silver; and long strolls in a conservatory where constantly burning stoves and a regiment of gardeners maintained a wilderness of flowers in eternal and artificial summer.

Like all illusions, it had been a very pretty one. Until it crumbled. Afterwards . . . no, what followed hadn't been pretty. Some of it, he had brought down upon himself, deliberately seeking the low, the dark, the debauched. The Hellfire Club, the stews of St. Giles, anything that would serve to obliterate the cloyingly sweet scent of false flowers from his memory. He wanted the noisome, the foul, the gritty, those seamy subterranean swamps of humanity too ripe to be anything but real.

Some of it had found him, and been almost more than he had bargained for, for all his vaunted sophistication. France. Teresa. Compared with France, the creative perversions of his friends in the Hellfire Club had been nothing but a tawdry pastime, the petty transgressions of bored boys. Sophistication, pitted against real evil, was about as much protection as a fine coating of gold leaf against a hurricane. France had toughened him, hardened him. It wasn't even the mob, crying with mad joy as the heads of their former masters tumbled into the straw. No, that was a good little malice, comprehensible in its own way. It was the Talleyrands, the Teresas, the men who coolly presided over the demise of civilization with an eye to nothing but what they themselves could glean from it, condemning former friends and lovers with no more ear to their cries than a butcher slitting the throat of a bleating sheep. If he had had any belief left in the innate goodness of human nature, it had bled out in France, into the straw beneath the guillotine, among the linens he shared with his lover, his accomplice, his éminence grise.

"I've changed more than you think," Vaughn said flatly.

She might have demurred, but he raised one hand, the great diamond on his finger winking a warning. Her eyes fixed on it with a magpie's fascination for shiny objects. "I believe we can spare ourselves the bourgeois joys of tender reminiscence. There is, after all, so little one would care to recall."

His wife tilted her head softly to one side. "That's not how I remember it . . . Sebastian."

Vaughn didn't move, but something in his face hardened, became as cold and glittering as the diamond on his finger. If she wanted to stroll down memory lane, there were certain avenues that bore exploring.

He raised a lazy eyebrow. "Whatever happened to—Fernando, was it?"

"François," Anne corrected sharply.

"Forgive me," Vaughn murmured. "François."

The man who had been fascinating enough that young Lady Vaughn had abandoned husband and rank in a precipitate midnight flight, along with the contents of her jewel box and a fair portion of what ancestral silver had survived the Civil Wars. He had been her music teacher. It was an embarrassing cliché, the wife running off with the music master. He supposed it could have been worse. It could have been the dancing master.

Anne's eyes dropped to the pale blues and yellows of the Aubusson rug. "François proved . . . uninteresting."

"You mean he left you after the money ran out."

Anne tossed her blond curls. "He wasn't what I had thought he was."

"People so seldom are," Vaughn said, with deceptive gentleness. "It is a lesson we all learn sooner or later. And after François?"

Anne looked away, over one shoulder, as though seeing people and places that weren't there. "There was an Austrian gentleman. He took me to Vienna with him. For a time."

"Until he tired of you," Vaughn translated.

She didn't attempt to correct him or deny it, but there were lines of strain around her eyes that hadn't been there before. He had seen that look on the past—but not on Anne. It had been in France, a marquis who had been run from hiding place to hiding place, cutting and weaving, always just evading capture, until at the end he had been caught and dragged forth.

Vaughn had barely known the man, but his eyes had stayed with him for weeks after, the eyes of a hunted thing, scarcely human.

"After that," Anne went on, speaking rapidly, "I moved to Rome. There was a cardinal who was kind to me."

"How fitting," said Vaughn softly. "A Protestant whore for a papist priest. What a charming pair you must have made. Does Babylon mean anything to you, my dear?"

Face twisting with annoyance, Anne made an impatient movement. With her, petulance always had won out over diplomacy in the end. "It wasn't like that!"

"Then what was it like?"

"You wouldn't understand. It's all different over there."

Vaughn ran a languid finger along the contour of his quizzing glass. "Then why don't you go back?"

"I can't—I don't want to," she corrected herself. Nervously working her fingers, the words came rushing out, "It's not just that. My current protector, he frightens me. I can't go on with this any longer. Sebastian . . ."

The sound of his name on her lips grated on his nerves. In the two years they had been married, she had always begun with his name when she wanted something, in just that tone. A long, drawn-out caress of a salutation, with the emphasis on the second syllable. Gambling debts, jewels . . . music lessons. Whatever it was, he had given it to her, not out of love—not by then—but out of boredom, because he had it to give, and it was easier to accede than argue.

"Even if I did want you back," he said, with deliberate cruelty, "there are obstacles. Your supposed death, for one."

"We could find a way around that," Anne said eagerly. "We could tell people that I was stunned in the carriage accident and lost my memory. I wandered off and—and was taken in by some kind farmers, who nursed me and treated me as their own. And then . . ."

"A touching tale, but with one slight hitch. In case you haven't heard, you were supposed to have died of smallpox."

"Oh," said Anne.

"It sounded less damning than the carriage accident," Vaughn said apologetically. "You do understand, I trust. It really isn't the done thing to die while eloping with your music master."

"Oh, yes, of course." Her eyes narrowed as she attempted to work out the problem, another familiar gesture, one he had found charming in the early days of their courtship. At the time, he had accepted it as indicative of deep thought. Later, he came to know it for what it was, the working of concentrated self-interest.

"Perhaps . . . ," she began slowly. "Perhaps you were so mad with grief that you fled from my room believing I was dead."

Lace fluttering, Vaughn raised a graceful hand. "Let me hazard a guess as to what happened next. Wandering through the countryside, you encountered that same ill-used farmer and his wife. They took you in, disposed of all your smallpox scars by means of a cunning folk remedy, and treated you as their own."

Anne regarded him dubiously, her nose wrinkling. "I'm not quite sure . . ."

Vaughn tapped his quizzing glass against his lower lip, as though in deep cogitation. "Just as they were on the verge of marrying you off to their cretin of a son—undoubtedly named Reuben, as cretinous farm boys invariably are—a fortuitous blow to the head awakened you to the reality of your station. You flung off your humble raiment, said suitably tearful farewells to all your favorite farm animals, and sallied forth into the world to regain your proper place."

"We might leave out Reuben," suggested Anne. "And the farm animals."

Vaughn let the quizzing glass drop. "Either way, it wouldn't fool a child. Which is not to say that it might not work on the half-wits who make up society. . . ."

Anne's face lit in eager response.

To his own surprise, Vaughn found he couldn't go on. Her naked desperation shamed him.

How inconvenient and unexpected, after all this time, to find himself moved by pity for his own renegade wife. But there it was. There was no sport left in baiting her, no profit in revenge. Instead, he felt nothing but a sickly sort of pity mingled with disgust—although whether the disgust was for him or her, he wouldn't have been able to say.

With an abrupt motion, Vaughn ended the game. "No, Anne. Has it never occurred to you that I might not want you back?"

"But—you have to!"

Turning away from her, Vaughn devoted his attention to the collection of Ming vases above the mantelpiece. His bones felt as old and brittle as the cracked china, silent witnesses of centuries of war and betrayal.

"I will pay you a large enough sum to ensure that there need be no more cardinals in your future. But I will not take you back."

"You can't do that." Anne yanked ineffectually at his arm, her nails scraping over the wool of his sleeve. "You married me. I'm your wife— till death do us part."

Vaughn looked at her coolly over his shoulder. "That could be arranged."

Anne's hand dropped, and she took a step back, her face twisted with inexplicable amusement, a tragicomic mask of humorless mirth. "*You* wouldn't. But he—" Anne caught herself, shaking her head so violently that her curls frothed about her face. "I'll go to my aunt. She'll make you see reason."

"Lady Hester? She still thinks I murdered you, you know. The poor old witch is half-mad. How do you think she'll feel to hear that you've duped her all these years, too?"

"I don't care." Anne's slippers slapped against the muted patterns of the carpet, weaving an uneven spiral between the door and the mantel. Her voice rose in a note Vaughn recognized well from the short span of their marriage, the shrill insistence of a child on the verge of a temper tantrum. "She'll have to listen to me. She'll back me. And then you—you'll have to take me back, unless you want there to be a scandal. The *ton* might ignore a woman alone, but they won't ignore Lady Hester Standish."

"Once, perhaps." When Anne had arranged her own precipitate departure, Lady Hester had still been a woman of substance among the ranks of the nobility. After her niece's supposed death, Lady Hester had gone from eccentric to something close to genuinely mad. All the affection she had lavished on her favorite niece, all her formidable mental powers, had instead been channeled into the radical politics that had once been merely a pastime. The *ton* had been first alarmed, then scornful, and finally, inevitably, bored. Whatever clout Lady Hester had once had, had long since dissipated in a jumble of incoherent speeches and revolutionary politics. "You've been away for a very long time, Anne."

Doubt flickered across the cerulean surface of Anne's eyes. "It hasn't been that long. There will still be those who know me, who recognize me. You can't deny me forever. Sebastian . . ."

There it was again, that grating repetition of his name, like an incantation meant to summon back the past. Vaughn was reminded of Glendower's boast that he could call spirits from the vasty deep. *Why, so can I, or so can any man,* Hotspur had responded. *But will they come when you do call for them?*

Vaughn bent his torso in an impersonal bow. "I suggest you leave before me. We don't want there to be a scandal, after all."

"This isn't the end of it, Sebastian. You must know that." With an attempt at bravado, she squared her fine-boned shoulders and tried to look imperious. "I'll give you a week to think it over."

Vaughn merely inclined his head in response.

She wasn't satisfied with that, he could tell, but some instinct of self-preservation taught her better than to argue. Some instinct or, from her tale, some past protector, less patient with her vagaries than her sometime husband. Her blue eyes narrowed, but she moved docilely enough towards the door, working out, Vaughn had no doubt, her next plan of attack. He doubted she would go to Lady Hester. At least, not yet. Lady Hester was a plan of last resort, the last charge of the cavalry.

In the open doorway, Anne paused, her hand on the gilded latch.

"Do you hate me that much—for leaving you?"

While they reminisced of days gone by, the concert must have ended. Down the length of the hallway, Vaughn could see the clustered groups of guests, waiting for their wraps, discussing the music, exchanging the latest on-dits. And, among them, Miss Mary Alsworthy, smiling disingenuously up at the besotted Mr. St. George.

With unerring instinct, Mary's blue eyes honed in on his, flicking from Anne to him with a look of scorn that burned like ice, before she pointedly returned her attentions to St. George, smiling up at him as though the fate of the kingdom depended on it.

"No," Vaughn said honestly. "Only for coming back."

Chapter Nineteen

But these are all lies: men have died from time to time,
and worms have eaten them, but not for love.

—William Shakespeare, *As You Like It*, IV, i

"Your watchdog is following us."

"My—?" Mary twisted to look, and saw only Lord Vaughn, cool and urbane, examining the set of his sleeves with an absorption that implied that everything else in the room was beneath his notice. His companion appeared to have departed.

Blue eyes narrowed, Mary turned back to St. George. "I would scarcely call him my watchdog."

"What would you call it, then, when I have had scarcely a moment to speak to you without his interruption?"

Mary shrugged helplessly.

Leaning a hand on the wall against her head, St. George's voice dropped. "Please forgive me for being so forward, but . . ." He hesitated, searching for words. "Is there something of which I ought to be aware? If you have an understanding—"

Mary dropped her eyes before St. George's earnest gaze, examining the braid trimming her sleeve with every bit as much attention as Lord Vaughn. "No," she said, addressing herself to her gloves. "We have no understanding."

That much, at least, was absolutely true.

St. George looked unconvinced.

"If your sentiments are engaged—" he began.

Mary cut him off with a quick movement of her hand. "Lord Vaughn," she said, making sure to pitch her voice loud enough to carry across the hall, "has been kind enough to take an avuncular interest in my affairs." Fluttering her lashes prettily at St. George, she added piercingly, "Bachelor gentlemen of a certain age often do."

Brushing the golden-brown curls back from his brow, St. George smiled ruefully down at her, the skin on either side of his eyes crinkling. "I hope you don't cast me in that category."

It had never occurred to her to do so. St. George, she supposed, must be at least as old as Lord Vaughn; there was a fullness to his form and a maturity in the lines of his face that only came with age. It was a good sort of maturity, the sort most women would find attractive, with a few lines adding depth and character to his undeniably pleasing countenance. Yet, next to Vaughn, he seemed like a boy, young and callow—and infinitely less interesting.

Unlike Vaughn, however, he was willing to come up to scratch. Nothing else mattered.

Mary forced herself to smile warmly up at him. "Never, my dear Mr. St. George. You defy categorization."

"There is a category in which I would greatly desire to be placed. Were you to be so inclined."

"And what might that be, Mr. St. George?"

In the hidden place between their bodies and the wall, St. George possessed himself of her hand.

Pressing it earnestly, he said, "That of your friend."

Mary managed to hold the corners of her smile in place. "But, of course, Mr. St. George," she said smoothly, drawing back on her hand. "I esteem myself honored in the friendship of so worthy and honorable a gentleman."

St. George's grip tightened around her fingers. "Your friend and—"

Behind them, someone cleared his throat, forcefully enough to scour the inside of a chimney.

"Miss Alsworthy," Vaughn drawled, standing at his ease with his quizzing glass poised at one eye. The glass flicked to her companion. "St. George."

St. George hastily dropped Mary's hand. "Vaughn."

Vaughn wagged the quizzing glass in St. George's general direction. "What a penchant you have, my dear sir, for conversing in corners. Are these country manners?"

St. George drew himself up to his full height, which put him at least an inch over Vaughn. "In the country, sir, we are accustomed to the luxury of completing a conversation unmolested."

"Indeed?" Vaughn affected an expression of polite interest. "What a charming, rural custom."

Ignoring him, St. George bent over Mary's hand. "I hope we may continue our conversation on a more auspicious occasion?"

Out of the corner of her eye, Mary could see the flash of Vaughn's glass as he dangled it languidly from one finger, the silver winking in the light. "I should like nothing better."

"In that case . . ." St. George pressed a kiss to the back of her hand, his lips brushing glove, not air. "I shall call upon you. Soon."

"Do," Mary said, the word sounding stiff on her lips beneath the lowering influence of Vaughn's cynical gaze. Fixing her attention firmly on St. George, she repeated, with a flirtatious smile, "Do."

Mary watched St. George depart, wishing she could feel anything at all. He carried himself well. Even if his coat was ill cut, the breadth of his back stretched pleasingly beneath the fabric and the candles caught the gold in his tawny hair. He was a respectable figure of a man, a solid one, a kind one, and she ought to feel something, if only gratitude for the prospect of rescue from spinsterhood. She ought to be relieved. But, instead, as she watched him clap his hat on his curly head, all she felt was a dull sense of resignation.

"Am I to wish you joy?" Vaughn's breath was warm against her ear.

"Coming from you," Mary said tartly, turning towards Vaughn, "it would undoubtedly be a barbed gift. Did you have something to say to me, my lord?"

"Other than the usual pleasantries?"

Tipping her head to one side, Mary indicated that she was not amused.

Vaughn cocked one dark brow. "Unless other affairs have intervened, I believe we have an outing to arrange."

"An outing," Mary repeated.

"To Hyde Park," Vaughn reminded her smoothly. "For matters of a martial kind."

So they were to continue with their association then. Having not heard from him for a week—Mary's lips tightened automatically at the memory—she had assumed that their bargain had ended. After all, he knew that the Black Tulip was to be at Hyde Park at the appointed day and hour. He didn't need her anymore. He didn't need her or want her—and she most certainly didn't need him.

Even now, though, the prospect of a day with Vaughn thrilled her. It was painful and embarrassing to be so drawn to someone who had already proven his indifference to her twice over. Yet there was no denying that words seemed sharper, colors brighter, ideas clearer, the very air more exhilarating when he was there, taunting, teasing, baiting. In short, being himself.

"I suppose my other affairs can wait the day."

"I am relieved," Vaughn said smoothly. "I should have hated to disappoint our friend."

"But you have so many friends," murmured Mary. "In all sorts of places." Down the hall, for example.

Vaughn regarded her lazily though his quizzing glass. "Some are more demanding than others."

Despite having opened the topic, Mary decided she didn't want to know. "What time do you call for me?" she asked abruptly.

"It will be early," Vaughn warned her. "Well before noon."

"I believe I can contrive to drag myself from my bed," Mary said with heavy sarcasm. "I'm scarcely such a hothouse flower as that."

To her surprise, instead of replying in kind, Vaughn just looked at her. His eyes, without their accustomed armor of the quizzing glass, dwelled on her face for what felt like a very long time.

"No," he said quietly. "I don't believe you are."

Mary couldn't figure out whether or not she had just been insulted. It was hard to be sure of anything under the dizzying force of Lord Vaughn's concentrated regard.

"Not all of us have hothouses," retorted Mary belligerently.

"You wouldn't want one," said Vaughn softly, his eyes never leaving hers. "They aren't all one thinks they would be."

Mary tossed her head. "As opposed to the common wildflower?"

"Never common," countered Vaughn, with just a glimmer of a smile. "And only a little bit wild."

There was a strange ache at the back of Mary's throat. Why wouldn't he just let her hate him? No, not hate; despise, revile, all those other socially acceptable emotions. Why did he have to look at her like that?

Because, she reminded herself bracingly, he was a rake, a rogue, and a seducer. They did that. The rake looked at a woman as though she were his sole hope for salvation—and then he went right on along to the next one, to the opera singer, the blonde in the back room, and heaven only knew who else.

"My lord Vaughn?" Lady Richard's country cousin interposed herself between them.

Lord Vaughn's face reverted to its habitual urbane detachment.

As one of Vaughn's women, the cousin was an unlikely choice. Her hair was straight, with no hint of a curl, an indeterminate shade between blond and brown that might have been pretty had she taken any pains with it. Her dress was equally plain, a high-necked blue muslin that wouldn't have looked amiss on a Quaker. The color was a pale blue so dreary as to be nearly gray, the sort of color that blended back into the wainscoting. Her only ornament was the locket she wore on a ribbon around her neck, a simple gold oval with a flower delicately worked in enamel on the front, a pretty enough trinket for a young girl, but nothing to draw the eye.

Mary made an effort to remember her name. It was something to do with sheep. Lambsdale, Oviston . . .

Whoever she was, she had placed a hand on Vaughn's arm as though it had a right to be there. It was a very elegantly shaped hand, with long, tapering fingers, a most inappropriate hand for a country bumpkin.

"Will you pardon me if I borrow Lord Vaughn for a moment, Miss Alsworthy?" she asked in a pleasant alto voice, unmarred by any regional accent.

Mary smiled brittlely. "Borrow?" She gave an affected little laugh. "My dear, you may have him for as long as you like."

"Shouldn't that be as long as I like?" countered Vaughn, looking like a self-satisfied pasha.

"I'm sure it will be," said Mary sweetly. "It is, after all, as *you* like it."

" 'As the ox hath his bow, the horse his curb, and the falcon her bells, so man hath his desires.' "

"If you can make any sense out of him, you have my commendations," remarked Mary to the cousin.

The cousin smiled demurely, revealing a set of even, white teeth. "I'm afraid you do me too much credit, Miss Alsworthy. I am merely the messenger. I come on behalf of Lord Uppington, who wishes to see Lord Vaughn in his book room. About the impending parliamentary session, I believe?"

Mary didn't believe it for a moment. It was difficult to imagine a more whiggish Whig than Lord Vaughn, whose ancestors had been among those responsible for the expulsion of the last Stuart king in 1688, while the Uppingtons were staunchly Tory. They were as firmly members of Pitt's faction as Vaughn was of Charles James Fox's.

It was, Mary supposed, not entirely inconceivable that Vaughn might wish to broker a deal with Uppington on an issue of interest to both factions. Given the weakness of Addington's government, there might even be plans afoot for a coalition, although Mary was hard pressed to imagine the ministry that could combine both Pitt and Fox.

Mary smiled prettily at Vaughn. "I certainly wouldn't want to keep you from your parliamentary duties. Good evening, Miss—er."

And with that effective parting snub, she was gone, wending her way back along the hallway with all the deliberate provocation of a latter-day Cleopatra. It only lacked a few flute boys.

"Flute boys?" queried Jane.

Vaughn regarded her blandly. "A momentary lapse in concentration."

"More than a moment, I would think," replied Jane, arching both her brows in obvious amusement.

"You wished—pardon me. *Lord Uppington* wished to speak to me?"

Jane took the hint. Forbearing to quiz him further, she indicated one of the two corridors branching off the entryway. "Shall we?"

In the entryway, Mary was being helped into her wrap by her new brother-in-law and sometime suitor, her back very pointedly turned.

Looking away, Vaughn found Jane's knowing eye on him. It was a distinctly irritating sensation. He was the one who was supposed to be doling out the sardonic looks, not the other way around. It was an unacceptable inversion of the established world order.

"After you, Miss Wooliston," he drawled in tones of exaggerate ennui.

Jane cast him a shrewd look, but said nothing. Instead, she took up a candle from the collection on the table in the hall and led the way down the right hand corridor. Her silence was more damning than any knowing comment.

Jane led him to a small parlor, lined with books and furnished sparsely with furniture as heavy and dark as the weather outside the window.

"Well?" Jane inquired, with an arch of one light brow.

It was, Vaughn had to admit, an effective trick. By never identifying the question, one got all sorts of interesting answers.

Dropping into a red-cushioned chair, he rested his palms comfortably over the arms. "Miss Alsworthy and I have a further appointment with your friend. We meet in Hyde Park, the day after tomorrow."

"His Majesty's review of the first division of the London volunteers."

"None other." Vaughn watched the drops of rain splatter against the windowpanes. "Are we meant to be party to an assassination?"

"I don't know." The words cost her an obvious effort. Jane's well-shaped lips pressed tightly together. "He managed to evade us at Vaux-hall."

"He?"

"I use the masculine pronoun for the sake of convenience. Nothing more."

Vaughn crossed his legs at the ankle, admiring the sparkle of his silver and diamond buckles. "I trust you investigated Rathbone?"

"Naturally." Jane circled the room, her muslin skirts whispering softly against her legs. "He possessed the usual revolutionary paraphernalia. Tattered tracts, treasonous correspondence with like-minded colleagues, a half-written treatise on political philosophy—none of it the least bit of use."

"No telltale manuscript by the bed? No sampler over the hearth embroidered with charming pictures of black tulips?"

"Rathbone isn't the embroidering kind," returned Jane. "His laboratory, however . . ." She paused, as though calculating how far to confide in him. "I believe you have some experience with natural philosophy, my lord."

Vaughn shook his head in demurral. "Only that of an amateur, a dabbler, a dilettante."

"That," commented Jane severely, "is far too many words to describe a nullity."

Vaughn accepted the rebuke with a casual inclination of his head.

"We found something curious in Rathbone's chambers," said Jane, watching Vaughn closely.

"Natural philosophers are curious sorts," provided Vaughn.

"We found vials of liquid mercury, several bowls of red crystals, lenses"—Jane ticked the items off on her fingers—"and a large canister, carefully stoppered, which, when we opened it, appeared to contain nothing at all. Yet someone went to the trouble of keeping it hermetically sealed with several layers of wax."

"An empty container?" Memory shifted and fell into place, an explanation far from simple but laughably prosaic. "Rathbone's experiments are beyond my humble powers, but I might be able to shed some little light on the discovery."

"Please do," invited Jane.

Vaughn ignored the light vein of sarcasm. "Have you ever heard of Priestley's treatise on air?" Without waiting for Jane's answer, he went on, "Apparently, like the rest of us, air is a deceiver. Rather than one element, it is several."

"Rather like the petals of the Tulip," mused Jane.

Vaughn acknowledged the point with a nod. "According to Priestley, by applying the right sorts of heat or chemicals, one could isolate the elements within the element, creating different sorts of gasses from the original air, all invisible to the naked eye. I can't imagine why one would want to," Vaughn added as an afterthought, "but there you have it."

"And Rathbone," concluded Jane, "was a student of Priestley."

"Precisely." Vaughn stretched out his legs before the fire. "Your empty container in fact was filled with a distilled element of some sort, which you unknowingly released back into the air whence it came. Tsk, tsk, Miss Wooliston. Weeks of scientific endeavor lost in the curiosity of a moment. Pandora's legacy lives on."

Jane frowned at him. "But what of the red powder? Miss Gwen believes it to be a new incendiary of some sort."

"A distillation of mercury, turned to crystal." Vaughn dabbed at his mouth with a lace-edged handkerchief. "I am unfamiliar with the process, but I believe it is one of the chemicals Priestley used in his experiments."

Jane looked like a cat who had licked at a bowl of cream to find it gone sour. "There were scorch marks on several of the tables, and yet not of the sort left by a candle."

"Your lenses," explained Vaughn. "One heats the chemicals with a so-called burning lens, by refracting sunlight through the lens to create heat and even flame."

Jane rested both hands on the windowsill. "In other words," she said, to the raindrops slipping down the glass, "there is a perfectly innocent explanation for all of it."

"I fear so," said Vaughn pleasantly. "As much as I regret to disappoint a lady."

"What a pity," said Jane wryly. "I had hoped it was an infernal machine in the making, rather than merely . . . empty air."

"I believe Priestley called it de-phlogisticated air," put in Vaughn helpfully.

Ignoring him, Jane took a slow turn about the room, coming to rest with one hand on the head of a bust of Aristotle. Her index finger tapped lightly against the great philosopher's carved cranium.

"Just because his scientific interests are legitimate doesn't mean that Rathbone isn't our man," said Jane, thinking aloud. "Even mad fanatics have hobbies."

"Stamp collecting, for example," put in Vaughn. "Collecting novelty porcelain."

Jane frowned at him. "Bedeviling one's friends and associates."

"I consider that less a hobby and more an avocation." Vaughn smiled serenely at Jane. "Every man needs something to give his life purpose."

"For now, I fear your purpose will have to be dogging Miss Alworthy's heels to His Majesty's review of the troops. I trust you shan't find it too onerous a task."

The gods planned their torments well: Sisyphus, doomed to roll the same rock eternally uphill; Tantalus, tempted with water, yet never allowed to drink; and he, poised as de facto bodyguard to the one women he wanted, but could never have.

It would, thought Vaughn grimly, be so much easier were she a member of the demimonde. Then he could simply make her his mistress, without regard to recurrent wives or the slings and arrows of the sharp-tongued harridans of the *ton*.

"I assume you will be there as well?"

"No," said Jane shortly. "I leave London in the morning. There are matters abroad that demand immediate attention."

Raising his quizzing glass to one eye, Vaughn regarded Jane in a silent demand for further information.

Jane regarded him right back. Her expression seemed to imply that she had no problem staring people out of countenance without artificial aids, and if he thought she was going to answer, he was quite mad.

"You're leaving us to the Black Tulip's tender mercies?" Vaughn drawled.

"Or the Black Tulip to yours," replied Jane blandly.

"In other words," suggested Vaughn, watching Jane closely, "you want me to keep the Black Tulip busy while you go about your business elsewhere."

Watching Jane's lips curve in a Sphinx-like smile, it occurred to Vaughn that Jane's assignment might have as much to do with keeping him busy as the Black Tulip. Their alliance, such as it was, was an uneasy one at best, and he knew Jane's associates continued to regard him with outright suspicion. The notion amused him. But he knew it would be useless to try to get Jane to say anything more on the topic.

Accepting defeat, Vaughn lowered his glass and leaned back in his chair. It was clearly well used, the cushions molded themselves obligingly to his body. "What do you believe the Black Tulip intends?" he asked.

"One." Jane held up a finger in illustration. "The Black Tulip does exactly what he claimed. He uses this opportunity to pass further instructions along to Miss Alsworthy."

"Unlikely," interrupted Vaughn lazily. "If the Tulip wanted a tête-à-tête, he wouldn't have tolerated the presence of an escort."

"He might, of course, stage a diversion to separate you from Miss Alsworthy. Or he might use more subtle means to communicate with her, such as a note tucked into her reticule, in which case your presence is immaterial."

"But you don't believe that is the case."

"No," said Jane heavily.

"Option two," provided Vaughn, holding up two fingers on her behalf. "The review is merely a diversion. The Tulip lures us to Hyde Park while he conducts his dastardly business elsewhere."

"By far the likeliest scenario," conceded Jane. "However, that's really option three. You missed one."

Vaughn raised a quizzical brow.

"An attempt of some kind on the royal family," prompted Jane, as though to a slow student. "Why your presence would be imperative for that, however, I can't think. Nor can I imagine how Miss Alsworthy would be of any use, unless the Tulip intended to use her to distract the guards protecting Their Majesties."

"But you find that improbable."

"Only a fool would attempt an assassination or a kidnapping in so public a place. The Black Tulip has proved that he is anything but a fool. On the other hand," she added thoughtfully, "killing off his operatives in Ireland was not a well-reasoned act."

Not well-reasoned was one way to describe it.

Vaughn's lips tightened as he remembered the sight that had greeted him in the drawing room of his cousin's town house in Dublin. He had seen Teresa in many poses over the years: dazzling a salon full of French radicals; prancing about disguised as a wild-haired adolescent boy; dressed in widow's weeds; naked in his bed. But nothing like that day in Dublin, with her head bent back as though her neck—that long, graceful neck of which she had been so proud—could no longer stand the weight.

There had been a blade protruding from her chest, but that he had only noticed later. It had been her face that held him. Her black eyes, flat, obsidian, filmed over in death, all the keen intelligence that had animated them gone. Her lips, pale and slack in her chalk white face, never more to debate or command or cajole. Not that Teresa had ever been much of a one for cajoling. Commanding had been more in her line.

There was nothing more she could say, nothing more that could be said. She was gone, as rapidly and perhaps with more justice than the men she herself had sent to the guillotine in the past. Her stiletto had pierced more than one man's ribs. Even so, the vision of her, cold and quiet, brought with it a raw ache that gnawed at his bowels like cheap French wine.

"Ill-reasoned indeed," said Vaughn dryly.

Lost in her own thoughts, Jane gazed off over Aristotle's head. "The Black Tulip is growing reckless. It makes him unpredictable."

"Reckless enough to fire at the King in the middle of Hyde Park?"

Jane flung up her hands in a gesture of controlled confusion. "Who can be sure? I had thought, when I saw the supplies in Rathbone's laboratory, that I might have found the answer."

"Ah," said Vaughn, moving gratefully away from the image of Teresa, stiff as a waxwork against a blood-dappled sofa. "You believed that the Tulip intended to surprise His Majesty and the rest of his family by setting off an infernal machine."

"It would make sense," said Jane seriously. "It would be far too easy for a revolutionary faction to have slipped one of their own among the volunteers to be reviewed and have him fire at His Majesty as he rides down the rank. His Majesty's guards will be prepared for that. But if there were to be a larger explosion of some kind, something akin to what we saw in Ireland . . ."

"Grenades," Vaughn supplied. "And rockets."

"Or some combination thereof," Jane agreed. "Even if the King himself emerged unscathed from an explosion, in the confusion it would be very easy for a rifleman to fire."

Vaughn regarded her approvingly. "Remind me to hire you the next time I need to assassinate someone."

Jane clasped her hands at her waist as demurely as a schoolgirl. "Only if he is French."

Vaughn's expression turned wry. "Pity." The only person he wanted removed just now was an English she.

You wouldn't, Anne had said. And she was right. He didn't like blood on his hands. It was a messy substance, blood, and damnably hard to remove from one's clothes and one's conscience.

It was, he reflected, doubly ironic that it was Anne who had brought him into Jane's toils.

Six months ago, the letters had begun arriving at the house in Belliston Square. Love letters, but not addressed to him. They had been written from Anne to her Fernando, or Francisco, or whatever the blasted music master's name had been. They arrived along with a demand for money, and the threat of publication if he refused.

There were only two people who might have possession of those letters—both of whom he had supposed dead, killed when their coach went over a cliff one stormy night in Northumberland. The music master. Or Anne. Within a week, Vaughn had had his answer. The carriage crash had been a sham. Anne's path led to Paris, to seedy inns and seedier taverns.

It was in France that he had first crossed paths with Jane. At the time, an alliance seemed the most reasonable means of progressing. Under Bonaparte's new laws, it was illegal for an Englishman to visit Paris. As the cousin to one of Bonaparte's most obsequious followers, Jane moved about the city unmolested. In exchange for Jane's help in locating Anne, Vaughn had agreed to lend his assistance in infiltrating Teresa's organization.

The arrangement had been expedient—and, perhaps, he admitted to himself, something more than that. It had been a chance for atonement. He had turned a blind eye to Teresa's activities in Paris, until the deaths grew too gruesome to ignore. And then he had left, simply packed up his bags and gone. In one fell swoop, it seemed, he could amend the omissions of his past, by putting an end to his sometime mistress's murderous activities and satisfying himself that his missing wife was gone beyond reclaiming. He would finally be free of both them.

Instead, Teresa was dead, killed under his roof, and Anne was back. So much, then, for redemption. And he was left with a mess of his own making. Once again, the gods laughed.

Steepling his fingers on his chest, Vaughn said casually, "That project with which I had required your assistance—there's no longer any need."

Jane regarded him steadily. "You mean—?"

"Break out the drums and sound the trumpets. The prodigal wife has returned."

Jane knew better than to wish him joy.

"What are you going to do?" she asked quietly.

"What else can I do?" Vaughn swept open both hands, lace fluttering. "I will be escorting Miss Alsworthy to His Majesty's review."

Chapter Twenty

Then straight commands that, at the warlike sound
Of trumpets loud and clarions be upreared
His mighty standard. . . .
Th' imperial ensign; which, full high advanced,
Shone like a meteor streaming to the wind
With gems and golden lustre rich imblaz'd,
Seraphic arms and trophies; all the while
Sonorous metal blowing martial sounds.

—John Milton, *Paradise Lost*, I

Lifting a hand to shield his eyes, Lord Vaughn scowled at the crisp autumn sunlight. "It's England," he grumbled. "Shouldn't it be raining?"

In the harsh noon light, the bags under his eyes were turning a perfectly lovely shade of purple, which contrasted nicely with the greenish tinge of his skin. Whatever he had been doing last night after his disappearance with Lady Richard's country cousin, it had clearly involved a great deal of spirituous liquor.

Mary regarded Vaughn's unhealthy color with no little satisfaction. Every now and then, justice really was served.

Mary shot him a smug, sideways glance. "It's a perfectly glorious autumn day. Don't tell me you aren't enjoying it."

"I might enjoy it more from within a carriage," commented Vaughn, nodding at the vehicles arrayed a slight distance away.

"In a carriage, we would be harder to reach," returned Mary, positioning her own sunshade more directly over her head. "And that is the sole point of this exercise, isn't it?"

"Isn't the pleasure of your company reason enough?" inquired Vaughn, in a way that suggested her company was anything but.

He had been decidedly surly ever since calling for her that morning, at the unhallowed hour of ten. True to her word, Mary had been dressed and ready, wearing her sturdiest walking shoes and carrying her thickest sunshade. Although the air was crisp, the skies were clear, promising the sort of perfect autumn weather that seemed nature's way of apologizing for the bleak winter days to come.

Aside from a raised brow, Vaughn had made no comment on either her punctuality or her attire. Mary had answered the brow with a brow of her own, and thus they had begun their journey in perfect silence, without so much as a good morning between them.

Mary had used the opportunity to study her companion. She had, she realized, only rarely seen him by daylight. Her acquaintance with Vaughn had taken place largely by candlelight, in the flare of the torches at Sibley Court, the lanterns at Vauxhall, the flickering candles of the Chinese chamber.

In the unforgiving morning light, with his skin sallow from lack of sleep, deep paunches beneath his eyes, and long furrows in his cheeks, Vaughn looked his age and then some. Even in his youth, his face must have been more distinguished than handsome, his cheekbones too sharp, his nose too aquiline for the Corinthian ideal of manly beauty. Mary compared him with St. George, broad of shoulder, sensuous of lip, quick to smile, and eager to please. St. George would never have greeted her with a raised brow and a shadow of a shrug. He would have helped her into the carriage, showered her with greetings, offered her a lap rug, and made polite commentary about the weather. The sunlight suited St. George.

Even so, Mary realized gloomily, even lined, sallow, and surly, she would far rather be sitting across from Vaughn than any other man of her acquaintance. It gave her more pleasure to exchange scowls at him than to smile at St. George, and his arrogantly raised eyebrow said more to her than the stumbling paeons of all her past admirers.

Mary had spent the rest of their short trip frowning out the window. Morning, she decided, was a highly overrated time of day. It made it far too difficult to ignore things one had no desire to see.

Leaving the carriage at the gates of the park, they had made their way on foot towards the martial display. Despite their early start, the park was already crowded with loyal subjects of the Crown, jostling and standing on tiptoe to catch a glimpse of their monarch as he reviewed the twelve thousand volunteers who were to help protect English shores from the vile French threat. By some miracle of military maneuvering, the twelve thousand troops had been drawn up into three sides of a square, as symmetrical as the joinery of a master cabinetmaker. It was impossible to get anywhere near the King. Mary saw him only as a bobbing white wig on horseback, distinguishable only by the star of the garter winking from his breast.

Having seen the press of people in the park, Mary could only imagine that the Black Tulip's object was exactly as he claimed, to give her further instructions. How the Black Tulip intended to find her was another matter entirely.

Mary staggered as someone bumped into her from behind, but it was only a lanky teenager elbowing his way to a better position.

Unfortunately, patriotism seemed to exist in an inverse relationship to the use of soap. As Mary and Vaughn picked their way gingerly across the park, the air around them was pungent with unwashed bodies, spilled drink, churned dirt, and the unmistakable scent of horse. In front of them, a small child dribbled a steady stream of drool down the back of its mother's dress. A crusting of crushed crumbs and spittle, long since dried, testified that this was by no means the infant's first offense.

The woman in front of her patted the baby's back, eliciting a ripe burp, redolent of sour milk. "'Ave you ever seen the like?" she demanded of her neighbor, who was chiefly notable for a towering ruin of a bonnet, the plumes cracked and sagging, the silk water stained. "Old Boney ain't going to mess with them."

"Don't reckon he would, dearie," her companion replied comfortably. With the affairs of nations thus so satisfactorily settled, she extracted a glass bottle from the pocket of her skirt and helped herself to a hearty swig of gin.

Vaughn turned a deeper shade of green.

"Shall we attempt to find some higher ground?" he asked, lifting his lace-edged handkerchief to his nose.

Holding on to the edge of her bonnet, Mary edged sideways, heading towards a relatively untenanted stand of trees a little ways away. "If you find this so unpleasant, there was no reason for you to come."

"Naturally," said Vaughn with heavy sarcasm, using his cane to clear her path. "Any gentleman would allow you to wend your way through this charming assembly alone."

"I'm sure Mr. St. George would have been delighted to accompany me. And been a good deal more good-natured about it."

"If good nature is all you demand, may I recommend the acquisition of a lap dog? You shall find its company just as stimulating."

"Pets bite," Mary said tartly, using her elbow to good effect on a group of teenage boys who showed no inclination to step aside. "And they don't generally come with estates in Warwickshire."

"I would advise against rushing into rustication." Vaughn slipped through the gap after her.

Mary employed her sunshade as a walking stick, not looking back. "I hear it's a lovely country. The climate is most salubrious."

"But the inhabitants leave something to be desired."

Mary arched a glance back over her shoulder, her eyes inscrutable beneath the brim of her bonnet. "Unless one desires the inhabitants."

Joining her beneath the tree, Vaughn plunked his cane down beside a tree root like a conquistador planting his flag. "You don't," he said, with altogether too much assurance.

"Isn't that for me to judge?" Mary shook out her crumpled skirts, paying particular attention to the smudges of something sticky just above the right hip. It had the texture and consistency of old oatmeal. Mary flicked experimentally at it with one gloved finger. She could feel

Vaughn's eyes on her, not the least bit deceived by her seeming inattention.

"Don't do it," he said shortly. "There is nothing more unpleasant than finding oneself inescapably yoked to a person for whom one has no regard."

Mary abandoned the stain. "Nothing more unpleasant? You have a very limited imagination, my lord. I can think of a great many things more unpleasant."

With one hand braced on the silver head of his cane, Vaughn radiated worldly skepticism. "Can you?"

"Yes, I can," retorted Mary. "And better than you. Do you know what it is to be a pensioner in someone else's house? Of course not! You're Lord Vaughn. You have houses and estates and—"

"Horses," supplied Lord Vaughn helpfully.

"Servants," finished Mary, with a quelling glance. "All rushing to do your bidding. Yours. Not someone else's. You don't know what it is to have to wait upon the whims of others. And all because no man has deigned to offer me the protection of his hand."

"Protection? An odd way of describing the institution of matrimony."

Mary's lip curled. "How else would you describe it? Marriage is protection against poverty, protection against all the carping old women who say, 'Oh, poor dear, no man would ever have her,' protection against the advances of unscrupulous cads who think nothing of taking advantage of a woman alone. Why else would anyone ever bother to marry?"

"One has heard that there are occasionally other reasons," interjected Vaughn mildly.

Mary bristled at the implied mockery. "Don't even think of talking to me about *love*. It doesn't make a difference, whatever your beloved poets say."

Vaughn's lips twisted into a humorless smile. "I, of all people, am in no position to do that."

"You, my lord? You're in a position to do whatever you like. You, after all, are a *man*." Mary imbued the simple word with enough venom to damn a dozen Edens. "And not just a man, but the great Lord Vaughn, master of all he surveys. You have only to snap your fingers, and your every desire is gratified."

Vaughn's gaze never strayed from her face. "Not every desire."

Mary waved aside his words with an impatient hand. "Most of them, at any rate. And then you have the consummate gall to stand in judgment over me for taking the only way open to me—I don't see any other, do you? I can marry or I can rot. It's not admirable, and it's not glorious, and I don't deny your right to mock. But I would think that some notion of noblesse oblige would mandate more condescension to your struggling inferiors."

Vaughn's brows drew together. "I never thought of you as anyone's inferior. Least of all mine."

"Ha!" There was something very satisfying about the short syllable. Mary was so pleased with it that she repeated it. "Would you treat an equal like a—like a common doxy?" She stumbled over the vulgar term, but there was no point in mincing words now. How else was there to describe it? He had used her that night in the Chinese chamber as he would any other female who came conveniently to hand, so long as that female was a pretty one. "Good enough to kiss, but never good enough to marry," she finished bitterly.

Vaughn looked at her in surprise, his brows drawing together over his nose. "That isn't it."

"No?" Breathing deeply through her nose, Mary crossed her arms across her chest. She supposed that hadn't been it for Lord Falconstone or Martin Frobisher or any of the other men who wrote her sonnets and tried to wheedle her out onto to balconies, but somehow lost all their eloquence when it came to the four simple words that made the difference between reputable and ruined. "Then how else would you describe it? It's all simple enough. The great Lord Vaughn wouldn't deign to sully his bloodlines with a mere miss. You need the daughter of an earl, at least."

The shadow of the tree branches above moved darkly across Vaughn's face. "Enough," he said sharply, turning away.

"Why?" Mary yanked on his arm, oblivious to the people milling around them, to the bands still playing on the parade ground, to the King trotting up and down along the row of his recruits. The Black Tulip could have been turning handsprings behind them and she would never have noticed. "Why flinch at it? It's your own choice. Are you too much of a coward to own it?"

"*Choice?*" Vaughn took a step back, the head of his cane catching the sunlight, making the arched neck of the silver snake glow like the idol of a pagan cult. "I suppose you could call it that. I chose to marry the daughter of an earl, just as you advise. I made that choice long ago, and I've been paying for it ever since."

That, as far as Mary was concerned, was so much blether.

Mary would have said as much, but Vaughn's curt voice went relentlessly on, like the lash of a whip. "I made a host of other choices, too. I chose to run away. I chose to ignore what was inconvenient. I chose pleasure over substance. I chose and chose and chose. After a time, Miss Alsworthy, do you know what happens? You run out of choices. There aren't any left. You're pinned in a web of your own devising."

"I don't believe that," Mary shot back before he could catch his breath. "You can't hide behind inclination by calling it compulsion. If you truly wanted matters otherwise, you could make them so. Why can't you just admit it? It's just that you don't want me."

"I don't, do I?" Vaughn rolled the head of his cane beneath his fingers. "How terribly kind of you to inform me of that. Otherwise, I might have continued to exist under the exceedingly uncomfortable delusion that I did."

Mary fought her way out of the tangled web of syntax. "I didn't mean like that," she countered. After all, he was male; they wanted as easily as they breathed. Hence the convenient construction of balconies off so many ballrooms.

Vaughn's fingers tightened on the head of his cane. "Nor did I," he said.

For a long moment, he held her gaze without speaking, simply letting the impact of his words sink in, before adding rapidly, as though he wished to get it over with as quickly as possible, "I won't deny that you're beautiful. No mirror could tell you otherwise. But there are beautiful women for the buying in any brothel in London. Oh yes, and the ballrooms, too, if one has the proper price. It wasn't your appearance that caught me. It was the way you put me down in the gallery at Sibley Court." Vaughn's lips curved in a reminiscent smile. "And the way you tried to bargain with me after."

"*Successfully* bargained," Mary corrected.

"That," replied Lord Vaughn, "is exactly what I mean. Has anyone ever told you that you haggle divinely? That the simple beauty of your self-interest is enough to bring a man to his knees?"

Mary couldn't in honesty say that anyone had.

Vaughn's eyes were as hard and bright as silver coins. "Those are the reasons I want you. I want you for your cunning mind and your hard heart, for your indomitable spirit and your scheming soul, for they're more honest by far than any of the so-called virtues."

"The truest poetry is the most feigning?" Mary quoted back his own words to him.

"And the most feigning is the most true. Now tell me I'm wrong. Tell me I'm lying. Tell me what I really want."

"I can't." Mary waited just long enough for Vaughn's silver eyes to light with triumph, before adding, "Because you didn't pause long enough to give me a chance."

Reaching for her as though to embrace her, Vaughn stopped himself just in time. His hands closing over her upper arms, he shook her lightly instead. "Do you know what it's been these past few weeks to constantly see you and know I couldn't have you?"

"It's no more than I've had to bear," Mary shot back, and only realized too late just how she had exposed herself. The look of satisfaction on Vaughn's face was all that was needed to show her that she had said too much. Seeking to distract him, she blustered, "You're just trying to evade my question, aren't you? If you had the choice—"

Vaughn's hands tightened on her shoulders. "Choice, again, is it? Let me assure you, once and for all. If I had my choice, there would be no need for any of this. If I had my choice, you would be buying your bloody bridal clothes. If I had *my* choice, Monday night would never have ended with a kiss."

"Bridal clothes?" echoed Mary.

"I would crown you with coronets and deck you with ancestral jewels. *If* I had my choice. But I don't." Vaughn's grip loosened so suddenly that Mary stumbled back against the tree. His face was hard and ugly in the unforgiving noon light. "I don't have that right."

Mary had to swallow hard before she could speak. Her throat was dry, and her tongue felt too thick for her mouth. "Why not?"

She had her answer. But not from Vaughn. Before he had time to answer, a shadow fell across the space between them.

"Because," said the newcomer, twining her arm possessively through Vaughn's, "he already has a wife."

Chapter Twenty-One

Phi: *Look where she comes again, credit thy Eyes,*
   Which did persuade thee that they saw her dead.
Er: *You cannot think, Alcander, there be Ghosts.*
   No, give me your hand, and prove mine flesh and blood.

—Aphra Behn, *The Forc'd Marriage*

The newcomer planted herself firmly in the space by Lord Vaughn's side. She came no higher than his shoulder, her blond curls bobbing against the black superfine of his coat like boats on a midnight sea. The broad-brimmed bonnet she wore cast a deep shadow across her face, leaving her as little more than a walking fashion doll, in a walking dress of fine burgundy wool, far more suited for the crisp autumn air than Mary's twice-turned muslin. Her kid gloves had been dyed to match her dress. The deep burgundy looked like streaks of blood against Vaughn's arm.

Or maybe it was merely that Mary's thoughts were bloody. Who was this ridiculous interloper? Mary waited for Vaughn to make short work of her with one of his cutting remarks, but Vaughn, for a wonder, said nothing at all. He appeared to be in the grip of an emotion too strong for words.

Instead, the bonnet brim lifted and fell as the lady in red raked Mary up and down with a distinctly appraising stare.

"I am Lady Vaughn," she announced. "And you are?"

"You," said Mary flatly, feeling her command of the English language escape her. "Are Lady Vaughn."

There must be other Lady Vaughns. Cousins, perhaps. Wives of minor peers or cadet branches of the family, preferably distinguished by alternate spellings, like Vaughan or Voyan or other Elizabethan execrations.

"Yes, that's right," said the little blond woman, in the tone of one speaking to the mentally impaired. "I'm so delighted to see that my husband has been entertaining you in my absence."

Her "husband" looked as though he would rather be entertaining himself with a good, hearty throttling. His hands flexed around the head of his cane hard enough to bend the silver, as he breathed heavily through his nose, in the manner of dragons and other fire-breathing creatures.

But he didn't say anything to deny it. Not a word.

"Haven't you anything to say?" Mary demanded. "Anything at all?"

The self-professed Lady Vaughn smiled with sickening sweetness beneath her broad-brimmed bonnet. "Knowing Sebastian, he's probably said quite enough already, haven't you, Sebastian? He never could seem to help himself. You really must forgive him, Miss—oh dear. I'm afraid I still don't know who you are."

And didn't much care, if her tone was anything to go by. Mary might as well have been a weed in the garden, a misplaced chair in the morning room, a broken biscuit on the tea tray.

I married an earl's daughter, Vaughn had said, not ten minutes ago. The faded blonde in front of her held herself with the careless imperiousness of one born to the peerage. It wasn't, as Mary well knew, the sort of demeanor that could be learned, no matter how hard one tried to imitate it.

But Lady Vaughn, the former Lady Anne Standish, youngest daughter of an earl, was dead. Everyone knew that.

Mary looked frantically at Vaughn, but there was no surprise on his face, no indignation, no denial. Just a venomous, killing rage—the rage of a cornered creature, knowing himself caught, with no recourse but to sting.

Mary's stomach twisted.

"You are?" prompted the alarmingly corporeal Lady Vaughn.

"No one who need concern you," Mary said in a brittle voice. "Isn't that right, my lord? I was nothing more than this month's entertainment."

Lady Vaughn's gloved fingers left dents in Vaughn's sleeve. "Men will have their little amusements."

"No one would know better than you, would they, Anne?"

Lord Vaughn spoke at last, but the words weren't anything like what Mary had hoped to hear. The intimacy of that single word, that "Anne," hit Mary like an arrow to the gut, ripping through any last hope she might have had of its all being a hoax, a mistake, anything but what it was.

Her back arrow straight, Mary looked up over the blonde's bonnet, straight at Vaughn. "It's true, isn't it? You are married. To her."

Vaughn's eyes shifted briefly downwards to the bonneted head. "Such as it is."

Pain sharpened Mary's diction, lending her words an icy edge. "There isn't much room for doubt. Either you are or you aren't. It's as simple as that."

"Just what I've been telling him," chimed in Lady Vaughn. "Only with Sebastian, nothing is ever simple, is it, my dear? He delights in complication."

"Not this complication," clipped out Lord Vaughn.

Mary looked from one to the other, Lady Vaughn smug, Lord Vaughn looking daggers, and suddenly felt like the servant wench in a French farce, a side character used by the author to create complications in the midst of the main action. The operative word being "used," as Vaughn had used her. What for, she wasn't entirely sure, but it seemed to have something to do with the battle of wills being played out around her, between Lord and Lady Vaughn, earl and countess, linked by blood, by birth, by marriage bonds, leaving no place at all for her. Even in the richness of their attire, they were a match for each other.

It would make a brilliant woodcut, thought Mary with the flippancy of despair. Something by Gillray, clever and cruel. He could call it *The Wife's Return*.

"When you told me I was to be a pawn," said Mary, in a hard little voice, "I hadn't realized that this was to be the game."

"It wasn't," said Lord Vaughn tersely. "Believe me."

Mary smiled sweetly up at him. "I would sooner place faith in Signor Machiavelli. At least he was an honest rogue. Good day, Lord Vaughn. *Lady* Vaughn." Taking up her sunshade, she shook it ostentatiously open, using it as a barrier between them. "I shan't intrude upon you any longer. Good day."

She didn't look back.

Behind her, she could hear Lord Vaughn's voice, calling her name. Mary ignored it.

She concentrated on putting one foot in front of the other, heel to toe. Step after step she walked, head held high, looking neither left nor right, consciously deaf to the sounds of a minor scuffle between Vaughn and Vaughn's wife. Oh, but that voice was hard to blot out, an insistent buzz at the back of her ears, droning the word "wife" over and over, like a worm boring its way into her brain.

A wife. Mary's legs carried her forwards without destination through the fringes of the crowd, past the gaily covered booths that had done a brisk business earlier in the day selling pies and gingerbread and commemorative programs. This was one day she didn't want to commemorate. If she could, she would wrap it up in a little ball, along with the entire past month, wadded up like last month's washing, and fling it all into the Thames, to be drowned and forgotten.

The recollection of every thoughtless word, every heedless deed, every shameful, baseless hope made her cringe. How they must have laughed at her, night after night, flinging herself at a married man in the hopes of a title that was already taken.

Had they met to mock her? Memory presented her with the image of the Chinese chamber, with two glasses ready prepared, two glasses for an intimate tête-à-tête. And then she . . . Mary's cheeks burned with the memory of it.

Perhaps they had placed bets on her, the earl and countess, wagering on her virtue as one would on a horse at the Derby. Mary jabbed her sunshade into the ground as she walked, wishing it were a spear. Stabbing was too good for Vaughn. He deserved to be hung, drawn, and quartered like the basest of traitors, with his head stuck up on a spike outside Almack's as a warning to other would-be rakes and seducers.

Or perhaps they should simply take her head, Mary thought with disgust, and stick it on a spike as a warning to other credulous maidens not to fall into the arms of the first would-be widower who wandered along.

Stupid to believe he cared for her. Stupider still to allow herself to care for him.

And yet, she would have been willing to swear that what he had said today he had meant honestly—at least as honestly as Lord Vaughn understood honesty—every last, unromantic syllable. Would he have told her about his wife? Was that what he was trying to tell her when that hideous little midget of a blond thing interrupted?

"Miss Alsworthy . . ."

Surrounded by the thunder of her thoughts, it took some time for it to register that someone was calling her name. Not aloud, as Vaughn had done, but in an insistent whisper, like the whistling of the wind.

Thoroughly disoriented, Mary stumbled to a stop, twisting her neck in search of the source of the sound. All around her, she saw nothing but empty booths, bunting askew, whose owners, having sold their wares, had pressed forward with the rest of the crowd to watch the King address his troops.

The King. Mary's spine stiffened. In her preoccupation with Vaughn, she had forgotten entirely about the King, his review, and the purpose of their visit.

"Miss Alsworthy . . ." Her name came again, from the narrow corridor between two abandoned booths.

Mary turned slowly towards the sound, wondering what would happen if she put up her sunshade and walked briskly away. After all, what had she to do with the Black Tulip, now that all her obligations to

Vaughn had been extinguished? Let Vaughn's wife bedazzle the Black Tulip with her charms. And if the Black Tulip didn't like blondes, that was Vaughn's problem. He was the one who had married one.

"Miss Alsworthy . . ." There was a distinct tinge of irritation to the whispered call.

An irritated French spy was a dangerous French spy. One didn't need to be the Pink Carnation to know that.

Cursing Vaughn and his heirs unto the ending of the world, Mary moved slowly towards the two abandoned booths. The ground beneath her feet was churned and muddied, littered with broken biscuits, crumpled bits of paper, and lost hair ribbons as she picked her way carefully into the shadowy tunnel created by the two booths.

"Yes, *mon seigneur?*" she murmured in tones of proper submission, as she poked her head in between drunken billows of bunting. The sour smell of spilled ale mixed with mud made her stomach churn. It was just one more unpleasant aspect to a thoroughly unpleasant day.

"I want you to turn around," rasped the harsh whisper. "Not all the way around," it added, just in case she might be idiot enough to do a full rotation.

When the Black Tulip said turn, one turned. Mary obligingly rotated, keeping one hand tightly on the shaft of her sunshade. This time, she resolved, if she had to, she could disarm the Black Tulip with a sharp jab from the steel tip. With the proper show of obedience, he wouldn't be expecting her to turn against him. A blow to the toe would send him staggering and leave him clear for a hearty whack to the head. It was a maneuver she had been forced to employ once before with a particularly importunate suitor. It had been wonderfully effective.

Once she had handed the Black Tulip into the custody of His Majesty's government, she could get on with more important matters. Namely, killing Lord Vaughn.

Behind her, the Black Tulip approached, with a curious rustle of fabric, like the slithering of a giant serpent. In the narrow space, the sound was magnified, oddly loud in contrast to the din of hoofbeats and clattering drums that drifted from the center of the park. Fabric whispered against fabric as something brushed against the back of her skirts.

"You summoned me, *mon seigneur*?" she trilled.

"How well it sounds on your tongue," the all-too-familiar voice purred in her ear, setting the hairs on her neck on end. "You make an excellent courtier. Although you might do even better as Queen."

Odd sentiments for a republican. But the Black Tulip's politics were none of her concern. At least, they wouldn't be, once she was done with him.

"I've always thought so," agreed Mary calmly, keeping her back still and straight. "But no one has offered me a crown as yet."

"Only a fool waits for offers," chided the Black Tulip. "If you want what is yours, you must take it."

"And what does *mon seigneur* want of me?" Mary asked sweetly. Out of the sunlight, the air felt surprisingly cold, raising gooseflesh on her arms beneath the thin fabric of her spencer.

It was the wind that made her shiver, she assured herself, nothing more. They weren't alone in an abandoned corner of Vauxhall this time. It was broad daylight, with a thousand troops mustered half a mile away. The idea of the Black Tulip attempting anything at all in such a setting was ludicrous.

"The time has come," murmured the Black Tulip, "for you to prove your devotion to our cause."

"I desire nothing more," parroted Mary obediently. "Had you anything in mind?"

"Oh, just a trifling task." There was a deep purr of satisfaction to the Black Tulip's voice that made Mary instinctively take a tighter grip on the shaft of her sunshade. "Nothing too taxing."

Lord Vaughn had a great deal to answer for. "How might I serve my lord?"

"There is a troublesome creature who has been plaguing me for some time now," said the Black Tulip meditatively. "Someone who makes the mistake of attempting to meddle in my affairs."

As he spoke, something pressed against the small of her back, something hard and cold, shaped like a circle. A million miles away, she heard the click of a trigger being cocked.

This couldn't be happening. Not to her. Not in the middle of Hyde Park on a sunny autumn day with thousands of people milling around just in front of her, with bands playing and the King riding up and down the rows of his troops, with his fat son, the Duke of York, bobbing along beside him. The babble of a thousand voices pressed against Mary's ears, shrill and painful, and the sunlight seemed unnaturally bright, as if to highlight everything that she might never see again, the vivid crimson of the Duke's uniform, the gaudy reds and blues draping the makeshift wooden booths, the yellow thread patterning the hem of her dress. She could smell mud and ale, decaying leaves and unwashed bodies, mundane and unpleasant and yet suddenly so infinitely desirable, all of it.

Steeling herself to stillness, Mary said carefully, "To meddle with your affairs would be a very unwise thing to do."

"Indeed," agreed the Black Tulip genially, as the barrel of the pistol pressed through the thin fabric of her dress. "Most unwise."

With a suddenness that made her giddy, the pressure lifted from her back. Reversing the pistol, the Black Tulip held it out to her, neatly balanced in the palm of a gloved hand. It wasn't particularly pretty. There was no elegant silver work or tracery, no fanciful curlicues or detail. It was simply what it was, an instrument of death, wood and iron in its most compact form, offered on a black-gloved hand.

Mary stared senselessly at it, not comprehending what he meant her to do.

"Well?" urged the Black Tulip. "Aren't you going to take it?" The gloved hand hefted the pistol in a practiced weighing of death, turning the weapon over with the deftness of long familiarity. "This pistol belonged to another lady before you," he said conversationally.

"Did it?" asked Mary, gathering her wits back around her and reaching for the object. If the Black Tulip were fool enough to hand her a weapon, she certainly wasn't going to refuse it.

The Black Tulip moved it neatly just out of her reach, leaving Mary grasping at empty air. "Her loyalties became ... confused. We wouldn't want that to happen to you, now would we?"

"Confused?" Her trick with the sunshade made considerably less sense when the object happened to be holding a pistol. There had to be some way of getting the pistol away from him. . . . "Might I see it?"

The Black Tulip ignored the request. "She was given a task, but she refused to see if through. She wouldn't kill the man she was meant to kill. So I killed her," he concluded matter-of-factly.

"Did you?" Mary's throat felt very dry.

"One can't have that sort of insubordination in the ranks," said the Black Tulip regretfully.

"No, of course not," Mary agreed, as the pistol wafted negligently in front of her.

"It's death on morale. It was a pity, though. She had proved so satisfactory until then."

"Mmm," said Mary, keeping an eye on the trajectory of the traveling firearm.

"You asked to be allowed to prove yourself, so I give you the opportunity to finish the task your predecessor left undone."

"How very magnanimous of you." If she could only just grab it out of his hand, and then turn it on him.

"I want you to kill Lord Vaughn."

Chapter Twenty-Two

Alas! the devil's sooner raised than laid.

—Richard Brinsley Sheridan, *The School for Scandal*

"You want me to kill *Lord Vaughn?*"

Mary forgot that she was supposed to be facing forwards and was only returned to her proper position by the application of the pistol to her side. It was very frustrating having a conversation with someone back to front, especially when that someone was a homicidal French spy with a primed pistol in one hand.

With the pistol prodding her in the ribs, Mary hastily returned to what the Black Tulip deemed an acceptable position, staring straight ahead, out across the park, her view half-veiled by strands of bunting. The Black Tulip had chosen his hiding place well. From outside their dark cavern, even she in her white dress would be all but invisible.

"Lord Vaughn?" Mary repeated incredulously, addressing herself to a pigeon flapping overhead. "I thought you wanted me to kill the King!"

The pigeon expressed its opinion of that misapprehension by promptly relieving itself on the next booth over.

"My dear Miss Alsworthy, wherever would you get such an absurd idea?" The Black Tulip indulged in a rich chuckle. "Kill the King in the middle of Hyde Park? You would have to be mad."

He was calling her mad? That was rich coming from a man who skulked about in dark corners whispering melodramatic statements in peoples' ears, urging them to shorten the life span of peers of the realm.

Mary shook her head in confusion. "Please don't think me disrespectful—or disobedient," she added hastily. "But I really don't understand. I can think of many reasons one might like to kill Lord Vaughn. I can think of many reasons why *I* might like to kill Lord Vaughn. But I can think of very few reasons for you to wish to kill Lord Vaughn."

"Can't you?" There was a challenge in the Black Tulip's tone that made little drops of sweat break out along Mary's arms.

Well, there was that little matter of his doing errands for the Pink Carnation and attempting to plant her in the Black Tulip's service, but aside from that . . .

"You poor fool," said the Black Tulip, not unkindly. "Didn't you think I knew what you were about?"

"I don't know what you're talking about."

"When Vaughn appeared with a black-haired woman, I knew exactly what he intended. It wasn't exactly subtle. A petal to replace those I had lost. Your master made a fatal miscalculation. I have no more need for petals. Not anymore." There was a note of finality to the Black Tulip's voice that sent a chill down Mary's spine.

"Haven't you thought it might be the other way around?" Mary pressed every ounce of persuasion she had ever possessed into service. "That I might be using him to get to you?"

"Then prove it to me," said the Black Tulip pleasantly. "Prove to me that he means nothing to you. Kill Vaughn."

"I have no objection to killing Vaughn on principle," Mary lied. "I just don't really see the point. It seems like a waste of good bullets."

"Come now, Miss Alsworthy. We both know exactly what Lord Vaughn is."

"A liar, a cheater, and a cad?" Mary suggested. "A shameless seducer? A remorseless reprobate?"

"Nothing more than a clever front. An effective one, I'll grant you, but not effective enough to fool me." There was no mistaking the note of self-congratulation in the Black Tulip's voice. "Vaughn overplayed his hand in Ireland. No one but he could have gotten that information from the Marquise. And no one but the Pink Carnation could have used it.

"I have certain plans," continued the Black Tulip softly, "that are about to come to fruition. I cannot afford any interference from jumped-up floral arrangements."

"Plans?" inquired Mary innocently.

"Kill Lord Vaughn," said the Black Tulip, "and then you can be privy to my plans. Not before."

"Do I have any guarantee that you'll include me in your counsels once I kill Lord Vaughn?" demanded Mary daringly. "Or will you kill me, too, once I've rid you of your nuisance?"

"I don't deal in guarantees, Miss Alsworthy. If you want a guarantee, speak to a merchant. I will tell you this, though. The Pink Carnation is not part of my plans."

Mary noticed he had made no promises regarding her own mortality.

"Surely," she suggested, with one eye on the pistol, "you would do better to let Lord Vaughn lead you to the Pink Carnation. To kill off an accomplice might be satisfying, but wouldn't you rather pluck the entire flower?"

The Black Tulip's free hand twined in heavy loop of hair beneath her bonnet and tugged, hard, forcing her head back at an unnatural angle. "Do not attempt to play me for a fool, Miss Alsworthy."

The sharp tilt of her throat made it hard to speak. "I—don't—see—what's—so foolish," Mary rasped. "Wouldn't you rather the real spy?"

The pressure of the roots of her hair increased, pressing back until spots swam in front of her eyes from the pain. Then the Black Tulip released her so abruptly that her head snapped back, leaving her gasping hopelessly for breath, with one hand at her throat.

"You really don't know, do you?" There was a distinctly unpleasant quality to the Black Tulip's laughter.

"Know what?" she gasped, rubbing her throat. When she saw to the Black Tulip's downfall, she was going to make sure it was a painful one.

"Vaughn has played *you* for a fool, Miss Alsworthy."

That wasn't precisely news, but Mary suspected that the Black Tulip wasn't talking about Vaughn's matrimonial status.

"You don't mean to imply—"

He did mean. "Would Vaughn be anyone's accomplice other than his own?"

"I don't believe it," said Mary stubbornly, despite the fact that she had once voiced a similar objection to Vaughn herself. "Vaughn is not the stuff of which selfless heroes are made."

"Consider well, Miss Alsworthy. Vaughn's prolonged absences from England. His recent trips to Paris. His interference with *my* agents. And, of course, your charming self. Now tell me that Vaughn is acting for another."

For a moment, Mary almost wondered if he might be right. If Vaughn had lied to her about so crucial an item as a living wife, why not about other things as well? It would be an excellent cover for a spy to pose as his own accomplice. But try as she might, she couldn't make the identification stick. It was impossible to imagine Vaughn adopting a flowery sobriequet. If he had, it would have been something exotic and absurd, like the Crimson Chrysanthemum or the Remorseless Rhododendron. Not a humble flower like a pink carnation.

"I can't possibly think of a worse candidate for Pink Carnation," Mary protested. "Vaughn isn't the least bit patriotic. What about his revolutionary friends? His connections with the Common Sense Society?"

"Nothing but a sham. Don't you know your history, girl? The Vaughns have been in bed with the House of Hanover since the day the first German George hoisted himself onto the throne of England. Vaughn's grandfather slaughtered Scots at Culloden for the second George and his father served as advisor to the third." The Black Tulip's gloved hand tightened on her arm, leaving dents that would undoubtedly turn into bruises. "In return, they've received anything they could desire. Honors, titles, monopolies, concessions. Don't think your Vaughn isn't well aware of what he owes to the Crown."

"He isn't my Vaughn."

"Not for want of trying, is it?" asked the Black Tulip, in a way that made her want to jab the parasol into his toe then and there. His breath feathered against her hair as he leaned forward confidingly. "He has a wife, you know."

Oh, how she knew. But that little detail faded to triviality next to the magnitude of the Black Tulip's threats.

"Sooner or later, he will take her back. And then where will you be? Used and abandoned. One of a hundred forgotten conquests. Our interests coincide, Miss Alsworthy. I am offering you the ideal opportunity for revenge. Those don't come along every day."

Mary made a show of pretending to consider. "You do make an excellent point. If you give me some time, I'm sure I can think of a perfectly smashing plan for disposing of our mutual adversary. I want to make it something painful. And slow."

"You'll have to settle for painful."

The Black Tulip gestured with the pistol, the sunlight glinting dully off the thin iron barrel. Mary instinctively pulled away, but the Black Tulip had another target in mind. The point of the pistol settled, with all the finality of a lowered spear, on the figure of a man making his way alone through the litter of the abandoned stalls. His high crowned hat cast his face into shade, but there could be no doubt he was looking for someone, as he stalked through the debris, craning his head first one way, then the other, his lips pressed together in a tight line of annoyance. His normally immaculate cravat was askew and his urbane stroll had been abandoned in favor of a brisk stride.

His wife was nowhere to be seen.

Mary's heart tightened as she watched him stalk from one stall to the next, using his cane to wrench aside the bunting, struggling with a fierce and entirely inexplicable wave of protectiveness. She wanted to straighten his wretched cravat and smooth out the worried lines beside his lips and hustle him away to someplace where inconvenient wives and homicidal spies could never find them.

He couldn't look that awful and not have meant what he had said before. Wife or no wife.

The problem was keeping him alive long enough to find out.

"There he is," said the Black Tulip, in a voice rich with satisfaction. "Looking for you."

"Looking for his wife, you mean," Mary said acidly, in an attempt to play for time.

The Black Tulip refused to be diverted. Mary found the stock of the pistol pressed into her palm. When she would have taken it from him, the Black Tulip's hand closed around hers.

"Put your hand here, on the stock. Yes, just so." The movements of his fingers mirrored hers, keeping her hand carefully in place. "It fits itself nicely to your hand, doesn't it?"

"Oh, beautifully," Mary simpered, wondering when he would take his hand away from hers. One step, one pivot, that was all it would take, if only he would let go.

But the Black Tulip showed no sign of relinquishing his position. It was his hand that raised the pistol, his other arm that came around her to brace it, holding her pinned in the pincers of his arms.

"You have baited your trap very nicely, Miss Alsworthy," he murmured approvingly. "Now it is time for the kill. All you need to do is point the pistol and shoot."

Pressing against the force of his arm, Mary forced the barrel of the pistol downwards, away from Vaughn. "As gratifying as it would be to slaughter the conniving cad right now, it does occur to me that poison would be a better choice. With all the claret Lord Vaughn drinks, it would be the work of a moment to drop something into his glass. I could do it tonight. Think of the fine pedigree of poisoning. So much more tasteful than guns. Guns are so . . . crude, don't you agree?"

The tip of the pistol slowly rose again, pointing at the unsuspecting figure of Lord Vaughn. "You wanted to prove yourself to me, Miss Alsworthy. All you need to do is level and shoot. It's as easy as that."

Mary struggled to angle the barrel back down. "A pistol shot is so loud, *mon seigneur*. You wouldn't want to draw attention to yourself like that, would you? After all, you have so much of your great work still to accomplish. Bonaparte wouldn't know what to do with himself without you."

"If you won't do it—" The Black Tulip's hand tightened over hers, gluing her fingers to the stock of the pistol.

"It's not that I won't," Mary amended hastily, wrestling him for control of the pistol. "But shouldn't we just strategize a bit first? Methods and all that? You know what they say. Shoot in haste, repent at leisure. . . ."

"—then I shall just have to do it myself."

Without any further ado, the Black Tulip wrenched their joined hands into position, leveling the pistol at Lord Vaughn's unprotected back with the casual aim of a master marksman.

"Adieu, Lord Vaughn. Or should I say the Pink Carnation?"

In a single, brutal movement, the Black Tulip pressed her finger down against the trigger. Mary's elbow jerked ineffectually back, but the Tulip's grip was too strong to dislodge.

The force of the recoil kicked Mary straight in the shoulder, knocking her back against the Black Tulip. The arms holding her abruptly disengaged, and Mary went stumbling sideways, tripping over a long hem.

Mary didn't pause to pursue the Black Tulip; her one concern was Vaughn. Coughing, eyes watering from the acrid black smoke, Mary fought her way free of the bunting, just in time to see Vaughn fall heavily from his knees to his elbows and from there to the ground.

Next to him, Vaughn's cane rolled once, then twice before sliding to a rest in the trampled brown grass.

Chapter Twenty-Three

...from morn
To noon he fell, from noon to dewy eve,
A summer's day, and with the setting sun
Dropt from the zenith, like a falling star.

—John Milton, *Paradise Lost*, I

"Vaughn?" Mary skidded across the muddy field. "Vaughn?"

Vaughn's hands were splayed on the ground on either side of him. His only response was a low groan. He made an effort to move, his shoulder muscles bunching beneath the fabric of his jacket. Squirming sideways, he attempted to lever himself up, moving only inches before his arms gave way again. A wet trail marked his path, glistening burgundy against the faded grass.

Dropping to her knees on the ground next to him, Mary stripped off her gloves. Wadding up the leather, she pressed it hard against the hole in his back. The makeshift bandage did little good. Despite the tear in the back of his coat, the blood seemed to be seeping from beneath him, wetting her knees through her dress as she knelt beside him.

Seeing her, Vaughn tried again to hoist himself up onto one arm.

"Don't," Mary said harshly, grappling to keep her grip on the wad of leather, slimy with blood. "You'll only hurt yourself more."

Vaughn's clouded eyes shifted across her face. "Didn't mean—" he managed to force out between cracked lips. "Never wanted—"

"I know," Mary said quickly. "I do. Don't fret yourself."

Vaughn's eyes shifted downwards, taking in the dark stains, the steadily spreading puddle of blood. His lips peeled back from his teeth in a parody of his old smile. But before he could say anything sarcastic, his eyes rolled back in his head, and he went still.

Holding the wadded gloves hard against his back, Mary hunkered down beside him, bending her ear to his lips, listening anxiously for the sounds of life. His breath brushed her cheek, and she could have cried with relief. He was only unconscious, not—Mary's mind shied away from other possibilities.

But he was still losing blood, the precious fluid seeping into the ground at her knees. Without loosing her grip on the sodden gloves, Mary used her other hand to ease his left arm upwards, tilting him to the side. And there it was, a matching wound on the other side, just below the arm, tearing through shirt, waistcoat, coat. The fabric was so sodden, it was hard to tell exactly where the damage was.

Vaughn's cravat would make the best bandage, but the intricate knot defied deconstruction, especially with only one hand. Inspired by desperation, Mary emptied out the contents of her reticule, sending coins spinning dizzily in the dirt. Wadding up the soft fabric, she stuffed it beneath the wet patch on his chest, letting the weight of Vaughn's body do the rest.

It wasn't enough, though. She needed something to hold both pads in place. Mary let go for just a moment, and the sodden gloves on his back slid slowly sideways. Lurching forwards, Mary pressed them back into place. With her right hand occupied, she wriggled out of her spencer, wishing that fashion had called for slightly looser garments this season. One-handed, clumsy with haste and fear, she folded the back of the jacket over to make a thick pad. Holding the sodden wadding on his back in place with her elbow, she painfully scooted one arm of the spencer beneath him, leaning across him to yank it out the other side, the bloody gloves pressing against her breast. Edging back, she positioned the folded portion so that it would cover both sides of his wound, holding the already blood-soaked padding in place.

With the sleeves pulled tight, there was only just enough room to make a knot. The material, designed for fashion rather than function, slipped free as she tried to tie it off. Cursing beneath her breath as the material scooted away from her blood-slick fingers, Mary grasped the ends and pulled them fast, tugging them as tight as they would go.

Rocking back on her knees, she regarded Vaughn helplessly. Would he bleed less if she turned him onto his back? Or would the movement merely make him lose more blood? Letty would probably know, Letty who bandaged cuts and soothed banged knees and did whatever else one did with small children who had a habit of falling onto sharp farming implements. But Mary had never paid the slightest attention to any of that. Blood, after all, stained one's clothes.

"Do you need help, dearie?" Caught squatting ignominiously on her haunches, Mary glanced up to see crooked feathers towering over her head, like a great, black bird of prey.

The feathers were attached to a crooked bonnet, and the bonnet, in turn, to a raddled face from which wafted the strong scent of gin. It was the same woman she had seen before, the one who had been standing just in front of her in the crowd, watching the King ride up and down the ranks.

Remembering the brush of fabric against the back of her dress, Mary shied violently away. What better disguise than a raddled lady of the night? The broken bonnet cast her face into permanent shadow, and the reek of gin would keep away any but the most hardened sot. For a woman, her shoulders seemed unnaturally broad; they blocked the sun and sent a long shadow falling across Vaughn's helpless form.

"No," said Mary fiercely, shielding Vaughn with her body. "We're quite all right."

The woman—if it really was a woman—shrugged. "Suit yourself."

Hoisting her bottle to her lips, she wandered back towards the main crush of people. But Mary noticed that she stopped not far away. One hand held the bottle aloft, but the other was hidden by the tipsy fall of her shawl, long enough and thick enough to hide any manner of things, from a bottle . . . to a pistol.

It probably wasn't her, Mary belatedly concluded. There had been no gin smell around the Black Tulip, and goodness only knew that she had been pressed close enough to him—or her—to tell. But the Black Tulip might be anyone, dressed as anything.

Mary crouched protectively over Vaughn. No matter how dangerous moving him might be, she had to get him out of the park and back to the relative safety of Vaughn House. With all the crowds milling about, there were too many opportunities for the Black Tulip to finish the job.

"You. Boy!" Without leaving her protective crouch, Mary reached out and grabbed a small boy by the scruff of his pants.

"Yes, miss?" Staring google-eyed at the broad streaks of blood decorating Mary's dress, the urchin shrunk back as far as his waistband would allow him to go.

Mary hastily scooped up her fallen coins and thrust them in front of him. "If you find me a sedan chair and make it come here right now, all of these are yours."

"All, miss?" The boy's eyes lit as visions of gingerbread danced through his head, greed trumping caution.

"All," Mary repeated emphatically, waving the handful of shiny metal back and forth. "But only if you come *quickly*. Understand?"

"Yes, miss!" the boy was already in motion, racing for the gates. Mary fervently hoped he was running for a chair, and not just away. With Vaughn's blood streaking her hands, she looked like the sort of person who would snatch up small children and bake them into pies, or whatever it was that parents used to frighten their children these days.

Scrubbing her hands hastily against her skirt, she eased one hand gently beneath Vaughn's head. The short hairs prickled against her fingers. His head weighed against her hand like lead, entirely inert.

"I don't care," she whispered to him, leaning her lips close to his ear. "I don't care how many wives you have. If you pull through this, you can have a hundred more. Just don't die. Please."

If he heard her, he gave no sign.

Where *was* the boy with the chair? There were so many places for a would-be assassin to hide among the crowds. Even the very tree above their heads. In the background, the martial clamor rattled on, with the clatter of hooves, the *rat-tat-tat* of the drums, the shrill cry of the horn. No one would notice a cry in the midst of the cacophany. Even the sound of a shot would be entirely inaudible beneath the gabble of the crowd and the screech of the pipes and drums.

"I've brought 'em," the boy announced.

Behind the boy stood two men, in the traditional livery of the chairman, a loose blue kersey coat over black breeches, with large cocked hats shading their faces. Between them, they held a black box with long, springy poles threaded through metal brackets on the side. It was a far cry from Vaughn's own sedan chair, painted in shiny black lacquer and chased with silver, but it would have to do. Closed up in the box, he should be safe from harm—or, at least, safe from further harm.

"There was an accident," Mary said imperiously, emptying her handful of coins into the boy's palm. The boy scampered happily away, taking the remains of her quarter's allowance with him. "Move him gently."

The chairman regarded her laconically. "It'll be extra if he bleeds on the cushions, like."

"It will be nothing unless you move him," said Mary acidly. *"Now."*

With a shrug to show what he thought of uppity wenches, the chairman leaned over, his blue kersey coat flapping about his calves, and hoisted Vaughn up by the armpits.

"Both of you!" snapped Mary. "Gently!"

With an expression of extreme martyrdom, the second chairman reluctantly grasped Vaughn's legs. Together, the two men shifted him through the opening between the poles into the chair. Ignoring the chairman's protests that his vehicle was meant for one, Mary climbed in after him, pressing Vaughn's head protectively against her shoulder.

"Vaughn House," she commanded, cutting through the man's protests. "In Belliston Square."

"Don't think I know where Vaughn House is?" muttered the chairman rebelliously beneath his breath, but he picked up the front poles as his comrade picked up the back, hoisting their burden into the air.

Easing an arm around Vaughn's shoulders to hold him steady, Mary fussed over his bandage. The chairman's cavalier treatment had shifted it upwards, and the wadded mass that had once been her reticule was sticking out beneath one end, heavy with blood.

Vaughn, she had no doubt, would have a perfect quotation for the occasion, something about a pound of flesh, or taking one's price in blood.

Mary blinked, hard. From the dust in the road, of course. It was a singularly dusty drive, and the windows of the sedan chair didn't keep the dust out as they ought.

On the street, as if from a continent away, people went about their business, unaware that inside the sedan chair the entire world hung pendant over a dark abyss, suspended by nothing more than the fragile thread of Vaughn's weak breathing. From the gates of the park, weaving through the traffic with the ease of long practice, rode Lady Hester Standish, looking like a self-satisfied cossack in her fur-trimmed red habit. Mary caught a glimpse of black boot beneath a muddied hem as she rode by, her legs on a level with the window.

On the opposite corner an ink seller hawked his ink, as black as Vaughn's hair, dulled now with dirt and sweat and the sticky moisture from her bloody hands. A drably dressed man, ledger clamped under his arm, scurried in the front of the chair, causing the chairmen to veer sharply to avoid him, eliciting a low groan from Vaughn as he was flung against the side of the chair.

Mary clutched him closer, silently urging the chairmen on. Once away from the congestion around the park, the trip to Vaughn House went quickly. When the chairmen started to let down their burden at the foot of the stairs, Mary poked sharply at the chairman's back.

"Inside," she ordered. Leaning out the window, she addressed the two liveried servants holding open the door. "Your master has been hurt. Call a surgeon."

The white-wigged servants shifted uneasily at their posts as the chairmen lumbered through with their human burden.

"What are you waiting for?" Mary snapped at the one nearest her window. "Don't just stand there goggle-eyed. Your master needs a surgeon. Go!"

The man's mouth opened and closed like a guppy. Vaughn's footmen had evidently been chosen for appearance rather than intelligence. Aunt Imogen would approve.

It was with some relief that Mary noted the approach of the same superior personage who had done his best to deny her access two weeks before. It would have been beneath his dignity to scurry. Instead, Vaughn's butler strode forward, every lineament radiating outrage at this crude invasion of his well-polished precinct.

"Lord Vaughn has been hurt," Mary said crisply. "He needs to be placed in his bedchamber. Where is it?"

The butler stared owlishly down at the window of the sedan chair, clearly less than pleased to be having a conversation with a conveyance. "This is most irregular, madam. If madam would be so good as to—"

Mary froze him with a glance. "Is your dignity worth your master's death?"

The butler stepped aside. "Up the stairs, third door on your left."

Accepting this new direction philosophically, the chairmen began to ascend the great, spiral stair, which twined around a fourteen-foot-high statue of Hercules wrestling with snakes. The chair tilted backwards at a dizzying angle as they spiraled upwards. Through the window of the chair, Mary could see Hercules, with his club in one hand and the neck of a snake in the other, lion skin slung over one shoulder, spinning around and around. At long last, the chairmen reached the landing, bringing the chair level. Stiff-legged, they marched down the hall to the third door on the left, where the butler, who must have raced up the back stairs to get there before them, thrust open the door.

"The surgeon?" Mary demanded though the window of the chair.

"Has been sent for," the butler assured her, indicating to the chairmen where they were to set down their burden.

Mary had only a confused impression of large seashells and a great deal of blue velvet before the chair came to a stop in the middle of the room, the chairmen's dusty boots leaving dark prints on the pristine pastels of the carpet beneath their feet. They set down the chair with a thump. The butler reached out a hand to help her out, but Mary wafted him aside, motioning him to take Vaughn instead.

"He needs two men to move him," she directed. "Whatever you do, do *not* take him beneath the arms."

"Right stroppy one, ain't she?" muttered the chairman.

The butler ignored him, saying impassively, "Yes, madam. You." He snapped his fingers at the chatty chairman. "Take his feet."

"And there's another one for you," grumbled the chairman, but he did as he was told.

Together, the butler and the senior chairman eased Vaughn between the front poles, carrying him up to the bed, which rested on a raised dais in the French style. Braced between them, Vaughn looked like a prop in a play, a wax figure of a man. One hand fell limply over the side, the once-bright white lace grimed with dirt and dried blood. Only the diamond on his bloodless finger gleamed with its accustomed luster, and its very dazzle seemed a mockery.

Mary scrambled out of the chair after them. Kicking her skirts impatiently out of the way, she lurched to her feet and hurried up the two steps to the dais, as the butler settled Vaughn upon the impeccable blue silk counterpane, moving with all the grave deliberation of an undertaker laying out a corpse. He looked remarkably small in the vast expanse of the bed, his skin nearly as pasty as the two marble nymphs propping up the elaborately curved seashell that formed the headboard.

Vaughn's fingers flexed weakly against the silk of the counterpane.

All but bowling over the butler to get to his side, Mary grasped his hand. His fingers felt miserably cold.

"Mary . . . ," he said weakly.

Mary's throat constricted uncomfortably.

"I refuse to enact a touching deathbed scene," she said harshly. "You're not dying."

Vaughn's lips twisted up in the ghost of a smile. "If you . . . say so."

His eyes drifted downwards, taking in the blood streaking the front of her formerly white gown.

" 'Who would have thought the old man would have so much blood in him?' " he murmured, and lapsed back against the pillow, his face as white as the linen beneath his head.

"Madam?" It was the butler, at the foot of the dais. "The surgeon has arrived."

A portly man in a plain black coat and breeches shouldered around him, using his battered leather bag to clear the way in front of him, as though he were used to forcing his way through to the scene of accidents. His wig was askew, sitting sideways on his wide forehead. It was an old-fashioned wig, of the woolly variety. It had presumably better suited the sheep.

Seeing Mary, the surgeon stopped short, looking her up and down with professional detachment.

"Is this the patient?" he asked.

Considering the bloodstains streaking her gown, his question was not entirely unjustified.

"The patient is over there," Mary said, all but shoving the surgeon up onto the dais. "There was an accident. Involving a bullet."

The doctor shot her a sideways glance from beneath his wig, as his hands busied themselves untying Mary's makeshift bandage. "I find such *accidents* generally occur at dawn."

"This one didn't," Mary said flatly. "My . . . cousin had taken me to see the troops in Hyde Park. One of the recruits was overexcited, and accidentally fired into the crowd."

If the doctor questioned the story or the relationship, he gave no indication of it. He was too busy cutting through the matted layers of cloth covering Vaughn's chest, peeling them carefully back. Despite his old-fashioned wig, he did seem to know his trade. His eyes were keen as he poked about at Vaughn's side, muttering to himself as he did. Whatever he was doing caused Vaughn's hands to clench the sheets, drops of sweat standing out against his brow as he arched with pain.

"There will be worse to come," said the doctor, in response to Mary's indignant stare. "You might want to remove yourself, Miss . . . ?"

"Isn't there something you can do for him?" demanded Mary. "To relieve the pain?"

Rummaging in his bag, the doctor produced a small brown bottle. "Tincture of opium mixed with spirits of wine. Use it sparingly, unless you want him sleeping until the next trump."

There was no time for such niceties as glasses. Tipping back his head, Mary lifted the small bottle to Vaughn's lips.

The doctor did something else to Vaughn's side, and he jerked beneath Mary's hands, sending a stream of thick, reddish brown liquid cascading down the side of his lips. Blotting it with the end of the sheet, Mary examined Vaughn's face anxiously. His eyes were closed, and his breathing was irregular, but he managed to open his cracked lips wide enough to mouth what looked like "thank you" before his body arched again with pain.

Mary rounded on the doctor, who lifted a bloody sponge from the wound and dropped it with a cavalier plop into the slop jar.

"Your friend was fortunate," commented the doctor, drawing the edges together and skewering them with a thick needle threaded with cotton thread. Vaughn's body twitched in response. "It's a good, clean wound."

It looked anything but clean to Mary, with blood sluggishly oozing between the jagged edges of flesh. The acrid scent of raw alcohol, mingled with the baser tones of blood, made her stomach churn.

Tying off a stitch, the doctor admired his handiwork. "The bullet went straight through without shattering."

"The bullet *is* gone?" asked Mary.

"Oh yes," agreed the doctor, rolling Vaughn over to get to the hole on his back. Taking his scissors, he snipped neatly away at what remained of Vaughn's jacket and shirt, clearing the area over the wound. "The bullet didn't have far to travel, just through this area above his collar-bone, here. He was quite lucky it wasn't lower."

At Mary's look, he elaborated, "The bullet went through the fleshy part of his shoulder. Painful, but seldom fatal. Had the bullet struck a few inches farther down, you would have had no need for my services." The doctor poked professionally at Vaughn's back. "Had it struck here, it would have gone right through his heart."

Chapter Twenty-Four

Oh do not die. . . .
But yet thou canst not die, I know;
To leave this world behind, is death,
But when thou from this world wilt go,
The whole world vapors with thy breath.

—John Donne, "A Fever"

"You mean it would have killed him," she said.

"Instantly," agreed the doctor. "Or the next thing to it. As I said, your friend is very fortunate."

He glanced speculatively up at her over Vaughn's body as he pronounced the word "friend."

"My *cousin* and I," Mary emphasized, "are both very grateful for your prompt assistance."

The surgeon eased the long end of a bandage around Vaughn's side, coaxing it beneath his back. "A curious man," he said conversationally, "might wonder how, if your cousin was watching the recruits, he came to be shot in the back."

"A clever man," returned Mary pointedly, "knows better than to ask profitless questions."

A veteran of countless illegal duels, the surgeon didn't need to be warned twice. Tying off the end of a bandage, he patted Vaughn's side with a professional air. "He'll need the stitches out in a day or so. You'll want to give him cold compresses for the fever."

Mary looked at Vaughn's gray face, his forehead clammy with sweat. "What fever?"

"They all get fever," the surgeon said cheerfully, closing his bag with a distinct click. "The fever kills more than the bullets. You just have to hope it won't be too high."

"How very encouraging." Doctors were such nasty little men, all puffed up with their Latin phrases and useless diagnoses. One would think he could at least offer to do something about the fever, rather than just predict it. "Is there anything one can do to bring the fever down?"

"You could bleed him." The doctor produced a small brass box from his bag. At a touch, the box sprung open, revealing twelve sharp blades, positioned with all the care modern medical science could afford. "Bleeding will release the corrupt blood and lower the fever."

Mary glanced down at the pile of blood-soaked cloth on the floor by the bed, the remnants of Vaughn's shirt and jacket. "He's lost enough blood already."

The surgeon refrained from giving the appropriate medical lecture. It would only be wasted on a woman. Shrugging, he took up his bag. "Hot and cold compresses, then."

Mary looked to the butler, who was waiting by the door. "Your fee will be seen to." She nodded to the butler. "If you would?"

The butler moved smoothly forwards to usher the surgeon from the room.

"If you're quite sure about the bleeding . . . ," the surgeon tossed over his shoulder.

"Quite sure," Mary said firmly.

She stayed sentinel by the side of the bed until the surgeon was safely out of the room. Sprawled on top of the coverlet, Lord Vaughn was by no means an inspiring sight. He looked, in fact, rather as though he had come out the wrong side of a barroom brawl, with his coat and shirt half torn away and the dark stain of opium-enhanced wine snaking down his cheek and onto his chest. Blood streaked his chest below the white bandage the doctor had wound around his shoulder, where red already showed in an ominous circle against the white.

Vaughn's skin showed surprisingly dark against the white band, dusted with dark hair. There was the line of an old scar near the join of his shoulder, a crescent-shaped slash, as though someone had aimed for his heart and missed. Apparently, this wasn't the first time someone had attempted to kill Lord Vaughn. Mary shouldn't have been surprised. A decade ago, London had been more wild, with duels fought by dawn on Hampstead Heath and gangs of toughs ready to prey on inebriated gentlemen. And heaven only knew what he had got up to on the Continent. Vaughn's chest, seamed, scarred, and lightly muscled, suggested that he had been more than equal to any adventures.

It would be too absurd for him to have survived so much only to be felled by one little bullet in the domestic dullness of Hyde Park. It was just the sort of cosmic joke Vaughn would appreciate. Only this time, it was on him.

"Madam." It was several moments before Mary realized that the insistent noise buzzing behind her ear was a voice, and that it was intended for her.

Dragging her gaze away from Vaughn, Mary realized that the butler—what *was* his name?—had returned and was standing just behind her.

He would be entirely within his rights to suggest that she leave. Aside from thrusting her own way into the house, her position was entirely anomalous. Despite her lies to the surgeon, she wasn't cousin, or ward, or wife. She was a nameless woman—a nameless woman with a tendency for appearing at inappropriate hours of the night, in whose company the master of the house had been severely wounded. And even if she were a proper sort of guest, her presence in the master's bedchamber would be highly improper.

Without turning her head, Mary said briskly, "The surgeon says his temperature will rise. Make sure there are cold cloths ready."

"Yes, madam," said the butler.

"He should probably have port, to thicken the blood. And brandy, for the pain. Not at the same time," Mary added as an afterthought. "I doubt he would like that."

"Indeed, madam," agreed the butler. As a door, cleverly cut into the paneling, eased open, the butler added, "I have taken the liberty of calling his lordship's man to make his lordship more comfortable."

"There's little hope of that," said Mary, but she allowed herself to be shepherded away from the bedside to make room for the valet.

The valet limped his way to the position she had just vacated, emitting noises of distress. Whether the clucking was over his master's condition or the state of his boots was largely unclear. Placing a basin of hot water on the nightstand, he set about wiping the dried blood from his master's chest with a care that satisfied even Mary's anxious eye. Over one arm, he had a pile of clean linen cloths, which he used to wipe Vaughn's chest clean. The tattered remnants of Vaughn's coat were eased away, to be replaced with a clean linen nightshirt.

The butler stepped discreetly in front of her before the valet could reach Vaughn's unmentionables.

"If I might be so bold . . ."

Mary prepared to do battle for her right to stay, regardless of Vaughn's state of undress.

". . . perhaps madam would be more comfortable in a fresh garment?"

Of all the things Mary had expected the butler to say, that had not been one of them.

Her dress did itch awfully. Vaughn's blood had seeped straight through the thin muslin to the chemise beneath. The fine lawn was sticky with it. The damp patch chafed unpleasantly against her chest. And then there was the broad stripe across the front of her dress at her knees, where she had knelt beside him, and several lighter streaks in the area of her torso where she cradled him to her in the carriage. There were dark crescents beneath her fingernails and a casual glance in the mirror revealed alarming streaks across her face.

"Thank you," Mary said, in a tone that was almost an apology. "I would like that very much."

The corners of the butler's lips shifted in what, in another man, might have been a smile. For a moment, he looked almost human.

"There are garments that might be of service in the countess's chambers."

He tilted his head in the direction of a connecting door Mary hadn't noticed before, set into the paneling on the opposite side of the room, next to the massive marble mantel.

"No." The reaction was instinctual. The notion of wearing *her* clothes made her skin crawl. "No, thank you—I don't know your name."

"Derby, ma'am. If madam would prefer, there is a dressing gown in his lordship's dressing room that might serve the same purpose while madam's dress is being freshened."

"Thank you, Derby. That will do very nicely."

While Derby took himself off through the door in the paneling, Mary ascended the dais and occupied herself in scaring away Vaughn's valet. It took only a few moments of concentrated glowering before the valet scurried away, ceding his place by Vaughn's side.

He had tucked Vaughn neatly up among the linens, with a blanket pulled all the way up to his chin and a tasseled nightcap perched on his closely shorn head. Given the obvious newness of the nightcap, Mary had no doubt that this was a victory the valet had not achieved while his employer was conscious. In proper deference to Vaughn's feelings, she plucked off the nightcap and tossed it beneath the bed. Then she rolled down the covers at his throat, giving him more room to breathe. She might not know anything of nursing, but smothering the patient surely wasn't the way to go about it.

Behind her, Derby laid a robe of heavy silk brocade neatly across the back of a chair.

One didn't fraternize with servants, but Mary heard herself say, "The surgeon says the wound is a clean one. He should recover quickly."

Derby's stern features relaxed in an expression that was first cousin to a smile. "I am sure madam will ensure that it is so."

And with that, the door clicked shut behind him.

Mary took up the robe he had left her, but she found herself oddly reluctant to leave her post by the bed, as though if she failed to keep proper watch, someone might slip in and steal Vaughn away. Instead, she sat by the bed and watched as the angle of the light through the window slowly shifted across Vaughn's bedspread, moving in tandem with the hands of the clock on the mantel. The fierce orange light of late afternoon lit the edges of the coverlet with a demonic glow before it, too, faded into dusk.

He looked so vulnerable in the large bed, with the ominous red splotch on his bandage showing above the covers. Every time his sleeping face contorted with pain, every time she heard the uneven rasp of his breath in drugged sleep, her heart clenched as though the Black Tulip held it in his fist. It hurt like a dozen bullet wounds to know that she had brought him to this. Oh, there had been times when she would have liked nothing better than to humble Lord Vaughn, to bring him low—and no time more than that afternoon—but not like this. Never like this.

The events of the afternoon replayed themselves before her a thousand times, only in the reprise she always managed to thrust aside the Black Tulip's arm at the crucial moment, so the bullet went wild, or distract him long enough to drive her sunshade into his toe, making him drop the pistol. And at the end, there was always Vaughn bounding up to her, smoothing the hair out of her face, touching her cheek with the back of his hand, as though he had never seen anything so infinitely precious and telling her—oh, everything he had told her before his wife's appearance but a thousand times over. And without the angry snarl.

Mary looked down at the limp hand lying on top of the coverlet, and frowned at her own foolishness. Girlish daydreams were all very well, but they wouldn't keep Vaughn safe from the Black Tulip. It was sheer luck that the shot had been too high; the Black Tulip couldn't be trusted to miss the next time.

There had to be some way to get to him before he could get to Vaughn. But how? She didn't even know that he was indeed a he. That had definitely been a skirt she had felt behind her. She rather doubted that the Black Tulip was stalking Hyde Park dressed in a cassock, despite his clerical appellation. Either he was a woman, or he had chosen to disguise himself as one for the purpose of sowing confusion. Had he been wearing a dress in Vauxhall? Mary would have been willing to swear he hadn't.

Well. Mary picked at the embroidery on the arms of the chairs as she stared at the sun setting over the bare branches of the trees in Belliston Square. She would just have to tell servants to keep a watch out for anyone suspicious, male *or* female. The butler seemed a sensible sort, he could be enlisted to set up a guard. And a guard would be set, whether Vaughn liked it or not. Mary's face settled into an expression of raw determination her sister would have recognized in an instant. She knew Vaughn would try to shrug off the danger as soon as he was healed enough to shrug. That was all very well, but she wasn't going to let him die for a bit of male bravado.

Even so, setting a guard only delayed the problem; it didn't solve it. The only way to truly solve it was to kill the Black Tulip. And they couldn't kill the Black Tulip until they knew who he was.

As the purple autumn sunset faded from the tops of the trees in the Square, Mary rose, stretching her cramped legs. In the great bed, Vaughn slept on in drug-induced slumber, his right arm flung up over his head like a little boy's. His features were softer in sleep, with the dusk casting a soothing veil over the lines drawn by pain and time.

His color seemed better, but Mary wasn't sure whether that was just an illusion created by the dim light. Mary touched the back of her hand to his forehead, careful not to wake him. The dreadful clamminess was gone. His forehead was warm and dry, and his breathing was easier than it had been. The fever would come next. But, for the moment, he was sleeping peacefully.

Moving stiffly, Mary stepped carefully down off the dais, catching at the balustrade for balance. Her knees objected to the movement. She felt as ancient as Methuselah, her legs and back stiff from sitting, her eyes dry and aching from staring, hour after hour, at the still figure in the bed.

She knew she ought to change, as Derby had advised. She ought to have done it hours ago. The sooner she left her dress to be cleaned and pressed, the sooner she could go home. So far, the only people who knew of her presence at Vaughn House were Derby, who wouldn't speak; the valet, who didn't speak; and the surgeon, who had been paid well not to speak. The other servants had seen her only through the dirty window of the sedan chair, not well enough to make out anything other than that she was a woman, a description that undoubtedly applied to many of Vaughn's acquaintance. But the longer she stayed, the greater the risk became. To stay the night would be ruin.

Wobbling a bit, she padded across the carpet to the door to the hall. Just outside the door, where she couldn't fail to see them, someone had left two trays. On the first stood two decanters, one filled with a ruby liquid that could only be the requested port, the other a deep amber that marked it as finest smuggled French brandy.

The second tray was clearly not intended for the inhabitant of the sickbed. It held two porcelain pots. One pot was short and rounded, accompanied by a silver tea ball and a dish for slops; the other was taller and cylindrical, with a quaint, conical lid. Both the shape and the smell identified it as a chocolate pot. There was one cup to go with each pot, both matched to the same set, a feminine pattern with delicate purple flowers on a fluted background. On a matching plate had been placed several slices of cake and an assortment of biscuits.

Next to the food, more homely but all the more welcome, the same considerate hand had left a basin and ewer. Both the water in the ewer and the tea in the pot were still so hot that steam rose and misted across Mary's face as she bent to pick up the tray. Derby must have returned several times to replace the water as it cooled. It was no more than a well-trained servant would do, but Mary was obscurely cheered by the gesture.

Setting the tray down on a small table, Mary slopped a generous amount of water into the basin, plunging her hands into the steaming water up to the wrists. It felt like heaven to finally wash the crust of blood off her hands. Once her hands were finally clean, she dipped a cloth directly into the ewer, scrubbing at the smudges on her face.

With Vaughn's robe still draped over her arm, Mary moved softly across the room, to the door in the wall. Unlike the door that led into the dressing room, there was no attempt to hide its outlines. A grand plaster pediment was mounted above the door frame, the two sides of the triangle broken in the middle to make room for an overflowing basket of flowers borne by two simpering nymphs. The architect might as well have put up a sign announcing, THIS WAY TO OFFICIAL CONSORT: GO FORTH, BE FRUITFUL, AND MULTIPLY.

A fine job Lady Vaughn had done of that, Mary thought scornfully. She hadn't even produced an heir.

There was a key in the lock, a fanciful key adorned with a series of interlocking curlicues, with a silk tassel fluttering from the end, a key intended more for ornament than use. Vaughn had used it. Trying the handle, Mary found the door to the countess's chamber barred fast, locking out the past. Taking up a candle, Mary turned the key, hearing the click as as the tiny mechanism shifted. She had to push hard against the door before the stiff hinges gave way, creaking open into the shrouded silence of the long-closed room.

Shouldering the door shut behind her, Mary ventured into the room, her booted feet dark blots against the light pink and yellow Aubusson carpet. The drapes were all drawn and clearly had been for some time, their tasseled edges weighted with a decade's worth of dust. Mary rubbed the once costly brocade between her fingers. It felt gritty to the touch. Letting the drape fall, Mary dusted her fingers off against her skirt.

Aside from the funereal film of dust, years of darkness had kept the rooms well preserved. In the small circle of light cast by her one candle, the colors stood out as true as they must have ten years ago, without any of the fading that came of sunlight and use. Unlike Vaughn's chambers, the walls had been painted rather than hung. The long panels depicted a pastoral paradise, largely populated by plump putti, whose purpose appeared to be to hover happily over the humans, dropping wreaths on their heads and garlanding them with flowers. Idealized shepherdesses herded improbably fluffy sheep, while amorous shepherds played ballads on lutes that were always in perfect tune. On the ceiling, in an elaborately scrolled oval, happy lads and lasses danced eternally around a ribbon-decked maypole.

One would have thought an earl's daughter would have better taste.

Tossing her head, Mary set her candle down on the countess's dressing table, draping the robe over the back of a chair. Unused to undressing without a maid, she wriggled with difficulty out of her bedraggled walking dress, dragging it up from the hem over her head. Bloodied and begrimed, the fabric was stiff and uncooperative. It stuck halfway over her head, causing Mary to wonder whether there might not have been something she was meant to unfasten first. A few determined tugs and it pulled free, leaving Mary flushed but triumphant.

As she stood in her petticoat, stays, and chemise, her attention was caught by one of the painted panels behind the dressing table, a dark-haired shepherd playing his lute in tribute to a simpering blond shepherdess. Lifting the candle, Mary leaned closer. It was a time-honored compliment to paint one's patron into a picture. The dark-haired shepherd had something of the look of Vaughn, although it was impossible to imagine Vaughn in a half-draped toga, perched on a rock, playing a lute. His shepherdess was a dainty little thing, with long, blond curls that bounced down below the broad sash at her waist. There was a decidedly hungry gleam in the shepherd's eye as he watched her.

Had Vaughn looked at Lady Anne like that?

Mary set down her candle again with a thump. She hated that sickly shepherdess with her self-satisfied expression and her greedy little hands. She hated her for her dreadful taste in interior decoration, for her noble pedigree, for her unchallenged right to occupy the chambers that Mary could enter only as guest. How had Vaughn proposed? Had he gone down on one knee and mouthed the appropriate and traditional words of love? Had he meant them? Or had it been a family arrangement, an alliance between two great houses, with documents to sign instead of poetry and property dispositions instead of kisses?

Mary viciously hoped for the latter. She hoped that during the short span of their marriage, the Vaughns had been all that was à la mode, with their separate bedchambers, separate lives, and separate loves, only coming together in their paired portraits to stare down at posterity in a lie of love.

Sinking down into the tufted stool before the countess's dressing table, Mary rubbed her hands hard over her eyes. She was being absurd! It shouldn't matter how Vaughn had felt about Lady Anne. All that mattered was that they were married, that Lady Anne had the right to be here and she didn't. Not Lady Anne, Lady Vaughn. Mary realized she had been unconsciously thinking of the woman by her courtesy title, as if she had never married, never shared Vaughn's bed, never taken the place Mary wanted to occupy herself.

Mary glanced sideways at the robe draped over a chair. Even now, in her petticoat, stays and chemise, if she wrapped the robe tightly around her undergarments, she could maintain a semblance of respectability.

But what was the purpose of respectability? She had already been nearly ruined once, for a man who meant nothing to her and a title that did. Better now, to be ruined in truth for the sake of the man she wanted, the man she—Mary shied away from the word. The man she loved. There. She had admitted it. She loved him. Was that so very strange? She loved him for all the dark and dismal reasons he loved her, for all his vices and inconsistencies, his selfishness and his pride, his inconvenient honesty and his devastating wit.

Reaching back, Mary untied the tapes at her waist. Her petticoat slid down over her hips, crumpling on the floor around her feet. Stepping daintily out of the pile of fabric, Mary kicked it aside. Her stays came next. One tug and the light canvas corset joined her petticoat on the pink and yellow pattern on the ground.

Bending over to tackle her boots, she tugged at the knots in the laces. Without her stays, she felt marvelously free, her unconfined waist bending without the press of whalebone. She kicked off one boot, then the other, flexing her feet in their silk stockings like a dancer at Covent Garden. She was sure her legs were as good as theirs.

Vaughn could be the judge of that.

With a flick of her fingers, Mary undid the bows on her garters, letting the blue ribbons flutter to the ground. With quick, precise movements, she rolled down the silk stockings over her calves, until she stood in Vaughn's wife's room in nothing but her chemise. Above the dressing table, her mirrored lips curved in a red, dangerous smile. The fine lawn whispered easily over her head, floating to the carpet like an emblem of fallen virtue.

The silk of Vaughn's robe slithered sensuously over her skin as she slid both arms into the broad sleeves, cinching the heavy fabric closed with its own broad sash. The brocade was the color of expensive wine, the color of the claret in Vaughn's glass that night in the Chinese chamber, embroidered with exotic Oriental dragons who swished their golden tails through a burgundy forest and played hide-and-seek in the folds around Mary's legs. As the fabric washed over her, Mary remembered that night, with the candlelight flickering off the porcelain plaques and the gold thread in the crimson cushions, in that doorless, windowless, jewel box of a room, and Vaughn, more exotic and glittering than any of it by far, his hair disheveled and his shirt open, drinking to her only with his eyes—with his eyes, and lips, and a hundred indecipherable endearments.

On an impulse, Mary reached up and drew the pins from her hair, letting it tumble down around her shoulders. She had been too vain of her hair to succumb to the current fashion for short curls. Loosed, it fell nearly to her waist, heavy and straight. Rather than use the countess's brush, with its telltale blond hairs still caught in the bristles, she combed her fingers through the tangles, feeling the heavy mass shift across her shoulder blades, black on crimson.

She rubbed her cheek against her right shoulder, enjoying the sleekness of the silk. The fabric smelled like Vaughn, with the tang of claret and sandalwood, exotic and familiar all at once.

She scarcely recognized herself in the mirror, with the dressing gown open at the neck and her hair falling free around her shoulders. The girl reflected in the candlelight was exotic and wanton, with the crimson of the robe casting an echoing color in her cheeks and lips, contrasting with the pale skin of her throat and hinting at more interesting valleys below. She had worn ballgowns cut far lower, and yet she had never felt so bare.

She had never worn silk next to her skin before, without layers of linen and lawn, cambric and canvas forming a barrier in between. The fabric slid fascinatingly around her legs as she walked towards the door, every ripple a caress. The girl in the crimson silk didn't stride; she swayed, as the heavy fabric nipped at her heels and played peek-a-boo with her calves. The fibers of the carpet tickled the soles of her bare feet.

As she slipped through to the earl's chamber, leaving behind a decade's dust and decay, she wondered what Vaughn would say when he saw her. And what she would say to him.

Or perhaps there would be no need for words at all.

Chapter Twenty-Five

"What are you still doing here?"

The voice, hoarse but distinct, came from the tousled
linen on the great bed on the dais, giving the impression of animated
and disgruntled bedding.

Mary shut the door of the countess's chambers carefully behind her,
disposing of her candle on the table by the door.

"You're not supposed to be awake," she said softly. "I gave you
enough opium to stun a goat."

"A flattering comparison," rasped the voice from the bed.

"Don't complain," admonished Mary, wending her way across the
room, the heavy silk undulating around her legs. "It might have been
an elephant."

Lifting his head from the pillow, Vaughn said, with great effort, "Hellfire Club . . . Played with opium . . . unexciting."

Mary had to lift up the long ends of the robe to ascend the two steps to the dais. "So those stories *are* all true."

Vaughn's head dropped back against the pillow as though the effort of holding it up were too much for him. His eyes drifted closed. "Not as interesting . . . as they sound."

"You can tell me more later." Mary settled herself on the edge of the bed, her long hair brushing Vaughn's pillow. His forehead felt warm to the touch, although that might have been nothing more than the heavy blankets. "After you rest."

Vaughn's gray eyes, filmed with pain and opium, moved speculatively from her unbound hair to the deep V left where the robe crossed at her chest. But he declined to comment.

"Is there any water?" he asked in a dry croak.

"Port?" suggested Mary, reaching for the rounder of the two decanters. "You lost a great deal of blood."

Vaughn moved his head slightly to the side, the movement barely making a dent in the pillow.

"Water," he repeated.

"If that's what you want . . ."

Mary shook back her too-wide sleeve, allowing him to admire the effect of her white arm against the deep red silk as she poured water from the crystal jug Derby had left on the tray with the decanters. There was no glass for it, so Mary poured the water into the brandy glass, looping both hands around the rounded bowl as she lifted the glass to Vaughn's lips.

Giving her an inscrutable look, Vaughn reached for the glass himself, using his good right arm, although even that movement made him grimace with pain. His fingers seemed to have trouble closing around the bowl, and the glass would have fallen if Mary had not been there to catch it when he released it.

As Mary replaced the glass on the tray, Vaughn struggled to push himself up on his elbows, going an unfortunate gray with the effort.

"Stop it!" Mary scolded, flinging herself into the breach. "You're supposed to be lying still."

"Would you?" croaked Vaughn, sliding back down into a bank of goose down.

"No," admitted Mary, extracting a pillow and giving it a good hard whack before replacing it behind him. "But that's beside the point. I'm not the one who was shot."

Vaughn's eyes gleamed a dull obsidian beneath his lowered lids. "You might have been."

"I refuse to argue hypotheticals with you while you're ill," said Mary loftily.

"Really?" murmured Vaughn. His voice might be barely audible, but he still managed to exude sarcasm from every pore. The fingers of his right hand fluttered in what was meant to be a wave. "What's all this, then?"

Even weak and drugged, Vaughn didn't miss a trick. He had, Mary realized, deliberately declined to comment on her scandalous state of undress in order to spring the argument on her when she would least expect it. She didn't know whether to cry with relief, laugh, or smack him.

Smacking him would have to wait, so Mary combined the two earlier options. Smiling crookedly, she said, "It's a robe. Your robe, in fact. Derby was kind enough to lend me the use of it."

Vaughn's brows drew together over his nose. Only Vaughn could contrive to look down his nose while almost entirely prone. "That's not all."

"Actually," said Mary airily, struggling with an absurd urge to laugh, "it *is* all."

Vaughn was not amused. "I can't marry you," he said flatly.

Mary brushed back a short lock of silvered hair. One of these days, she would have to ask him whether the silver was a matter of nature or art. Given the unalloyed darkness of the hair on the other portions of his body, she suspected the latter. "I know. You told me earlier."

Vaughn scowled forbiddingly. "My wife—Anne—she's still alive."

Mary smiled blandly down at him. "I met her, if you recall. Right before you were shot."

Vaughn pressed his eyes tightly together.

Mary leaned hastily over. "Is it your arm? Do you need more opium?"

"Anne," said Vaughn on a low groan. "Of all the damnable . . ."

"Ah," said Mary, leaning back. "I do agree with the adjective. How is it that she comes to be alive when you were meant to have murdered her years ago?"

"One . . . only wish," murmured Vaughn hoarsely. Filling the brandy glass with water, Mary held it to Vaughn's lips. He drank gratefully before falling back again against the pillows. When he spoke again, his voice was clearer. "She ran off more than ten years ago. Music master. I believed—I hoped—she was dead."

Mary paused with the glass suspended above the tray. Brandy was beginning to seem like a very good idea. For her. "The tomb in the family vault?"

"Empty."

"And the rumors?"

"All false." Vaughn's lips twisted into a whisper of a smile. "But so entertaining. They added . . . a certain cachet. Kept the debutantes away."

"You," said Mary in fond exasperation, "are quite mad."

Vaughn's smile winked out like a snuffed candle. "And quite married."

Mary set the glass down on the tray, concentrating on the sparkle of crystal against silver. "How long have you known?"

Vaughn wasted no words. "Vauxhall."

The purple-red of the port reflected against the silver base of the tray like Homer's wine-dark sea, treachery in its unfathomed depths, capable of swallowing ships and their crews whole, with no one ever the wiser. Vauxhall. That had been when Vaughn had gone from flirtatious to indifferent. No, not indifferent. Distracted at first, and then deliberately rude. All due to the appearance of one small, cloaked figure.

"So, you see . . . you should leave me. Go home." Vaughn pointedly turned his head on the pillow in a deliberate gesture of renunciation, presenting her with a profile as imperious and as cold as that of an emperor on an antique coin. As he turned, she could see the brownish stains on the bandage that tied beneath his arm.

"No," she said, very simply and very clearly.

Rolling his head slowly back over, Vaughn regarded her with narrowed eyes. Like most autocrats, he was unused to being disobeyed. It would do him good, Mary decided giddily. He needed a little less deference in his life. With her choice made, she felt oddly light and free. There was no turning back now, no thinking of what lay ahead or behind. There was just Vaughn. And that was enough.

"I'm not leaving you," Mary elaborated. She added, with false nonchalance, "I can't, in any event. Derby is having my dress cleaned and pressed."

Vaughn's elbows made dents in the goosedown as he pressed himself up against the pillows. "Don't you understand?" he demanded hoarsely. "It isn't going to change. She isn't going away this time."

"Neither am I," said Mary calmly, reaching behind him to plump his pillows. "Do you think you could move just a bit to the left? Ah. There. Perfect. I haven't had much experience of nursing, but I hear that one is supposed to pay special attention to the patient's pillows."

Even the poorer for several pints of blood, Vaughn wasn't that easily put off. "Why?"

Mary considered prosing on about the pillows, but thought better of it. There was no way out but through; the admission had to be made, and the longer she put off making it, the harder it would become.

"Because I want to." Now that the moment had come, Mary realized that the flippant answer wasn't entirely honest. If one was going to tear out one's heart and lay it at someone's feet to be trampled on, there was no point in doing it by halves. "Because I want *you*."

Vaughn didn't say anything. He just looked at her, like a spectator at Astley's Amphitheatre, waiting to see what absurd stunt might come next.

"I want you," Mary repeated, her voice gaining strength with each word. "Not your title. Not your money. Oh, I won't deny those would be lovely—but if I can't have you with them, I'll have you without them. That's why."

Vaughn's fingers moved weakly on the counterpane, as though missing the comforting presence of his quizzing glass. "How very . . . impractical of you."

"I know." Shrugging, she raised both brows, challenging him to contradict her. "I've never done anything so utterly idiotic in my life."

He returned her gaze impassively, arrogant even in illness, his stark features affording no encouragement, no quarter. One would have thought he could have spared her a nod, a smile, any kind of acknowledgment that she had just laid her future into his hands in the single most selfless gesture she had made in her life.

But, then, he wouldn't be Vaughn.

Why couldn't she have felt this way about any of her other suitors? St. George, for example. Someone with a good disposition and a tidy income and no inconvenient spouses tucked away in the wings. But then there was Vaughn. Always Vaughn. He blotted out the others— like a plague of locusts, thought Mary irritably, darkening the sky and consuming everything in his path.

"I could have saved myself a great deal of bother today by just shooting you myself, instead of fighting with the Black Tulip for your blasted life," Mary informed him. "But for some reason, I like you alive. Alive and tormenting me." Folding her arms across her chest, Mary glowered down at him. "Heaven only knows there's no reason in the world I should. All you do is sneer and mock and quote ridiculous bits of Shakespeare at me. Half the time, I think you make them up."

Naturally, that got his attention.

Before Vaughn could muster a protest, Mary jabbed a finger at him. "You're rude and autocratic and—and married! Good heavens. You can't get any worse than that. Even Turnip Fitzhugh has the benefit of bachelordom."

Vaughn made a face. "No. Not Turnip. Please."

"No," agreed Mary, "not Turnip. Although Turnip has thirty thousand pounds a year and it would be child's play to get him out on a balcony. I could be established. I could be married. But then there's you." She let that sink in before going on, before confessing the rest of the horrible truth. "Next to you, everyone else seems dull. Everyone else seems pale. It's like water after wine."

Vaughn's lips twisted into a smile. "I didn't think . . . you indulged."

"I didn't," Mary said shortly. "Until you."

Vaughn's eyes held hers, unreadable beneath their heavy lids. Without the slightest hint of mockery, he said, "Neither did I."

For a wounded man, Vaughn had a surprisingly strong grip. His right hand caught the loose end of the robe and tugged. Since she had a choice of sitting or losing her robe, Mary sat, landing heavily on the side of the bed.

"Your bandages," said Mary anxiously, as the movement dislodged the covers, revealing the expanse of white linen wrapped about his chest.

"Never mind my bandages." With a bemused grimace, Vaughn shifted himself up against the pillows. "Was ever one in this humor wooed? Come here. Please."

Mary didn't move from her perch on the side of the bed. With victory in her grasp, it was easy to be ungracious. She raised both brows. "I thought you wanted me to go away."

Vaughn smiled crookedly. "I find that I'm not so noble as I had hoped. You can vouch that I did try, although it went sorely against the grain."

"I prefer you as you are—tainted and tarnished."

Vaughn's good hand tangled in her long, black hair. "Rotted black to the core, you mean."

"More of a light gray," Mary corrected. "Practically silver."

"'Love looks not with the eyes, but with the mind,'" quoted Vaughn, lifting one eyebrow in silent challenge.

There was only one way to stop Vaughn when he started abusing Shakespeare. Mary didn't scruple to employ it. With her long hair flowing down around them, she employed the excellent method recommended by Mr. Shakespeare and stopped his mouth with a kiss, and let not him speak neither. His lips were dry and cracked beneath hers, not soft as they had been the other night. Where there had once been claret, she could taste the metallic tang of blood where he must have bitten down with the pain of the surgeon's probing. Mary welcomed the chafing, the sharp taste of blood where once there had been wine. He was hers, every bruise, every flaw, with blood on his lips and the musty aftertaste of opium furring his tongue.

There was a raised patch of skin just below his collarbone, where he had been wounded once before, and survived. It was a long, thin wound, slippery as snakeskin against the skin of his chest. Mary's hand slid sideways, exploring the contours of his muscles, the texture of his skin, the curious ridges and bumps of his bones, cataloguing them all for her own private inventory.

With one deft move, Vaughn twitched free the bow at her waist, his hands slipping beneath her robe. Inch by inch, the caress of silk gave way to skin, as his hands slid slowly up from her waist along the curve of her ribs, unfettered by all the layers of clothing that had thwarted her more adventurous suitors in the past. Unhindered by corset or stays, Vaughn's hands brushed delicately past her unbound breasts, the slightest whisper of a touch, but all the more tantalizing for that. Mary's breath caught in her throat as he circled back with deliberate slowness. Mary arched her neck, soaring miles above Belliston Square on her own private cloud as Vaughn leaned forwards to brush a kiss against her pulse.

She plummeted abruptly back to earth as Vaughn pulled away, doubling over with a pained grunt.

"Vaughn?" Shoving her hair out of the way, Mary leaned anxiously over him, calling herself a thousand nasty names for having forgotten that there were such things as stitches and that amorous activities tended to dislodge them. With Vaughn looking at her like that, touching her like that, it had been so dangerously easy to forget. "Are you all right? Are you bleeding again?"

"This," rasped Vaughn, clasping both hands to his side, "would be considerably more entertaining were I master of all my faculties."

Mary scooted sideways off the bed, holding her robe together with both hands. "I'm ringing for Derby."

Vaughn's head inched up. Although white about the lips, he managed to say, with commendable sangfroid, "While he is an admirable butler, Derby would be decidedly de trop. Don't you agree, my dear?"

"I'm not letting you tear open your stitches. You need sleep, not—" Mary gestured broadly. She didn't see any brighter red among the brown stains, but it was hard to tell with Vaughn's hand clamped over the area. At least, if he was bleeding, it couldn't be heavily, or it would have seeped through his fingers, as it had before, during those nightmare hours in the park.

Moving very carefully, Vaughn eased himself back against the pillows, keeping one hand clasped against his side. "You won't refuse a wounded man?"

"Precisely why I am refusing you."

"What if it's a dying wish?"

Mary shivered. "Don't say that."

"Would it matter . . . that much?"

"Do you have to ask?"

"Yes." Vaughn's lips twisted in a ghost of a roguish smile. "For my vanity's sake."

"Your vanity does quite well enough without my help. But, yes." Mary snuggled back down next to him, taking care to stay to his good side. "It would matter. A great deal. When I thought you were dying . . . that I had killed you . . ."

"Ah, yes," said Vaughn, raising an interested eyebrow. "What was that about fighting with the Black Tulip for my miserable life?"

Mary gave him the expurgated version. "He thinks you're the Pink Carnation and he wants you dead."

"Good Lord, not *again*," groaned Vaughn.

"Again?" demanded Mary. "Do you get mistaken for spies frequently?"

"Oddly enough, yes. I stumbled upon the Pink Carnation during one of my trips to Paris. Or, rather," he admitted, "the Pink Carnation stumbled on me. I was having a spot of bother with Fouche's lot, from which the Carnation was good enough to extract me. In return . . ." Mary felt his chest ripple beneath her cheek as he shrugged.

"What exactly might that spot of bother have been?"

Vaughn settled back more comfortably against the pillow. "It is rather amusing when one considers it. The Pink Carnation was operating under the mistaken impression that I was our elusive Black Tulip—it's the wardrobe, I imagine," he added as an aside. "There's no other explanation for it."

"Hmm," said Mary, but forbore to comment.

"The French, on the other hand, had somehow come by the absurd conclusion that I was embroiled in the affairs of the Pink Carnation. They began to make Paris rather unpleasant."

"I've heard the guillotine often is."

"Fortunately, the Pink Carnation captured me before Fouche did. Once we had straightened out the small matter of my intentions, the Carnation graciously condescended to take on my business in France. In return, the Pink Carnation has called upon me for certain small favors. You were one of them. I resisted strenuously," he added.

Mary chose to ignore that bit. "So the English think you're working for the French, and the French think you're working for the English."

"A delightful little tangle, isn't it?"

"We seem to have a number of those," Mary said ruefully.

Vaughn rested his cheek against the top of her head. When he spoke, she could feel his breath rustling against her hair, like the wind through the leaves in the Square. "I wish I could do it all over, start again."

"Without an Anne," Mary finished for him.

"Without an Anne," Vaughn agreed.

"If it hadn't been her, it would have been someone else," Mary said philosophically. Remembering something that had nagged at her before, she pulled back just far enough to see Vaughn's face. "Who was Teresa?"

The old guards clamped down across Vaughn's face. "Never my wife."

"Clearly."

Mary could feel the moment when Vaughn's tense muscles relaxed beneath her cheek, as her silence won out over reticence. "She was my lover. In Paris."

"Your mistress," Mary translated.

"Not as such," replied Vaughn thoughtfully. She could feel his chest shift beneath her cheek as he settled back further against the pillows. "The term never suited her. She would never have admitted to being anything other than an equal partner."

"You cared for her." Mary did her best to keep her tone neutral.

"I admired her," Vaughn corrected. "She was clever. Strong-willed."

"Beautiful, too, no doubt," said Mary acidly.

She could hear the smile in Vaughn's voice. "Very."

Shifting out of the circle of Vaughn's arm, Mary swished her hair back over her shoulder. "I can't imagine how you could bear to part with her."

"She was also," said Vaughn very delicately, "an agent of the French government."

"Oh." There didn't seem to be anything else to say. Mary looked down at him, at the deep circles beneath his eyes and creases in his cheeks, tokens of years in which she had had no part. Years of Hellfire Club outings and trysts with French spies and heaven only knew what else. "Did you know that at the time?"

Vaughn raised one eyebrow. "In the beginning, it wasn't really a consideration."

Mary folded her arms across her chest, very conscious of the robe hanging open with the belt lost somewhere among the bedclothes. "I'm sure you were too swept away by her manifold charms to care."

Vaughn considered that for a very long time. "Not really," he said, after a pause that seemed to go on forever. "The question never arose."

Mary's skepticism must have been readily visible, because Vaughn raised his good hand in a gesture of graceful helplessness.

"Paris in '91 was . . . different." His eyes drifted past her, fixing on a fold of the blue velvet bed hangings as his memory roamed back a decade along the twisting streets of Paris. "Oh, the Bastille had been taken and the mobs had marched on Versailles, but it all still felt like a game—a dangerous game, to be sure, but what's the joy of playing for low stakes?" His lips twisted in reminiscence, a smile with a sting in its tail. "We used to place bets on which concession the King would make next, which ridiculous acts the Assembly would pass, which district would be the next to go up in arms." His eyes darkened. "We never thought they would kill the King. And then the Terror . . ."

His gaze settled on Mary's face, where she sat as still and solemn as a marble statue of Justice. With an effort, he mustered something of his old urbane demeanor. "As you can see," he said, with a nonchalant shrug that might have been more convincing but for the lines of strain around his eyes, "events took me somewhat by surprise. As they did us all."

"But not her," Mary supplied, sticking doggedly to the main point.

"Who can say? It may have been her goal all along, or she may merely have seen her chance and seized it. I only knew the extent of it once the Terror was well under way. By then . . ." Vaughn let his silence speak for itself. "Having no desire to tangle with a pack of maddened ideologues, I chose the route of least difficulty to myself. I left."

Mary ignored the self-condemnation and seized on what she saw as the more important point. A woman scorned was always dangerous; a woman scorned with a habit of executing her enemies was even worse.

"Will she be back to haunt you, too?"

"No."

Arms akimbo, Mary shook back her hair. "You seem to have a talent for inspiring resurrections."

Despite himself, Vaughn's cheekbones lifted with amusement. "Setting me up as your savior?" As Mary made a face at him, he shook his head, his amusement fading. "There'll be no resurrection this time. Teresa is dead. Quite genuinely and indisputably dead."

"How?" Mary asked apprehensively. She had a suspicion she wasn't going to like the answer.

Vaughn's face was grim. "She was killed this past summer, by her own master. The Black Tulip."

"That's why," Mary said abruptly, her nails digging into the feather tick. "That's why you told me the Tulip was running short of petals. Let me guess: She had black hair, too."

"Yes." The candle threw strange shadows across Vaughn's face, throwing one cheek into relief, the other into shadow, like the parti-colored costume of a harlequin in an Italian commedia dell'arte. Only there was nothing lighthearted about Vaughn's expression. His hand sought hers among the bedclothes, his fingers closing tightly over hers. "I should never have got you involved."

The outlines of the trees, silhouetted in relief against the walls, reminded Mary just a little too much of that deserted copse deep in the heart of Vauxhall gardens. She could very well have done without ever having made the acquaintance of the Black Tulip. Of course, if it weren't for the Black Tulip and his machinations, she wouldn't be here with Vaughn.

"You didn't know me then," she said mechanically. "I was expendable. Anyone would have done the same."

Vaughn's thumb brushed caressingly across the vein at the base of her wrist. "Spoken like a true pragmatist," he said tenderly, but Mary's mind was too full of other concerns to be distracted by compliments.

"The other petals," Mary asked apprehensively. "Did you . . . know them, too?"

"Certainly not in that way."

Vaughn's voice was getting hoarser again. Reaching for the carafe of water, Mary measured a generous portion into the glass and offered it to Vaughn with both hands, like a feudal page serving his lord a ritual draft. "For a time, I thought you were the Black Tulip."

Vaughn's eye crinkled at her over the rim of the glass. "Am I to take that as compliment or insult?"

"Neither," said Mary primly, placing the glass back on the tray. "Merely common deduction. You were recruiting black-haired agents—"

"On behalf of the Pink Carnation," Vaughn corrected.

"I had only your word for that. You do not"—Mary's blue eyes slanted down at him—"inspire confidence."

Vaughn drew her down again into the comfortable hollow by his side, the mattress already dented with the shape of her body, as though she had been there always. "I'll simply have to resort to other means to impress you with my sincerity."

"I won't be easy to convince," warned Mary, as she curled into the crook of his arm, stifling a yawn against the back of her hand. It had, when all was said and done, been a very long day.

Vaughn's fingers stroked lightly down her shoulder. "Then it's fortunate that I shall have a lifetime to wear you down."

Chapter Twenty-Six

And now good-morrow to our waking souls,
Which watch not one another out of fear;
For love, all love of other sights controls,
And makes one little room an everywhere.

—John Donne, "The Good-Morrow"

The room was so still that Mary could hear the ticking of the clock on the mantel and the gentle whisper of Vaughn's breathing, in and out, in and out. Outside, there was the rustle of the leaves in the square and a rhythmic creak where someone had left a shutter unlatched and the wind was batting it back and forth, playing with it for its sport.

"From another man," said Mary quietly, "I would have taken that as a proposal of marriage."

Vaughn's fingers tightened on her shoulder. "In any other circumstance, it would have been." She could feel the movement as his head turned on the pillow, staring out towards the window. "It might still be."

Mary marched her fingers idly up along his chest, toying with the dark hairs in her path. "I didn't think a wife was that easily disposed of."

"Generally, no." Vaughn's tone was conversational. They might just as well have been discussing the prospects for the new management of the Covent Garden theatre, or whether it might rain on Sunday. "There have always been ways. The madhouse, the attic—the Continent."

Mary caught the subtle change in tone on the last word. "You think you can persuade her to go back?"

"It's a tempting thought," Vaughn confessed. "Out of sight and out of mind. I tried that once already. It didn't serve."

"With enough gold," suggested Mary, "she might be persuaded to stay out of sight."

"We would have no guarantee—other than her word."

Mary's lips curved in memory of a long-ago conversation. "Which you value as you would your own."

Vaughn rested his chin against the top of her head. "Precisely the problem. The moment necessity struck, she would return. I won't have her cast a cloud on our children's parentage."

"Children," Mary repeated. She lifted her head, bumping Vaughn's chin in the process. "Children?"

Wincing, Vaughn said dryly, "They are the natural consequence of marriage."

Mary raised a brow. "I've heard that marriage isn't necessarily a factor."

"In our case, it is." Vaughn tucked her head once more safely beneath his chin, his good arm holding her tighter. "I would hate to see the title go to my cousin by default."

"You had no children by—" Mary found she couldn't quite bring herself to pronounce the name. To say it made it real, like introducing an extra party into the bed. "—her," she finished lamely.

"No," said Vaughn, but there was a telltale pause before he spoke the word.

Mary shifted her head to look up to him, achieving a very good view of the underside of his chin. There was very little to be learned from it, other than the fact that he had missed his usual evening shave.

"After I learned that she might still be alive, I went to Paris. I retraced her steps, as best I could. It had," he added with a tinge of bitter humor, "been a very long time."

"But you succeeded," Mary said. It wasn't a question.

"Success?" Vaughn turned the word over on his tongue, examining it from every angle. "I suppose you might call it that. I followed her trail to a cheap boardinghouse—or what had once been so before it reverted to a private residence. Finding the business less than lucrative, the proprietress practiced a secondary trade."

Vaughn paused, giving Mary time to think over his meaning. There were so many secondary trades it might be, but two in particular came to mind. She had heard of women who disguised their brothels as boardinghouses—young ladies weren't supposed to know of such things, but one heard the rumors. And then there were those places where one went to get rid of unwanted children. There had been that girl, two Seasons ago . . . The story had been garbled in the retelling, but the point had been clear enough.

"There was a child," said Vaughn, with chilling finality. "Whether it was mine or his, I don't know. It makes no difference now."

The thought of it made Mary a little ill, although whether it was the act itself or the notion of Vaughn's child by another woman, she couldn't say for certain. "You're quite sure?"

"Are we ever afforded the luxury of certainty in this life? The woman kept no written records, if that's what you mean." Vaughn's head rustled against the pillow. "If there had been a child, Anne would have trotted it out. She would never have neglected so convenient a tool. At the time, it would have seemed only an impediment."

"So she took steps to get rid of it."

"She did get rid of it," Vaughn corrected, and Mary found herself shamed by the flood of relief that washed over her at those uncompromising words. To have a mysterious wife barring her way was bad enough, but a child would be that much worse, making demands upon Vaughn, threatening the rights of her children.

Their children. How quickly those hypothetical shadows had become flesh in her imagination. The thought of anyone threatening their patrimony made her nails curve into claws. She would rake out the throat of anyone who came near them. Even though they didn't exist yet, and possibly never would.

"She killed her own child. Your child."

"No," said Vaughn, his voice heavy with gallows humor, "she hired someone else to kill her child. Anne never performed for herself what she could order someone else to do for her."

A woman who would kill her own child as an encumbrance wouldn't scruple to take aim at an inconvenient husband—or hire someone to do so. Something niggled at Mary, a connection she couldn't quite place.

"Would she inherit anything were you to die?"

"Not enough. The estate is entailed upon my nearest male relation— a cousin. Currently, the bulk of my personal fortune goes to my mother."

Mary's head lifted in surprise, pulled to an abrupt stop as her hair caught under Vaughn's arm.

Vaughn's eyes glinted with amusement in the uneven candlelight. "Did you think I had leapt into the world full grown, like Minerva from Jove's head?"

Since that wasn't terribly far from what she had thought, Mary could only shrug feebly. It was almost impossible to imagine Vaughn as a small child. The closest she came was a miniature adult in an impeccable cravat, wagging a rattle at his nurse in lieu of a quizzing glass.

"My mother," explained Vaughn, "is hale and hearty and fully occupied in lording it over the family pile in Northumberland. It's all still quite feudal up there, and Mother plays the role of chatelaine to the hilt. I have no doubt she would happily defend the castle against an invading army if the occasion called for it."

Mary extracted her hair from under Vaughn's arm and levered herself up on one elbow, just far enough to see his face. "What do you think she'll think of me?"

"I think you'll get along famously." Vaughn smiled wolfishly. "Eventually."

Before Mary could delve into that equivocal statement, Vaughn went on, "If my mother were to predecease me, the money gets parceled out in various bequests, none of them to Anne. She is, after all, supposed to be dead."

"That would pose a problem," agreed Mary, relaxing against him. "How very foolish of her."

Vaughn's lips brushed the top of her head "I'm sure you would have planned it much better. If she can prove her existence, she has her dower rights—but it would make little sense for Anne to kill me merely to acquire a dower house and a quarterly allowance."

"Unless *she* wanted to marry again," Mary pointed out. "In which case, it might be worth her while to have you out of the way."

"No," said Vaughn. "More's the pity. She wants to come back. As countess."

Resting her head against the side of his chest, Mary pondered that unwelcome information. If the Lady Anne chose to return as countess, what was there to be done about it? It would be the easiest course for Vaughn to accede and take her back and breed his pure-bred heir, an earl's son begat on an earl's daughter. After the initial flurry of shock from the *ton*, he could go back to life as it would have been, as though the last thirteen years had been nothing more than a wrinkle in time. In contrast, she had no official position, no claim, nothing to hold him. If he chose that route, this night in his bed would be her last, and there would be nothing she could do about it.

"Would you take her back?" she asked quietly.

As though he sensed something of what she was thinking, Vaughn's hand moved possessively through her hair. "Even were matters not as they are? No. Matters being as they are—absolutely not. You won't be rid of me that easily."

Mary rubbed her cheek against his chest. "Perhaps she thought in a weakened state, you would be more likely to agree."

She could hear the smile in Vaughn's voice. "Just as you prevailed upon me in my weakened condition?"

"You seem suspiciously eloquent for a man at death's door."

"Never underestimate the healing power of love's gentle balm," intoned Vaughn in saccharine tones.

Mary looked up at him, her brows a straight, dark line above her eyes. "Is it?" she asked seriously. "Love?"

"It isn't the opium," replied Vaughn.

Mary waited, unwilling to let him off that easily. After a very long moment, as Vaughn's arm grew heavier and heavier beneath her neck and the ticking of the clock grew louder by the moment, he spoke.

"Yes," he said heavily. "I suppose it is."

"Much against your will," Mary supplied for him.

"Rather like you." Vaughn's lips quirked in a twisted smile. "Diamond cuts diamond. Two hard-hearted souls rendered fools by Cupid, brought low like lesser mortals. I find myself experiencing absurd urges to go out and slay dragons on your behalf." He dismissed the problem with a nonchalant wave of his hand. "Don't worry. I'm sure they'll pass in time."

"Twenty or thirty years," Mary agreed, yawning. "By then, all the dragons will have died natural deaths, asphyxiated by their own smoke."

"One can only hope," agreed Vaughn. "I've never aspired to the heroic."

"Are you sure you haven't any other wives roaming about?"

"Quite sure. After the first one, I was taking no chances."

"Except on me," Mary corrected sleepily.

"Except on you," agreed Vaughn. His voice made a pleasant burr in the back of Mary's head. "You are the exception that proves the rule."

Mary mused over exceptions and rules, while the words blurred and shifted in her brain, leading off along all sorts of irrelevant byways. In the end, she contented herself with murmuring, "That's nice."

"Tired?" Vaughn's breath ruffled her hair.

"No," Mary said emphatically. And she wasn't really. She was just a little bit . . . The last sound she remembered hearing was the soft burr of Vaughn's chuckle reverberating through his chest.

When Mary woke the first time, the last of the candle guttered within a wall of wax, sending uneven shadows flickering across the silk lining the walls. In a sleepy stupor, Mary's eyes followed the swaying shadows, idly watching their progress across the wall as she struggled to remember where on earth she was. There was a heavy weight across her chest that, upon examination, turned out to be a leanly muscled male arm, entirely devoid of any sort of clothing. Ah. Mary's lips curved into a sleepy smile. Vaughn. That was all right then.

Burrowing comfortably among the blankets, she sank back into the head-shaped patch in the pillow, and was just drifting happily back into slumber when reason finally caught up with her.

Mary's eyes snapped fully open. She was in bed, unclothed, with Vaughn. Gazing disjointedly around her, Mary remembered that this had seemed like a very good idea the night before, under the cloak of darkness, with morning miles away.

It was tempting to think of nestling back in the curve of Vaughn's arm, beneath the burrow of blankets they had created for themselves, subsiding into the sleepy warmth of the bed, next to the even rise and fall of his breathing. Vaughn occupied the bed as he did everything else, like a conqueror presiding over a subject land, arms and legs flung any which way.

Outside, the sky above the trees was still night dark, but with the indefinable gray tinge to it that signaled dawn soon to come. Within the hour, the first gray light would permeate the sky. The street vendors would creep from their burrows to set up their stalls and hawk their wares; servants would roll heavy-eyed from bed to build the fires and black the grates. In no time, the street would be thick with curious passersby and her reputation would be even more of a nullity than it was already. No matter what promises Vaughn had made in the night, it wouldn't be fair to force his hand that way.

It did briefly occur to her, as she squirmed reluctantly out from under Vaughn's arm, that she had been willing to force Geoffrey's hand in a far more dramatic fashion. But that was different. She hadn't really cared what Geoffrey thought about her in the end, so long as she got him to the church on time. Vaughn, on the other hand . . . Mary winced as several strands of hair parted company with her head. Even her hair turned traitor and clung to him, preferring to stay in bed with him than go with her. She would take him on whatever terms she could have him. Mary winced away from consideration of the consequences; there would be time enough to think of that later.

Scooping her hair out of the way, Mary conducted an anxious check of Vaughn's vital points. The bandage was still firmly around his chest, and while there were ominous brown stains on both the bandage and smearing the sheets beneath him, none of them looked new. His head was warm, but no warmer than one would expect after a night under a down comforter. Like a cat, Vaughn clearly had nine lives. They would have to see that he didn't risk any more of them. There was no telling how many he had already used up.

Shivering in the morning chill, Mary scooped the discarded robe off the floor and wrapped it firmly around as she tiptoed to the door. The faithful Derby didn't disappoint her. Just outside the door, her clothing had been folded in a neat pile, cleaned and pressed as promised. Even with his ministrations, there were dark stains in the fabric where Vaughn's blood had set. Those would be amusing to explain to her little sister. There was no hope that it could be hidden from her. Nothing that passed through Pinchingdale House escaped Letty's eye.

The canvas stays felt stiff and clumsy on her ribs after the glorious freedom of silk. It had been so easy to untie, but struggling back into it was another thing entirely. After several uncomfortable moments with her arms contorted behind her back, Mary came up with the cunning notion of shifting it around, lacing it up the front, and then wiggling it around to the back. As she was engaged in this laborious process, she heard a rustle of bedclothes. Twisting her head over her shoulder, she saw a disheveled head peering over the mound of sheets and blankets.

"Fleeing my bed?" Vaughn demanded groggily, groping for the carafe of water at the side of the bed. "You'll make me feel unloved."

"Sleep," Mary urged, twitching her stays into place. "It's not morning yet."

"Then there's no reason for you to go," he yawned. "'"Tis true, 'tis day, what though it be? O wilt thou therefore rise from me?'"

If he could indulge in quotations before breakfast, he was clearly feeling better. Mary yanked her dress down over her head. "I will call to see how you're getting on," she promised. "Properly chaperoned, of course."

Brows drawing together, Vaughn pushed himself up against the pillows, wincing as the movement pained his side.

"Are you having second thoughts?" he demanded. "If you are . . ."

"No," said Mary briefly, and watched as he relaxed. "No. Just a care for consequences. If anyone were to see me here, before you settle matters with your wife . . ."

"I hate it," said Vaughn grumpily, his dark hair sticking up around his head. "I want to parade you through the halls of St. James, flaunt you at the theatre, and keep you in bed all bloody day. Not in that order," he added.

Seating herself on a silk-upholstered chair, Mary laced up her boots, tying off the ends in neat knots. "Soon enough," she said soothingly, wishing she really believed it. "For now, sleep. We'll talk tomorrow. Today, rather."

It wasn't his sincerity she doubted, but his ability to bring it about. Even for the great Lord Vaughn, a properly wed wife was a rather large impediment. And there were even more pressing concerns to tend to. Such as keeping him alive.

"I'll fix it," Vaughn muttered, his voice indistinct among the bedclothes. "Somehow."

Without approaching the dais, Mary tied the strings of her bonnet beneath her chin. "I'll send Derby in to you if I see him. Someone should watch over you until the danger of fever is past."

"I'll send for my solicitor. Hargreaves. He'll know how to go about it. These lawyer chaps always do. Heretofores and wherefores and more stratagems than a battalion of scheming Greeks."

Mary paused at the foot of the dais, looking up at the bed. It took all the resolve she had not to climb the two steps, sit down beside him, take his hand. From there, she knew, it would only be a short slide to slipping down beside him.

"Send for the physician first," she advised briskly. "You'll be no good to either of us otherwise."

The doorknob was a hard lump beneath her palm. It was only through sheer force of will that she forced herself to turn it, breaking open their enchanted nest, where the rumpled bedsheets, the robe on the floor, the very movement of the shadows on the wall were all redolent of Vaughn. If only she could draw the drapes, pull closed the bed curtains, and keep the world permanently at bay while they drowsed together in perennial night.

But dawn would come. It was only a matter of time before the candle drowned in its own wax, before the sun poked insolently through the drapes, before the world once again was too much with them.

Taking a deep breath, Mary drew the door shut behind her, shutting out Vaughn's voice, halfway to sleep, murmuring, "There must be a way. . . ."

Outside, in the hallway, all was dark and still. The candles in the sconces had long since been snuffed and there was no natural light to make her way. Mary felt like the heroine of a fairy tale after the enchantment had faded, making her way out of a palace where all had been lights and revelry, but, by the cock's crow, turned dark and deserted, like fairy gold that turned to dust by the light of day. Mary found her way to the main stair by memory and touch, keeping one hand running lightly against the wall until she found the banister. Down, down, down she went, her flat-heeled boots making a dull slapping sound against the shallow marble treads. She didn't think it was fairy gold that Vaughn was offering her. Not intentionally, at any rate.

If he were free . . .

Mary let herself out through the garden, keeping her bonnet close around her face as she slipped through the formal parterres that either Vaughn or one of his ancestors had laid out in the French style behind Vaughn House. The garden had already been readied for the colder weather. The marble statues were shrouded in burlap sacking to protect them against the elements, anonymous but for the odd bits of appendages that stuck out at the edges, a daintily arched foot here, a long tail there. The fountain in the center had been drained, already taking on that frostbitten grayish white tone common to stone in winter, and the base of the boxwood shrubs had been carefully banked with a preparation of bark and wood chips to protect them from the coming winter frost. Only the gravel beneath Mary's feet remained unaltered, constant season in and season out.

It was ridiculously easy to slip out of the house and through the garden gate. Which meant, thought Mary, casting a look of deep misgiving over her shoulder at the serried ranks of shrubs behind her, that it would be just as easy for someone to slip in.

From Vaughn's garden, it was only a short way back to Grosvenor Square. Mary stayed to the alleyways and dark corners, brooding over the problem of the Black Tulip. What if they put it about that Vaughn had died from the bullet wound? Mary instantly discarded that idea as unworkable. His heir would descend like a buzzard; curious members of the *ton* would throng the gates of Vaughn House; and Mary rather doubted Vaughn would meekly consent to play dead for the length of time it would take to find and kill the Black Tulip.

Entering by the servants' gate, Mary let herself quietly into her brother-in-law's house. The servants' hall was empty and quiet, the grate still thickly spread with last night's ashes. Vaughn could retreat for a month to his estates in Northumberland—but who was to say that the Black Tulip wouldn't have agents there, too? Accidents were so easily arranged in the country. There was something that nagged at her, something the Black Tulip had said that didn't quite make sense.

To be fair, there was a good deal the Black Tulip had said that didn't quite make sense. With her skirts quietly whispering against the worn back stairs, Mary tried to recapture those unpleasant moments before the Black Tulip had pressed her finger down on the trigger, sending Vaughn tumbling headlong into the grass. Mary hastily wrenched her mind away from that image, trying to force herself to focus on the Black Tulip's voice, the murmur of words in her ear. What was it he had said? Something about *your Vaughn,* followed by ... Memory clicked into place, the Black Tulip's voice clear in her ears. *He has a wife, you know.*

She knew, all too well. But how had the Black Tulip?

Creeping up the back stairs, Mary slipped through the green baize door into the front hall, where the Greek gods and goddesses in their arched niches scowled down at her. Mary scowled back at them, her mind busily belaboring the possibility of a connection between the Black Tulip and Vaughn's curiously resurrected wife. Was it sheer co-incidence that Vaughn's wife and the Black Tulip had both been in Hyde Park at the same time, with a bullet meant for Vaughn?

In the corner of the room, one of the statues lurched to life and stumbled towards her.

Mary instinctively lurched back, arms coming up in self-defense, before realizing that it wasn't a statue, but her sister, draped in a volu-minous shawl over what was clearly last night's dress. Tripping over the fringe of her shawl, Letty stumbled to a halt. Rubbing the sleep out of her eyes, she blinked blearily at Mary.

"Thank God," she said heavily, catching at the foot of a statue of Artemis for balance. She moved as though her limbs pained her, which wasn't surprising, considering that the marble bench she had been occu-pying lacked cushions, arms, or back. "You're all right. You *are* all right?"

"Yes." Mary moved warily into the room, keeping a watchful eye on her sister. Letty looked far worse that she did. Her upswept crown of curls had been squashed to one side from leaning against the wall, and the weave of her shawl had imprinted itself across one cheek. "I'm per-fectly well."

Letty closed her eyes. "Thank God," she repeated.

Her wide blue eyes roamed with dismay over the splotches on Mary's dress, the disarranged hair shoved up under her bonnet.

"How did you—no. Where did you—" Something in Mary's face must have stopped her, because she broke off with a strangled laugh. "Never mind. It doesn't matter. It's enough that you're back. And safe. Really, it is," she repeated, as though trying to convince herself.

Her very freckles looked like they were about to pop off her cheeks with the strain of keeping her flood of questions from bursting forth.

"You are the eldest, after all," Letty added, rather desperately, twist-ing her hands in the fabric of her skirt in that way she always had when she was anxious. "There's nothing I can tell you that you don't know already. And it's your life. I can't organize it for you."

She looked pleadingly at Mary. Her shawl trailed down drunkenly over one shoulder like a Scotsman's ceremonial plaid, and her hair stuck out to the right, but there was a certain heroic dignity about her as she lifted her chin and announced, "I'm not going to ask."

Mary had never been so fond of her little sister as in that moment. Crossing the room to her sister, she bent, and kissed her lightly on the cheek.

"Thank you," she said, and then she turned and went upstairs to bed.

Chapter Twenty-Seven

"What was Dempster planning to do, sell the papers on the black market?" I made a face at Colin over my wineglass. "Is there even a black market for old documents?"

As far as I could see, his theory about Dempster's raiding his archives for monetary gain was as full of plot holes as a Gilbert and Sullivan operetta.

Colin made a face right back, only he looked cuter doing it. "It's not the documents themselves that are worth money to him; it's the identity of the Pink Carnation."

"How?" I demanded. "It's not as if the French would still be willing to pay money for that information. Not unless he's living in even more of a dream world than I am."

"He might be, for all that," said Colin. "But that's not the point. The French might not be willing to pay that sort of money, but there's more than one publisher who would."

"For the identity of the Pink Carnation," I said flatly. "Now you're the one living in a dream world. It's certainly big news from a scholarly standpoint, but why would anyone else care? And scholars don't generally make up a big portion of the book-buying market."

"History sells. It sells well. And the Pink Carnation is just the sort of figure to catch the public imagination. Especially since . . ."

"Yes, yes, I know," I said hastily, glancing quickly around to make sure no one else was listening. "The whole woman thing. A new heroine for our times, blah, blah, blah."

"And real," Colin stressed. "Not a made-up heroine, but a real one, with documentary proof to back it up."

"I see," I said slowly. Dempster's crazy motive was beginning to seem less crazy by the moment. "There'll be History Channel programs, a made-for-TV movie . . ."

"Book deals, movie deals . . . ," Colin continued.

"Maybe even a *20/20* special," I finished grimly. Certainly enough to make it worth Dempster's while seducing a pretty and somewhat neurotic twenty-something to obtain access to her family's papers. "Damn. But why would he get the money? Why not you, as the keeper of the papers? Why would all the rights suddenly belong to him?" As you can tell, my knowledge of intellectual property rights is not exactly extensive.

"As long as he publishes first, it doesn't matter who owns the papers. I can only protect the papers themselves, not the information in them. If he wrote a book about the Carnation, and the BBC based a program off his book, he's the one they would have to pay."

I mulled that over for a moment. "Even if he succeeded in conning Serena—or me—into giving him access to the information, he's not the only one who knows the secret. You know, I know, your aunt knows . . . How does he guarantee one of us doesn't scoop him?"

Colin twirled his glass so the wine swirled in a circle like a burgundy sea. "While I would hate to admit to knowing how a mind like Dempster's works, I would guess that he's banking on my and Aunt Arabella's having our reasons to keep the story quiet. We wouldn't go out and publicize it for the very same reasons we haven't done so all these years. As for you," he added, before I could get my mouth open to ask him just what those reasons might be, "it's common knowledge that the academic press moves as slowly as the windmills of the gods."

I couldn't fight with that one. A friend of mine had had the same article waiting for publication for two years. Not a book, mind you. An article. All of twenty-five pages including end notes. The journal with her article in it had been supposed to come out in spring of 2001. It was now autumn of 2003. She was still waiting.

Colin set his wineglass down with an authoritative clink. "By the time you got your dissertation written, all your footnotes in place, and your manuscript placed with one of the university publishing houses, he would have time to publish five times over. And I would be willing to wager," he added delicately, "that Dempster's book will be written in a rather more sensational style."

"Are you impugning my writing style?" I demanded.

Colin raised both brows. "Popular nonfiction doesn't have footnotes. At least, not as many."

"Fair enough," I said. "I'll grant you all that."

"And," added Colin, "even presuming that it doesn't play out precisely that way, it doesn't matter. The point is that Dempster believes it could."

"How do you know so much about what Dempster believes or doesn't?" I challenged.

"He did date Serena for nearly a year. I had a good deal of time to observe."

And it hadn't been all pleasant observations, either, from the set of his mouth.

"Okay," I said. "I'll buy your argument. Dempster believes that your family papers are the key to making his fortune."

"He has," Colin pointed out, "expensive tastes."

"I did get that." Those socks hadn't come cheap. "And an archivist's salary is probably peanuts. Anything interesting always is."

Colin raised his glass. "Do I detect a hint of bitterness?"

"Call it world-weary resignation."

"At the advanced age of—?"

"Well past the age of consent, if that's what you're worried about," I shot off, and then went bright red again. Why do I always say these things without thinking? "How old is Dempster?"

Colin accepted the change of subject, although a faint smile played around his lips. "Too old for my sister."

"Clearly." I paused to consider the problem of Serena. "What about one of your friends for her?"

Being a boy, this idea had obviously never occurred to him before. "For what?" he asked warily.

"To date, of course! That's the whole point of an older brother," I explained. "To provide eligible friends. If you hadn't been remiss in your duty, she would never have been reduced to dating Dempster."

After I'd spoken, I realized that wasn't the most politic comment I might have made, under the circumstances, but fortunately Colin took it in the spirit in which it was intended. "And your older brother?" he asked. "Did he play his role properly?"

"I didn't have one," I admitted mournfully. "I asked my parents for one, but they pointed out that by the time I was born it was too late to remedy the situation. What about Martin for Serena? He looks like he could use a little cheering up."

Colin looked skeptical. "They've met dozens of times over the years. If anything were going to happen, wouldn't it have happened?"

I was too in love with my theory to let it go that easily. "But there was that other woman was Martin was seeing. And, besides, he might have felt inhibited because Serena's your little sister."

"So," Colin said, with the air of a man turning over a flawed theoretical theorem, "what you're saying is that as Serena's brother, I ought to fix her up with my friends, but because she's my sister, none of them will be able to date her."

He had a certain point there. I chose to ignore it.

"Details, details," I said airily. "Is it just the two of you?"

It was. And by an amazing coincidence, it was just the two of us in my family, too, me and Jillian. He had a sister; I had a sister. He was the eldest; I was the eldest. By the time our main course arrived, we were positively swimming in similarities—and in red wine, but that had nothing at all to do with it. Clearly, our compatibility was of a higher order. He watched TV; I watched TV. . . .

There, some differences arose. We discovered that we both liked

Blackadder, but he confessed to an unaccountable fondness for *Red Dwarf* (what is it with men and spaceships?), and refused to see any merit in *Monarch of the Glen*.

"The young laird returns to restore the family castle?" Colin said scornfully, stabbing at his lamb shank. He had, manlike, gone straight to the largest hunk of meat on the menu. "Not bloody likely."

I looked pointedly at him.

"Mine isn't a castle," said Colin hastily.

"Uh-huh."

"And I'm not Scottish."

"Of course," I purred.

"And my housekeeper doesn't fancy me."

"Ha!" I said. "You *have* watched the show."

Colin rapidly changed the subject.

We both agreed that the current craze for reality television was a blight upon civilization.

"Imagine having your private life laid out for public view," I said with a shudder of distaste. "And doing it to yourself like that. Do people have no shame?"

Colin, it turned out, had a guilty passion for American television, especially old *Law & Order* reruns. I wondered if he secretly fancied himself as a tough New York cop, much the way I secretly fancy myself as a 1920s dowager with a lorgnette, neither of which species really exists anymore. It was really rather cute. Admittedly, at that point I would have found anything Colin said really rather cute.

By the time the check had been proffered and neatly snatched up by Colin (ten points to him on the first-date scale), the entire evening was encased in a warm haze of tannins and flickering candlelight. It felt like we had lived half our lives at the little red-draped table in the corner of the restaurant, rather than a mere two-and-a-half hours.

As we strolled out the door into the drab November night, it seemed the most natural thing in the world for Colin to sling an arm around my shoulders.

"So," he said, with a devilish grin that would have made any maiden's heart go pitter-pat, "when did you decide it wasn't just my archives that interested you?"

"Did I say that? Hey!" I squirmed away as he applied pressure to my waist that felt like it would have been meant to be a tickle if I hadn't been wearing a heavy layer of quilted Barbour jacket over an equally thick sweater. But it was the thought that counted. "All right, all right. I think it was our midnight cocoa."

"Ah," said Colin wisely. "I always knew my culinary skills would win me a woman one of these days."

"Oh yes," I agreed. "The way you stirred that cocoa powder into hot water was entirely irresistible."

We paused just in front of the little Pakistani convenient store, grinning foolishly at each other. It didn't seem possible that this was the same place where I bought my milk and the odd candy bar. The light from the window shone benevolently over the pavement, sprinkling it with a thousand tiny stars.

"You know what it really was?" I said.

"Not my hot chocolate?"

Was that what they were calling it now? Fortunately, I had just enough of an internal filter left not to say that out loud. No point scaring him away before I'd even gotten a first kiss out of him.

"No," I said firmly. "That night was the first time I saw you smile. Before that, you just kept scowling at me. But then you smiled, and—" I shrugged helplessly. "Well, it looked good on you."

Colin reprised the facial expression in question. "I couldn't help it. You looked so delightfully absurd in Aunt Arabella's old nightgown, banging into the walls trying to find the kitchen."

Absurd wasn't quite the reaction I had being hoping for. I would have preferred sexy, stunning, irresistible. Even cute would have done. But the way he looked at me as he said it made the actual adjective irrelevant.

"You called me Jane Eyre," I reminded him.

"Singularly ill-advised on my part, if that makes me Mr. Rochester."

"No wives in the attic?" I asked.

"You can check next time you come down to Sussex, just in case I overlooked one."

The way the conversation was heading reminded me of that day's research. I almost piped up with the news about Lord Vaughn's re-appearing wife—but then thought better of it. This was one date where the Pink Carnation wasn't going to be a third party. For once, it was just the two of us. No French spies, no ambitious archivists, no un-expected interruptions.

Besides, having just assured Colin that I liked him for more than his archives, it seemed a little tactless to bring them up again so soon.

"When did you decide that I wasn't an evil interloper?" I asked, snuggling into the crook of his arm and tipping my head back at an im-probable angle to look up at him. I achieved an excellent view of the side of his jaw.

"Hmm." Colin considered. "I guess it would have to be seeing you in that ridiculous, oversized nightgown with your toes poking out at the bottom. You looked like a Victorian orphan."

"I thought I looked like Jane Eyre," I said indignantly. After all, if one is going to be likened to literary characters, they should at least be heroines, preferably of the attractive variety.

"Who was a Victorian orphan," Colin pointed out smugly.

"Fine," I grumbled. "So she was. But I draw the line at being gover-ness to your illegitimate ward."

"She'll be so disappointed."

I slapped him companionably on the arm as we crossed the curb to-wards the row of narrow white houses that took up one side of Craven Hill Gardens. There wasn't much of a garden about it, just a narrow patch of green in the middle, surrounded by an iron fence, against which we put our garbage out to be taken away.

"Well, this is me," I said, as we drew up in front of Number 9, which looked exactly like all the other numbers.

I floundered about for the right thing to say next. *Kiss me, you fool!* would be to the point, but not exactly subtle. I couldn't invite him to see my etchings because I didn't have any etchings. It didn't seem quite right to invite him downstairs on a first date. Moral considerations aside, there was no need for him to view the bra I had left dangling over the back of a chair, the dirty dishes in my sink, and the big pack of tampons next to the toilet. I hadn't had time to shave, there were undiscovered cultures growing in my hair, and Grandma wouldn't approve.

"Would you like to see the hallway?" I blurted out.

"I can imagine nothing I would enjoy more," Colin said courteously. Too courteously. He was laughing at me. And who wouldn't? I might as well have asked him if he had any interest in inspecting my fuse box. It would have been just as subtle.

My fingers fumbled with the key, and I nearly dropped it before getting it into the lock on the second try.

"Need a hand?"

"Nope, fine," I said, triumphantly shoving open the door, which had a tendency to stick. It gave way with a suddenness that sent me staggering.

"Voilà," I said slightly breathlessly. "Welcome to my humble hallway."

Well, the building's hallway, at any rate. On the radiator, the day's mail had been left out for the residents to sort for themselves. Straight ahead was the staircase that led down into my basement flat, carpeted in a drab blue, mottled with mud and spilled coffees. The bulb in my stairway was out again. If I didn't know better, I'd think goblins ate them. Since grown-up graduate students aren't supposed to believe in goblins, the more likely theory was that the people in the other basement flat purloined the bulbs for their private use. Either way, the dim light somehow made the blue-flowered wallpaper seem even bluer, creating a general impression of Victorian dinginess.

Sticking his hands in the pockets of his Barbour jacket, Colin looked around, from the streaked mirror above the radiator to the cracked and peeling wallpaper. It was a far cry from Selwick Hall.

"It's very . . . blue," he said.

"So it is," I agreed, nodding furiously. Couldn't fault his color sense there.

His gaze fixed on mine, in a way that made the hallway seem a good deal smaller and warmer than it actually was.

"But not," said Colin softly, "as pretty as you."

And before I could point out that "you" rhymed with "blue," Colin leaned that crucial inch forward and I turned into a great big pot of goo. In fact, I'm sure I would have thought of goo, had I been doing any thinking. As it was, my attention was focused on more important things, like staying upright and not sending us both toppling backwards into the radiator, which would have had the unfortunate corollary of putting an end to the kiss. It wouldn't have done much good to the mail, either.

Don't ask me to recount the mechanics of it. I can't remember them. All I know is that somehow, my head tilted back when it was supposed to tilt, and our lips met the way that lips are supposed to meet, and our noses didn't cause us any trouble at all. His hand fit very nicely in the small of my back, just as if it had always been meant to be there, and it took a full five minutes at least for my hair to work its way into his mouth.

We parted to arm's length, beaming at each other as though one of us had just said something very clever. My lips were tingling and my cheeks were bright red and one of my contact lenses had definitely worked its way up under my eyelid. I felt utterly splendid.

"I like your hallway," said Colin, spitting out a strand of my hair.

I beamed at him. "Me too."

There had never been a lovelier color than blue.

Reluctantly, Colin released my shoulders and took a step back. "Shall we do this again sometime? Like tomorrow?"

Hooking the strap of my shoulder bag with my thumb, I hoisted it back onto my shoulder. "Maybe tomorrow night, I'll even let you see my flat," I said archly.

Colin arched an eyebrow. "Is it blue, too?"

"No." I tagged along after him to the street door, leaning against it as he stepped out onto the stoop. "It's beige. Very exciting."

Colin smiled in a way that made me very glad I was leaning against the door. "I'll look forward to it."

"Me too," I said breathlessly. "Oh, me too."

Chapter Twenty-Eight

He which hath business, and make love, doth do
Such wrong, as when a married man doth woo.

—John Donne, "Break of Day"

"Anne? In league with the Black Tulip?" Vaughn raised an eloquent eyebrow. "My dear girl, the bullet went through my shoulder, not my brain."

Under the usual layers of linen and wool, the area in question ached like the very devil. Tailored to be formfitting, his coat had not been meant for the extra padding of a bandage, even one stripped down to the very minimum. His valet's tentative suggestion of a sling had been summarily dismissed with all the derision it deserved. A Vaughn put weakness on public view? Unthinkable.

His head ached, his arm ached, he had a wife on the loose, and he had been summoned to Pinchingdale House at the inhuman hour of noon to discuss the fact that a crazed French maniac was out for his blood. In short, he was not in the best of moods.

His sarcasm didn't even raise a welt on its intended victim. Mary crossed both arms across her chest and stared him down. "How else would the Black Tulip know you had a wife?"

"The man *is* in the business of collecting information."

And the devil only knew that Anne wasn't exactly being subtle. Vaughn only hoped she hadn't trumpeted her resurrection to anyone else just yet. He had already made an appointment with his solicitors for the following afternoon, to discuss the troublesome matter of a reappearing wife. The less gossip she generated, the better.

As Mary drew breath for what was clearly another well-reasoned and completely irrelevant argument, Vaughn neatly cut her off by sliding his good arm around her waist. "Must we continue with this tedious topic? I can think of far better uses for a darkened room."

Mary shoved at him without conviction. "As tedious as it may be to you, I happen to find your continued existence a matter of some concern. One would think you might, too. Immortality doesn't come to you along with the earldom, you know."

"I should hope not," Vaughn teased, sliding his hands up her arms to her shoulders. His bad arm twinged in protest, but it was worth it just to see her tilt her head up at him with that sloe-eyed glance that was more effective than a hundred other women's come-hither stares. "Or I would never have inherited."

Mary gave him the sort of look Vaughn imagined Queen Elizabeth must have bestowed upon her courtiers. Right before sending them to the Tower. "You know very well what I mean."

"Could it be," Vaughn asked delicately, "that you are worried about me?"

Mary's eyes shifted away in an evasion that was as near a victory as Vaughn was going to get. "I don't know why I should be, since you clearly aren't the least bit worried for yourself."

Hearing what she hadn't said, Vaughn gathered her closer, resting his cheek against her hair. Despite her irritable words, she came into his arms without protest, leaning against him as though she needed the comfort, too.

Vaughn rubbed his cheek against the sleek fall of her hair. It smelled faintly of expensive French perfume, a sophisticated extraction of flowers that had long ago ceased to have anything to do with nature.

"There must be a way out," he murmured.

"Of course there is," came the crisp voice from beneath his ear. "We question your wife."

Frowning, Vaughn pulled back to look down at her. "It won't do any good."

"Oh, won't it? You just don't want to admit that someone who once shared your bed might want to murder you."

Vaughn dropped his arms and took a step back. "I never said anything of the kind."

Mary arched both brows. "Then why are you so reluctant to admit that your wife might be involved?"

"Because"—Vaughn clasped his hands behind his back and strolled towards the window with exaggerated deliberation—"Anne has all the political inclination of a stoat."

"Even stoats might be bribed."

Vaughn made a great show of examining the weave of the draperies. Dull stuff. The Pinchingdales had never had any flair for fashion. The same could not be said of his sometime spouse. "I doubt the French treasury could afford her."

"There is another possibility," Mary's cool voice said behind him.

Turning, Vaughn spread both hands wide in a gesture of invitation and derision. "I am all agog. Divine revelation? Possession by demons?"

"Lady Hester Standish," said Mary crisply.

"Definitely a demon."

"You did say that she had revolutionary leanings."

"With which she inspired my dear not-quite-departed wife? You forget. I did know Anne quite well at one point. She had no interest in her aunt's theories."

That has been one of the many little disappointments of their brief marriage. At the time, Vaughn had thought of himself as something of an intellectual—a philosopher, a wit. He had lost that delusion several years ago and moved on to the more attainable role of cynic.

"No," said Mary, her eyes brilliant even in the dim room. "But she does presumably have an interest in her aunt. What if Lady Hester is our Black Tulip?"

"What if the King were a rosebush?"

"A *rosebush*?"

"I was," said Vaughn with dignity, "simply underlining the absurdity of the notion. Lady Hester is sixty if she's a day—"

"But remarkably spry."

"—and has not, to my knowledge, been abroad for the past fifteen years."

"To your knowledge," countered Mary. "That doesn't mean she hasn't been. She only opens her house for the Season, just like everyone else. Where is she for the rest of that time?"

She did have a point, although Vaughn was damned if he was going to concede it. "Presumably, she retires to the country. Just like everyone else."

"But how can you be sure that's where she goes?" Mary argued. "I've certainly never been invited to a house party there. Have you?" Taking his silence for assent, she went on, "I saw Lady Hester at Vauxhall and again at Hyde Park."

"You also saw Turnip Fitzhugh."

"Not in Hyde Park."

"If I were the Black Tulip," pointed out Vaughn, "I would take pains not to be seen."

"Unless you expected others to use that reasoning," said Mary triumphantly. "In which case you would take pains to be seen as much as possible. Hiding is so obvious."

The tangled logic was making Vaughn's head ache. Or perhaps it was the aftermath of the opium. "You seem to have overlooked the slight problem of sex. Isn't the Black Tulip meant to be a man?"

Mary exuded smugness and French perfume. "Yesterday, the Black Tulip was wearing a dress." Looking remarkably pleased with herself, Mary swished herself and her skirts onto an overstuffed settee. "It all adds up quite nicely. Lady Hester's voice is low enough to be taken for a man's, and her features are mannish enough to pass for a man if she had to. Her long absences from town could hide trips abroad. And she is the person most likely to command her niece's allegiance."

Vaughn lowered himself onto the settee next to her, saying slowly, "As far as Lady Hester knows, Anne is dead."

Scenting victory, Mary seized her advantage. "As far as *you* know, as far as Lady Hester knows, your wife is dead. You don't know that she really knows that at all. It might well be quite the opposite."

"I never should have got out of bed," muttered Vaughn. "It was so wonderfully peaceful there."

"So is a tomb."

Vaughn extended his arm along the back of the settee. "A bit melodramatic, don't you think?"

"No," said Mary soberly, shifting to face him. In the dim light, her beautifully chiseled face was as pale and serious as an ancient statue. "I had my hand on the pistol when he shot at you. I saw—"

Breaking off, she looked briefly away. Her back was as straight and her face as serene as ever, but her hands gave her away. They were twisted into a knot so tight that the veins on the back of her hands stood out like blue worms.

When she spoke again, her voice was carefully light. "He's not going to stop at an appendage, you know. I haven't compromised myself just to have you killed off."

The back of Vaughn's throat tightened with a painful brew of admiration and tenderness. Admiration for her indomitable will and impressive self-control. And tenderness . . . well, because he couldn't seem to help it. It was just there, whether he wanted it to be or not.

But it wasn't in him to put any of that into words, any more than it would have been in her to acknowledge it.

Instead, he grazed his knuckles lightly across her cheek, saying with his touch what he couldn't in words.

"You haven't compromised yourself at all," he said, mirroring her tone of urbane detachment. "Not yet, at any rate. I must be losing my touch."

"I don't know why I even bother with you," Mary agreed, tilting her head back and looking him challengingly in the eye. In the depths of her gaze, something desperate glittered, something desperate and anxious, brilliant with the fierceness of unarticulated fear.

The answering spark lit in his eyes, blazing through his veins like wildfire, urgent and reckless. His voice dropped to a seductive drawl as his fingers tangled in her hair, pulling her closer. "Then I'll just have to remind you."

She laughed deep in her throat, a low sound of anticipation and triumph that set his blood pounding, and turned the question of her seduction from academic to inevitable.

Until a broadside of light assaulted his eyes and his own name was cracked over him like the blast of a cannon.

In the harsh morning light streaming through the window, a dark form loomed like an avenging archangel, seven feet tall, with a flaming sword in his hand.

Vaughn released Mary so quickly that they both nearly tumbled off the settee.

As his eyes adjusted to the light, the figure in front of the window shrunk to human proportions, and recognizable ones, at that. It was the master of the house himself, Mary's former suitor and current brother-in-law, looming in front of the window with one hand still holding the drape he had just yanked back. It wasn't a flaming sword in Pinchingdale's other hand, but Vaughn's own stick, which he held aloft in a way that boded no good to either Vaughn or his cane.

"What are you doing?" demanded Mary.

"I found this in the hall," Pinchingdale bit out, brandishing the stick like an angry aborigine.

Regaining his accustomed poise, Vaughn held out one hand. "How kind of you to return it to me, Pinchingdale," he drawled. "But it was really quite unnecessary. I would have collected it when I departed."

Pinchingdale's lips tightened, but he managed to hold on to his temper. Vaughn's opinion of him went up a notch. A small notch, but a notch nonetheless.

In carefully controlled tones, he inquired, "May I ask what you're doing here, Vaughn?"

Before Vaughn could give the obvious and inflammatory answer, Mary intervened.

"I invited him to call," she said shortly.

That piece of intelligence did little to sweeten Pinchingdale's disposition. "*You* summoned *him*."

Under other circumstances, Vaughn might have objected to being referred to in that sort of tone, but he was too busy watching Mary, who lifted her chin and skewered her former suitor with an imperious stare. "There were certain things I needed to discuss with Lord Vaughn."

Pinchingdale looked pointedly from one to the other, from Mary's tousled hair to Vaughn's rumpled linen. "A proposal of marriage, one hopes?"

For a brother-in-law, Pinchingdale was altogether too damn proprietary.

"I had heard that you prefer to deal in elopements," said Vaughn silkily.

"I am asking you, Vaughn, as one *gentleman* to another, to have a care for Miss Alsworthy's reputation."

Lifting his quizzing glass, Vaughn trained it on the other man with deliberate insolence. "As you did?"

The words sizzled in the air between them like a flaming gauntlet.

"Hello!" Pinchingdale's little wife stuck her freckled face around the door. "Why are the drapes closed?"

The rest of her followed her face around the edge of the door, garbed in a cheerful, flowered muslin that would have looked more the thing for the country than the town. It was a source of ongoing amazement to Vaughn that she and Mary had sprung from the same family. There was only one possible answer. Mary was quite definitely a changeling.

Rising, Vaughn acknowledged her presence with a carefully calculated bow. "So people won't shoot at us through the windows," he explained. "Naturally."

"If you would like to be shot at from within the room," said Pinchingdale shortly, "I would be more than happy to oblige."

"I don't think that would be very good for the wallpaper," said Letty, moving to slip her arm through her husband's in a gesture that was one part affection and two parts restraint.

"Blood does stain so," agreed Vaughn.

"A risk I would be willing to take," said Pinchingdale grimly, but Vaughn noticed that he made no effort to extricate his arm from his wife's. That might have been because she was holding on to it with both hands.

"You needn't bother," said Mary in a voice whose edges cut like glass. Rising with a dignity that commanded the attention of all, she placed herself deliberately between Vaughn and her former suitor. "Why kill Vaughn, when the Black Tulip is planning to do it for you?"

For all Pinchingdale's other flaws, no one could accuse him of being dim. His expression changed in a moment from anger to reluctant comprehension. He would, Vaughn had no doubt, have far rather blasted his brains out for seduction of his sister-in-law than joined forces with him over a common enemy. But Pinchingdale was nothing if not honorable, and when England called, he obeyed.

"Ireland," said Pinchingdale grimly.

"Among other things," said Vaughn, deriving great enjoyment out of watching Pinchingdale squirm. It was almost worth having received that bullet in the arm. "The Black Tulip has added two and two and emerged with forty-five. He thinks I am the Pink Carnation."

"But that's absurd!" exclaimed Letty. Flushing, she added, "I didn't mean . . . It's just that, well . . ."

"I couldn't agree more," said Vaughn genially. "I only wish the Black Tulip felt the same way."

"An ingenious story, Vaughn, but do you have any proof?"

Mary drew herself up to her full height. In her white gown, she looked like an avenging goddess who had forgotten her helmet and breastplate. "Isn't a bullet in his shoulder proof enough?"

"It isn't actually in my shoulder at the moment," clarified Vaughn helpfully. "It only stopped in passing."

Pinchingdale cast his eyes briefly up to the ceiling, as though seeking for divine intervention.

He received a response rather more quickly than one would expect.

A new tread sounded in the doorway, and a footman appeared, bearing a letter on a silver salver.

"A message for his lordship," he intoned.

Pinchingdale moved to take the letter.

"His *other* lordship," corrected the footman hastily, thrusting the tray towards Vaughn.

Pinchingdale cast him a startled look. "How is it that you're receiving notes in my home, Vaughn?"

Scooping up the folded piece of paper, Vaughn cracked the seal. "I can only assume that whoever it was must have followed me here."

Letty reached the drapes seconds before Mary.

"I do need some light to read," said Vaughn mildly.

Without further ado, Mary snatched the letter from him and held it up to the light herself. It was short; no longer than three lines, and whatever it was made a grim smile spread across Mary's face.

"Ha," she said.

Vaughn cast her a sardonic look. "As edifying as that syllable was, would you care to elaborate further?"

Mary waved the letter in the air like a triumphal banner before relinquishing it into his outstretched hand. "This proves my theory. It's from *her*. She wants to see you."

"I don't follow," said Pinchingdale, as Vaughn skimmed the three lines of the note.

It was, indeed, from Anne. They had much to discuss, she said. She hinted at a deal. A deal certainly hadn't been in the cards yesterday, when she staked her claim at Mary's expense. Yesterday, when the Black Tulip seized the opportunity opened by his confusion to put a bullet through him. Unless the Black Tulip hadn't so much seized the opportunity as created it himself. With the help of Anne.

"Who is *she*?" asked Letty, moving straight to the meat of the matter. Her brows drew together as she cast a startled look at her husband. "It couldn't be—"

"No," said Pinchingdale. "It couldn't be the Marquise de Montval. She was quite dead."

Little did they know that dead was often a negotiable category.

Shaking out the lace of his cuffs with studied nonchalance, Vaughn braced himself for the inevitable. They would have to be told about Anne. Vaughn had a feeling that Pinchingdale was going to be even less pleased at the notion of his sister-in-law canoodling with a married man than he had been when that man was merely one's resident roué.

"If you must know . . . ," Vaughn drawled.

"The writer is a former lady friend of Vaughn's," Mary broke in, crisply and clearly.

That was one way of putting it.

Vaughn looked at her sharply, but Mary angled her head pointedly away, refusing to meet his eye.

Pinchingdale's keen gray eyes followed them both, reaching the obvious and erroneous conclusion that the woman in question was a former mistress of Vaughn's and that Mary did not approve.

Brava, Vaughn thought. It had been beautifully done.

With her nose firmly planted in the air, Mary went on, "I believe that she has been colluding with the Black Tulip."

Pinchingdale's eyes narrowed. "You and the Black Tulip seem to share a great many of the same lady friends, Vaughn."

"Only one other," Vaughn said shortly. Something in the expression on Pinchingdale's face moved him to defend Teresa's memory. Such as it was. "She was a clever woman."

"And a vicious killer."

"Everyone has their little flaws."

Mary clapped her hands sharply together. "Boys," she said pointedly. "Might we get on?"

"Yes," Letty jumped in before the two men could shift their bad humor to Mary. "What does the note say?"

Vaughn's eyes dropped to the few sparely written lines, not at all like Anne's usual diffuse style, although it was undeniably her hand. "She asks for an assignation. This afternoon."

"Where?" asked Pinchingdale, abandoning private quarrels for the public good. At least, for the moment. Vaughn had no doubt that

Pinchingdale would like nothing better than to haul out the family horsewhip the moment the Black Tulip had been safely dispatched.

The address wasn't one Vaughn recognized. "Her lodgings. They appear to be in Westminster."

"It's clearly a trap," Mary put in. "An attempt to finish what the Black Tulip failed to accomplish yesterday."

"That does seem like a reasonable conclusion," seconded Pinchingdale.

"Then what do you suggest I do about it?" Balancing his snuff box in one hand, Vaughn neatly flicked open the lid, as though the entire discussion were one of merely academic concern. "You are, after all, meant to be the expert on this sort of affair."

If Pinchingdale caught the implied insult, he chose to ignore it. "Keep the assignation," he said briefly. "Keep it, but go armed."

Letty nodded decisively. "I like it. They wouldn't expect you to walk knowingly into a trap."

"That," interjected Mary, "is because no sane person does."

Inhaling his snuff, Vaughn coughed delicately. "Then it ought to be perfect for me."

"Perfect idiocy, you mean. I'll come with you."

"Aren't you forgetting something?" said Letty matter-of-factly.

"And what might that be?" Mary asked icily.

"Lady Euphemia's play."

"Oh," said Mary.

"You are the princess," added Letty apologetically.

"Catch the prince's eye and you might be a real one," drawled Vaughn.

"Isn't there the small matter of his wife?"

"A trifling difficulty."

Mary sighed. "If only."

Chapter Twenty-Nine

Ay, now the plot thickens very much upon us.
—George Villiers, second Duke of Buckingham, *The Rehearsal*

Vaughn went to his assignation doubly armed. He had a sword at his hip and Pinchingdale up a tree.

He hadn't intended either Pinchingdale or the tree. But whether it was for Mary's sake or, as Pinchingdale claimed, because he had as much of an interest in catching the Black Tulip as Vaughn did, Pinchingdale had insisted on following along.

"I should think," Pinchingdale had said, with a brow raised in challenge, "that you would be glad of the extra protection."

"I would," Vaughn had replied, just as dryly, "if I could be sure that you intended your bullets for the Black Tulip, rather than me."

Having ascertained that they understood each other, they had departed for Anne's lodgings in relative harmony—if, by harmony, one meant guarded silence. By prearrangement, they took separate routes, just in case anyone was watching. Vaughn went in his own carriage with the Vaughn crest emblazoned on the doors, rattling conspicuously along, while Pinchingdale took whatever shadowy and circuitous route pleased him best.

Their destination turned out to be a narrow, three-story building constructed of yellowing brick, lying hard by the jumble of medieval structures that made up Parliament. The wrought-iron railings had been painted a teal blue, presumably to complement the bright blue of the door, but the harsh elements of the English climate had already taken their toll. The peeling paint gave the railings a scabrous appearance, as though they were suffering from an acute case of leprosy. The rest of the structure appeared equally neglected. The small panes that made up the sash window were dark with accumulated grime. If Anne was, indeed, working for the Black Tulip, the French government's largesse did not extend to a generous housing allowance.

On the other hand, grimy windows had the benefit of concealing a multitude of illicit activities.

Reaching for the knocker, Vaughn lifted it fastidiously between two fingers and let it fall. The reverberations had scarcely stopped before the door was shoved open and a hand on his sleeve yanked him unceremoniously over the threshold. Behind him, the door slammed definitively into its frame.

The pressure on his bad arm made Vaughn see spots, but his other hand went unerringly to the hilt of his sword.

"There's no need for that!" said a husky voice indignantly.

As Vaughn's eyes adjusted to the gloom of the hallway, the white blur in front of him resolved itself into Anne, wearing a dress cut too low for afternoon, looking decidedly piqued to be facing several inches of cold Spanish steel. Before sheathing his sword, Vaughn took a quick inventory of his surroundings. The hallway was a narrow rectangle, windowless, furnitureless, and devoid of places to hide. A flight of stairs rose steeply to a small landing on the second story. Doors on either side opened onto sparsely furnished rooms, one on each side. They appeared to be empty. Vaughn wasn't prepared to risk his life on appearances.

"No blunt object descending towards my brain?" he queried satirically. "No pistol leveled at my heart? I'm disappointed in you. You might have run me through twice over by now."

"You've got it all wrong, Sebastian." Anne blinked up at him, the image of wounded innocence. "I've been trying to save you."

"An interesting way you have of showing it," said Vaughn mildly, keeping one hand on the hilt of his sword and an eye on the stairs.

"Why else would I have come to the park yesterday?" said Anne sulkily. "*I* was the one trying to get you away. She was the one who shot you."

Vaughn snapped to the alert. "Lady Hester?"

Anne looked at him blankly. "What has Aunt Hester to do with this?"

"Less than I thought, apparently." So much for Mary's theory about Lady Hester's career as the Black Tulip.

His wife tossed her short blond curls. "I only came to the park to get you away before you got hurt. And you wouldn't have been hurt if you'd only come with me instead of running off after *her*."

"And how would you happen to know all that?" Vaughn asked silkily.

"He told me."

"He?"

"Come into the drawing room?" Anne tugged on his sleeve, once again unerringly choosing the wrong arm.

Wincing, Vaughn followed her up the narrow flight of stairs. The Black Tulip might have picked his tools more wisely. As a conspirator, Anne was an utter failure. Visibly nervous, she kept glancing back over her shoulder as they climbed the stairs.

"You do realize," said Vaughn conversationally as they arrived at the landing, "that if you precipitate my demise, you don't get anything at all. As far as the lawyers are concerned, you're dead, you know. You'll have a very tricky time proving otherwise."

Anne cast him a wounded look as she ushered him into a small drawing room, meagerly decorated with the sort of drab furnishings one expected to find in hired lodgings. A settee with faded upholstery, two matching chairs, and a small writing desk in the corner. The pictures on the wall were equally generic, cheap etchings and muddy scenes of what looked like they were meant to be Venetian canals, painted by someone who had been no nearer Venice than Cheapside. With one exception.

Propped on the mantel, someone had placed a portrait miniature in a baroque frame so rich and elaborate it stopped just short of being a reliquary. The frame was pure gold, worth more by itself than all the other items in the room, the metal contorted into a complicated pattern of roses and thistles. On top, like a crown, glistened a red rose painstakingly constructed of ruby petals and emerald leaves.

The gentleman in the portrait miniature, while handsome enough, faded into insignificance in contrast with the casing. His head was covered by the closely rolled white curls that Vaughn could remember his own father sporting back in his youth, pulled back into a tight queue at the back with a wide black velvet ribbon. He wore a white stock and a blue sash crosswise over something that looked, if Vaughn wasn't much mistaken, like armor, a symbolic nod to an earlier age. An order of some sort dangled from the sash, detailed in brushstrokes so fine as to be nearly invisible.

Something about the miniature stirred a memory, long buried. Eyes narrowing, Vaughn rummaged through a mental catalogue of acquaintances. He knew he had seen that face before, but where? In Paris, in Rome, in Constantinople?

In Ireland?

"Port?" Anne offered, holding out a glass in a hand that trembled.

Like the miniature, the glasses were at odds with the general air of dust and dereliction. A large rose had been engraved on one side, while a thorny plant wrapped its stem around the bowl. The rich hue of the liquid turned the petals of the rose a deep blackish red.

Holding up the glass, Vaughn sniffed at it delicately. Placing it pointedly back on the table, he flicked fastidiously at the cup. "I believe I'll pass. Drink before dinner can be so injurious to one's health."

Crystal chimed against crystal as Anne clattered the stopper back into the decanter. "I haven't been trying to kill you, Sebastian, really. *He* thinks I am, but that's all part of the plan. He thinks he's using me, but it's really quite the other way around. I only used him to get back. To get back to you," she clarified.

Vaughn found this newfound devotion rather unconvincing, and said so. "I find this newfound devotion rather unconvincing. You are, after all, the one who bolted."

Anne's thin fingers were playing with the stopper, easing it in and out of the neck of the decanter, as if she could stop up time or release it like the port in the bottle. "I only bolted because of you. You and Henrietta Hervey."

"Who in the blazes was Henrietta Hervey? Did she run off with a dancing master and set a fashion?"

"Music master," corrected Anne. "And you were the one she kept running off with. You had a very irritating habit of consorting with her in gazebos."

Oh, that Henrietta Hervey. "One gazebo. Singular."

"And Harriet Hounslow and Helena Heatherington . . ." Anne ticked them off on her fingers.

"Aspirates must have been the rage that season."

"I certainly wasn't."

"Was that what it was all about?" Vaughn asked incredulously. "My neglect? You had your own distractions, as I recall. Several of them, in fact."

Anne shrugged. "I was bored. Oh, don't laugh. I know it was idiocy. I know that now. At the time . . . I wanted someone to be enraptured with *me*, me and only me. François promised complete devotion. We were going to be like gypsies, frolicking in the meadows and living for love alone."

"I can't see you lasting very long in a meadow."

"I didn't. Neither did he."

"As fascinating as it is to roam the halls of memory, we appear to have strayed somewhat from the matter at hand—your gentleman friend. Your current gentleman friend," Vaughn specified. "The one who wants to see me dead."

"He approached me in Rome, where I was . . . well, rather at loose ends." Vaughn didn't need any translation to explain what that meant. "I wanted very badly to come back to England. He offered me riches beyond counting, anything I wanted, if only I would come back with him and do whatever it was he wanted me to do to get your attention. It seemed almost too fortuitous."

"Things that seem too fortuitous generally are."

"I know that," said Anne defensively. "I did realize that once I'd done what he asked, I was more likely to get a knife in my ribs than riches beyond counting."

"So you decided you were better off with me than him."

"I always intended to use him to get to you," Anne insisted. "That was the plan from the very beginning."

"Hmm," said Vaughn. He had his doubts about that.

"His promises were utterly improbable. Titles, lands, jewels . . . He kept saying that when he became King—"

"King?" Vaughn said sharply. "We are speaking of the same person, aren't we? Chap who works for the French? Likes to call himself the Black Tulip?"

"Oh yes," said Anne airily, as though it weren't the very person the English secret service had been seeking for well over a decade. Anne had always been brilliant at ignoring anything that didn't concern her personally. "But he isn't really a republican, you know. He only threw in his lot with them out of a personal grudge. That's what he told me."

Vaughn began to wonder if he were still asleep, drifting through a particularly realistic opium dream. But if he were going to dream under the influence of opium, it would be of Mary, preferably without clothing, not of a barren parlor in an unfashionable neighborhood where his unwanted spouse fed him absurd tales.

"That must have been quite a large grudge," he commented, "to countenance the overthrow of a kingdom."

Anne donned her thoughtful look. "He said something about an eye for an eye, that the French King had refused to help his father regain his kingdom, so he had made sure Louis lost his."

Outside, a tree branch creaked, undoubtedly Pinchingdale trying to hear better. Glancing towards the window, Vaughn's eye fell on the portrait miniature, surmounted by its crimson rose, interlaced with roses and thistles. In his golden casing, the bewigged man smiled benevolently over the room, regal as a king.

His father's kingdom. Roses and thistles. The images whirled and settled, falling together into a new, unsettling, and nearly impossible pattern.

With a sudden swift movement, Vaughn seized on the glass of port, upending the contents onto the ground, where the dark liquid seeped into the warped boards of wood that covered the floor.

"Sebastian!" protested Anne. "It's not poisoned, really."

Whether the brew was poisoned or not was immaterial. He had seen what he needed to see.

Empty, he could make out the words engraved below the rose and thistle. Entwined in an elaborate monogram were the initials *CR*, followed by the word "fiat," the common Latin command for "let it be done."

CR stood for *Carolus Rex*, the Latin name for Charles the King—or, in this case, a Charles who never was king. Prince Charles Edward Stuart, Jacobite Pretender to the English throne, had tried once to regain his kingdom by the sword and seen his hopes brutally crushed on the battlefields of Scotland. He had died years ago, while Vaughn was still a boy. He had died a ruined man, crushed by the weight of his failed hopes, abandoned by his wife, practically pickled in alcohol. That was the man in the portrait, painted before disappointment and drink had taken their toll, wearing armor in token of his eventual reconquest of the kingdom he believed to be his.

He ought to have recognized the rose and the thistle, the most common of Jacobite symbols. But why would he have? The last Jacobite rebellion had been crushed half a century ago, and all the Pretender's attempts couldn't put an army together again. There had been talk of another invasion in Vaughn's youth—but the French King, already depleted by his efforts in the Americas, had refused to bankroll it.

It couldn't be Charles Edward who waved the Jacobite standard this time. That would be a far more impressive resurrection than Anne's. If he had lived, he would be well over eighty.

But Vaughn knew now who that portrait reminded him of. The resemblance wasn't immediately apparent. One had to mentally remove the old-fashioned white wig, broaden the cheekbones, lower the forehead.

He had always assumed that the Black Tulip was, like Teresa, a confirmed idealogue, a madman with a cause. And so he was. Only the cause wasn't at all what Vaughn had assumed it would be.

"What is his name?" Vaughn demanded harshly. "His real name?"

"J-Jamie. Jamie Stuart. But he prefers to be called Your Highness."

Vaughn grabbed Anne by both shoulders. "Where is he?"

"At—at Lady Euphemia's estate in Richmond. For the play. When he heard the royal family were going to be attending the theatricals tonight . . ."

Vaughn didn't wait to hear more.

Mary was at Richmond

"Don't you see?" Anne's voice rang with satisfaction. "I've kept you clear of it. I saved you. Sebastian? Sebastian! Where are you going?"

Vaughn took the stairs two at a time. Behind him, he could hear Anne panting as she trotted down the stairs after him, but her breathless commentary didn't make a dent in the hideous scenarios unraveling through his mind. He knew what the Black Tulip was capable of; he had seen it before. But not Mary. It couldn't be allowed to happen to Mary.

"For goodness' sake, Sebastian . . . ," Anne demanded breathlessly behind him.

Vaughn slammed out of the front door as though a dozen demons were at his back. The water stairs, he decided. A boat would be far faster than trying to go overland, and they were hard by the Thames and the dock that served Parliament. As he pounded down the front steps, a figure dropped lightly from a tree, to land on the ground beside him.

"He's in Richmond," Vaughn said tersely, never breaking stride or looking at the man beside him. "With Mary."

Pinchingdale didn't need to be told twice. "A boat will be fastest."

"My thoughts precisely."

A flurry of white muslin caught up to them just short of the water stairs, and tugged on Vaughn's arm. Vaughn shook the restraining hand off.

"Him—tree!" gasped Anne, waving an arm at Pinchingdale.

"I'll perform the introductions later." Since it didn't seem like he would be able to get rid of her, Vaughn boosted her hastily into the boat. Perhaps she could be used to distract the Tulip. If she didn't decide to turn coat again, that was.

Pinchingdale hopped lightly down beside her, eyeing his shipmate in a way that suggested his wife was going to get a full account later on.

Swinging his sword out of his way, Vaughn swung down beside them, slapping two coins into the palm of the waiting boatman.

"Richmond. As fast as you can."

MARY STOOD SHIVERING in the wings of Lady Euphemia McPhee's personal theatre. Built to rival Garrick's temple of Shakespeare, the marble edifice was certainly impressive. It was also cold. While Lady Euphemia had blithely installed trapdoors for *Hamlet* (should she ever want to play Hamlet) and all sorts of complicated machinery for manipulating scenery or dropping Greek gods from the sky, she had neglected to include any fireplaces.

As a princess of Briton, Mary was draped in flowing white samite edged with cloth of gold. That translated to white muslin hung with yellow tassels that looked like they had recently come off someone's drapes, presumably Lady Euphemia's. Her long black hair, falling free to her waist, had been adorned with a filet of purest gold. In other words, painted pasteboard, to go with the equally "golden" armlets that encircled her bare arms just below and above the elbow, detailed with what Lady Euphemia and Aunt Imogen fondly believed to be ancient Druidic runes. What the Druids had to do with St. George, Mary wasn't quite sure. But, then, neither was Lady Euphemia. It was, she had explained airily, poetic license.

Onstage, *A Rhyming Historie of Britain* had only just begun, and the shuffling of feet was already louder than the voice of the narrator.

From the front row, Mary could hear her mother's voice, with more carrying quality than anything on the stage, announcing, "*Such* a clever woman, Lady Euphemia! And connected to the royal family, you know. . . . My daughter is playing a princess. Not my daughter who's a Viscountess, but the other one."

Rubbing the gooseflesh on her arms, Mary wondered how Vaughn was getting on with the Black Tulip. She would have given anything— well, nearly anything—to be out of her ridiculous draperies and in a carriage to Westminster, crouched next to a window with a pistol in her hand. Even the sight of Turnip Fitzhugh being tugged across the stage in a large rowboat failed to divert her.

Mary irritably shoved her hair back over her shoulder, twitching at the prickle of the ends against her bare arms. She wasn't sure what she was more afraid of: the vengeance of the Tulip or Vaughn being left alone with his wife.

The Tulip, she concluded after some reflection. Definitely the Tulip.

Onstage, Turnip's bearers had dropped their tow ropes with more than a little relief, depositing Turnip right in the center of the stage.

Funny that she had never noticed before just how much Turnip sounded like Tulip. All that wanted changing was the middle.

It was hard to imagine anyone who looked less like a deadly spy than Turnip Fitzhugh. According to the script, Turnip was meant to be Brutus, founder of Britain, who had fled the rack of Troy to found a mighty kingdom in a new land. With his toga falling off one shoulder (much to the appreciation of some of the older women in the audience, including Aunt Imogen), and his face screwed up in a squint as he tried to read Lady Euphemia's lips as she mouthed his lines at him, Turnip looked more like one of Shakespeare's rude mechanicals than a mythic hero.

Hitching up his toga, Turnip proclaimed, "I am bravest Brutus. From funny Troy I flee."

"Sunny Troy!" hissed Lady Euphemia.

Turnip nodded vigorously. "From funny, *sunny* Troy I flee," he declaimed proudly. "Go I now to a new place, where King I shall see— er, be."

"Heaven help England," muttered someone in the audience.

From the look on Lady Euphemia's face, Turnip's dynasty was destined to be a short-lived one.

In the wings behind him, Mary could see the other actors queuing up and servants who had been pressed into service as stagehands bustling about with scenery and props for the coming scenes. It was an eclectic collection of props, ranging from a very large ham haunch (for Henry VIII), to a scaffold (for King Charles), and finally an immense bust of George III (for George III), garlanded with flowers and balanced on a wheeled plinth. If the royal family did put in their promised appearance, the bust was due to be ceremonially rolled out, accompanied by fireworks and the entire cast singing "God Save the King" in three-part harmony.

Despite the absence of the royal family, George III was already on the move. Over Turnip's artistically bared shoulder, Mary saw His Majesty's head go past, nose first, making for the back of the stage with a speed that resulted in a near collision with a miniature version of the Spanish Armada.

The servant wheeling him was bent nearly double with the effort. That was curious in itself, since the statue was made of plaster, hollow inside. Lady Euphemia had originally intended to fill it with doves, which would burst out and flap picturesquely around His Majesty. At least, that had been the plan until St. George had pointed out that if the doves didn't expire from their captivity and make a nasty stench inside the sculpture, one was likely to soil the royal shoulders. Lady Euphemia had regretfully reconsidered, and the bust remained empty.

Or it should have been. Then why was the man having such trouble? His neck was pulled so far into the neck of his livery that it looked like his stock was eating his chin and a white wig with rolled curls on the side effectively shielded the rest of his face. But in his efforts, the wig had slipped, revealing a sliver of close-cropped black hair, a gaunt cheek, and a long aquiline nose.

Creeping as close to the stage as she dared, Mary squinted across the way. The man had moved into the shadows, bearing the King's bust along with him, but his profile was unmistakable. The sallow skin, the long nose, the oddly sunken cheeks that made her think of John the Baptist in the wilderness . . .

What in the blazes was Mr. Rathbone, vice-chairman of the Common Sense Society, doing in the wings of Lady Euphemia McPhee's pet theatre, dressed in the McPhee livery, making off with the head of George III?

Mary rather doubted that he'd had an abrupt reversal of fortune and decided to go into service.

He might, of course, be indulging in a bit of amateur espionage, gathering information to send off to his sister society in France, that society with the long name that Vaughn had reeled off with such nonchalance.

As Vaughn did everything.

Mary hastily recalled her mind from the recollection of Vaughn's other talents, and back to Rathbone, not nearly so pleasant a subject, but far more pressing. The cast of Lady Euphemia's fiasco was replete with the sisters, daughters, and wives of men of influence, the scapegrace younger brothers of members of Parliament, the cousins of the King's advisors. Any one of them might let something slip in the casual chatter as he waited in the wings, any one might have information he wasn't supposed to have.

But why make off with the King's head? Was he using it as a shield? An excuse for his presence? An act of petty sabotage? The last seemed the most likely. It would be just like Rathbone and his group of petty revolutionaries to expend their energies in symbolic statements, like replacing the King's bust with one of Bonaparte, or sticking a large red, white, and blue cockade in the royal wig.

No matter what he was doing, it couldn't be good. Mary took quick inventory of events on the stage. At the rate Turnip was blundering along, she had a good ten minutes at least, as long as Lady Euphemia didn't bludgeon Turnip to death with the script before he got to the end of his part.

Oh, well. If that happened, it should take them some time to clean the blood off the stage.

Setting her pasteboard circlet more firmly on her brow, Mary slipped quietly through the wings, weaving her way past Charles II's spaniels, who nipped at her heels, and a pillow-stuffed Henry VIII, who attempted to nip at something else entirely. Mary gave him the sort of look reserved by princesses of Briton for impertinent mortals.

There were plenty of men in the McPhee livery scuttling about, but no large plaster head. Casting a glance over her shoulder to make sure no one noticed her departure, Mary slid into the narrow space behind the backdrop, where spare scenery was propped against the wall and props laid out on a long, wooden table.

Rathbone was there, bent over the plaster head, running a long piece of string out of the royal nostrils.

Mary paused at the very edge of the backdrop, considering her next move. Despite his gaunt frame, Rathbone was still considerably taller than she was; she still hadn't forgotten the discomfort of being backed into a corner by him at the Common Sense Society. And there they had been surrounded by people. Revolutionaries, but people, nonetheless.

He might not be too happy to be surprised at his task. And if he were the Black Tulip . . . Mary surreptitiously rubbed her hands along her arms. She still bore the bruises.

Glancing quickly around, her gaze fell on the table of props. The swords were all pasteboard, flimsy things that would bend at a touch, and Robin Hood's bow had a broken string. But in the midst of it all hulked Henry VIII's ham haunch.

Mary crept closer, resting one hand on the bony end. Beneath its pink and red paint, the ham haunch was solid wood. The narrow end made a convenient handle. Closing her hands around it, Mary hefted it experimentally in the air. Muttering to himself at his task, Rathbone never turned around. Adjusting her grip, Mary raised the ham haunch over her head, and swung it down.

The haunch connected with Rathbone's head with a satisfying crunch, bowling him over sideways. He thudded against the bare boards of the floor and was still.

Gathering up her draperies, Mary leaned forward to inspect him for signs of sentience. He seemed most convincingly inert. Still alive—she could tell that from the uneven rasp of his breath—but his closed lids and the darkening bruise on his temple suggested that he wouldn't be a bother to her for quite some time. Laying the ham haunch within easy reach, just in case she needed it again, Mary knelt down beside the fallen man and used two fingers to peel back one eyelid. The pupil stared straight ahead, devoid of recognition.

Feeling rather smug, Mary rose, brushing her hands on her skirt. If she'd only had a ham haunch to hand the other day when the Black Tulip appeared . . . Ah, well, one couldn't be expected to foresee every eventuality.

Bending over, Mary lifted the string that had fallen from Rathbone's hand when he toppled over. The waxed twine was oddly gritty to the touch, dotted with dark flecks like bits of sand.

Grimacing, Mary rubbed her fingers together to dislodge the residue. Dirt? Or something else? Either way, she didn't like the feel of it on her fingers.

For whatever reason, Rathbone had threaded the string through the enlarged nostrils of the larger-than-life-size bust. Twisting sideways, Mary peered into the royal nose. There was something inside, several somethings, in fact.

Straightening her aching back, Mary eyed the bust. There had to be some other way to get to the inside. Whatever was in there was too large to have been shoved in by the nose. And Lady Euphemia's doves would have needed an outlet, too, short of striking the King's head with a mallet. That would hardly be a spectacle calculated to please the King, seeing his head broken open in effigy.

Of course! Shoving her own hair hastily out of the way, Mary reached for the tail of the King's wig. The headpiece lifted easily off, revealing the cavity below. Inside, in the large, empty space between the King's ears, someone had packed a curious contraption contrived of three small wooden barrels, banded together with metal strips, nestled in against four cylindrical flasks sealed with wax. The whole had been padded around with shreds of paper and cloth, like the nest of a very peculiar bird. The string Rathbone had been unrolling with such care had its origin in the barrel in the middle.

Utterly baffled, Mary frowned down at the King's head. Whatever the contraption was, it was clearly not meant to be in there. But what was it?

"That is," said a voice behind her conversationally, "what is commonly known as an infernal machine."

Chapter Thirty

. . . his form had not yet lost
All her original brightness, nor appeared
Less than Archangel. . . .

—John Milton, *Paradise Lost,* I

Mary dropped the plaster wig.

It clattered ominously behind her as she whirled to face the newcomer. Eight feet tall, he loomed in front of her, a martial apparition straight out of a stained-glass window. A red Crusader's cross burned against a cloth of gold tunic. Plumes bristled from a silver helmet, a regular cascade of crimson plumes, soaring into the air like the flames of a bonfire. In one gloved hand, a long spear reared halfway to the ceiling, its point towering a head above its bearer.

Mary pressed back hard against the statue, the royal nose jammed uncomfortably against her spine, until the apparition swept off his plumed helmet, reducing his height by a good foot and providing her with a view of a familiar and welcome face.

"Oh, Mr. St. George!" Mary said with a sigh of relief. "Were you looking for me? I hope I haven't missed our cue."

Without the distracting red plumes, St. George dwindled comfortably to his usual dimensions. Dressed as his mythic namesake, he was decked out in a sleeveless tabard over a flowing shirt and a pair of very tight black tights. Like Aunt Imogen, Lady Euphemia appreciated a good leg, and St. George was in possession of two of them, if not quite so good as Vaughn's. The tights ended in a pair of ridiculous turned-up shoes, with the toes curled up into points, another of Lady Euphemia's pseudo-medieval creations.

Mary smiled warmly at St. George, hoping that he wouldn't notice the body on the floor. If she could hustle him back into the wings, away from the fallen man and the mysteriously laden statue . . .

Her luck seemed to be out. Setting down his helmet, St. George squinted at Rathbone's crumpled form. Bending, he picked up the discarded ham haunch, turning it curiously over. Mary watched uneasily as he hefted it in one hand, as though testing its weight.

"Yours, I believe?" he said pleasantly.

"Only borrowed," Mary said, rapidly considering and discarding various explanations and excuses. "I believe it's meant to be Henry the Eighth's."

Unfortunately, St. George wasn't moved to discuss Henry VIII's gustatory habits. He continued to look at her, so quizzically that Mary felt herself flushing beneath the paint Lady Euphemia had smeared on her face.

With an aborted gesture at Rathbone's body, she said quickly. "I saw someone skulking around backstage. I was so rattled that I struck out without thinking. Silly me." She attempted a laugh, but it came out as hollow as the plaster head of George III.

"Is that Mr. Rathbone?" asked St. George neutrally.

"Yes," admitted Mary, her back still blocking the King's effigy. "I'm afraid your sister is going to be without an escort tonight."

St. George waved that consideration aside. Strolling in a circle around Mary, he nodded at the giant head behind her. "I take it you found Rathbone playing with that?"

"The very thing," Mary agreed, as St. George lifted the lid and peered into the innards. "What was it you called it?"

"An infernal machine," St. George explained helpfully, replacing the King's queue neatly in its place and hiding the mysterious bundles once more from view. "Like the one someone used to try to blow Bonaparte to bits four years ago."

"You mean it's an incendiary device," Mary translated, taking an automatic step away from his Majesty's otherwise benign face.

"I prefer the term infernal machine," said St. George. He didn't move from his own position, his hand resting familiarly on top of the King's head, like a man with a pet mastiff. "It has a far more winning ring to it, don't you think?"

There was something rather odd about the way he was looking at her, not with the boyish admiration he had shown over the past several weeks, but with a fixed intensity that made Mary distinctly nervous.

It occurred to Mary, for the first time, that every time she had seen Mr. Rathbone, it had been in the company of Mr. St. George. It was St. George's sister Rathbone was meant to be courting; a sister Mary had never seen, much less met.

"Certainly a more sinister one." Keeping her face and voice pleasant, Mary took what she hoped was an inconspicuous step in the direction of her trusty ham haunch. "I hadn't realized you knew so much about mechanical devices, Mr. St. George."

"I don't," he said, with his old self-deprecating smile. "That was what Mr. Rathbone was for."

"I—see."

She didn't like what she saw at all.

"You do see, don't you?" He was still smiling, his teeth very white in the dim corridor. "You see altogether too much, Miss Alsworthy. And at very inconvenient moments."

"I can un-see it, if you like," said Mary brightly, edging towards the ham haunch. "It's dreadfully dim back here, you know. It makes it terribly hard to see anything at all. I'm very good at not seeing what doesn't need to be seen."

Reversing his grip on his spear, St. George brought it down it so that the bar stood as a barrier between Mary and exit, effectively cutting her off. The pennant on the end, emblazoned with a St. George cross, fluttered in a parody of patriotism.

"I'm afraid it's too late for that, Miss Alsworthy," he said, with genuine regret. "Pity. I would as soon destroy a work of art."

Reaching across the bar, he grazed two knuckles across her cheek in a fleeting caress.

It was all Mary could do not to flinch from his touch, but long experience had taught her to hold her ground.

"Then why do so?" she suggested, in her throatiest voice.

Undulating forwards, she would have insinuated herself up against him, but the banded shaft of the spear stood between them, catching her hard in the stomach. Suppressing her involuntary gasp, she ran a finger teasingly along the embroidered line of the red cross on his tabard. "Let there be no more games between us, no more pretense. I know who you are. And you know who I am."

Letting her eyes go limpid, she slid her the flat of her palm up his chest in a deliberately provocative caress. It didn't have much effect on her captor, but if there was a pistol hidden on his person, it was exceptionally well disguised. "Isn't it time you admitted me to your counsels . . . *mon seigneur?*"

"No," he said simply, but he made no move to back away. Mary took that as a good sign.

Mary pressed closer, flirting as though her life depended on it. Which it did. It was not an uplifting thought. The only glimmer of hope she could find in the situation was that if the Black Tulip was backstage with her, he couldn't be stalking Vaughn. Which meant that Vaughn was safe. At least, for the moment.

Mary redoubled her efforts, shrugging her shoulders together to make her tunic dip in the middle. If that didn't soften him, she didn't know what would. She lowered her voice, made it soft and caressing, "Think of all the trouble you could have saved, *mon seigneur*, if only you had confided in me. Had you told me your plans, I would never have incapacitated your agent."

With a casual movement, St. George took her hand and removed it from his chest, with as much emotion as if he were plucking off a burr. Holding it high in the air, his hand closed around hers in a bruising grip.

"Yes," he said. "You would have."

Mary let her lashes dip down to veil her eyes—a necessary gesture to keep him from seeing the fear that filled them. "You still doubt me, *mon seigneur?*"

St. George's lips twisted in a cynical expression that sat oddly on his genial features. "Oh, there's no doubt, Miss Alsworthy. I know exactly who you serve."

"Myself mostly." Mary tilted her head coquettishly, sending her long, straight hair swishing against his arm, releasing a faint scent of exotic French perfume, calculated to enslave the senses. "But you, if you'll let me."

"No, Miss Alsworthy, there's no more arguing it. You failed your test. You failed your test yesterday, when you refused to pull the trigger."

"A momentary hesitation," Mary protested. "I haven't much experience of guns."

"You serve *him*," countered St. George, unimpressed. He added, with a chilling combination of scorn and pity, "You serve him because you've fallen in love with him. Others have made that mistake before you. With the same result."

Mary opened her mouth to argue, but something in his face blunted her words. There would be no more arguing. The Black Tulip had made up his mind.

Mary swallowed hard and straightened her spine, dropping her coquetry like an outgrown mask. The battle would have to be won on other grounds.

"Are you going to kill me?" she asked conversationally.

"Not yet," replied the Black Tulip, with equal sangfroid. "Lady Euphemia would notice if you weren't onstage to play your part. I want nothing disrupting my plan."

He had spoken of his plans before, in Hyde Park. Mary glanced thoughtfully at the large plaster head of the King, fitted with its incendiary device, before looking back up at the Black Tulip, her sapphire eyes keen with comprehension.

"You intend to kill the King tonight, don't you? The incendiary device—pardon me, the *infernal machine*—is to be aimed at him."

The Black Tulip regarded her approvingly. "You are a quick study. To answer your question, yes. The sealed casks contain a little something Rathbone concocted for me, an extract of air that magnifies the properties of fire."

"In other words," clarified Mary, watching him closely, "a very big explosion."

"Big enough to consume the entire brood of Hanoverian usurpers," said St. George, with great satisfaction. "It should be more entertaining than doves, don't you think?"

"That's why you talked Lady Euphemia out of putting the birds in the King's statue," said Mary. It wasn't a question.

"I had planned to blow up Parliament, in a tribute to Guy Fawkes, but when this opportunity arose, it seemed too good to pass by. Ever since the Gunpowder Plot, they do have an inconvenient habit of inspecting the cellars before the King gives his speech."

"Very inconsiderate of them," agreed Mary sarcastically. "And then? Once the King and Queen and all their offspring are blown to little bits, what then? Do you declare a republic in the name of France?"

"No." St. George's eyes burned with such intensity that Mary would have taken a step back if Rathbone's fallen body weren't blocking her way. "I reclaim what is mine. My kingdom. My throne."

"Yours?"

"Mine," St. George repeated. "Mine by right of birth."

Knowing that she was taking a calculated risk, Mary said, with deliberate provocation, "I didn't think the King had by-blows."

One large hand pinned her about the neck, pressing hard against her throat. "You insult my birth. Be born to that Hanoverian scum—never. My father was of the true line."

He released her so abruptly that Mary stumbled back, gasping, nearly tumbling over Rathbone's inert form in the process. She wondered, belatedly, whether it might not have made more tactical sense to fall. If she were to dive for St. George's legs, bringing him down with her . . .

St. George drew himself up to his full height. "My father was a

Stuart. King Charles the Third, by grace of God—though the Lord knows, he was shown little enough grace while he lived." His eyes were dark pools, churning with bitter memories. "Even the Pope refused to acknowledge him. It broke him. It humbled him. The rightful King of England and they all scorned him and left him to rot in a pit of drink and debt."

Mary refrained from pointing out that the drink and debt might well have been Prince Charles Edward's own doing.

"Bloody Louis wouldn't help him he when he asked. I remember it well. The look on his face when the word came. He hadn't the money, Louis said. Dear Cousin Louis." St. George's voice dripped scorn. It occurred to Mary with mild surprise that if St. George was telling the truth about his origins, King Louis of France really would have been his cousin, somewhere on his father's side. "But he had plenty of money for jewels for his Austrian whore. Louis wouldn't help us, so I helped Cousin Louis. I helped him right off his throne."

"Is that why you did it?" Mary said softly. "Joined the revolution?"

St. George gave a sharp laugh. "It certainly wasn't *liberté, egalité,* and *fraternité*."

His inflection made a mockery of the revolutionary ideals.

His French accent was much better than hers. It would be, Mary thought inconsequentially. If he were the son of the exiled Stuart pretender, he would have spent his childhood kicking about France and Italy. No wonder his Italian had been so fluent.

"Does Bonaparte know all this?" asked Mary carefully.

"Of course," said St. George, baring his teeth in a feral grin. "It works out very nicely for him, don't you agree? A monarch with right of blood on the throne, and he's spared the trouble of ruling England himself."

Put that way, it did seem rather a bargain for Bonaparte. If not necessarily for England.

There was one glaring flaw to St. George's plans. Mary wondered if St. George had spotted it. True Stuart pretender or not, there was no reason men would flock to his standard, just because the immediate royal family had been assassinated. There would be plots and counter-plots, factions and cabals, and at least a dozen other claimants to the throne, all pressing their right. In short, civil war.

Wonderful for Bonaparte, not so wonderful for either England or the latest Stuart pretender.

Had St. George realized that, or was he so consumed by the thought of the throne that it never occurred to him that he might be Bonaparte's dupe? From the noble glow on his face, Mary suspected he hadn't. Like all exiles, St. George seemed to believe that at the sight of their rightful king, the people would fling down their arms and follow him, strewing rose petals and singing hosannas. Other monarchs had made that mistake before. Including his father and grandfather.

Through the fabric of the backdrop came Lady Euphemia's voice, raised insistently, "And then one dark night, there came a poor princess in perilous plight."

"Ah," said St. George. "There's our cue. After you, my dear."

Using the spear as a prod, he sent her reeling in the direction of the backdrop. They were supposed to enter stage left, but with a spear in her back, even a wooden one, Mary wasn't about to be picky. Grasping the folds of the curtain, she scrabbled for the break in the middle.

"—came a poor princess in perilous plight!" Lady Euphemia repeated loudly, as Mary stumbled out onto the stage through the gap in the curtains, blinking in the sudden glare of the footlights.

Lady Euphemia gave her a look that clearly indicated that Mary wasn't going to be offered starring roles in any future productions.

That was the least of Mary's worries.

In front of her, the theatre was a sea of swollen faces, distorted by the glare of the footlights. What would they do if she walked calmly to the center of the stage and announced that there was a madman who thought he was the Pretender to the throne in the back of the stage, and that the King's head was packed full of explosives? Nothing. Well, not nothing. There would be whispering and laughing and no one would do anything at all.

St. George, hidden behind the curtains, would have plenty of time to shove his infernal machine into the audience, light its fuse, and blow as many people as possible into tiny bits. In the audience, Mary could see a slew of familiar faces, yawning, laughing, whispering, sleeping. Innocent. Unsuspecting. Her mother and father were in the first row with Letty, her mother's mouth open as she prattled on into her husband's ear, while her father nodded, not hearing a word of it. He had clearly taken the precaution of donning his earplugs before the performance.

Frowning, Mary tried to catch Letty's eye, indicating with a jerk of her head that she should get their parents out of the theatre. Letty tilted her head and opened her eyes wide, indicating confusion. Mary's lips pressed together in frustration.

She wasn't the only one feeling frustrated. A loud harrumphing noise echoed from the prompter's pit.

Mary hastily struck a tragic pose, one hand outstretched in supplication in the general direction of the audience, eyes lifted to the heavens—or where the heavens would be, if there wasn't a large dome in the way. There was no need to feign desperation.

"Oh, is there no hero, no valiant knight, / Who will charge out and put the dragon to flight?"

Lady Euphemia bobbed her head up and down in time to the lines, beaming in open appreciation of her own poetry.

Pat on his cue, St. George strode onto the stage. Good. On the stage she could see him. On the stage he was away from his infernal machine. Mary's brain churned with fevered schemes, including "accidentally" tripping him as he crossed downstage. If he took a tumble off the platform and just happened to land head first, that should put him out of commission long enough to dismantle his infernal machine and use her brother-in-law's influence to bring the conspirators to justice. St. George and Rathbone would be hanged for treason, and Vaughn would finally be safe. Married, but safe.

There was one slight hitch. St. George didn't cross downstage. Mary could hear the restless shuffling and whispering from the audience rising to new heights. Still in her pose, Mary twisted her neck to peek over her shoulder. St. George stood like a stone effigy of a medieval warrior, looking as shocked and unsettled as Hamlet confronted with his father's ghost. Lady Euphemia emitted a veritable chorus of harrumphs, but to no avail. St. George's eyes were fixed in disbelief on something, or someone, in the audience.

Blinking against the glare of the footlights, Mary followed his gaze. At first, she saw the figure haloed through the red haze of the lights, so that he seemed lit by supernatural fire as he advanced purposefully down the central aisle, the red light catching the hilt of his sword, dancing along the silver lace on his cuffs, scintillating off the great diamond on one hand.

Mary's blood rang in her ears like a fanfare of trumpets as Vaughn strode up to the stage, a sword at his hip and retribution in his gaze. He grinned, a daredevil expression that issued as clear a challenge as the traditional glove.

In one well-practiced motion, Vaughn drew his sword, the steel sliding smoothly out of its scabbard to glitter with deadly luster in the glare of the footlights.

"Good evening, St. George. Or shall we say . . . *en garde?*"

Chapter Thirty-One

"**D**amn you, Vaughn!" exclaimed St. George, rattled out of role. "You were supposed to be dead by now."

"No, no!" intervened Lady Euphemia, stomping onto the stage. "That's not your line. You were supposed to say—"

Elbowing Lady Euphemia out of the way, Vaughn sprung up onto the stage. "A common problem, it seems. A good corpse is so hard to find nowadays."

Bracing his spear in both hands, St. George sent it whipping through the air with the competence of a man who knew his way with a stick. "Not so hard as you might think, Vaughn. If one knows how to make them."

Vaughn regarded St. George's fancy spear-work with a jaundiced eye. "Haven't we had enough of theatricals? Drop that spear."

St. George brought his spear up in a defensive angle. "Never."

"Never say never," replied Vaughn suavely. His sword sliced through the air in a silver arc.

Unfortunately, the blade connected with the wooden end of the spear and stuck there, like an axe in a chopping block. The shock of it reverberated straight up Vaughn's sword arm. It didn't do his wounded shoulder any good, either. Favoring his left side, he stumbled back a step, cursing.

A broad grin of satisfaction illuminated St. George's face, lighting it to devilish handsomeness. "What was that you were saying, Vaughn?"

With some difficulty, Vaughn wrenched his blade free, taking a chunk of wood with it.

"I say, Vaughn," called out a loud voice from the audience. "Are you meant to be the dragon?"

"Can't be," replied the unmistakable tones of Percy Ponsonby. "Green, y'know. Dragons, I mean."

"Dragons," said Vaughn, his eyes locked on St. George as they circled one another on the stage, "come in many different colors. Eh, St. George? Or should I say . . . Jamie?"

"You can call me . . . Your Majesty." St. George jabbed with the spear.

Vaughn leapt lithely out of the way, opening a long rent down St. George's sleeve with a quick side slash.

"I don't think so," Vaughn retorted, his silver eyes glistening dangerously. "Not for the by-blow of a second-rate pretender."

"No, no, no!" protested Lady Euphemia, waving her arms about in the prompting pit. "The Pretender doesn't come on until the second act when we do the reenactment of Culloden."

"By-blow?" demanded St. George. "I advise you to watch your words, Vaughn."

"I don't see why," Vaughn drawled, feinting at St. George's shoulder. "A bastard is a bastard by any other name."

A shocked murmur ran through the audience, who were paying far more attention than they had to any of Lady Euphemia's carefully planned verse. Most seemed to be laboring under the delusion that the production had taken a shift for the better, and were loudly applauding every insult, with speculation on how it was meant to turn out.

"Five pounds on the dragon winning!" someone called out, setting off a flurry of competing wagers.

At the back of the room, Mary caught sight of her brother-in-law, following Vaughn's path to the stage with a look of grim determination on his face.

Sliding off the stage, Mary grabbed her former fiancé by the arm. "St. George has an infernal device behind the backdrop."

Geoffrey's brows drew together. "Explosives?"

Mary nodded. "Packed inside the King's statue. Can you get the audience out?"

"I'll deal with the audience if you clear the wings," said Letty promptly, squirming around her husband's side.

No further words were needed. Geoffrey made for the wings, hauling Lady Euphemia out of her pit with ruthless efficiency. Letty's methods were rather more conspicuous, but just as effective. Scrambling up onto a chair, Letty shouted over the din, "The Prince of Wales has refreshments on the lawn!"

The words "Prince of Wales" and "refreshments" worked their magic. Both the social-climbing and the hungry stampeded to the exit, wanting first crack at the heir to the throne and the lobster patties, respectively. There was much elbowing and shoving and poking with canes as London's elite displayed the savage spirit of their Saxon forebearers.

Leaving them to it, Mary hurried back towards the stage, where Vaughn and St. George exchanged blows and insults. She didn't like the way Vaughn's jacket seemed to be clinging wetly to his left shoulder. If the idiot would insist on fencing with a fresh bullet wound . . . St. George, on the other hand, was in prime fighting condition, his cheeks flushed with the exercise and a grin lifting the corners of his mouth. He was more broadly built than Vaughn, more heavily muscled. Vaughn was leaner and quicker—but for how long? The loss of blood was already taking its toll. He managed to jump over the sweep of St. George's spear, designed to trip him up, but there was a sluggishness to the movement, and he staggered as he landed on his feet again.

Taking advantage of his momentary imbalance, St. George raised the spear with deadly efficiency and dealt Vaughn a powerful whack on his wounded shoulder.

Going gray, Vaughn doubled over, his breath whistling sharply through his teeth. The point of his sword scraped the boards of the stage. Mary didn't think; she acted. She sprinted forwards, intent on throwing herself between them. If she couldn't stop St. George, at least she could slow him down.

"Sebastian!"

The hoarse cry hadn't come from Mary's throat, but that of another woman, fighting her way against the horde of departing guests. Breaking free from the throng, she struggled up onto the stage, using her elbows to lever herself up. Mary could hear the sharp screech of tearing fabric as a splintered edge of wood pulled at her dress. Her blond curls were disarrayed with her exertions; the porcelain prettiness of her complexion marred by red splotches on her cheeks, but Mary knew her instantly.

"Don't even think of it!" snapped Mary, making a grab for the Black Tulip's confederate.

Lady Vaughn was too speedy for her. Scrambling past, she launched herself, not at Vaughn, but at the Black Tulip. Flinging herself at St. George, Lady Vaughn latched on to the arm that held the spear, hanging heavily on to it with both arms so that the wooden shaft missed Vaughn's side and scraped across the floor with a sound like nails on a windowpane.

The Black Tulip was not amused. With a wordless growl of annoyance, St. George sent her flying with a careless backhand, stumbling backwards into one of the footlights. The glass lamp toppled over and smashed, shards of glass sparkling as they scattered, like spray from a fountain.

Off balance, Lady Vaughn tottered for a moment, arms flailing in the air, before losing the battle with gravity and falling heavily over another footlight, banging her head painfully against Turnip's discarded boat, which had been pushed to a resting place at the edge of the stage.

"Another broken vessel," commented St. George bitterly, feinting at Vaughn. It was unclear whether he meant the woman or the glass. He didn't spare so much as a glance for her fallen form.

"You seem to attract a number of those," taunted Vaughn, ducking and weaving, seeking an opening where the long reach of the spear wouldn't thwart his aim. "Why is it that you think they all desert you in the end, St. George? Could it be your looks? your breath? your mad dreams of conquest?"

For all his brave repartie, Vaughn's voice rasped in a way that made Mary distinctly nervous.

He was tiring, the strain showing in his voice and his movements, increasingly sluggish as he ducked St. George's blows. Unhealthy sweat beaded his brow, and his coat was damp with another sort of liquid entirely. Vaughn might have the real sword, but what was two feet of metal compared with eight feet of solid wood? There was no way Vaughn could get close enough to St. George to run him through without getting past that shifting barrier of painted wood. It was too heavy to send flying with a flick of his sword—an attempt bent back his wrist and nearly his sword—and too long to dart past.

Seized by a sudden inspiration, Mary slipped past the crumpled body of Vaughn's wife and snatched up a long oar from the interior of Turnip's Trojan boat. It must have been purloined from someone's rowboat; rather than a pasteboard imitation, it was the real item, a long shaft of wood with a rectangle on one end. It wasn't a ham haunch, but it was nearly as long as St. George's spear, and that was what mattered.

With her oar at the ready, Mary circled the fighters, looking for an opening. St. George was too tall to hit over the head unless he bent over first. She doubted he would be that obliging. A glancing blow to the head wouldn't do more than distract him. That moment of distraction might be all that Vaughn needed to get under St. George's guard and run him through. But watching Vaughn hop over a long sweep aimed at his shins, Mary had another idea.

St. George knew he had the winning hand. With a triumphant snarl, he pressed forwards, the spear lifted to be brought down upon

Vaughn's unprotected head. Dropping to one knee, Mary stuck the oar out in front of St. George's legs. An expression of tremendous surprise crossed his face, and he seemed to hover in the air for a very long moment. The spear went spiraling harmlessly into the air, bumping and skidding across the boards of the stage before rolling neatly off the edge.

St. George fell forwards with a tremendous thump that wrenched the oar clean out of Mary's hands. Vaughn leapt agilely back out of the way as St. George hit the ground spread-eagled, an arm stretched out on either side. A small explosion of dust motes rose and settled around him.

A faint groan emerged from the vicinity of the floorboards.

Planting one foot on St. George's back, Vaughn grinned at Mary. "Well done, dear girl."

"Thank you." Mary shrugged her hair back over her shoulders, for the first time aware of her tattered and dirtied draperies, disarranged to the point of indecency. She had lost the filet somewhere along the way, and her armlets had all bunched up around her wrists.

From the expression on Vaughn's face, he didn't seem to mind.

"My very own Boadicea," said Vaughn softly. "You could set a fashion among warrior maidens."

Mary spread her empty hands. "I'm afraid I've lost my spear."

Vaughn's eyes glinted with amusement. "I'd be more than happy to loan you one."

Mary could feel the warmth in her cheeks as she cast a reproving glance at him over St. George's fallen body.

The warmth wasn't just in her cheeks, though. All of her felt uncomfortably warm, with a prickly sort of heat that wasn't just from bawdy double entendres or the intimacy of Vaughn's gaze. In the sudden silence, she could hear a curious crackling noise, a crackle and hiss like paper being crumpled.

With a sick lurch at the pit of her stomach, Mary remembered Vaughn's wife toppling over, with the shattered glass of the broken footlights radiating out around her.

Licking her dry lips, Mary pivoted slowly, following the low trail of flame from the shattered footlights across the stage.

It ate merrily away at Lady Euphemia's prized red velvet curtains, devouring any fallen props in its wake. The flames were already licking delicately at the base of the backdrop, blackening the bottom of the painted castle. Adventurous shoots of flame wriggled upwards, scaling the castle walls.

Behind the backdrop lay the Black Tulip's infernal machine.

"Quick!" Using both hands, Mary pushing Vaughn off the stage ahead of her. He landed on both feet. Barely.

"It won't—" Vaughn began, slightly out of breath.

"An infernal machine," she said tersely, grabbing him by the hand and dragging him along behind her, anxious to put as much space as possible between them and the stage. Heaven only knew if Rathbone's contraption worked. If it did, she didn't want to find out. "Backstage."

She was too busy forging straight ahead to see the change in Vaughn's expression, but she felt it as he rocked to a sudden halt, breaking her grip. With a sharp phrase on her lips, Mary turned, just in time to see Vaughn's face, frozen like Lot's wife turned to salt, in an expression of guilt and horror.

"Anne," he said heavily. Before Mary could do anything to stop him, he wheeled back towards the stage.

Mary caught futilely at his sleeve, her fingernails grazing his sleeve with a hideous rasping noise.

"Don't—" she begged, but the sound of her own plea was drowned out as a thunderous rattle shook the stage and the world cascaded into flame.

Chapter Thirty-Two

Let me not to the marriage of true minds
Admit impediments....

—William Shakespeare, Sonnet 116

I will live in thy heart, die in thy lap, and be buried in thine eyes—
and, moreover, I will go with thee to thy uncle's.

—William Shakespeare, *Much Ado About Nothing*, V, ii

Mary woke herself with coughing, and wished she hadn't. Everything hurt. Her throat was raw, her head ached, and her bare arms stung as though they had been scratched by nettles. Even the inside of her eyelids felt gritty.

It was with great effort that she dragged them open to see a grimed face hanging over her, lit from behind with a red glow like a bonfire of brimstone. Dark figures scuttled about the infernally illuminated landscape, some standing, chatting and sipping punch, others darting back and forth with buckets. Mary winced at the sound of hundreds of voices raised in excited chatter, which competed with the hiss and crackle of the flames, and an echoing in her ears like a thousand bees buzzing. And about them all gusted great clouds of smoke, acrid with ash, searing the back of her throat and kindling the panicked memory of fire and thunder and a sudden pain that had turned the red flames to black.

The concerned face dipped closer, blotting out sight and standing as a shield against memory.

"Vaughn?" Mary tried to say, but it came out as a cross between a croak and a rasp, so she had to content herself with coughing again.

Vaughn, his cheeks streaked with ash, pressed his eyes shut, drawing in a deep breath in a way that made Mary's berth on his lap rock like a ship at sea. His eyelids looked very white against his blackened face. They were, she noticed belatedly, sitting on the ground. Not on a rug or a blanket, but right on the grass, with grass stains undoubtedly seeping into Vaughn's fawn-colored pantaloons, and Mary cradled up against him like a child in her nurse's arms.

"Do you know who I am?" he demanded roughly.

Mary made an incredulous face at him, or tried to. For some reason, the motion made the side of her face sting abominably. She put a hand up to it, and looked in some disbelief as her fingers came away wet with blood.

"You were grazed by a piece of flying masonry," said Vaughn brusquely. "Now who am I?"

Mary scrubbed her fingers together to get rid of the stain. "You're Vaughn, and as autocratic as ever," she rasped, pleased to see that her voice had returned to her, even if she did sound like an old crone. "What happened?"

Pressing her closer, so that she could smell the acrid whiff of ash and the sickly sweet scent of blood on his waistcoat, Vaughn laughed roughly, a wild laugh of relief. "What hasn't?" he asked. "Your infernal machine went off—"

"Not mine," Mary croaked hastily, and Vaughn pulled her closer in a movement that from anyone else would have been called a hug.

"The infernal machine, then." His voice was hoarse, too, but not as bad as hers. Just a little rough around the edges, like an Irish whiskey. "It exploded and brought the whole dome down with it."

Dimly, memory returned. Taking Vaughn's hand and pulling him off the stage, trying to get as far away from the explosives as possible. And then Vaughn, stopping, trying to go back—

Mary drew in a painful breath. "Did she . . . ?" she asked, not sure she wanted to know the answer.

"No," said Vaughn bluntly.

His eyes strayed towards the remains of the pavilion, belching smoke and flame. Tiny dollhouse figures darted forward, tossing their little droplets of water on the flames. The burning, writhing thing that had once been Lady Euphemia's theatre responded with little hisses and puffs of scorn, before blazing right back up again. "At least, I don't see how. She was directly beneath the dome when it fell."

The rectangular hall that had housed the audience was still largely intact, although the roof was already beginning to come down on one end. The bulbous dome that had covered the stage was entirely gone, collapsed in upon itself like an interrupted soufflé. Red flames, darker than Mary had ever imagined flames could be, flared out of the crumpled edifice, and the whole was cloaked in a writhing black cloud of smoke, like a medieval painter's vision of the torments of the damned.

A woman, unconscious beneath it, wouldn't have stood a chance. Even if the falling stones didn't kill her, the smoke or flame would.

"I am sorry," said Mary hoarsely.

Vaughn looked down at her with a curious expression of his face. "No, you're not." His lips twisted in brutal self-mockery. "And the most damnable part of it is that I'm not, either."

Mary would have protested, but Vaughn wasn't looking at her anyway. His gaze was fixed far away from her, on the burning rubble of Lady Euphemia's theatre.

"What a tombstone that is," he said softly. "What an epitaph. Fifteen years married and not even missed. Crushed out like the inconvenience she was. Poor Anne. I can't even hate her anymore. Hate might have been closer to love."

Streaked with soot, lit by the lurid glow, his features stark with self-loathing, he looked more than ever like Milton's Satan, doomed forever to be his own hell. Mary's heart ached for him, for the bleakness that shrouded his expression like the thick black smoke upon the pavilion.

"My wife's life snuffed out, and I haven't even the will to mourn her. The most I can muster is pity, the poor cousin to emotion. Anyone deserves better than that. Everyone deserves at least one person to mourn."

Thinking nasty thoughts about women who ran off with their music masters, returned to blackmail, and got themselves smothered under several tons of smoldering rubble, Mary struggled up on her elbows, managing to drive several holes into Vaughn's stomach in the process.

"She was dead already," she said staunchly. "Fourteen years ago. You can't be expected to mourn her twice."

Something in her voice brought Vaughn back from the hazy realms in which he was wandering. His eyes refocused on her face. His lips twisted in a cynical smile, but his hand was gentle as he smoothed the tangled hair back from her brow.

"My hard-hearted Mary," he said tenderly. "Always quick to seize on whatever is most convenient."

Mary winced and pulled back as the great diamond on his finger tangled in the knots and snaggles in her unbound hair. "Just because it's convenient doesn't mean it's not true."

Vaughn rested his forehead against hers, gritty with dirt and ash. "True," he agreed. "But even so."

It was very hard to argue with someone whose head was right up against yours, but Mary tried.

"I won't have you tormenting yourself," she said tartly, somewhere in the vicinity of his left ear.

Vaughn lifted his head and smiled at her, a genuine smile through the grime and fatigue. "No, that's your job, isn't it?"

There was such a wealth of meaning in his voice that Mary felt, suddenly, more than a little bit wobbly and oddly unsure of herself. She looked at him uncertainly. "Is it?"

Whatever Vaughn might have said was lost, as a sound like a convulsion of the earth erupted above them. Shifting her gaze hastily up, Mary saw that it wasn't an earthquake or a reenactment of Pompeii—Lady Euphemia devoted her energies purely to English scenes—but her sister's husband, clearing his throat loudly enough to do that organ permanent damage. Similarly smeared with soot, Geoffrey looked tired, and harried, and distinctly put out at Mary's using Vaughn's lap as her own private chaise longue.

"Is Letty all right?" Mary asked hoarsely, heading off any comments about her undeniably compromising position.

"Yes." Geoffrey's harried expression briefly lightened. "She is organizing the bucket brigade."

The stiff muscles of Mary's face involuntarily quirked into an answering smile. "I should have known it wasn't Lady Euphemia."

"Letty has matters well in hand," said Geoffrey proudly, turning to look back at the small figure of his wife, who was bustling up and down the line, making sure everyone had buckets, and understood they were to pour the water on the fire and not on one another.

Unwisely drawing attention to himself, Vaughn broke in, "Has there been any sign of—"

"St. George?" said Geoffrey, blessedly misinterpreting Vaughn's concern. "I don't see how anyone else might have got out. He was the Black Tulip, I take it?"

Vaughn nodded in assent.

Geoffrey allowed himself a grim smile. "Lady Euphemia is convinced the bomb was set by French agents determined to stymie her patriotic pageant. She's quite chuffed about it, despite the loss of her theatre."

"The more reasonable assumption," countered Vaughn, "would be an enraged poet determined to stop such an execration taking place ever again."

Geoffrey shrugged. "She's planning to publish the verse in a memorial volume and present it to his Majesty as a gift."

"Good God," shuddered Vaughn. "With allies like these, who needs the French?"

Geoffrey turned a jaundiced eye on Lord Vaughn's seating arrangement.

"You seem to have adopted certain French manners," he said pointedly. With the air of a man making a great concession, he added, "Given the events of the afternoon, no more need be said. But you might want to rectify the situation before anyone else notices."

"I don't see anything the least bit improper about it," said Vaughn blandly, as if it were entirely normal to be having a conversation sitting cross-legged on the ground with a woman on one's lap. He smiled down at Mary. "Do you, my dear?"

Mary narrowed her eyes impartially at both men in a universal condemnation of masculine folly. Neither of them paid the least bit of attention to her.

Geoffrey folded his arms across his chest in the classic pose of offended guardian. "*You* may not see anything wrong with it, Vaughn," he began darkly, "but as for the rest of civilized society—"

"Since," Vaughn smoothly overrode him, "Miss Alsworthy has done me the honor to agree to be my wife."

"Mmph," said Geoffrey, or at least as near as Mary could tell.

"Of course," Vaughn added, with a devilish glint in his eye that belied the studied indifference of his voice, "we *could* always elope . . ."

Geoffrey's soot-smeared countenance went stonier than Lady Euphemia's fallen columns.

". . . but I think St. George's, Hanover Square, is much nicer, don't you?"

Geoffrey looked like he wanted to say something decidedly improper. Calling on the reserves of self-control that made him one of the War Office's more trusted agents, he gritted out, "Have you set a date yet?"

Vaughn waved a dirty hand. "Sometime soon. You can tell your wife to start making the arrangements. Once she's done with the buckets," Vaughn added generously.

"Brilliant," said Geoffrey, and turned on his heel, presumably to report the news to his wife, although from the stiff set of his back, he looked as though he might first seek out a discreet spot where he could punch something in private and pretend it was Vaughn.

Vaughn watched his future relation's retreating back with unconcealed pleasure. "Poor Pinchingdale. He's spent months trying to make me out to be the Black Tulip. It must kill him that our offspring will be first cousins."

"There is one ever so slight problem with your plan," Mary pointed out.

Vaughn looked quizzically down at her.

"What might that be?" His face darkened as he inclined his head slightly towards the smoldering theatre. "There can be no further impediment."

The expression on his face made Mary sorry she had spoken, but she shouldered gamely on. "You seem to have forgotten that I can't have agreed. Since you never asked me."

Vaughn arched a sooty eyebrow. "Do I need to?" he asked mildly.

Mary had meant to return a lighthearted answer, the sort of sophisticated riposte to which she was accustomed, but the airy words wouldn't come.

Instead, she found herself saying, with schoolgirl earnestness and a tongue that was suddenly too thick for her mouth, "Are you sure you want to?" Mary's eyes searched his blackened face. "After—"

She inclined her head feebly towards the burning building. The movement made her head ache. A cheer went up among the clustered members of the *ton* as a still-standing section of wall went tumbling down, crashing into the rubble in an explosion of smoke and ash. Mary caught the involuntarily flicker of Vaughn's eyes in that direction, the fleeting look of pain he couldn't quite suppress as the stones thudded down, a cairn for his wife's grave.

Vaughn's hand tightened around hers. "The real question is, are you? The women in my life seem to have an uncomfortable time of it."

He might not mourn for the woman who had left him thirteen years ago, but what about the woman who had turned against the Black Tulip for him today and lost her life in doing it? He had turned back for her, in that stony trap of a building. The last word on his lips, before the theatre had exploded, had been *her* name. Whatever he might claim, Anne's ghost was still there, an impediment in death as well as in life.

Unless someone contrived to exorcise it.

"Woman," Mary corrected.

"Huh?"

Mary squirmed to a sitting position, ignoring the reverberations the movement sent through her battered skull. "One woman. Singular. You are not allowed any others. Any discomfort or deadly danger is reserved solely for me and me alone. I'm not sharing you. Any bit of you."

Eyes bright, Vaughn lifted her hand to his lips.

"Bossy, aren't you?" he murmured over her knuckles. "The vows haven't even been said yet."

Mary regarded him challengingly. "Haven't they?"

"In more ways than you can imagine," Vaughn said soberly, thinking back over the past few weeks. "Pledged first in wine, then in blood, and now in ashes. I can't imagine a more thorough set of vows than that."

"More thorough than your first?" asked Mary.

"You," said Vaughn, twining his fingers through hers, "are first and last, alpha and omega. I've had enough of letting the past rule me." When Mary still looked uncertain, he added, with deliberate levity, "Think how much I'm giving up for you. Loose women, French spies . . ."

"Ha!' exclaimed Mary. "What about all *I'm* giving up for you? Adoring suitors, sonnets to my elbows . . ."

"I can think of better things to pay tribute to," said Vaughn, and did.

It was unclear whose lips were sootier, but neither seemed to mind. The taste of blood and ashes only lent urgency to their kiss, a reminder of all they had nearly lost. With a happy disregard for his bad shoulder and assorted other aches and pains, Vaughn wrapped his arms around Mary and kissed her so thoroughly that most of the grime surrounding his lips transferred itself from his face to hers, like a misplaced beard.

"What was that about sacrifice?" he asked blandly, once he had got his voice back.

Mary blinked. "I don't remember," she said, "but tell me again."

Vaughn was more than happy to oblige.

They parted to an arm's length, smiling foolishly at each other. Vaughn noted that Mary's hair was filmed with ash, matted and tangled into a coiffure that wouldn't have looked amiss on one of Macbeth's witches. Despite his best efforts, her bare arms and neck had been scraped by flying bits of debris, and the less said about the remains of her royal robes, the better. Dried blood streaked the left side of her face, and the soot had lent her a rather remarkable mustache.

He had never seen anything lovelier.

A bath, however, would not be amiss. Preferably for both of them. At the same time.

"The devil," said Vaughn. "I've left my carriage in Westminster. We'll have to prevail upon your sister to take us back."

"Once she's finished with her buckets, you mean," said Mary, struggling to her feet, and holding out a hand to Vaughn.

He took it without the sarcastic commentary Mary had half-expected, silently accepting her help and pulling heavily on her arm as he rose. She didn't like the sallow look of his skin beneath the soot on his face, or the stickiness matting his shirtfront.

"At least we don't have to worry about the Black Tulip trying to kill you anymore," she said, following her own private train of thought, as they started slowly and more than a little unsteadily towards Letty and Geoff.

"No," said Vaughn thoughtfully. "Only your brother-in-law. Who will, if I marry you, be my brother, too. A terrifying thought. More terrifying for him than for me, I imagine."

Occupied with other matters, Mary brushed Vaughn's badinage aside. "Do you think he really was the son of Prince Charles Edward?"

"It doesn't matter whether he was or not," said Vaughn matter-of-factly. "The Act of Succession bars that entire line from the throne."

Shading her eyes from the glare, Mary squinted at the collapse of Lady Euphemia's theatre, a monument to the ruins of more than one failed ambition. Whether he might have been king or not, his grave was the same. "I suppose it's all immaterial now."

"Much as he is," commented Vaughn. "He can congregate on a cloud with his Stuart ancestors and commiserate on how much they were misused. They were an ill-fated line. James I had the Gunpowder Plot, Charles I died on the scaffold, Charles II died childless—"

"If we don't get you back to London soon," Mary broke into his catalogue of royal woes, "the same may be said about you. I'm sure you ripped your wound back open, carrying me."

Vaughn, feeling a little more light-headed than he would have liked to admit, looked debonairly down his nose at her. "Taking care of your investment, are you?"

"Not as well as I ought," said Mary, catching his arm as he wobbled. "You've gotten rather battered over the past few days."

"Worth every wound," said Vaughn gallantly, but he stumbled as he said it.

As she steadied him, Mary's magpie eye was caught by something glinting in the grass. It glittered too nicely to be one of the Lady Euphemia's pasteboard creations. Mary's own armlets had been lost somewhere long since, and her gold trim was blackened by smoke. But whatever it was that lay fallen in the grass still gleamed true gold.

"What do you think that is?" she asked, pointing.

Holding on to her arm for balance, Vaughn leaned over to scoop it up. "Scrounging for pocket change?" he said lazily as he clapped it into her palm. "I assure you, I'll make you a better allowance than that."

Holding the piece in the air so that the red light of the flames reflected off its surface like a sunset, Mary filed away the promise of an allowance for later.

"Don't you recognize it?" she asked, turning the gold piece slowly this way and that for Vaughn to see.

On one side was a blasted oak, with new shoots beginning to grow out of the burnt and broken trunk. On the other, a warrior drove a spear into the unsuspecting hide of a blurry blob at his feet. There was a hole bored into the top, by means of which someone might attach it to a chain. The lettering around the edge of the medal read, SPES TAMEN EST UNA.

" 'There is still one hope,' " Mary translated, a line forming between her brows. "That's what St. George said it meant when he showed it to me." Holding the coin gingerly between two fingers, she looked anxiously at Vaughn. "Do you think . . . ?"

Vaughn plucked the medallion out of her fingers and tucked it safely away in his waistcoat pocket.

"Of course not," he said, with a surreptitious glance at the smoldering rubble. "It would have been impossible."

"Impossible," Mary echoed, squinting at the flames. "Undoubtedly."

Chapter Thirty-Three

The medallion had lodged in a corner of the box, half-obscured by a packet of letters from Vaughn's mother. Wiggling the coin free of its cardboard moorings, I balanced it in the palm of my hand. It wasn't a large object. At a rough guess, it was about the same size as a five-pence coin, but the alloys were purer than the muddy brown five-pence pieces in my pocket. After two hundred years, the Jacobite keepsake still shone pure gold.

Turning it over in my hand, I kicked myself for not having figured the answer out myself. After all, hadn't I done a paper on Jacobite iconography my first year of grad school? I knew the answer to that one. I most definitely had. It had completely ruined my Christmas break, since Harvard adheres to the charming habit of having exams and paper deadlines post-Christmas, thus ensuring a harried holiday, where the mistletoe gets mixed in with the reference books.

To be fair, *spes tamen est una* wasn't one of the better-known Jacobite mottos. It came late, well after the heyday of Jacobite enthusiasm, once the cause had already pretty much petered out. If I remembered correctly, it hadn't been one of Bonnie Prince Charlie's mottoes at all. Instead, it had been used as the message on a medallion he had commissioned for his daughter, Charlotte, in the hopes that she would take up the Stuart cause, and one day take her rightful place as Queen of England.

At least, everyone had always assumed that it was Charlotte those medals were commissioned for. Maybe some of them even had been.

But what if Bonnie Prince Charlie really had had a son? It wasn't impossible. Bonnie Prince Charlie had eventually married a princess with a long German title, but that hadn't been until the 1770s. According to the less sympathetic biographies, Charles Edward had spent most of his declining years drinking himself senseless to drown out the memory of his failure to attain his throne. His longtime mistress, Clementina Walkshaw, had abandoned him . . . when? Sometime in the 1750s, I thought, which would put her defection after the disappointment of the failed '45 rebellion, when his dipsomania was beginning to get a bit much, even for the most devoted of mistresses.

During that gap between Clementina and Louise von Something-or-Other, a clever woman might have maneuvered him to the altar. If St. George had been just about forty in 1803, that would place his birth in the early 1760s, the perfect timing for a hypothetical secret marriage. And if that was the case . . .

We would never know. Or maybe, someday, someone might go back and track it all down, but it wasn't going to be me. At least, not until I got the dissertation done. The Black Tulip's true identity didn't quite fit into my dissertation, which was, after all, supposed to be on the structure, methods, and cultural implications of English spying organizations, but it would make a very juicy article. I could think of several scholars who would turn a very satisfying chartreuse at the sight of it.

Who would have ever thought that the Pink Carnation's deadliest enemy wasn't a hardened revolutionary, but a thwarted Pretender? Now that I knew the answer, I realized I had missed all sorts of clues. Even St. George's assumed name was a private joke. Bonnie Prince Charlie's father, James III, had been styled the Chevalier de St. George. An obvious alias for his grandson and namesake.

If the Black Tulip really was James III's grandson.

I had all sorts of other questions, too. Had he really died in that fire? One assumed he must have. How would St. George, directly under the dome, have made his way out again? It was only in fiction that the villain, hideously scarred, returned to wreak revenge. But then how on earth did that coin make it onto the grass outside the burning pavilion and into Vaughn's pocket?

"Ah, Eloise!"

I hastily tucked the medallion away, not into my pocket, as Vaughn had, but back into the corner of the box, hoping my body had blocked the glint of gold.

Turning my chair with a hideous screech of metal against linoleum, I smiled at Dempster. It took some effort to make that smile convincing. Ever since hearing the Serena story the previous Saturday, Dempster hadn't been high on my list of favorite people.

Once again, Dempster was almost too nattily attired, in a blazer bearing the emblem of a famous prep school—or, at least, that was what it was meant to suggest. I had no idea if it did or not.

"How goes the research?" he asked fulsomely, like the lady of the manor visiting the small garden of a tenant farmer to see how the peas and potatoes were getting on. Don't ask why the image was lady of the manor rather than lord of the manor; it just was.

"I can't make heads or tails of most of this," I said cheerfully, with a wave at the box of documents, sounding as American as I knew how. "It's just so much paper!" I was tempted to add a "like, you know?" but decided that would be overdoing it.

Dempster smiled tolerantly. "Perhaps I might help you understand it better. Over a coffee?"

I clapped my hand to my mouth in false distress. "Oh, dear! I can't. My boyfriend is picking me up at—" I made a show of checking my watch. "Six. So just about now."

"Your boyfriend?"

I blinked disingenuously up at Dempster. "Yes. We have dinner plans with a friend of mine. I think you might know her."

Dempster rose to the bait like a trout breaking the water. It was beautiful to behold. He was one of those people who can never resist trying to prove he knows as many people as you do. I had been counting on that.

"Who?" he asked, visibly cycling through his mental Rolodex of useful connections.

"She was actually a school friend of a very good friend of mine," I said, rambling happily on, while Dempster looked benignly on. It wasn't an expression that sat well on him. It made him look mildly bilious. "But we've gotten to know each other since I came to London. You know how these friend-of-a-friend things are. And then you have to go back and trace the friendship web to figure out how you got to know each other in the first place."

Dempster looked so muddled that I almost felt sorry for him. Almost.

"Which one was the old school friend?"

Hmph, if he couldn't handle a simple friendship genealogy, how could he be expected to master the complex interrelationships of historical personages? "My old school friend is Pammy Harrington. She's the one who introduced me to the friend I'm meeting up with tonight. The one I understand you know. Rather well, in fact."

"Oh?" The man was too dense to even realize what was up. No, "dense" isn't the right word. It just never occurred to him that any report could be less than favorable. He preened in anticipation of a second-hand compliment.

"Yes," I said sweetly, bringing the game to a close. "I believe you two might even have dated. Serena Selwick."

The wattage of Dempster's smile visibly dimmed.

"Oh," he said. "You know Serena. She's a lovely girl."

"Yes, she is," I agreed.

The silence crept in and expanded between us, like the Blob. I could tell Dempster was dying to find out just what and how much I knew. Serena wasn't the sort to go around complaining about old grievances, but still . . . you never knew. A guilty conscience makes for an overactive imagination.

I smiled, gently.

It had the desired effect of making him even more nervous. Dempter fiddled with a corner of his pocket handkerchief. "Have you known Serena long?"

"Not terribly long," I said, and watched as the tension in his well-tailored shoulders lightened. "But it's hard not to feel protective of her. She's so delicate. And defenseless. One of life's innocents."

"That's very noble of you," said Dempster, unsuccessfully trying to reroute the conversation.

"Not really," I said cheerfully. "It's not entirely disinterested on my part."

I gave him just a moment to let that sink in. Naturally, he judged my motives by his own. The color came back into his cheeks as he leapt to the obvious assumption that I must just be using my friendship with Serena to get to her family papers. After all, wouldn't anyone?

I could see his opinion of me going up by leaps and bounds.

"You see," I added, before he could say "archives," "I've just started dating Serena's brother, Colin."

"Did I hear my name?" drawled a familiar voice.

Lounging against the doorjamb, looking dubiously at the worn linoleum and weak tracking lighting, was none other than the man himself, managing to make the rest of the room look small and stuffy.

I'm not sure how long he had been standing there—I had been too busy tormenting Dempster—but from the suppressed smirk on Colin's face, it had been more than long enough. He did a fairly good job of suppressing his smirk. His one dimple, the one in his left cheek, wasn't even in evidence. But I knew it was there.

He also managed the drawl very well, almost up to Vaughn's standard. He must have been practicing before he came.

"Ready?" he asked, smiling at me and pointedly ignoring his sister's flummoxed ex-boyfriend, who was doing an excellent guppy imitation, his lips going in and out with little bubbles of air.

"Just about," I said brightly, jumbling my notebooks and papers back into my bag. I held out a hand to Dempster. "Thank you so much for the use of the archive. I really appreciate it."

Dempster looked from me to Colin. One had to give him points for persistence. He rallied valiantly. "Will I see you here again next Saturday?"

Traipsing across the room, I slid an arm confidingly through Colin's. "I don't think so," I said breezily. "I can't think of anything more here that I would need. But thanks. And good luck with your projects!"

"You know where to find me," Dempster called out manfully behind us. "If you need any help, that is."

I turned around just enough to waggle my fingers good-bye as Colin nudged the door closed behind us, effectively cutting off any further farewells.

My bag, as it is wont to do, thumped down my arm into the crook of my elbow. Without breaking stride or saying a word, Colin reached out and appropriated it, shifting it to his far side. He held it that way boys do, not using the strap, but grasping it by the top, so no one can suspect they might be wearing it.

I beamed at him in gratitude. No matter how used to carrying your own bags you get, it's still nice to have someone else do it for you. Of their own accord, without your having to ask.

He was, as a friend of mine would say, good people.

"So," I asked, smiling up at him as we climbed the stairs from Dempster's archival dungeon, "do you feel spiritually cleansed?"

"That's not quite how I would have put it," he said dryly, sauntering along beside me through the long drawing rooms, under Vaughn's knowing eye. Our footsteps clumped pleasingly against the parquet, two pairs in perfect tandem. Well, not quite perfect tandem. Colin's stride was much longer than mine, and his shoes thumped while mine clicked, but our steps still made a pleasant rhythm together, nonetheless.

"You know what I mean," I said.

The smirk Colin had been so successfully repressing all that time escaped and spread across his face, complete with dimple. "The look on Dempster's face when you told him you were friends with Serena—I wouldn't have missed that for the world. Excellently done, by the way."

"Thank you," I said, sketching a slight curtsy that might have been more effective if I hadn't (a) been wearing pants, and (b) still been walking. "I do try. It was indeed beautiful to behold as he watched all of his plans go poof, right up in smoke."

Strolling into the entrance hall, beneath the shadow of the massive Hercules, we contemplated Dempster's downfall in mutual satisfaction.

Colin held open the front door, moving aside for me to precede him. I hastily turned up the collar of my jacket as the first blast of frigid air hit me.

"We aren't very nice people," I said ruefully.

"Dempster isn't a very nice person," said Colin calmly.

He had a point there.

I shook my head thoughtfully. "I still can't believe he really thought he could use me to get to you—to your papers, I mean."

Hunching his shoulders into his jacket against the bitter pre-Christmas cold, Colin looked down at me sideways. "Did you find what you were looking for in his?"

I nodded vehemently, watching my breath make little puffs in the air. It had gotten much colder, just over the past week. It was December already, and frosty enough to show that the weather knew it. "You'll never believe who the Black Tulip really was."

"Not the Marquise de Something-or-Other?"

"Nope. A Jacobite Pretender."

"I didn't think we still had those in the nineteenth century."

"There's a reason for that," I said, with as much pride as if I had routed the last remaining Stuart all by myself. "The Pink Carnation."

"Was there nothing she didn't get her fingers into?" asked Colin admiringly, if ungrammatically.

"Not much that I can see," I said proudly, sticking my hands into my pockets and wishing I'd remembered to bring gloves. "Of course, I've only covered a fairly small space of her career so far. There's a whole lot that's attributed to her later on, and I'm guessing only about half of it is probable."

"Shouldn't she improve as she goes on?" asked Colin, considering the question seriously. "With increased experience and a larger network of agents, there's no reason she shouldn't have been able to do more."

I hunched my chin into my turtleneck in an attempt to keep it warm. "Yeah, but could she defy the laws of time and space? It's one thing to be responsible for putting down French plots on either side of the Channel—"

"A lot of Frogs on the other side of the Channel," intoned Colin in *Fawlty Towers* tones.

I made a face at him. "Fine. She can have France. I'll even grant her Portugal and Spain. But India? And Russia? I just don't buy it."

"Why not? People did move around, even all the way to India and back."

"But the timing never quite works. How could she be in India to deal with a Mahratta rebellion and in France to try to stop Napoleon's coronation all at the same time?"

"Delegation?" suggested Colin. "Deputies?"

"Possibly," I said, frowning. "But which was where when?"

Colin's eyes crinkled in that way that never failed to make my stomach do flip-flops. "Will the real Pink Carnation please stand up?"

"Something like that," I agreed. "I've even seen assertions that the League of the Purple Gentian got back into business later on, but I'm assuming that must be a typo."

"Or not," said Colin mysteriously. Before I could quiz him on it, he asked, "Where are you planning to look next?"

"I haven't really thought about it," I admitted. "I've been so focused on the Black Tulip for the past month, that now that I know exactly who he was, I'm not sure where to go next."

"What about Selwick Hall?"

I was so wrapped up in my own train of thought that it took a moment for his meaning to seep through. As I looked blankly up at Colin, he elaborated: "We still have papers you haven't seen yet. There are heaps I've never looked at, and I doubt anyone else has, either. Except maybe Aunt Arabella," he added as an afterthought.

"Are you sure? I wouldn't want you to think I was pulling a Dempster and using you just for your papers."

Colin grinned down at me. "I've come to terms with the fact that you're just using me for my body."

Naturally, after that, it was impossible to say anything at all for quite a few moments. But while London is full of convenient cul-de-sacs for lovers' meetings, the climate isn't nearly so accommodating.

I defy anyone to stand outside and smooch in forty-degree weather with a stinging drizzle beginning to come down.

Among other things, the cold was making my nose run. I swiped surreptitiously at it with one hand as Colin wedged my bag under one arm and wrenched at the Velcro fastenings of his umbrella.

Putting up his umbrella over both of us, Colin looked inquiringly down at me. "What do you think? Would you like to come down to Selwick Hall for a week and root about in the library?"

Was the Black Tulip French?

Oh, wait, he wasn't. But he'd been working for them. Besides, the Stuarts had quite a few French Princesses in their family tree, like Bonnie Prince Charlie's great-grandmother, Henrietta Maria, who had been Louis XIV's aunt. Either way, the answer was crystal clear.

"Are you sure you wouldn't mind having me?"

Colin gave me a look. It was a very eloquent look. I capitulated instantly—rather like the French.

"I can't think of anything I would like better," I said honestly.

"Brilliant," said Colin.

In a contented silence, hand in hand, we strolled off into the stinging December rain.

Historical Note

Some of you may be asking what a Jacobite Pretender is doing as the villain in a Napoleonic novel. (Or if you aren't, you should be.) As with everything else, you can blame that on Lord Vaughn. Of all my characters, Lord Vaughn is the most rooted in the eighteenth century. His manners, his mores, his mind-set—all look back to the heyday of the Whig aristocracy, to an era of refined wit rather than Romantic excess. Both the barge on the Thames and the pleasure gardens of Vauxhall, while still in use in the early nineteenth century, bear the savor of the prior century, just like Vaughn.

Like Vaughn, Jacobitism also properly belongs more to the eighteenth century than the nineteenth—which made it just the right sort of foil for Vaughn. The Jacobite cause, which gave successive Hanoverian Georges nasty nightmares, had its origin in the expulsion of James II from the throne in the Glorious Revolution of 1688. Glorious for some, but not for James's descendants, who spent the next century in ineffectual attempts to regain the throne. James II's son, known variously as James III, the Chevalier of St. George, or the Old Pretender, made a bid for the throne in 1715. After that failed, his son, Prince Charles Edward, popularly known as Bonnie Prince Charlie, made another attempt in 1745, which was brutally squashed on the battlefields of Scotland. Although the cause largely petered out with the death of Bonnie Prince Charlie in 1788, half-hearted plots continued to be made and toasts drunk well into the nineteenth century. George III cannily neutralized Charles's brother, the would-be Henry IX, by putting him on the royal payroll in 1801, thus forestalling any rebellions out of him, but Bonnie Prince Charlie's illegitimate grandson was still touting his right to the English throne as late as 1850.

Like Eloise, I spent a semester in grad school reading up on Jacobite activities and iconography. The motto *spes tamen est una* was indeed the slogan on a medal struck by Bonnie Prince Charlie for his child and heir—only that child was his illegitimate daughter, Charlotte, whom he created with the Duchess of Albany, rather than his apocryphal illegitimate son, James. Might Charles have had an illegitimate son of the right age? As Eloise pointed out, it's not an impossibility. His long-term mistress, Clementina Walkinshaw, left him in 1760 (driven away by his drunkenness, or so the story goes), leaving a convenient twelve-year gap until his marriage in 1772 to a German princess of irreproachable lineage, Louisa of Stolberg-Gedern (who also eventually left him). A child born during those twelve years would be just the right age to be the Black Tulip. . . .

For those interested in learning more about Jacobitism in all its aspects, including its survivals into the nineteenth century, I highly recommend Paul Monod's excellent monograph on the topic, *Jacobitism and the English People*.

A few other legitimate historical characters and organizations were pressed into service for the purposes of this story. Thomas Paine was, in fact, a master corset-maker before becoming a writer of incendiary pamphlets. His pamphlet on the expected invasion of England by Bonaparte (imaginatively titled "To the People of England on the Invasion of England") wasn't actually published until 1804, but I took the liberty of moving it up a few months for dramatic effect. Joseph Priestley and his allegiances and experiments were also taken from his life. Priestley was, indeed, hounded out of England after his infamous "gunpowder" comment, and he did isolate "dephlogisticated air" or, as we now call it, oxygen. The Common Sense Society, named after Paine's famous pamphlet, was loosely based on the Revolution Society (lambasted by Edmund Burke in his *Reflections on the Revolution in France*), of which Priestley was a member. Priestley's disciple, Rathbone, the Common Sense Society, and the Société des Droits des Hommes were entirely my own inventions, and not to be blamed on anyone else.

About the Author

Lauren Willig holds graduate degrees in both law and history from Harvard and is a second-year litigation associate at a New York law firm.